A CAPTURED CAULDRON

RULES FOR COMPULSORY BREWS

SIDE QUEST ROW SERIES
BOOK 2

R.K. ASHWICK

LASKELL

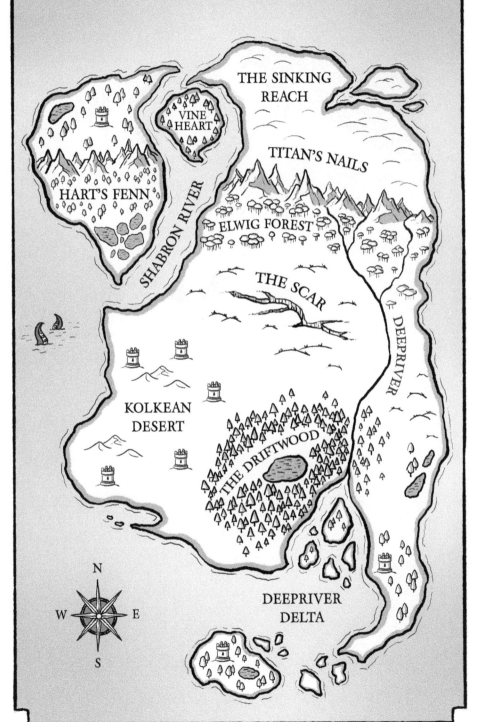

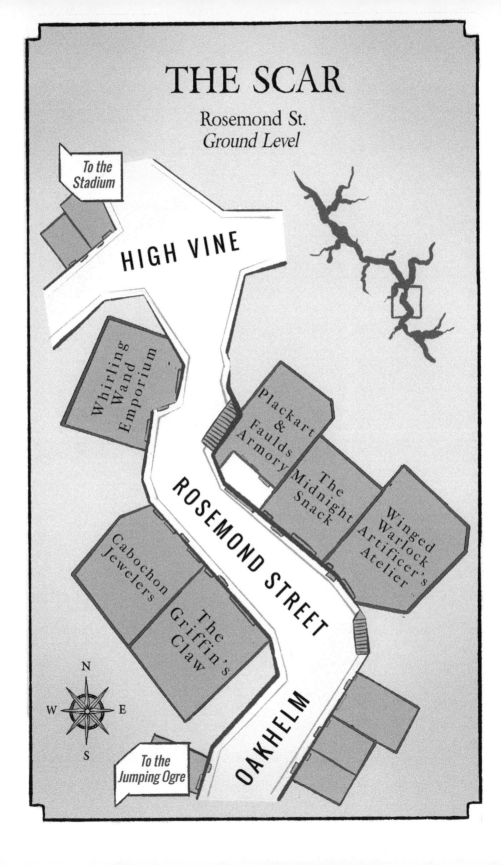

CONTENTS

RULE 1:

SAFETY FIRST

Dawn

CONTRARY TO HER NAMESAKE, Dawn loved sunset more than sunrise on Rosemond Street.

She couldn't help it—her wand shop was tucked into the corner of Rosemond and High Vine, giving her the perfect view of the little street at dusk. Much like her wands, the place was beauty and chaos wrapped into a narrow bundle. Crowds rushed toward home or taverns after a long workday, their faces burnished in the last golds and pinks the sun had to offer them. Some popped their heads in to chat with her or the other shopkeepers; others hurried along, an evening quest on their minds.

No matter the city's pace, its bustle in the warm, waning light promised Dawn the same things every time: the peace of a day ended, and the excitement of a night begun.

After dusting her cabinets one more time—a wandmaker with dirty cabinets wasn't worth her wood—she flipped the store sign to *Closed* and hurried into the street. Despite her best efforts, she was running late today. The last sliver of sunlight had already risen to the upper edge of the chasm above, leaving her in the sleepy shadows on the ground level of the tiered city.

But she couldn't rest now—not when she had a promise to fulfill to one Ambrose Beake.

"Sherry?" she called, peering into another shop carved into the chasm wall: an open-air forge, dusty and warm. "Is Ames already in there?"

A soot-streaked woman looked up from her workbench, her hair matching the gray of the ashes all around her. Despite the mess, the work she held in her gloved hands was nothing short of immaculate: a polished steel helmet, every rivet steeped in protective enchantments and self-healing spells. A daunting masterpiece for any other armorer—but a simple day's work for her.

"Afraid so." Sherry jerked her head toward the shop next door. "He rushed in right when Viola closed. Speaking of which..."

She flipped her own store sign from *Kettle's On* to *Off Fighting Dragons*.

"Will you be going in to help him?" Sherry continued, dusting off her gloves and releasing gray puffs into the air. Dawn kept a careful distance—the road dust had already half-ruined her new pink skirt, and she wasn't about to fully ruin it with the equivalent of forge burps.

"I told him I would," she said. "He's really panicking this late?"

"Oh, you know Ambrose this time of year. Boy's like a pygmy dragon with its head chopped off."

"I'll reattach his head, then. Got it." Dawn picked up her skirts and hurried on.

"Buy him a cookie for me, would you?" Sherry called after her. "Viola can put it on my tab!"

Dawn gave her a final wave, then ducked into Ambrose's refuge for the evening—the new bakery on Rosemond Street.

The Midnight Snack had taken the place of Eli's old potion shop almost a year ago, and Dawn could hardly see a hint of what it used to be. While Eli's shop had been bright and flashy, filled with crystal and light woods, Viola the baker had embraced the comfort of darkness. She had draped deep velvets in jewel tones across the walls, emphasizing the perpetual glow of enchanted glass stars on the ceiling. As if the atmosphere wasn't already conducive to post-dessert naps, she had also moved in the plushest of furniture, rivaling even Grim's well-worn couch. Rich pillows, squashy cushions, throw blankets over soft couches... Every merchant on Rosemond Street had their favorite spot, and every merchant had fallen asleep in it at least once.

(Currently, Grim held the record for fifteen accidental naps in the corner armchair.)

But Viola's final addition to the shop had been a staggeringly plain choice: a vast corkboard, studded with sparkly pins in moon and star shapes.

"Don't worry, it'll fill up," the gnomish baker had said to Dawn on opening day, her smile accentuating her wide cheeks. "It's a great place for local stuff. Announcements, notices, missing pet fliers. That sort of thing."

True to her word, customers had taken to it immediately, filling it with art show posters, theater schedules, *Help Wanted* signs, little doodles...

And, in the after hours when Viola was cleaning up, Ambrose's plans for Potion Con.

"Thank the gods you're here," his voice shot from across the room. "Day one is *ruined*."

Ambrose paced in front of the corkboard, where Viola's glittery moon pins now presided over a flurry of schedules, lists, and notes. The papers fluttered like birds each time the half-elf passed, his pale, ink-stained hands darting to various points on the board.

"It's always the panels," the potioneer hissed. "They moved my panel on antidotes to tomorrow *morning*, which means I can't attend the wand demonstration with you until the afternoon. But if I try to catch the later demonstration, I risk being late for the debates." He took a harried breath, his blue hair falling in front of his face, and turned to Dawn with pleading eyes. "Thoughts?"

Dawn did her best not to laugh. This sort of Ambrose-specific nuttery happened every year Potion Con came to the Scar. He wanted absolutely everything the three-day potioneering convention had to offer—every panel, every talk, every demonstration. He would pore over the schedules for weeks and think, and think, and think...

But over the years, she had become an expert in reining in all those thinks.

She floated over to the side table near Ambrose, laden with mini sugar cookies gone ignored. "First"—she held up a cookie, rainbow sprinkles shining in the light of the glass stars—"eat this."

Ambrose nodded reluctantly and took a bite. While he brushed crumbs off his navy waistcoat, Dawn took a cookie for herself and perused the ink-marked schedules. Despite all his scribbles, she could read them perfectly—a natural consequence of him showing her the papers every day for the last week.

"Second"—she tapped the schedule in the center—"you gotta be on time for the debates. That's non-negotiable. What if Xavion picks the first debate slot?"

Ambrose hummed through a mouthful of cookie. "Precisely."

"You can't let them debate someone else."

"Absolutely not." Ambrose began scribbling on the papers again. The frenzied glint in his eyes faded, and he slowly returned to his perfect, steady posture. "I'll nix the wand demonstration from my list, then. Thank you."

Dawn grinned. Pygmy dragon head successfully reattached. "So, you're done planning for the con, then?"

Ambrose blinked at her. "No. This was just day one."

All right, fine. Pygmy dragon head...sort of reattached.

She reached for a second cookie to bolster herself, but a voice from the front counter stopped her.

"Hey, before you eat all my day-old cookies..." Viola popped up from behind the glass counter, a tray of colorful pastries in hand. "Wanna help me get rid of these cupcakes?"

Dawn dropped the cookie instantly. Ambrose hesitated, eyeing the corkboard. "I really should—"

"Get some fuel for those day two thoughts!" Dawn finished for him, dragging him over to the counter. The cupcakes on the tray were her absolute favorite. Passionfruit and coconut, daintily topped with sugared edible flowers, and—*oh*, the passionfruit curd inside—

She threw a handful of coins into the day-old jar—specifically set up for after-hours visits like this—then grabbed a cupcake. Viola hopped up onto a stool behind the counter, her grin as bright as the sugared petals. "Thought you might want some," she said proudly, smoothing out her skirt.

When it came to fashion, she couldn't have been more different from Dawn. She eschewed lively Scarrish patterns and colors in favor of black dresses, not caring if flour formed white runes on the fabric. Her monotone didn't stop at her clothing, either. Black eyeliner ringed her eyes, glittering black nail polish punctuated the tips of her fingers...and just under her folded gnomish ears, tiny black bat earrings fluttered in constant circles.

But when it came to her mood, Viola was an echo of Dawn's cheery pink top.

"You gotta tell me what the magic feels like this time," she said with a wiggle. "It's a day-old, so it won't be as strong, but I think you'll still like the new spell. Go on, take a bite!"

While Ambrose carefully unwrapped his cupcake, Dawn dove in and took a large bite from the pile of frosting.

The magic struck her instantly. The distinct scent of a sea breeze, salty and cool, wafted under her nose, while the warmth of a beachy sun tingled across her brown skin. She eagerly took another bite, and the soft vanilla cake added more notes to the breeze: hibiscus, citrus, coconut...

"Fascinating," Ambrose said, chewing slowly as he examined the frosting. "You were able to fit both scent and feeling into one illusion cake?"

"Just finished tweaking the recipe yesterday." Viola spun around on the stool, her black braid swinging behind her. "I'm hoping it'll be a bestseller this winter."

With a delighted hum, Dawn closed her eyes and stretched out her arms, pretending to bask on the invisible beach. As she leaned back, something clattered from her skirt pocket to the floor.

"Dawn, you dropped your..." Ambrose knelt down to pick it up. "Wait, what is this?"

She opened her eyes and brightened. "Oh! I wanted to show you this." She snatched it from his hand and set it on the table—a small wand, carefully carved and modestly appointed with a single raw crystal at the tip. Clapping her hands together, she nudged Ambrose's shoulder in excitement. "Guess where it's from."

"Hm." Ambrose set aside his cupcake wrapper and pointed to the wand, playing into her little game. "May I?"

"Sure, sure."

He picked up the device with long, delicate fingers, analyzing it from every angle with his signature little frown. Though he wasn't wearing his typical potion robes, he looked every inch the studious potioneer, his gaze not missing a single detail.

"It isn't yours," he finally said. "The maker didn't polish it enough, and there are far too many irregularities in the carving. And *you*"— he tapped the crystal at the end—"have access to crystals of far higher quality than this."

Dawn nodded eagerly. "So...?"

Ambrose's pensive frown went deeper—then he lit up, mouth agape.

"An apprentice?" He gasped. "Did you actually pick one?"

"You're half-right!" She plucked the wand from his grasp and flicked it twice; red sparkles spiraled out of the tip, then vanished in a multitude of tiny starbursts. Good velocity and consistent performance from an amateur's wand, all things considered. "Got this as a part of someone's application today."

It was a historic time for Dawn's Whirling Wand Emporium—she was now on the hunt for an apprentice, and applications had already poured in from every corner of Laskell. The resumes practically glowed: top marks at school, previous wand experience, prior apprenticeships...

Viola pointed to the wand. "So, this applicant's the front-runner, right?"

Dawn slumped, thinking of all the other stunning candidates. "Right now, she is." She sighed. "But how am I gonna pick just one?"

"I hear that," Viola grumbled. "I've been debating on these new recipes for a week."

She propped her ankle up against the velvet stool beside her, the chestnut wood of her prosthetic lower leg sinking into the fabric. From socket to pylon, all up and down the wooden leg, paintings of cupcakes sparkled. Chocolate cupcakes with pink frosting, pink cupcakes with chocolate frosting; then all pink, all chocolate...

"Banneker said that if I let the paintings sit for a while," Viola mused, "I'd feel their aura and know which one to pick."

Ambrose snorted. Dawn ignored him.

"How about that one?" She pointed to the all-pink confection. She could already picture it in Viola's glass displays: a mouth-watering combination of strawberry and raspberry, topped with bright, chunky sprinkles. Maybe with a magically fizzy finish, or a cute little spell that changed the buyer's nail color—

Viola grinned. "You *would* pick that one."

Dawn pretended to primp her curly mohawk. "Am I wrong?"

A familiar voice chimed in. "You? Never."

Beside her, Ambrose relaxed instantly, as if the cupcake's beach illusion had only just struck him.

Eli Valenz stood at the bakery's entrance, fully dressed for his adventurer training that evening: leather jerkin, bracers, a belt made to hold weapons and potions... It was a far cry from his shop owner's vest and dangling earrings, but Dawn adored the new look. He looked comfortable. Strapping, even. Someone bards would soon sing about, once he started going on big quests.

Ambrose could see it, too—his gaze roved slowly over Eli, and Eli returned the silent gesture. Dawn bit into her cupcake again, a strong hint of jealousy warring with the sweet icing on her tongue. Insufferable, the both of them.

"What's this?" Ambrose finally strode over to Eli, pointing to the little automaton in the man's arms. At first glance, Tom the Automaton looked like an oversized beer mug, until one noticed the broom head, fork arms, and legs made of daggers and wheels. With a soft smile, Ambrose bent down to look Tom in her eyeless face.

"Is this the little scamp who spilled my coffee this morning?" He tugged her out of Eli's arms and planted a kiss on the top of her head. Eli raised his eyebrows.

"Anything for the taller scamp who cleaned up the spilled coffee?"

"Hm." Ambrose looked him over once more and feigned thoughtfulness. "No."

He leaned in and gave him a quick kiss anyway. With a tilted grin, Eli pulled him back in for a second, deeper one. Dawn chewed faster, jealousy now overpowering any last hint of the coconut and sea breeze. Gods, when had she last been kissed? Months? She couldn't even recall how her last date had gone, and she wasn't likely to have another one soon. Questing season was upon them, and when the adventurers emptied the city, it was time for merchants to tidy: tidy their shops, tidy records, tidy all those apprentice applications coming in...

She stared at the wand on the counter. That was it—she'd have an apprentice soon. A helpful apprentice who would be eager—no, *ecstatic*—to tidy things for her.

Perhaps her dating days could return, she thought in excitement. Perhaps she could start this month. This weekend, even. She had more than a few acquaintances coming to town for Potion Con. What a perfect time to reconnect. Brush up on her flirting technique. Grab a drink or two at the after-parties...

"Oh, almost forgot." Eli finally let go of Ambrose and dug around in the pouch on his belt. "Got today's paper for you. Thought I saw the name of one of your Potion Con buddies in an article."

He held out a folded broadsheet, which Ambrose snatched eagerly.

"Sandon? Or Evie?" He set Tom on the ground. "No matter, I'll take a look. Thank you."

As he wandered off to scrutinize the broadsheet, Eli sauntered over to Dawn, while Tom whirled in wide circles around his legs.

"Can this little hazard stay with you and Ember while I'm at training?" he asked, nearly tripping over her on her last revolution. "If you don't want to, Sherry said she can take her—"

"No, I got her! Ember will love the company." Dawn scooped Tom up mid-spin, careful to keep the dagger legs away from her new skirt. Her phoenix salamander Ember would indeed love the company—he enjoyed sitting on Tom's head while the automaton roamed the shop. "Will you hear about your quest today?"

"What quest?" Viola perked up. Eli tried to give a humble shrug as he leaned against the counter, but his grin told a different story.

"I should hear today at training if I get assigned to my first quest out of the city limits," he said. "Oren said he'd have the assignments ready to announce by the end of the week."

And the bard songs would be rolling in within the year. Dawn looked forward to learning the words to all of them.

"Ooh, a *big* quest!" Viola gave a delighted clap. "If you need travel rations for the journey, I make a mean cracker. Don't let my sponge cakes fool you."

"Who said I wasn't going to fill my pack with sponge cakes?"

Dawn peered over Eli's shoulder at Ambrose, who had his back to them. "Ames, what healing brews go best with cake?"

He didn't respond.

All of his Potion Con excitement had evaporated, leaving behind a ramrod posture and tight silence. Something instinctively churned in Dawn's gut.

"Ames?" she called again. He whirled around, his hands folding the broadsheet quickly.

"I'm sorry?" he said. "Oh, the quest. Yes, of course I'll brew him something for it."

His weak response didn't work—Eli's gaze immediately went to the paper. "What'd the article say?"

Ambrose swallowed. "Nothing."

As if to undercut his blatant lie, a little statue on the counter flashed a frenetic white.

Every shop on Rosemond Street had one such statue—a small rose of glass and wood, linked to all the other shops for relaying messages and alarms. One brief flash of white indicated a single message. Several indicated a healthy conversation.

A lightning storm of them signaled a disaster.

"Don't listen to them," Ambrose blurted out as the rose statue blinked a near-constant white. "I assure you, it's not a problem—"

Dawn grabbed the tiny scroll under the statue and yanked it open.

Sherry: Barnaby kidnapped! Did you read the article?
Banneker: Hold on, wasn't he supposed to be on a panel with Ames?
Grim: Fourth kidnapping in three months. I don't like it.
Sherry: And of course the convention has no official statement
regarding security, can you believe—

When Dawn read the messages aloud, Ambrose scoffed. "I'm sure it's mere conjecture."

"Doesn't sound like conjecture to me," Eli said. "What did the article say?"

Ambrose reluctantly handed the paper over to him. "It's Barnaby Walsh," he muttered. "An inkmaker up in the northern quarter. He was supposed to be on a panel with me at Potion Con. The one about cross-disciplinary research and tactics, which, by the way, I was highly looking forward to because..." He held up a hand to stop himself. "The article claims he has been kidnapped and will not be at the convention."

Viola skittered around the counter, her prosthetic punctuating her movements with tiny clinks against the wood floor. "I don't get it," she said, standing on tiptoe to look at the article in Eli's hand. "Who would kidnap an inkmaker?"

Dawn, Ambrose, and Eli all shared knowing glances. Viola looked between all of them in confusion. "What? I'm really asking, who would—"

The door swung open with a loud creak. They all jumped—then relaxed upon seeing a familiar orcish silhouette filling the doorframe.

"Hey, Grim," Viola said with relief. "Would you like a—?"

"Sit," they grunted. "S'time we talk."

Dawn winced. She knew what was coming. She had gotten this lecture as an apprentice, as had Ambrose. Even Eli had gotten the talk during his first month on Rosemond Street—though with a rival potioneer to contend with, Dawn was sure he had other things on his mind at the time.

But Viola seemed to understand the gravity of the situation. She gathered a stack of day-old chocolate cookies and clustered in with everyone at the nearest table. Grim took a seat at the head of the table, their hulking frame barely fitting in the little chair. Between their permanent frown and the two tusks poking out from their lip, the jeweler's demeanor intimidated many a customer. As a result, they rarely had to deal with obnoxious hagglers or smart-mouthed clients.

Dawn was incredibly jealous.

"I presume you've heard of Aphos?" Grim began, their ring-encrusted fingers tapping the table.

"In passing," Viola said, squirming like she was failing a test. "It's...the city beneath the city, right?"

"That's what they call themselves," Grim said. "It's a market town hidden deep in the lower parts of the chasm, for those who can't exactly buy and sell what they need in our topside markets. Thieves, assassins..."

"Kidnappers," Eli muttered. He sat with Tom on his lap and shoulder-to-shoulder with Ambrose, who was doing his level best to appear unbothered by the kerfuffle—but he leaned toward Eli anyway, like a flower to the sun.

Not having anyone to lean against herself, Dawn simply sat there, trying not to think about the nightmares she'd had about Aphos as a young apprentice. About criminals crawling out of sinkholes and cisterns, lurking in shadows, scurrying in tunnels under her feet...

"Aphosians," Grim continued, nodding to Eli, "have their own corner on the underground market. For their illusion spellwork, mostly. You see a device with a kraken branded on it, it's theirs. But their community doesn't always have the specialized skills they need for a certain product or job—"

"So they kidnap people." Viola swallowed. "People like us."

Despite Dawn's attempts to block her childish nightmares, her palms began to sweat. Everyone at this table, everyone on Rosemond Street, had unique skills. Dawn herself had honed hers to a fine point and had no problem showing them off through her various trophies and certificates. But in the shadow of that accomplishment was a threat: that one day, Aphos could find her abilities particularly...valuable to them.

The same thought must have been running through Viola's head, for her eyes wandered over her shop, full of glitter and comfort. "But I —I mean, they wouldn't want..."

Grim held up a hand in reassurance. "Rosemond Street is safe. We haven't had a threat in years. I'm only telling you so that you watch out for yourself when you're out and about around the city. Particularly this time of year."

Eli's face darkened. "Questing season," he said, his grip on the newspaper tightening. "There are hardly any adventurers left in town. If anyone wanted to hire someone to rescue Barnaby—"

Ambrose laid a firm hand over Eli's. "Barnaby won't be down there forever," he said, voice taut. "Aphos lets people go once they're done with their forced commission. Don't they?" He looked at Grim in a silent command to reassure his boyfriend. The orc took a cookie but left it unbitten, instead waving it as they spoke.

"Aphos has no interest in harming their resources, nor are they inclined to feed and house them forever. I'd bet twenty talons your Mr. Walsh reappears in his ink shop a week from now, no worse for wear."

Viola, for her part, took a cookie and stuffed the entire thing into her mouth. "Ames, are you still gonna go to Potion Con?"

Ambrose scoffed. "Of course I'm going."

Dawn would've bet twenty talons on that response, but Eli didn't seem so reassured. "Maybe I should go with you—"

"My dear, you're about to go on a quest."

Dawn wiped her palms on her skirt. "I could tag along with him."

Ambrose gestured to the corkboard. "No, we made a plan. You have a different schedule for day one. That wand demonstration—"

"I can skip it!"

"No." Ambrose extricated himself from the packed table. "I appreciate all the concern, but..." He huffed and straightened his waistcoat. "Potion Con is perfectly safe. I will be attending as normal, and *you*" —he pointed to Eli—"will be going on your quest. Which, by the way..." He dug up his pocket watch. Eli cursed and stood abruptly, launching Tom from his lap.

"All right, well"—he gave Ambrose a kiss, then narrowly avoided tripping over Tom on his way out the door—"just—stay safe, all of you? I can't help you if I'm fighting fey raptors in the Vineheart next week!"

Dawn gasped. "Is that what the quest is going to be?"

"With any luck." Eli tried to grin back, but the gesture was weak. "Oh, Viola, if there are any leftover cinnamon rolls, could I—?"

Viola waved him along. "Go. I'll pack one for Ambrose to take back for you."

"You're the best!"

Eli took off down the street, leaving the others to pick up the shards of the evening's peace. Grim finished their cookie and began a low conversation with Viola about gingerbread recipes. Dawn continued fiddling with the gifted wand, working out her lingering anxiety.

And Ambrose stood before the corkboard once more, hands on his hips, Tom whizzing around his ankles.

"All right." He swallowed. "Scheduling day two..."

RULE 2:

(RE)SET EXPECTATIONS

Eli

ELI CROUCHED LOW BEHIND A ROCK, his boots sinking into the soft sand. Everything was uncomfortably warm here. The stone against his palm, the evening light reflecting off his sword. His jerkin soaked up the heat, sending beads of sweat dripping down his neck. Gods, this armor was going to stink later—

He shook away the wandering thoughts, dug his feet into the sand, and focused on the prey before him.

A giant fey raptor stalked lightly across the sand dunes, its long talons leaving behind no footprints. Its needlelike beak, however, struck sharp holes into the ground, digging for bugs and other prey. And all the while, its feathered ears twisted, constantly on the lookout for even a hint of danger.

"Check that weak spot inside the right thigh," a voice whispered next to Eli. Hickory, an orc with green skin and an axe she affectionately called Trudy, crouched beside him, giving crisp, silent hand signals to two other adventurers behind an adjacent rock. "Hold steady. Burt's gonna go for the kill."

Eli held still for Burt's entrance—and nearly missed it by blinking. The adventurer skittered out from behind a rock in an instant, his tiny gnomish feet nimbly dodging the dry twigs scattered across the ground. The fey raptor lifted its head—but Burt had already vanished behind another rock, as silent as the still air.

The raptor's ears twitched once, twice...then it resumed its own little hunt in the sand. Eli let out a slow breath and reminded himself to loosen his grip on his sword. There was no reason for him to be so tense—the creature wasn't real. It was merely an illusion of a fey raptor. Its wispy sides were transparent in the lights of the practice pit, and its ephemeral beak never caught more than air in the sand. But between its knife-sharp talons and poison-tipped tail feathers, the illusory beast was still enough to give him nightmares.

Hickory gave another hand signal to Burt, who nodded and crept back out of his hiding spot with his bow. If the creature scared him, he didn't show it—he kept a careful eye on its twitching ears, moving silently, arrow nocked...

Then the raptor turned, exposing its vulnerable right flank not to Burt, but to Hickory and Eli. Eli's heartbeat quickened. If the monster pivoted any further, it would spot Burt. But if *he* hit that spot first—

"I can get it," he whispered to Hickory.

"No. Let Burt do it."

The raptor cocked its head and spread its wings, as if testing the wind. Eli tensed—if it took off, they'd lose their shot. He swallowed and looked at Burt, who remained frozen in the beast's blind spot, arrow still pointed at the ground.

Patience, Eli recalled Oren saying. Patience and the right moment.

But his patience had evaporated with the heat. Sweat was pooling on his back, and Burt didn't have the right moment, *he* did, he could take it right now, he just—

The raptor peered at the sky and coiled its back legs, ready to launch—but Eli launched first. He jumped out from behind the rock, ignoring the twigs cracking under his feet, and raised his sword to strike the weak spot.

But the beast caught his movement too quickly—it hissed and

leapt out of the way in one fluid movement. The sword whiffed through air; Burt's arrow whizzed past Eli's head.

The monster turned and snapped its razor beak inches from Eli's face.

"Oh, come on!" Hickory groaned and vaulted over the rock. One hand axe thrown at the monster's face and it was done, the illusion flickering out while her weapon thumped into the sand. "*Really,* Eli?"

"Sorry!" He raised his hands in apology. "The weak spot was right there, I thought I got it—"

"Yeah, and *I* almost got your eye back there," Burt grumbled, trudging over to pick up his arrow. "You didn't even *try* to avoid the twigs this time."

Eli glanced at the broken twigs behind him and rubbed the back of his neck. "I figured if I moved fast enough..."

"No such thing as moving fast enough against a raptor, kid," Oren called from the platform above the practice pit. The elven trainer leaned against the railing, absently fidgeting with his knee brace. "Not when it's heard you coming. You either use stealth or you get your neck snapped."

Eli released an annoyed breath through his nose. Stealth had never been his specialty. Give him something to hit, something decisive, something to *act* on. But sneaking around on tiptoe? That was for the birds.

Or, well, the Burts.

"Reset?" Hickory called to Oren, eliciting a chorus of complaints from the other adventurers still hidden behind the rocks. This had been the party's fourth exercise against the raptor illusion—one more, and Eli thought he might melt in his armor. But this time, Oren shook his head and held up a piece of paper.

"Got your next assignments first," he said. Eli's heart leapt into his throat, and everyone else peeked out from their hiding places.

Oren had been teasing a big mission for weeks, one deep in the exciting, treacherous Vineheart jungle. Every training day, Eli hoped to bring Ambrose the news that he was about to go on his first big quest...and every training day, he came back empty-handed. But if today was the day—

"Is it the Vineheart assignment?" he called, but the party was too busy gathering in a loud gaggle. Oren slid down the ladder to join them and began calling out names.

"For this month," he said, rubbing the gray stubble on his jaw. "Twig and Otto, you'll be on boat escort duty on the Deepriver. Eel season and all. Harvest a few teeth if you can—they're selling well this season. Burt and Hickory..." Oren pointed to the pair beside Eli. "You're on the Vineheart quest. Top up your arrows before we go. There won't be any decent vendors on the road." He glanced at the bottom of the paper. "Eli, you're on deck for local quests this month."

As the others squealed and huddled to discuss their pending shopping trips, Eli deflated. Sure, he was just a trainee...but local quests? Guarding doors, escorting caravans? While everyone else was fighting river eels and trekking into dangerous jungles?

He'd rather go twenty more rounds with the fake fey raptor than go through that slog.

He jogged up to Oren, trying to sound as casual and unaffected as possible. "Hey, there's no chance they might need a third on that Vineheart assignment, right?"

Oren rolled up the paper, giving him a look that was both chiding and apologetic. "It's a big quest, Eli."

"I know—"

"And you're not quite ready yet," he said. "In the Vineheart, every choice is a matter of life and death. One wrong move"—he nodded to the mess of snapped twigs on the practice pit—"and you've lost a party member."

Eli's shoulders slouched. He had no argument against that.

Oren set a hand on his shoulder. "Work on your stealth skills while we're gone," he said. "I've already let the Guildhouse know you'll be in town for local jobs. There's a tourist at Potion Con who wants a bodyguard—that'll be easy money for you." He gave Eli a paternal smile. "Keep practicing, show us what you've worked on when we get back, and we'll bring you on the next quest."

Oren turned and climbed back up the ladder. Hickory bounded over to take his place beside Eli, her hand axe dangling at her side.

"We'll get you on the next one, Valenz." She nudged Eli's arm. "At least you get to go to Potion Con with the Griffin kid this way."

Eli gave her an unconvincing smile. The Griffin kid—all the adventurers called Ambrose that, even if they were younger than the potioneer. Most of them were shop regulars, and many of them remembered Ambrose's time as a gangly young apprentice. To them, he would always be the Griffin kid, even when he grew to be eighty.

"Yeah," he said weakly. "Ames'll be thrilled."

In truth, Ambrose would be thrilled for the same reason Eli wasn't. No jungle journeys or river cruises meant no danger for Eli, and no anxious heart attacks for the potioneer.

But it still wasn't the news he had been hoping to bring back.

"Hickory!" Oren called. "Let's go with that reset!"

The rest of the party groaned. Eli sighed and jogged back to the rock.

RULE 3:

ARRIVE EARLY

Ambrose

IT WAS the night before Potion Con, and Ambrose could hardly sleep.

Not because of the kidnapping news, of course. Potion Con was perfectly safe. So many people, thousands of eyes, plenty of guards. No, Ambrose was busy warring with his feelings—most of which he couldn't possibly confess to Eli.

He tossed and turned, finally nestling against his boyfriend's chest to soak in his warmth and listen to his steady breathing. Yes, it was terrible that Eli hadn't been picked for the Vineheart quest. Yes, he was missing out on experience and glory and gold and...whatever else came with slaying fey raptors.

But secretly, Ambrose held two guilty joys in his heart: one, that Eli was in no danger of being eaten by a fey raptor, and two, that he was going to attend Potion Con instead.

"Let me guess," Eli muttered at the breakfast table the following morning, his eyes barely open, hair mussed. "You're loving this."

Ambrose tried not to crack a smile—a wicked, guilt-ridden smile —as he poured coffee for both of them. "I am not."

"You're a terrible liar."

"I am..." He set down the coffee in front of Eli. "A tiny bit happy you're not galloping off into danger, yes."

"But I was *supposed* to be galloping off right now!" Eli gestured sharply to the window, his complaint emphasized by the miserable morning crackle in his voice. "I should be flying away on a griffin, not..." He slumped. "Babysitting some artificer at Potion Con."

Ambrose piled bacon onto his plate. "I am sorry. Truly, I am. But..."

Eli glared up at him. Ambrose quickly set an extra piece of bacon on his plate as an offering.

"It's just you've never been to the convention before," he continued. "I know it's not as exciting as fey raptors, but...I think you might enjoy it. A little."

He bent down and kissed Eli's forehead. Eli slurped his coffee noisily in response.

Fortunately for Ambrose, after Eli left to meet with his charge for the day, Dawn arrived at his front door with more genuine enthusiasm.

"Tessa's going to be at the wand demo today," she said, rattling off her acquaintances as they walked toward the convention arena. "And Kels said that she'd be at one of the after-parties tonight. You remember her, right? The leatherworker with the green braids?"

"I remember her fawning over you three years ago."

Dawn waved off his words, her nails immaculately painted in fresh, sparkling gold. "She wasn't doing that."

"She absolutely was." Ambrose smiled. Dawn had dressed more beautifully than the actual dawn this morning. She floated along in an amethyst silk dress that clung to her round figure, her eyelids dusted with a matching tone. And all down her long, pointed ears, rows of gold earrings chimed with her every step.

If she was planning to spark some romance today, there was going to be a bonfire by lunch.

They slipped into the morning crowds of the Scar, navigating easily around confused tourists and bleary-eyed Scarrish folk. When Ambrose caught sight of the convention plaza and the check-in tables, he had to restrain himself from picking up speed and losing Dawn in the shuffle. Just a few more minutes, and he'd be wading through the convention instead of the streets, meeting friends, preparing for his first panel—

A hand grabbed his arm. "Ambrose!"

He yelped and reeled back—but the hand was firm, yanking him out of the crowd, away from Dawn, and toward a series of...

Dainty café tables.

"Sherry!" Ambrose glared at the woman holding his arm, his heart still pounding. "What are you doing? I can't be late for the convention—"

"Ames?" Dawn burst out of the crowd, then smiled in relief. "Oh. Hi, Sherry."

"Hello, dear." The gray-haired woman released Ambrose's arm and plopped down at one of the tables, surrounded by an empty tea cup and half-eaten grapefruit. "I wanted to catch you before you went in. Have you got your schedules all sorted?"

Dawn patted her pocket; Ambrose held up his heavily notated paper.

"Good, good. Now, before you go, I've got something for you from Grim..." She dug into her worn skirt pockets. "They're off helping Banneker set up his vendor booth, but they wanted me to... Ah! Here we are." She proffered her open fist with the delighted energy of a grandmother offering a stale caramel. "Go on, go on. Take one."

Ambrose frowned. The two tiny objects in her palm were distinctly not caramels. They were simple round pins, one purple, one gold. He picked up the gold pin, and a bright little zip of magic ran up his fingertips. Of course—he should have expected something like this from Grim, given yesterday's hubbub.

"What's the enchantment?" he asked as he pinned the device to his potion robes, where it immediately camouflaged itself against the fabric pattern. Normally, he hated the idea of poking a hole in his robes, but he knew better than to argue against either Sherry or Grim over something so trivial.

"Just a simple location marker," Sherry said. "Not that Grim's looking to track you all day, of course. Or that they don't trust you, my dears. It's only if—"

"If we're in trouble," Dawn finished, fastening the purple pin to her dress. Similar to Ambrose's, it disappeared into the vibrant color of her dress in an instant. "Yeah, we know."

Sherry visibly relaxed the moment the pins went on, betraying the truth: the devices were far less for their safety and far more for her peace of mind.

"Thank you," she said, squeezing Ambrose's arm. "Do have fun, won't you?"

"Of course." He straightened his robes. "Will you be at the debates this afternoon?"

"I wouldn't miss it." Sherry beamed and shooed them along. "Now, go on and get out there. You've let me hold you up long enough."

Ambrose and Dawn continued on at a faster pace, the flow of traffic buoying them to the check-in tables and beyond. All around the plaza, potioneers, apprentices, students, and simply curious folk chatted in the check-in lines. Some of them eagerly waved to the pair, but they could only wave back and continue on to the entrance tunnel. Years of past experience had taught them well—if they began chatting in the plaza, they'd never make it to the actual convention.

"Here's the map." The cheery elf at the potion masters' table waved him along. "Check the back for the updated list of food options. Enjoy the con!"

Ambrose stepped into the tunnel and took a deep breath of the cool air while waiting for Dawn. The shade was a dependable promise of the excitement to come. He had hoped to share some of it with Eli, of course, but the chances of finding him in the crowd with his client were slim, particularly once the events began...

"Master Beake!" A mustachioed gnome approached him, tailed

closely by a very familiar, broad-shouldered man. Ambrose hid a delighted grin.

Luck was on his side—Eli had found him first.

"Yes?" he said, working to focus on the gnome's words and not the terribly handsome bodyguard behind him.

"Master Beake, how utterly splendid to meet you," the gnome said, shaking Ambrose's hand vigorously with both of his hands. "I'm Sebastian of Sunville's Bewitched Bags and Belts. I read your paper on your breakthrough use of esther last year. It was positively *inspiring*."

"Thank you very much. I—"

Dawn sidled up to Ambrose, neatly arranging her convention badge, and he glanced down the tunnel—it was these sorts of conversations that would ensure he never actually made it inside the event.

"I'm honored to hear that, truly," he continued. "I'm afraid I cannot be late for my first panel, but if you'd kindly accompany me to the main area—?"

"Of course, of course!" Sebastian started down the tunnel. "Far be it from me to make you late—oh, Master Zeda, there you are!" He waved to another potioneer in long, brown robes. "How fortunate, to find both you and Master Beake here—"

The group moved forward in a loose gaggle, Sebastian pinging between introductions and greetings while Eli fell into step beside Ambrose and Dawn.

"You seem to have a friendly charge," Ambrose observed, suppressing the urge to take Eli's hand.

Eli shrugged. "He'll be fine. Just gotta make sure he doesn't run off and get lost in the crowd."

"The place is packed already." Dawn looked around her. "Better keep an eye out for Xavion."

Eli rolled his eyes; Ambrose deflated. Xavion Demachel: talented potioneer, incorrigible egomaniac, and the one person at Potion Con who could sour his mood.

"They're likely farther inside," he muttered. "Signing autographs or something. Did you see that magazine article about them last month?"

Eli snorted. He knew all about Xavion, of course. With how many dinner conversations Ambrose spent ranting about them, there was no way he could escape the knowledge. "What, *My Time in Titan's Nails*?" he said. "The tell-all about their quest to find purple variegated ice flower in the mountains? Pile of dragon dung. Bet you twenty talons they've never even seen snow."

"Precisely. They wouldn't last a day twenty leagues from Titan's —" Ambrose stopped and centered himself. It didn't matter how many false articles Xavion had written about themself. He wouldn't let them get to him, not this year. "It doesn't matter. I'll see them soon enough."

But as he reached the end of the tunnel, his eyes roamed instinctively over the crowd, and he kept folding and unfolding the corner of his con schedule. Dawn hid her smile behind her map. "Mm-hm. It doesn't matter, huh?"

Ambrose glared at her. "They will *not* ruin my day."

"Sure."

"I mean it!"

She just laughed. "All right, all right. Meet you at the panel?"

Eli raised an eyebrow. In any other large outing like this, they would not be simply meeting at the panel. Ambrose would have neatly arranged in his head a list of potential meeting places. A spot for food if they were hungry, a café getaway if they hated the place, a pre-prepared excuse to leave early if necessary...

But this was Potion Con. There was no reason to fear.

"I'll meet you at the panel," he said confidently and stepped into the sunlight of the open sinkhole arena.

Every year, the convention expanded farther and farther into the Scar's famed Gods' Print Sinkhole. Booths and wooden partitions stretched across the vast, sandy floor, forming discussion rooms, demonstration areas, debate stages...

But recently, the convention had begun to crawl up the striped walls of the sinkhole, too—taking advantage of time-worn nooks and crannies and turning them into bars, relaxation spaces, and private event areas. As a result, every layer of the sinkhole buzzed with both sunlight and noise.

And when Ambrose descended to the floor, the noise spiraled into a fever pitch.

"There he is!" An orc tugged on his friend's sleeve and gestured with both arms. "Ambrose, over here!"

Ambrose grinned. "Mr. Wyndham, how are you?"

He had barely shaken that man's hand when another potioneer rushed up. "Master Beake, it's so good to see you," she said, a blush crossing her cheeks. "I don't know if you remember me from last year, but we'll be on today's panel together—"

"I remember." Ambrose gave her a small bow. "I'm thrilled they selected you to join. Your paper on Driftwood dragons and their role in shaping local ingredients—"

But he hardly had time to finish his sentence before another person approached, then another, and another. All friends from past conventions, all overflowing with updates and news and questions.

And Ambrose, for his part, brimmed with joy—particularly when he dared a glance at Eli next to him and found him gaping.

"Ames." Eli leaned in while Sebastian chatted with another artificer nearby. "What exactly is going on here?"

Ambrose bit back a smile. "What do you mean?"

"What do you *mean*, what do I mean?" he whispered, gesturing at the crowd. "You didn't tell me you were a celebrity!"

Ambrose scoffed. "I am not."

"Then what do you call all this?" he demanded. His eyes were as bright as his earrings, as if his suppressed smile was instead shining out of them. Ambrose bit his lip.

"I did tell you that you might enjoy Potion Con a little."

Eli leaned in closer, his voice lowering to dangerous levels. "Only because I have a crush on the convention's biggest star," he said. "I am seconds away from ditching this guy and following you around instead."

For a weak-willed second, Ambrose seriously considered begging him to do just that.

"I"—he fumbled—"I don't think your charge would appreciate that—"

"Oh, I see you've met my bodyguard!" Sebastian bounded jovially back into the conversation. "Apologies, I should have introduced you two earlier." He peered around Ambrose, and his gallant smile flipped into a concerned frown. "My dear boy, I'm terribly surprised you don't have one of your own, what with all these blasted kidnappings going on."

Ambrose held back an eye roll. "I appreciate the concern, but I'll be quite all right, thank you—"

"Ah, *there* he is."

Ambrose looked up, briefly grateful for the distraction—then realized who had spoken.

The newcomer was an unusually tall elf, bedecked in potion robes twice as dazzling and half as practical as those around them. A golden shimmer on their copper cheeks and across their pointed ears directed attention to their face, all sloping, sharp angles and toothy smiles. They approached Ambrose with all the grace of a shark with fashion sense, several admirers trailing behind like little bubbles.

"Master Beake," they said, bowing deeply in a parody of respect. "Finally, the convention can begin."

Ambrose stiffened. Eli quickly claimed his place not at Sebastian's side but at Ambrose's, shoulders square, smile tight and prickly. The elf was undeterred, their gaze roving over Eli in a flicker of interest. "A new...friend?"

"Eli Valenz," Ambrose said, "may I introduce you to Xavion Demachel, a Guild potioneer from the Driftwood."

"Charmed," Eli said charmlessly.

"Enchanted." Xavion showed every one of their teeth. "I was so hoping you'd make an appearance this year, as the man who finally melted Ambrose Beake's icy heart. Tell me, did you ever manage to sell that shop you blew up?"

Whispers shot through the observing crowd. Rage boiled in Ambrose's chest, and beside him, Eli clenched his fists—but Xavion was never one to make just one verbal jab.

"My dear Amby"—they shifted their gaze before Ambrose could respond—"I didn't see any of your work in the last *Potioneering Quarterly*. Slowing down, are you?"

Ambrose wished his gaze could transmute into knives. "I'm afraid I'm still waiting on peer reviews, unlike others I know."

Xavion gave a hum, flitting right over his counter-attack. "Perhaps you should try getting out in nature for a change. Going straight to the source of the magic."

Ambrose noticed the pen in their hand and glanced at their followers. Several were toting signed magazines with a unique illustration on the cover: Xavion's smiling face against a backdrop of snowy mountains.

"Oh, yes," he drawled, flicking his gaze over their immaculate robes. "Proper mountain climber, now, are you?"

Xavion grinned. "It's certainly more thrilling than a musty old potion shop."

Some of their admirers giggled; Ambrose thought his rage might spill out through his ears.

"Oh, like you ever actually—" he started, then reeled himself back in. This was precisely what Xavion wanted—a show of his anger to kick the convention off in their favor. He took a breath and set his hands behind his back. "I'm afraid I must go," he said, forcing every word to be steady and even. "I have a panel starting soon."

"Of course." Xavion waved him off as if they had been the one to dismiss him. "Will I see you at the debates this afternoon, Amby?"

Ambrose's next word was through gritted teeth. "Indeed."

"Excellent." Another bow, one last curious look at Eli, then they swept away, glitter floating off their robes as they went.

Eli folded his arms. "You're going to crush them at the debates, right?"

"That's the plan," Ambrose muttered.

Eli paused, then leaned toward him with a wicked grin. "You got this, *Amby*."

Ambrose shuddered. "Don't."

RULE 4:

MIX AND MINGLE

Dawn

DAWN MOPED BY A FOOD STALL, overpriced coffee in hand. How could there be so many people at Potion Con, yet none of them were who she wanted to see?

Tessa had gotten delayed due to weather and wouldn't arrive until tomorrow. Kels had chickened out on attending due to the kidnappings. Then there was Rin, whom she couldn't find at all, and Aurelia, who had decided to only attend day three...and now she was over halfway through the day, with absolutely no flirting prospects lined up for the evening.

She gave a huff. Water, water, everywhere, or however that stupid phrase went. At least the wand demonstration had been entertaining. And she *had* done some retail therapy and bought several bags' worth of crystals and wood samples from Vendor's Alley...

A thoughtful voice hummed next to her. "Someone's vibe isn't matching the aura of Potion Con today."

She took a loud sip of the coffee. "Hi, Banneker."

Banneker sidled up with a kebab in hand, its bright red sauce matching the hue of his hair. For having gotten up early to set up his booth in Vendor's Alley, the artificer hardly looked worse for wear. Even his freckles looked bright-eyed and bushy-tailed.

"I see you at least had fun at the Alley," he said, pointing with his toe to the bags at her feet. "Rest of the day not matching up?"

"Not quite." She leaned against the striped stone wall of the sink-hole, taking in the bustle of the open-air food court. "Was hoping more of my friends would be here."

"I get it." Banneker rubbed his pointed ear. "A few of my regulars decided not to come, with the safety concerns and all."

"How's your booth doing?"

"Oh, it's hanging in there," he answered modestly. Dawn knew that was a lie—when she had passed by his table earlier, half his devices had been marked as sold, with eager customers eyeing the remainder.

Banneker nudged her. "Hey, if you come back around to my booth, I've still got some free marbles to give out."

Dawn smiled. "Shouldn't you be trying to get those marbles back in your head?"

"No point. You know they'll just fall out of my ears tomorrow." He waved his half-empty kebab stick in the air. "Don't worry too much about your friends, my dudette. There's two more days of the con. Why don't you go relax for a bit, and we'll see you at the debates?"

Dawn's gaze wandered up the sinkhole walls, taking in the tiers of visitors mingling above the food court. Several of those higher nooks and crannies had been turned into overpriced bars, eager to get people primed for a rowdy debate session in the afternoon. Not that she could blame them; a drink sounded nice right about now. She dug up her schedule and gave it a once-over. The debates weren't for another hour—she could fit a cocktail in between now and then, easy.

"All right," she said. "I'll give it a shot. See you later?"

Banneker gave a wide gesture. "Go be one with the universe!"

She shook her head, drained her coffee, and wound her way across the sinkhole, passing by more booths, panels, demonstrations...

"And this here is Noodle. She's a rock pygmy dragon native to the area—"

"Now, this dreaming potion by itself will only last a few minutes, but if you combine it with this solution—"

"Get your quartzes here! Crushed, tumbled, and columns, pre-cleansed and ready to go! Griffin shipping options available!"

...until she finally found the stone-carved stairs leading into the convention's main bar: The Crazed Cauldron, its temporary wooden sign hanging crooked over the door. Dawn grimaced. Given the vastness of the arena, she likely had only a half hour to spare on a watered-down drink before she had to hoof it to the debates, but it was better than staring out at the food stalls and feeling sorry for herself—

The door before her slammed open, and a body came hurtling out.

"What the—?"

It took all her strength to hold onto the railing and not tumble back down the stairs, while the body in question sprawled on the floor at her feet, both panting and laughing. The woman looked a mess—rumpled tunic, dust-streaked vest, purple hair splayed over her tawny face—but she clearly didn't care. She grinned and waved up at Dawn from her spot on the dirty floor. "Hi."

Dawn blinked at her. "Hi?"

"Sorry about that." The woman staggered to her feet and dusted herself off. "Let me just clear this guy out real quick."

"What?" Dawn stood on tiptoe to look over her shoulder. The convention bar was a shambles. Chairs and barstools lay scattered on the floor while peaceful patrons crowded into the side booths, giving the woman and the aforementioned guy—a beefy human with a terrible sneer—space to brawl.

"Come on, Franz." The woman stalked back in, fists raised, smile wide. "If you really call that a punch, I'm gonna tell your editor about it and get you kicked off the adventuring beat."

The man lunged; she ducked, fluid as water.

"You—!" he garbled and continued swinging. She wove in and out of range, taunting him with her laugh—but her bravado had a shelf life. Franz's punches, as drunk as they were, veered closer and closer to her jaw, angrier and faster with every attempt—

Dawn didn't know why she did it. She could've—*should've*—just closed the door, returned to Banneker, and forgotten all about killing time with a bland cocktail. But when the man finally threw himself at the purple-haired woman, hands out, lips in a snarl, Dawn grabbed a glass of water from the bar and tossed it right into his face.

He spluttered in surprise, teetering halfway through his lunge. This was all the woman needed—she quickly ducked to the side and left her leg stuck out, letting him trip and smash his way down to the floor.

"All right, that's it!" The bartender hopped out from behind the bar. "Someone get Franz out of here."

Several other men—who were much braver now that the opponent was on the floor—leapt in and dragged Franz down to the lower levels, leaving Dawn with a stranger's empty glass and an odd sense of accomplishment.

"You too, Rory." The bartender glared at the purple-haired woman. "Out."

"He started it!" She gathered up the glasses scattered across the bar and, in a blink, had them neatly stacked before him. "And you can't stand him, either. Don't tell me you weren't looking forward to kicking him out."

The bartender reluctantly took the glasses. "You're an idiot."

She set both hands under her chin. "Your favorite idiot."

As he grumbled and wiped down the bartop, patrons slowly crawled out from the booths and began to flock around the bar. Dawn didn't realize she was still hovering by the doorway until the woman—Rory—approached her once more, her dishevelment a clear mark of victory.

"Hey." She nodded to Dawn. "Sorry again about that. You all right?"

Dawn stared at Rory's face, absorbing the details the commotion had previously hidden. Her foolish grin did nothing to hide the entrancing sharpness of her features—the angled cheekbones, the short, pointed ears, the eyebrows studded with onyx piercings. It would have been intimidating if her look hadn't been tempered by surprising hints of softness. Dawn's eyes trailed over the wavy lines in her undercut, the teardrop earrings tapping against her jawline, then down farther...to the undulating strokes of a moving tattoo, barely peeking out from her wrinkled collar to caress her collarbone.

Dawn swallowed, her face warm. Yeah. She was certainly all right.

"You know," she said, scrambling for a joke, "people normally wait until the debates to start punching people."

It worked—Rory laughed. "Seeing as I'm not a potioneer, I gotta take my fights where I can get 'em." She gestured to the bar. "Here, let me buy you a drink to thank you. I know the bartender—he's moonlighting from The Rose & Crown. Makes a fantastic dragon's tail. You like whiskey, uh...?"

She trailed off, waiting for a name. Dawn smiled. She was more of a rum girl herself, but for this woman? She'd take the whiskey neat.

"Dawn. And a dragon's tail sounds great."

They moved to a booth overlooking the arena, where potioneers still swarmed in tiny droves. Trying not to stare at the woman lounging across from her, Dawn watched the muted chaos below and took a sip of her drink. Just as Rory had promised, it wasn't half-bad. The dry wine atop the smoky whiskey created a delightful two-toned twist, both in the glass and on her tongue.

"Told you he was good." Rory leaned back in the booth, tapping her glass with chipped navy nails. "So, you a potioneer?"

"Wandmaker," Dawn said. "Mostly here with friends." Or at least she would be, if half of them had actually attended today. "What about you? You said you weren't a potioneer."

"No, I'm not smart enough for that. I'm a journalist covering the convention."

"Oh. Science beat?"

"Magical crime, actually." Rory tilted her drink toward the arena before taking a sip. "Interviewing all the tourists who shelled out for bodyguards this year. Not that there are a lot of them, but it's enough for a fluff piece." Her gaze settled on Dawn with a roguish half smile, one that sent a small tingle up Dawn's arms. "Did your friends bring any guards? I need a few more quotes for my story before I go."

"Nah, they're locals," Dawn said. "They don't need bodyguards." Then, in a desperate attempt at charm, something to match that smile— "I'd beat up anyone who tried to get close to them. You saw how I operate."

She held up her glass and flexed an arm. To her relief, Rory snorted into her drink.

"We can market that," she said, eyes glittering. "I can put an ad in the newspaper and everything. I happen to know a guy."

Sip by sip, their cocktails disappeared as they piled onto the joke. Full-page ads for Dawn's services, a glittery bodyguard uniform (pink and purple, of course), sparkling waterskins strapped to her thighs and arms—

Then the bartender pounded on the bartop, cutting their words short.

"Debates start in twenty minutes, folks!" he called. "Watch some smart idiots argue and punch each other, then come straight back here for happy hour!"

All around them, people eagerly hopped out of their seats and made for the debates. Rory set down her glass, smile faltering.

"Well, I've got a few more people to dig up for interviews." She checked her pocket watch. "Doubt anyone will be sober enough to give a good quote after the debates are done."

Dawn reluctantly slid out of the booth, wracking her brain for a way to keep Rory around a little while longer. If she could talk with her a bit more, she might be able to whisk her off to an after-party. A good one at The Jumping Ogre, or maybe at The Acid Splash in the northern quarter. Eli had enjoyed that place last time he—

Wait. *Eli.*

"Come to the debates with me," she blurted out. "One of my friends is working here as a bodyguard. You could interview him and his client. And one of my other friends is a big potioneer—he'll have something to say about the bodyguards if you want a dissenting opinion."

Rory's eyebrows rose. "Will he be in the debates?"

"He crushes it every year."

"How's his right hook?"

Dawn laughed—the one time Ambrose had thrown a punch, it hadn't worked out for him. Or...had it, in the end?

"Nonexistent," she said. "If he actually has to throw one this year, I'm buying everyone a drink."

"Punches, sources, *and* drinks?" Rory drained her glass, her eyes locking with Dawn's in a way that suggested none of those was what really intrigued her. "I'm in, water girl. Lead the way."

RULE 5:

SIMMER

Ambrose

THE DEBATE HALL had already filled by the time Ambrose arrived. Not that he was surprised—the energy of opening day meant there would be more fistfights than usual, and that was generally half the draw of the debates. Eager students and experienced potion masters alike gathered together with snacks and drinks. One man in particular had posted up in the corner, already surveying the sign-up booth and taking extensive notes—no doubt for the unofficial gambling rings about to form.

Rosemond Street, fortunately, had nabbed an excellent spot near the debate stage, erasing Ambrose's fear of being relegated to the back of the audience. Sherry and Banneker passed around a bag of caramel popcorn, while Dawn laughed with an unfamiliar woman beside her.

"No Grim?" Ambrose asked as he approached. Sherry shook her head.

"You know they hate watching the fights," she said. "Last time they attended, I caught them trying to offer lessons on uppercuts to the poor boys after. They can't stand to watch a bad punch."

"Couldn't be me," Dawn said through a mouthful of caramel drizzle. The newcomer beside her stuck her hand out to Ambrose.

"You must be Ambrose Beake. I'm Rory, with the *Scarrish Post*," she said with a wide, genuine grin. "Can't believe you were the friend Dawn was talking about. Half the folks I've interviewed today have mentioned you, I swear."

Ambrose gave Dawn a half-chiding look. "Roping me into interviews, are you?"

"*No.*" She started chewing her popcorn faster. "I just thought she might like to interview Eli. She's writing an article about bodyguards at Potion Con."

Judging by the way she glanced sidelong at Rory, that was most certainly not the reason Dawn had dragged her along, but Ambrose let it lie—far be it from him to get in the way of her pursuits. On the contrary, he made a mental note to casually mention Dawn's professional accolades to Rory before he went onstage.

"Has anyone seen Eli recently?" he asked, searching the crowd for a hint of black hair and broad shoulders. Just when he was beginning to fear that Sebastian had chosen not to attend the debates, the mustachioed gnome appeared amongst the many faces.

"Oh, there's Master Beake!" Sebastian called, then tugged on Eli's sleeve. "Are you quite sure we'll be all right to stand with your friends? I've never been able to stand so close to the stage before—"

"It'll be fine," Eli reassured him. "It's, uh...safer this way."

"Right, right. Brilliant idea." The artificer's head bobbled. Eli winked at Ambrose and made space next to Sherry. Ambrose fought the urge not to immediately push his way over and take his hand; instead, he nodded politely to Sebastian, then made his excuses to Dawn and Rory.

"I'm afraid I must go sign up and see what's in store for me," he said. "I'll be right back."

Ambrose made a point of never signing up a topic himself, not for any category. In his opinion, those who actively presented a topic were the brash ones, the ones who wanted to yell rather than communicate an informed opinion. He himself almost never planned to go up—but more often than not, someone would sign up a truly heinous take, and he would find himself verbally beating said point to death onstage a half hour later.

Unfortunately for him, this had become a well-known habit of his —particularly well-known by Xavion—and Xavion took it upon themself to taunt him with horrible opinions. That crushed silver-weed was more effective than dried. That uncleansed minerals couldn't be used in effect reversals.

(*That* particular topic, at least, had only taken five minutes to beat into the dirt. Xavion hadn't thought that challenge through.)

Ambrose strode up to the booth and searched for what his debate rival had posted today. With their greeting that morning, there was no possibility they weren't on the list. But as he flipped through the pages, Xavion's name wasn't appearing. Not when it came to ingredient theories, or research practices, or historical analysis...

He flipped to the last page, Dragon's Advocate, and sighed.

Dragon's Advocate was intended first and foremost as a learning tool. Two people argued a well-known and well-ascribed theory in the same way a jeweler tumbled a rock. Examining it from all sides, using creativity and problem-solving to unearth new perspectives on old ideas.

And today, Xavion had dared sign up an argument that, whenever it was brought up, threatened to cleave every panel and debate in two.

True illusions are impossible.

Of course they were. Everyone knew that. No one had ever been able to manage a full illusion that perfectly looked, felt, sounded, tasted, *and* smelled like the real thing. There were too many factors at play, too many magic components that could dangerously backfire against each other in pursuit of all of those aspects. Sure, some people could manage three of the five and make the illusion passable —Aphosian artificers had gotten the closest—but no one had actually achieved perfection.

And given the Guild's strict restrictions on such dangerous experimentation, no one ever would. Trying to argue against it was like arguing that water wasn't wet.

He bit his lip, his quill hovering over the paper. Xavion had done this on purpose. They had seen Eli, knew who he was, knew he would be in the audience. They wanted to watch Ambrose fail in front of him, and indeed, they were one of the only ones with a chance of doing so.

But Ambrose wasn't going to back away from a challenge simply because his boyfriend was watching.

And he wasn't going to fail, either.

He signed his name next to the topic, gave a short nod to the orc manning the booth, and walked back to his friends.

The Dragon's Advocate topics didn't take place until later in the debate slots, giving him time to frantically form an argument in his head while others sparred out loud onstage. One such debate turned into a clumsy fistfight, which rewarded both Eli and Dawn for their patience.

"Give him the chair!" Dawn yelled and passed Eli the popcorn.

"Keep your guard up!" Eli shouted before cramming a handful of popcorn into his mouth and offering Ambrose the bag. "Want some?"

"Hm?" It took him a moment to wrest himself from his thoughts. "No, thank you."

Eventually, the two potioneers shuffled offstage with nosebleeds and bruised egos, and Eli turned to Ambrose. "So, what'd you sign up for?" he asked, handing the popcorn bag over to Sherry. "Something fun?"

Well, it would certainly be fun for Xavion to watch Ambrose lose —which he would if he walked up there with nothing in his head.

"Something difficult," Ambrose admitted. Eli squeezed his hand.

"Good," he said. "That means it'll hurt them more when you destroy them." He glanced at Sebastian, who was deep in a conversation with the elf beside him, then started rolling up his sleeves. "Now, do we need a quick refresher on defensive stances?"

Ambrose tried not to stare at Eli's increasingly visible forearms. "Is that necessary?"

"Listen, I'm not letting you go up there and act like those idiots." Eli gestured to the potioneers now sitting in the medic's corner, mumbling retorts through handkerchiefs pressed to their noses. "Come on, what are the basics?"

Ambrose rolled his eyes and half-heartedly lifted his arms. Eli lifted them the rest of the way for him and put them into position while Ambrose recited. "Fists protecting the face, elbows tucked in..."

"That's right, and watch their shoulders to anticipate their punch." Eli held his wrists. "You remember how to slip?" He mimicked the ducking movement for him.

"In theory."

Eli kissed his knuckles. "Don't punch them back, not if you can help it. You wouldn't survive a brawl."

"Your confidence in me is inspiring."

Up onstage, the announcer cleared her throat. "Xavion Demachel, CPM, and Ambrose Beake, CPM."

Ambrose's heart thudded against his ribcage, as it always did before a debate. It didn't matter how many times he went up there, nor how many times he won. He could never quite get used to the number of eyes staring at him, watching and waiting for him to succeed...or fail.

Eli squeezed his hand once more before he went up, and Ambrose tried to hold onto that feeling, that warmth, for as long as possible—but the fear in his system struck as soon as he stood onstage. Did he have to throw up? Go to the bathroom? Run away screaming? All three? He had no argument, utterly no thought in his brain on how to even *pretend* that true illusions were possible—

But then Xavion ascended to the stage, smiling and waving to the crowd, and a surge of purified vexation tamped down all of Ambrose's other emotions.

He wasn't going to let this pompous elf win. Not in front of this crowd, and especially not in front of Eli.

They shook hands and stepped back from each other.

"Today's Dragon's Advocate topic, set by Demachel," the

announcer said, "is positing that true illusions are impossible." Her gaze flicked up from the clipboard. "And the sky is blue."

Laughter rippled through the crowd. Ambrose's stomach churned. Xavion was already smirking.

"Demachel," the announcer continued, "I'll allow you one minute to present your argument, and Mr. Beake will have one minute to counter." She nodded to both of them and walked away, eyebrows raised at Ambrose in a silent *Good luck with this one.*

Xavion began as they always did, with their smooth voice and leisurely, unruffled stroll around their half of the stage.

"We potioneers have been trying to enhance our world since the very birth of the art," they said, their robes swirling around their feet. "We are experts at revealing the truth of our surroundings or creating a comforting lie to hide what we cannot change. We have been in the business of both truth and lies ever since both concepts existed. But the only thing we cannot do"—they held up a finger—"is create a lie truly indistinguishable from the truth. A perfect illusion that in every single way imitates reality. Every attempt to do so has proven and will prove to be disastrous."

Again, there wasn't much of an argument here. Every first-year student knew this statement. Whether it was at an academy or an apprenticeship, it was drilled into them early so an errant teenager didn't try to defy the odds and combine five different brews into one very large explosion.

Unfortunately for all those well-meaning teachers, Ambrose had to provide some sort of counter-argument.

"I disagree," he said. A murmur through the crowd—who, of course, knew he had to say that, but their murmuring was another obligatory part of the debate structure.

"I don't disagree that every attempt has been disastrous," he clarified, keeping his posture straight as if he already knew his argument. "But I—I *do* disagree that it will always prove to be so."

"So, you have a solution?" Xavion asked.

"Not as such."

"Then what's your argument?"

Ambrose's cheeks went pink, a reaction he hated. Xavion didn't need any visual cue that he had no ideas whatsoever.

But he had a minute to counter—he might as well use it to talk himself through this mess.

"All of our existing illusion potions succeed because they focus on only a few key aspects of reality," he said, pacing about his half of the stage. "Trying to build a recipe that addresses every single aspect only ends in destabilization. There are too many factors to consider, too many ingredients that can and will react to each other in detrimental ways once you combine them."

Xavion folded their arms, watching Ambrose like he was cornered prey. "Yes, precisely."

"Similarly, drinking multiple potions to achieve all intended effects is ill-advised," Ambrose continued, grasping desperately for a path, a clue, anything to move his argument forward. "The body cannot tolerate that amount of magic. So, how can true illusions be feasible?"

"That's the question, Beake."

A smattering of chuckles from the crowd. The announcer glanced at her pocket watch. If Ambrose didn't form some kind of counter within the minute, he'd be shut down, the laughingstock of the next two days of the convention—

He blurted out the first thought that came to mind. "You don't combine the ingredients at all."

Xavion frowned. "What?"

Follow the logic, Ambrose told himself. That was all he could do at this point.

"Most multi-effect potions are the result of directly combining two solutions," he said. "But if one properly partitions and filters the solutions, controlling precisely what and how much actually interacts with each other, it could be possible to gradually form a stable multi-effect brew that addresses all aspects of a true illusion."

Xavion scoffed. "Past studies have tried everything—"

Ah—an easy counter. Ambrose straightened.

"No, they haven't. That's a core tenet of potioneering. There's always something out there we haven't used yet, or haven't used right, or figured out how to use. Like, like..." His mind flipped back through old experiments, past trials—

He saw Eli out of the corner of his eye. "Like esther."

Xavion rolled their eyes. "Yes, yes, we all know about your little dragon wing illusions."

Some more snickering from the people directly around Xavion. Ambrose didn't bother looking at them. A silly attempt at riling him up, easily ignored.

"No, that isn't—" He gestured to the air. "Every prior attempt at enhancing illusions has utilized Elwig sorrel as the connector, right?"

Xavion's eyes narrowed. "Yes."

"What if they used esther instead?"

Xavion didn't hesitate. "It's impossible," they said. "The brewing process is far too harsh. It would immediately break down the esther into a useless ingredient."

"Up until now, yes." Ambrose's words picked up speed. "But if you follow the principles of my expansion on Warren's technique for treating esther, it may be possible to keep it from breaking down."

The announcer clicked her pocket watch—a signal for Xavion to argue back.

"Oh, please," they sneered. "Your expansion last year was hardly more than luck."

"Was it luck when I was able to recreate it more than twenty times after?" Ambrose tilted his head. "Or was it luck when you mentioned using my technique in your interview in *Potioneering Quarterly* last month?"

Xavion's expression cracked, and they glanced nervously at the audience. "You must keep your obsession with me in check, Beake."

A small pattering of laughter. Ambrose looked at the announcer. "Tangent?"

The announcer nodded. "That's a warning, Demachel."

Xavion's sneer fully evaporated, and Ambrose could see them mentally reset themself. Having no tangent to distract with meant they actually had to counter Ambrose's argument—or risk a loss.

"Esther isn't strong enough to sustain the magic of an illusion," they snapped. "It becomes unstable in strengths above the fourth level."

"Bryant's research on fifth-level antidotes, though not yet peer-reviewed, suggests otherwise," Ambrose said smoothly. He had to respond faster now, keep Xavion from pivoting. He knew how they worked—the less time they had, the more frustrated they became.

"It's never been tested in multi-aspect illusions before—"

"According to a panel just this morning, it's being tested in decorative environmental illusions that are aiming for three aspects of realism." Ambrose gave an exaggerated frown. "Or were you still signing autographs when that panel was going on?"

Somewhere to his left, Dawn laughed and started coughing on popcorn.

"Tangent, Beake," the announcer warned.

Ambrose nodded. "Accepted."

Xavion straightened their robes. "How long would the potion even last?"

"Your position wasn't on how long it could last," Ambrose said lightly. "Merely that it couldn't exist."

Xavion strode forward, fists clenched, eyes sparking. "But it *cannot* exist!"

"Not now, perhaps." Ambrose stepped forward as well. "But five years ago, a potion for full-day flight didn't exist. When I first began studying, high-level lightning resistance was merely a theory." He found himself only a few feet away from Xavion, who was staring daggers into his face. He kept going. "Why defend something as an absolute when few such things exist in our field? Did you actually present the argument to test the limits of our current collective knowledge? Or did you do it just to embarrass me?" He leaned forward with a small, taunting smile. "You really must keep your obsession with me in check, Demachel."

Xavion surged forward, shoulders tight—but this time, the announcer held up both hands.

"All right, all right," she said. "Good arguments, both of you. Why don't we take five and regroup?"

Ambrose cursed inwardly. It was both a victory in getting the last word, and a defeat in that Xavion would have five minutes to think.

As he descended toward his friends, the announcer turned to face the audience. "Don't forget, folks, last event after these debates is the dragon Q&A panel in room E5! First event of tomorrow is the Brewer's Boozy Brunch with the organizers of the convention..."

Dawn beamed and grabbed Ambrose's arm. "Oh my gods, I thought they were gonna throw a punch—"

"They wouldn't." Ambrose rested against Eli, who dared a brief and only mildly unprofessional kiss on his cheek.

"Kinda wanted to see it," he said, his pride practically vibrating through their shared touch. "You coulda taken them down."

"Such newfound confidence," Ambrose answered weakly—the five minutes were ticking away loudly in the back of his mind. Sherry leaned in and touched his shoulder.

"Everything all right?"

"I..." He looked around, suddenly feeling every shift and buzz of the crush around him. "I need to get out of the crowd. Go think somewhere, prepare my next argument." He caught sight of the tunnel leading out of the debate hall and brightened. "I'll be right back."

RULE 6:

WATCH CAREFULLY

Dawn

DAWN WATCHED Ambrose melt into the crowd, his navy and gold robes blending in with the mass of other potion masters filling the space. His furrowed brow had returned, indicating he was already lost in thought, sorting out how to finish verbally beating Xavion to a pulp on the debate stage.

For a moment, she pondered going with him—as a sounding board or a familiar face, at the very least. After all, it wasn't against debate rules for her to coach him, nor to hang around and make sure he was safe and comfortable in the crowd...

Then Rory tapped her on the shoulder, and all thought of stepping away evaporated. Ambrose didn't need her help. This was Potion Con. This was *his* domain. He was almost as safe and comfortable here as he was at his own shop.

He could stew in his thoughts for a minute or so while she spoke to a beautiful woman.

"Real glad you dragged me along," Rory said, tugging a small notebook from her pocket. "No idea what those potioneers are talking about, but it's good fun." She flipped to a fresh page, strands of her short purple hair falling delicately over her eyes. "So, you said Ambrose was the dissenting bodyguard opinion?"

Eli looked up at the word *bodyguard*—then, to Dawn's dismay, made one glance between her and Rory, grinned, and passed the popcorn off to Sherry.

"Dawn." He cleared his throat. "Who's your new friend?"

He put such a blatant emphasis on *friend* that Dawn glanced at Rory in horror. But if the journalist caught the implication, she made no show of it—she looked up from her notepad and stuck her hand out.

"Rory Basha of the *Scarrish Post*, magical crimes beat," she said, the well-worn moniker forming one large word. "You're the body-guard, right? Mind if I ask you a few questions—?"

Before she could launch into her interview, the announcer gave a sharp whistle. Xavion ascended the stage once more, adjusting their glittery robes with no hint of a smile on their face. On the other side of the room, Ambrose reappeared from the hall, approaching the stage with stoic determination.

Dawn waited for him to look their way, as he always did before going up. No matter how nervous or angry or determined he was, he always had at least a ghost of a smile to pass along to them. She prepared to flash him a thumbs-up or mouth a *Go get him*—

But he didn't look. He just walked up onstage in an oddly stiff gait, his face strangely...neutral.

That wasn't like him at all.

Dawn nudged Eli. "Does Ames look...okay to you?"

"No," he muttered, already frowning. "You think he's nervous?"

"Maybe," Dawn tried. But that wasn't right, either—and judging by Eli's tense posture, they both knew it.

"All right." The announcer shifted in her seat as Ambrose and Xavion met again in the middle of the stage. "We've got time for a quick wrap-up. Master Demachel, you'll have a minute to state your follow-up to Master Beake's last assertion, then Master Beake will have a minute to respond. I trust you both know the drill beyond that." After a requisite murmur of laughter from the crowd, she nodded them along. "Shake and we'll get on with it."

Xavion extended their hand, nails shining gold. Ambrose held out his own hand with an inflexible motion, his gaze looking not at his rival but past them. Xavion stepped forward, eyes narrowed—

Their hand went straight through Ambrose's palm.

"What the—?" They leapt back. A flash of fear, then boiling anger contorted their features. "What is this?"

Ambrose disappeared.

His form didn't even flicker. One moment, he was there, and the next, he was gone, leaving a gasping audience and Xavion alone onstage.

Xavion fumed.

"Is this some sort of sick joke?" they demanded, glaring at the announcer with the heat of a dozen cauldron fires. "How *dare* that man! He should be banned immediately—"

But it wasn't a joke. Dawn knew that. Ambrose would never pull such a trick at Potion Con, not in a hundred years.

"Where is he?" she said, hating how much her voice shook. "Where's Ames?"

She didn't realize she was holding on to Eli's arm until he shifted past her, taking her trembling hand in his.

"Come on," he said, eyes on the hallway.

"But"— Sebastian called after him—"pardon me, but where are you going?"

Eli ignored him, as did the others; Sherry and Banneker were swift to follow, with Rory close behind.

"I'm sorry, but..." Rory said as they maneuvered through the wildly gossiping crowd. "Does he normally—?"

"No," Eli bit out the word. "No, he doesn't. Something's wrong."

Dawn had hoped she could catch her breath when they reached the edge of the crowd at the hallway—but the freeing sense of empty space did little to relieve her when Ambrose wasn't there.

"Ambrose?" Sherry called, her voice bouncing in the stone tunnel. Nothing.

"He couldn't have gone far," Banneker said uncertainly. Dawn wanted to laugh. As if he would run. As if he would just leave.

They kept going down the hall, picking up speed, calling Ambrose's name over and over again. There were no doors he could have gone through, no branching tunnels, nothing—

Until they reached the service tunnel.

More roughly carved than the others, this striped tunnel retreated into darkness, eventually connecting with other pathways that looped back to the Scar proper. Dawn searched the shadows, praying for a familiar shape or voice to appear...

A speck of white farther in caught her eye: a plain, rumpled cloth, cast aside in the middle of the tunnel like a discarded napkin. She walked toward it—

Banneker threw out a skinny arm, blocking them all from moving forward with an uncharacteristic command. "Stay right there."

He crept forward, then carefully lifted the cloth, gave it a sniff, and dropped it back down with a sharp flinch.

"Smells like a knock-out brew." His voice echoed in the dark tunnel. "A strong one."

Dawn's stomach flipped. Next to her, Sherry's voice wavered.

"It could have come from one of the medics," she tried. "Perhaps it just—fell out of their pack—"

"Wait." Eli squinted, then strode forward and picked up a glint of gold off the ground.

His muscles went taut all at once.

"It didn't come from a medic," he said, his voice pulled thin, his hand shaking. Dawn recognized the object in his hand immediately. The Guild-inscribed gold, the blue gem at the center.

Ambrose's signet ring.

She couldn't breathe. Ambrose loved that ring. He never took it off, not ever.

As she tried and failed to regain her breath, Rory cautiously stepped forward, hands raised.

"Hey," she said, her voice low and steady. "If you'll allow me..."

Their eyes all snapped to her.

"Don't touch anything else," she continued, "and don't go anywhere. I've seen this several times before on my beat—"

"Where?" Eli snapped.

Rory kept going, just as steady as before. "The illusion and the knock-out enchantment," she said carefully. "It's common with Aphosian practices, and if we're dealing with Aphos—"

Eli took off running.

RULE 7:

TEAMWORK REQUIRED

Eli

ELI SPRINTED down the dark tunnels, fear carrying his feet far from the others' shouts. All around him, crystal lamps sputtered to life, flaring on and off as he passed—but they revealed nothing other than his own shadow. There was no Ambrose, no evidence of Ambrose; not even a footprint to guide his steps.

He stopped and swore loudly, the tunnel amplifying the word as if putting out its own call for the missing man. This couldn't be happening. Ambrose had been right there, steps away, while he was guarding someone else—

His roiling thoughts sent him running again, picking a path blindly, hoping it would send him in the right direction. The tunnels gradually wound back around the arena, and through open alcoves in the wall, he could see Potion Con flashing past him. The food stalls, heady with the smell of oil and sugar. Panels, where potioneers and artificers droned. Vendor booths, still lively and chattering so late in the day.

No hint of icy hair there, either; no blue eyes meeting his in the crowd. Ambrose was gone, and none of these people even knew.

He picked up speed, panic rising as he neared the entrance, with the plaza beyond it, then the streets, then the entire city. Gods, if he disappeared into the city, if they had managed to get him out of the convention—

A massive figure stepped in front of him and caught him with beefy arms.

"Let go of me!" he shouted on instinct, immediately throwing a wild punch. The figure caught it easily but made no move to return the gesture.

"No use going out there, Valenz," Grim said. "He isn't there."

Eli slouched, nearly boneless with relief, and let out a breath. "So, you've found him?"

"Not yet," they said. Their words were pulled as tight as Eli's, edged with the same fear. "Sherry sent for me. Got here as quick as I could." They released Eli. "No use going out into the city alone. Let's get back to the group and sort this out."

Fear still writhed in Eli's chest, and part of him demanded to keep running. Going backward was useless; going backward was admitting defeat.

But Grim's lingering grip was as solid as stone, and his words were just as sound. If Ambrose really was out there, out in the stretching chasm city, there was no good Eli could do there by himself.

"Fine." He gritted his teeth. "Let's go back."

By the time they returned to the service tunnel, the place had transformed. Half the area was cordoned off with rope, while Potion Con officials and uniformed peacekeepers filled the remaining space. In the back, Rory interviewed one of the officials, her voice just as steady and professional as before.

"And when was the last time you had a security breach like this?" she asked. The official nervously tugged on his collar and glanced at a gnomish peacekeeper, who was busy pondering the enchanted knock-out cloth on the ground.

"It is far too early to conclude it was a security breach," the official said. "Our head peacekeeper will determine what may have occurred here."

Rory barely hid an eye roll and kept writing in her notebook. As she took notes, a gnome blew past her, black skirts swishing and curses rolling off her tongue.

"Damned arena," Viola muttered, both sand and flour dusting her dress as she glared down at the uneven planks under her. "You'd think these potioneers would have enough money to fund a better set of wooden boards." She huffed and joined the Rosemond Street huddle alongside Eli and Grim. "Any news? Came as fast as I could, but with this stupid path..." She stomped on the ground, the metal of her prosthetic rattling against the boards.

"No sign of him," Sherry said, her arm protectively around Dawn's shoulders. "Banneker's gone back to his booth to get..." She rubbed her forehead with a trembling hand. "Something, I'm not sure, but— but we don't have anything so far. No one saw what happened."

They silently clustered closer together. Eli gravitated toward Dawn, who had tear stains on her cheeks; she immediately leaned into him, words bubbling out all at once.

"I knew I should've gone with him," she blurted out. "It's all my fault—"

Eli wrapped his arms around her. "It's not your fault. I should've gone." It didn't matter that he had been guarding someone, or even that he was supposed to guard that person now. Aphos had gotten who they wanted, and it hadn't been his charge.

It had been his boyfriend.

"Okay, got my stuff." Banneker skidded to a halt near Grim, bags of tools swinging from both his shoulders. "Magical signature-tracking, footprint-finding..." He turned to the head peacekeeper. "Got anything so far?"

"Hm." The gnome stroked his thick beard. "Well, I have reason to believe..." He stooped and pointed to the cloth with great authority. "That this could be enchanted."

All of Rosemond Street blinked at him.

"Yeah, we know—" Banneker tried, but the peacekeeper held up a somber hand.

"It will require rigorous testing at my office," he said with great aplomb. "These things take time to ensure the correct data. But rest assured, I will be the one to find him. I am on the case. Now, about the missing man..." He frowned. "What did you say he looked like again? Green hair, was it?"

Eli looked to Dawn; Sherry to Grim; Viola to Banneker.

They clustered even closer together.

"Regroup at the street," Grim ordered.

"The bakery," Viola quickly added. "I'll have food ready for you—"

Sherry held Grim's arm. "You'll start tracking Ambrose's pin?"

"Already started," Grim said. "Banneker and I should have an esti-mate within the hour." Their gray eyes swiveled to Dawn and Eli. "If you two need to rest..."

Eli almost laughed, the cold sound rattling in his ribcage. He didn't need rest. He needed Ambrose Beake in front of him again.

"We'll be there," he said. Dawn nodded alongside him, holding his hand in a firm grip. "We're getting him back."

RULE 8:

DON'T PANIC

Ambrose

AT FIRST, Ambrose thought he was in a dream.

He didn't know where he was or when he was. With his pounding headache, he didn't even have a firm grip on *who* he was. All he knew was that the stone walls surrounding him weren't from The Griffin's Claw or Eli's place or Potion Con, and he could only assume that was less than ideal.

As he pushed himself to sit up, the dream quickly warped into a nightmare.

His wrists were bound with a thin rope, as scratchy and uncomfortable as the rough cot underneath him. Beyond the cot, his only companions in the tiny stone room were a metal door and a tray on the ground, bearing an apple and a cup of water. The room held nothing else—not even a window.

He screwed his eyes shut against his headache and tried to recall what had happened at the convention. His memories started innocently enough: he had walked away from the debate stage, looking for a quieter place to think for a moment. He had found an emptier spot in the hallway...

His memory wavered like a candle flame and his headache flared, discouraging him from remembering. He pushed past the pain, searching for the truth. Someone had approached him only a minute later...

A man called his name. It was strangely difficult to discern his features, apart from a deep voice, a pale complexion, and a strange amulet on his chest. He turned a dial on the amulet, and everything went fuzzy, the disorienting blur accompanied by a rhythmic clicking sound.

Before Ambrose could ask who he was, the stranger spoke.

"You're the one who completed the mayor's commission with the esther, yes?"

"Yes," he found himself saying. "Eli Valenz and I—"

The ticking from the necklace grew louder in his memory. Ambrose winced and tried to focus. He had asked something—yes, he had finally managed to ask for the man's name, and—

"My name isn't important right now," the man said. "I'm here on behalf of my supervisor. She is a patron of the potioneering arts, you see, and has taken a great interest in your work."

The noise from the debate area was suddenly muffled as if Ambrose had corks in his ears.

"And with that interest"—the man turned the dial on the necklace again —"comes an opportunity. One I think you will be quite open to under the right circumstances."

Alarms sounded somewhere in the back of Ambrose's mind, but something else in his head swatted them away, and he remained where he stood. "Really?" he murmured, his voice drowned out by the ticking.

"If you'll come with me?"

Ambrose tried to turn back to the stage, look behind him, shout, anything—but he couldn't control himself anymore, and he began to walk with the stranger.

They veered toward a dark service hall. Ambrose tried to back away from him, to catch the eye of anyone he passed and signal that something was wrong—but no one looked at him, not even when he brushed up against them.

The hallway darkened further, the crystal lamps not responding to their presence, and Ambrose's panic finally breached the surface. He couldn't speak beyond agreeing with the man, couldn't walk except alongside him. There was no fighting, no escape unless he bought himself time—

The man pulled out a reeking white cloth. There was no time left.

Ambrose managed to raise one hand while keeping the other behind him, working off his signet ring.

"Wait, please—" he mumbled, the words struggling to get out, but the cloth ended their fight. He heard the quiet ping of metal on the ground, then his own body crumpling onto the stone—

Ambrose opened his eyes, reeling back on the cot. He had been kidnapped.

He had half a mind to laugh—the very idea was like saying he had met a talking dragon, or had tea with the serpent living in the Scar's cistern. It was all completely ridiculous.

He frantically tested his rope bindings—and when that resulted in nothing but sore wrists, he scrambled for a way to ground himself. He needed information. Clues. That would settle the tightening in his chest, surely.

He took a deep breath and examined the walls first. They had the same striated pattern as the chasm, so his kidnappers hadn't taken him out of the Scar itself. There were no windows to denote time and no daylight coming from the crack under the door. For now, he assumed he had been out anywhere between several hours and a day.

Somehow, that new detail didn't reassure him.

He looked around the floor next, steeling himself for bones, rats, spiders, bloodstains—and found nothing. Just a bit of dust in the corner and his untouched tray of food before him.

With so little to go on, his search became more panicked. He pushed on the door next, checked every corner of the cot. Then the blanket, the tray, even the apple...but the blankness and silence of it all held nothing to distract him from his spiraling thoughts. Perhaps whoever had kidnapped him meant for him to stay here forever, to rot and become the cell's first skeleton. Then he'd never see Eli or Dawn or Rosemond Street again, and someone would have to sell his shop, and some uppity elf would turn it into a—a *skincare* boutique or something—

He forced out a calming breath. There would be no uppity elf, no skincare boutique, and absolutely no rotting. He would be back on Rosemond Street soon. He just needed to *think*.

He clumsily grabbed the apple and gnawed on it in thought. His kidnapper had mentioned an opportunity. An involuntary commission, most likely, from whoever his supervisor was. Certainly not Guild-approved by any stretch—

The Guild—*yes*, that was it. The Guild had a protocol for this sort of problem, didn't they? They had tried to drill it into his head as an apprentice, with mandatory lectures and additional stern warnings from Grim.

As his head pounded once more, he chased the mealy apple with a gulp of stale water. If it truly was a forced commission, the protocol was to agree to it, if he recalled correctly. The Guild did not advocate for heroics. No brave denial, no submission to torture. He had to agree so that he could get out of these bindings and this room, then delay the finished product as long as possible. Give the Guild—or, hopefully, Eli—time to find him and get him out.

It was simple, straightforward; something for his mind to latch onto. He could handle that.

As soon as he breathed a sigh of minimum relief, the door creaked open, letting his kidnapper into the tiny room.

Though the man's features had been fuzzy at Potion Con, he was quite clear here. Pale, square jaw, evaluating green eyes, and chopped brown hair, looking at his victim with neither interest nor pity. Ambrose blinked. The hallway was not the first time he had seen this man—he had been at the debates as well, taking notes in the corner. Planning his kidnapping even while Ambrose was safe in the crowd.

Ambrose decided not to let him speak first.

"Are you the man with the opportunity?" he said. The newcomer tilted his head.

"All business, aren't you?"

"Isn't that why you kidnapped me?" he replied coolly, trying to keep his hands from shaking.

"I can appreciate someone who's to the point." He gestured to the hallway behind him. "Follow me, then."

As they stepped into the hall, a shadow of a small figure ducked around a corner. The kidnapper glanced toward the shadow, rolled his eyes, and pushed Ambrose in the opposite direction.

He tried to memorize the turns they took. A left here, then down a flight of carved stairs, then right at an intersection...but it was no use. The hallways were just as windowless and nondescript as the room he had woken up in. Other than a few minute variations in the stone wall, he couldn't tell the various halls and stairwells apart.

The winding path sent his thoughts down a frightening road of their own. As far as he knew, several crime rings had a foothold in the various caves and sinkholes surrounding the Scar, but only one was large enough to command the depths below the city proper. And if he was *there*, escape would be impossible.

A terrified knot formed in his throat, and he quickly stopped his thoughts in their tracks. Best not to make assumptions just yet. He could be anywhere in the cave systems, after all. This man could belong to the Deadleaves or the Harfoots or the—

The man pushed open a door and ushered him into a large chamber. After so long in the cell and the cramped tunnels, this soaring room would have felt like a breath of fresh air if it weren't for its menacing atmosphere. Stalactites towered high above him, threatening to fall and pierce him if he made so much as a misstep. But they weren't the only things leering at him—deep carvings swirled along the wall in magically shifting waves, forming and unforming the shapes of massive, ancient creatures. Dragons, phoenixes, river eels, their teeth and claws all painted in gold...

Between the sharp carvings, the stalactites above, and the stalagmites hemming in the walls like guards, Ambrose got the distinct impression of walking into a giant open maw.

He struggled to swallow, his feet heavy, heart hammering. Though he knew little of Scarrish crime, this place was far too deep for the Deadleaves and far too opulent for the Harfoots. And the massive kraken symbol on the far wall, its golden eyes glittering maliciously above a line of thrones...

No, he was deep in the heart of Aphos. Just as he had feared.

"Cassius?" a flat voice called out to his kidnapper from the thrones. "Come forward."

Cassius bowed deeply, then pushed Ambrose forward without further ceremony.

The thrones—five of them, all gold, sharp-lined, and heavy— were empty, save for the one in the center. There, an older woman leaned impatiently against the golden arms of the throne. Everything about her swept—her posture, her hair, her dress. The rippling layers reminded him of the dress Eli's mother had worn to the festival last year, but in a brilliant blue, a vibrancy that had no place in a cave like this. Her deep violet hair, partially pinned up by a gold flower, exuded perfume as she shifted against the harsh metal lines of the throne.

Information, Ambrose frantically reminded himself. He could find some of it here, something that would guide his thoughts.

He took a second, different look at the woman. Judging by the light sneer under her rounded nose, this woman wasn't the passionate potioneering patron Cassius had made her out to be—and if that were the case, she likely had little to no experience in a workshop. Good. Even if she was sharp enough to run Aphos, he could likely slip a few lies past her. He could make up an impossible ingredient he needed, or construct some elaborate ruse about alchemical reactions to help delay the process. That would at least buy him a few weeks.

But Cassius, arms folded and face sullen...*that* man concerned Ambrose. He had been at Potion Con, watching the debates and assessing their abilities. He was the one who had chosen Ambrose; he likely knew enough to detect at least some of his lies.

The well-dressed woman turned a wavy, golden ring on her finger, drawing his attention back to her.

"This is the man for the potion?" she asked. Her Kolkean accent, while much thinner than Eli's and mixed with a Scarrish slant, gave her question a sharp, tilted edge.

"One perfectly suited to the task, I assure you, Madam Mila," Cassius said. Mila rattled off something in Kolkean. While half of it was far too fast for Ambrose to understand, his limited vocabulary gleaned from Eli allowed him a few broken phrases here and there.

"...unlike last time?"

"Smarter than the last—"

"He'd better be."

Cassius bowed again in response; Mila set her shoulders and looked directly at Ambrose. He steeled himself in kind, reassuring himself with an array of Guild-approved replies in his head. *Yes, I can do it; I'll need a few months, at least; can I please have a sandwich at the earliest opportunity, etc.*

"A true illusion potion," Mila said. "Can you do it?"

Everything in him recoiled, and all thought of agreement fell out of his head.

"Absolutely not," he retorted. Cassius sighed. Mila's eyes narrowed.

"So, you're not capable?"

"He is," Cassius interjected. "I heard his argument myself. He can do it."

"What, my debate?" Ambrose would have gestured in anger if his hands weren't tied. "That was all *theory*. A completely amoral theory, by the way. The—the consequences of attempting such a brew would—"

"I want one in six months," Mila cut in. Ambrose whipped back around to her, his bound hands throwing him off-balance.

"No." He stumbled. "Release me at once. I *refuse* to do such an insane thing—"

Mila clicked her tongue. She didn't even need to look at Cassius this time—he began rattling off names. Sickeningly familiar names.

"Eli Valenz has a fairly simple routine, wouldn't you say?" Cassius said lightly. "He's at the practice pits at least four days a week."

Ice filled Ambrose's veins. Cassius kept going.

"He has dinner with an artificer named Banneker once a week, who in turn has tea with a jeweler named Grim twice a week. One Dawn Kerighin never seems to leave her workshop, and there's an armorer named Sherry who—"

"Stop," Ambrose snapped, his hands shaking. "*Stop.*"

Madam Mila gave him a tight, thin smile, just as a carving of a lion shifted past her on the wall. This was why the Guild instructed a quick agreement. Avoid endangering himself and avoid endangering anyone else.

Agree and delay, he told himself, clenching his jaw. Agree and delay.

"One potion in six months?" he said. "Then you'll let me go?"

"One potion, six months, and the instructions to replicate it," Cassius said. "And we won't harm you or the others."

"On my honor," Mila said.

Given that she led an underground crime syndicate, her sense of honor meant little to Ambrose—but they knew about his friends. They knew about Eli.

He let out a long breath. "Fine. I'll do it."

Mila nodded and swept out of the room without a sound. Cassius pushed on Ambrose's shoulder and led him back into the tunnels, out of the gaping maw of Madam Mila's throne room.

His thoughts scrambled for purchase as they walked. If this was anything like Aphos' past kidnappings, they would deposit him home after he made the potion. So, all he had to do was make a fake vial, convince them it was real through some level of glitter and smoke and trickery, then go home before they recognized the ruse—

As the cell door approached, he ran back through Cassius' words and almost stopped in his tracks.

Cassius had never vocally agreed to release him after the delivery of the brew.

"Wait." He slowed his pace, willing the cell door to stretch farther away. "You *will* let me go home after I make the potion, correct?"

Cassius yanked open the door and shoved him inside. Ambrose tried whirling around, but he was too slow—the lock had already clicked into place.

"I don't recall mentioning that," Cassius said, his smirk audible through the metal.

"But you—" Ambrose slammed his shoulder against the door. "You let the others go!"

"The others?" Cassius drawled. "Ah, yes. Mapmakers, artificers, and the like. But this potion you're making is quite important to the Madam. This is no temporary commission, I'm afraid."

Ambrose stiffened. He didn't want to ask, he *shouldn't* ask— "And if I can't make it?"

"Like I said," Cassius drawled, "Eli Valenz has a fairly simple routine."

He strolled away, footsteps echoing down the hall. Ambrose slid down and slouched with his back to the door, fear and anger turning into an exhausting slurry in his chest. Glitter water and trickery weren't going to get him out of this one.

He steadied his breath and looked up at the ceiling. There was no information there, no reassuring details, but somewhere above, far above, Rosemond Street still bustled. They'd have learned something was wrong by now. They'd be looking for him.

Perhaps a fake potion couldn't get him out of here, but...Rosemond Street certainly could.

RULE 9:
GATHER THE INGREDIENTS

Dawn

DAWN HAD NEVER FELT SO unsettled in Viola's bakery before.

Normally, having all of Rosemond Street crammed into The Midnight Snack prompted a celebratory air. The floating stars twinkled a little brighter; the velvets absorbed their laughter. But today, the bakery felt as dim and empty as if they weren't there at all. As if the place understood the sudden Ambrose-shaped hole in the group and couldn't coalesce enough light or comfort to fill it.

And in the absence of such comfort, none of the merchants could sit still.

While Viola hastily threw together a plate of pastries, Banneker sat cross-legged in the middle of the floor, hurriedly fidgeting with a copper, sand-filled dish. By the front counter, Grim and Sherry spoke in hushed tones, constantly asking Viola or Banneker if they needed assistance. And Eli—

Dawn's heart cracked just looking at him. He paced near the windows, twice as taut as he had been at the convention. He had made his apologies to Sebastian, guided the poor gnome safely home, then walked straight to the bakery.

And hadn't stopped walking since.

"I should've been there," he mumbled, continuing along his tight path by the window. At his ankles, Tom stared in confusion at the empty potion shop across the street. "I should've been next to him, he was *right* there—"

"You had a job," Dawn tried weakly. She was sitting atop the closest table, swinging her feet just to feel the motion, feel something other than her stomach lurching. She had been seconds from following Ambrose before she had gotten distracted. By Rory. By a pretty face.

"You had a job," she repeated, her voice cracking. "I didn't. *I* should've followed him—"

"It wouldn't have mattered," Grim cut in, approaching with a tray of tiny cakes made even tinier by their massive hands. Petit fours, perfectly shaped and iced, garnished with candied lavender. "If Aphos really took him, you could've been standing right next to him and not have noticed. That's how they've worked in the past—"

"And that's how they worked today," Banneker finished. "I'd recognize their signature anywhere."

He tugged a small metal device out of his pocket. At first, Dawn thought it was one of the fidget toys he often made when he was bored—but Sherry's raised eyebrows quickly corrected her.

"Banneker," she said warily, "where did you get that?"

He held up a chiding finger. "Never ask a dudette her age nor a dude where he got his contraband."

He twisted the kraken-branded circle atop the device. Every piece was made of a different metal, making the contraption difficult to visually parse. "Managed to get my hands on this a few years ago," he said. "It's not one of Aphos' flashier pieces, but it gets the job done. You just think about what you want, and..."

He closed his eyes, and an instant later, a second Banneker appeared on the other side of the copper dish, mimicking the real Banneker's posture. They both opened their eyes and pressed their hands together—the hands met, rather than passing through each other.

"It won't hold for long, but it's almost a true illusion," Banneker said, his voice betraying his own fascination. "They've managed to get touch, sound, sight, and smell almost perfect in most of their devices. Set 'em up right as decoys or distractions, and your targets won't realize it's a fake until it's too late."

As Eli shifted his pacing to inspect the illusion, Dawn's insides twisted into a knot. Part of her wanted to scoff, to claim that she wouldn't be fooled by such a trick.

But someone had created an illusion of her best friend and she hadn't noticed until it was too late.

"How?" she asked, morbid curiosity getting the better of her. "How do they do it?"

Banneker's shoulders slumped. He twisted the circle again; his twin disappeared. "Don't know," he admitted, rattling the device. "I try to reverse engineer these suckers whenever I get my hands on one. They self-destruct every time. And it's not just me—Grim's tried, too."

Sherry shot a look at Grim, who shifted uncomfortably.

"I've, uh, never done that," the orc muttered. Eli, still pacing, blew past them both.

"How do we know it was actually Aphos, though?" he asked. "Someone could have just bought the device from them and used it to kidnap Ames."

"If it is Aphos," Banneker said, "I can confirm that right now."

He pulled the copper dish toward him, placed a golden gem on the sand, then gently blew on it. The gem flashed and the sand whirled into the air—but rather than falling, the grains remained in place, forming a strange optical illusion. Dawn had to tilt her head to understand the sand sculpture before her.

"Is that...the Scar?" She slid off the table to examine it more closely. The structure was indeed a little model of the chasm, hovering in front of Banneker's face. As she leaned closer, the gem matching Ambrose's pin floated upward off the dish. She willed for it to go somewhere she recognized, somewhere she could run to in an instant—

It hung below the ground floor of the chasm instead. Hovering south, far below Rosemond Street, below the layer cake of the chasm city.

Ambrose was underground. Deep underground, where only one community held sway.

Sherry shook her head, holding her arms, her face going pale. "No, no, *no*—"

Dawn's head began to swim. Eli let out a string of curses, whirled toward the door on instinct, then whirled uselessly back. "What do we—?" He gestured sharply to the gem. "How in the gods-damned hells do we—"

"Here." Viola grabbed a petit four from the tray and held it out to him with surprising ferocity. "Eat this first."

The command made him freeze. "What?"

"Just eat it," she repeated, her gaze sweeping out to the others. "*All* of you."

Dawn reluctantly picked up a cake alongside Eli, her stomach roiling at the idea of eating anything—but she did as the baker asked and nibbled on a corner.

The cake's effect was instantaneous. As soon as the icing melted on her tongue, a breeze of relief swept through her chest. By the time her teeth struck the strawberry jam and vanilla cream in the middle, her shoulders had unwound, her muscles relaxed. She no longer felt the need to fidget, and next to her, neither did Eli—he stopped moving for the first time in an hour.

"There," Viola said proudly. "Better?"

Mumblings of "Thank you, Viola" rippled through the bakery.

"Just doing my job." She took away the tray. Sherry took a deep breath, then leaned against Grim, her face less pinched than before.

"Why?" she finally asked, her eyes fixed on the floating gem. "Why did they take him? What on earth do they want him for?"

"Doesn't matter. They won't get it," Eli said. "We know where he is now. Let's form a group, go down there, and get him back."

Dawn grimaced at the words, and Sherry did the same. It was an easy assertion to make for someone who hadn't grown up in the Scar.

"We can't just go down there," Banneker answered for all of them, waving his finger around the gem. "There's a reason I don't have this area mapped out. Even without all their guarded entrances, Aphos' area is a maze of tunnels and sinkholes. If we just run down there, we'll get caught in seconds."

"But..." Eli's eyes shone in frustration. "But he's so close. Couldn't we just—?"

Something tapped gently on the bakery window. Dawn turned; Tom was still looking out at Ambrose's shop, her fork hands on the glass.

"No, he isn't there..." Dawn gently picked her up, aiming to turn her away from the street—but the empty darkness of The Griffin's Claw caught her gaze and wouldn't let go, dragging up memories she had fought down for almost a year.

This wasn't the first time Ambrose had found himself alone underground—and the last time had been her fault, too. Flashes of that night quickly welled up, unbidden. Of her leading the way into the sinkhole, eager to find her magical moss. Of a broken bridge and her reckless determination to keep going.

Ambrose had been right that night. Right to throw the potion bottle into the sinkhole, to beg her to stop the search. But she hadn't been thinking straight, hadn't been for months, and she had stepped away from him, pulled out her teleporter, and—

A knock sounded on the bakery door. Everyone in the room jumped.

"I'll get it," Viola said, grabbing a rolling pin before marching up to the door. "Excuse me, we're closed right now—"

But the newcomer wasn't a customer.

"My good madam." The bearded detective from Potion Con stood in the doorway, heroically silhouetted by the crystal streetlamps outside. What's more, he seemed to know it, for he cleared his throat and gave an unnecessarily sweeping bow to his new audience.

"I am here," he continued, "to reassure the good folks of Rosemond Street that the Potion Master's Guild has officially selected me for the Ambrose Beake case."

When no applause or sighs of relief emanated from the bakery, he bravely carried on.

"And," he said, stroking his beard, "I do believe I have confirmed..."

Another dramatic pause here. Dawn fought the urge to throw Tom at him.

"That Mr. Beake is no longer in the convention arena," he said proudly.

Viola closed the door in his face.

"All right," she said. "What's next?"

Grim straightened, immediately settling into their role as street meeting leader. They didn't have their typical clipboard nor their neat list of agenda items, but the silent shift was still comforting.

"The Guild said they'll send someone to cover Beake's shop," they began. "In the meantime, we'll keep the tracker running in case Aphos moves him out of the Scar."

"We must find a way to send him a message, too," Sherry said, "to tell him we're getting him out of there."

Eli circled around the sand sculpture, his words picking up speed with his steps.

"And if he can communicate back," he added eagerly, "he could tell us more about where he is. Maybe we could teleport down there and bypass those tunnels entirely."

Banneker gave a hesitant hum and lay down on the floor, hand outstretched to poke the floating gem. "Aphos won't let just anyone whizz in and out. They've got some kind of barrier down there, some-thing only they can teleport in and out of. Believe me, I tried once when I was drunk." He winced at the memory. "Zero outta ten. Do not recommend."

Dawn twisted a thin stack of rings on her index finger, the airy taste of the petit four fading too quickly on her tongue. Ambrose was likely only an hour's walk away, as the dragon flew, but that didn't matter. They couldn't teleport and they couldn't walk in. They had no map, no leads, no communication...

They had nothing, and she had nothing to offer.

She was about to ask for another calming cake, double-strength this time, when another knock rattled the door. Banneker scrambled to his feet; Viola huffed and grabbed her rolling pin once more.

"Hold on," she said, pushing up her sleeves—but when she glanced out the window, she scrunched her face in confusion and opened the door a crack.

"Excuse me, but we're closed today—"

"Oh, I understand," a voice responded quickly. "Are you the owner of this shop? I was wondering if I could ask a few questions about the potioneer across the street."

Dawn froze. Why did that voice sound familiar?

"Not today." Viola started to close the door, but the voice was insistent.

"Ma'am, I'm a journalist on the magical crimes beat, and I understand the potioneer across the street has been kidnapped—"

Magical crimes beat?

Dawn stepped forward. "Rory?"

Viola let the door swing open, revealing the tawny, purple-haired elf. She waved awkwardly. "Hi."

"You know her?" Viola asked.

"Yes. I mean, kind of," Dawn added quickly. "We, um—" No use explaining the bar fight right now. "We...met at the convention. Before Ambrose was kidnapped."

"I'm so sorry to hear about your friend," Rory said, stepping into the shop to address the group at large. "I'd like to ask a few questions, if possible. I understand the event is very raw for you, but I can't tell you how fast memories can fade or change, particularly for events like this. Any details you recall could be extremely valuable."

Dawn's guilt increased tenfold at the sight of the journalist, gnawing angrily at her insides. *This* was the pretty face that had distracted her. If she hadn't invited her to the debates, maybe she would have retained her scrap of sense and followed Ambrose into that tunnel.

"You'll have to come back later," she said, her emotions sharpening the words. "We're not answering questions right now."

"But—"

"She's right," Viola said firmly, gesturing to the street. Behind Dawn, Eli turned to Grim.

"How quickly can we find a way to talk to Ames?" he asked.

"Not sure. We'll need to be careful about it," Grim said. "Aphos is likely watching him closely—"

Rory's eyes widened. "Aphos?" she repeated. Viola tried closing the door, but Rory shoved her foot into the doorway, keeping it jammed open.

"So, you know?" she continued. "You have confirmation it was Aphos that took him?"

Just like when she had fought Franz at the bar, her eyes lit up with a wild sort of light, and before Viola could move, she had squirmed her way into the shop.

"Look, if you're trying to break him out yourself," she rambled, "you're going to run into trouble. I've been reporting on Aphos' movements for years, and they've only increased their security over the past few seasons. Their secret entrances have been rotating every month, and with the Deadleaves' presence growing, their cant has evolved to encompass a lot of passphrases from..." Her eyes landed on the sand model of the Scar, and she gasped. "You *tracked* him?"

No one had time to stop her—she rushed forward and crouched to examine the gem. "Yeah, they've got him deep in their domain, all right. The Deadleaves are usually farther north, and the Harfoots ceded that territory almost twenty years ago. If they didn't teleport him straight in with their own devices, they probably went through the entrance over..."

She looked up, caught onto the comparative silence of the rest of the room, and straightened with a sheepish laugh.

"Sorry." She took a respectful step back, glancing at Dawn. "I— I've just been on this beat for ages. If he was really taken to Aphos... maybe I could help. You know, advise on the situation."

Banneker tilted his head. "You can do that as a journalist?"

"Sure." Rory waved a hand, then quickly added, "I mean—I can't actually go down into Aphos for you. Too risky for undercover work." She straightened. "But I can still help you. I know I can."

Dawn only curled further in on herself, her hope and guilt sparking against each other like a wand gone wrong. They needed the help, there was no denying that. But to see this woman here all the time, reminding her of what she had done, why Ambrose was down there—

"Thanks," she tried, "but I think we can figure it out—"

Eli stepped in. "No, let's hear her out. If you know anything about Aphos, we want to hear it. All of it." He looked at Grim for confirmation, who reluctantly nodded.

"Don't think we have much choice," they said, their voice carrying an air of finality. "We'll take the help as long as you're willing to give it."

Rory's face lit up. "Yes!" she blurted out, then immediately tried to adopt a more professional posture. "I mean—yes. Happy to help. Help you"—she smiled at Dawn—"find your friend."

The terrible sparks in Dawn's chest sputtered and smoked.

RULE 10:

FIND A LAB PARTNER

Ambrose

Ambrose didn't realize how much he enjoyed the concept of windows until the following morning.

At least, he guessed it was morning. Without sunlight or his pocket watch to refer to, his only indication that a day had passed was Cassius' change of clothes. Yesterday, he had dressed like any other Scarrish citizen—tunic, vest, a pair of sturdy boots against the chasm dust. Today, he had shed that part of his disguise, along with any scrap of patience.

"Come along," he called sharply to Ambrose, his blue coat flowing around his knees as he strode through the tunnels. When he snapped his fingers, a heavy gold ring glinted in the crystal lamplight, and a brief wave of golden light flashed through his sleeve. Ambrose wrinkled his nose. Of *course* this man had illusion magic sewn into his clothing.

"Your lab work starts today," Cassius continued. "The slower you walk, the less time you'll have to brew."

Ambrose glared at the man's shoulders and kept his pace exactly the same.

The tunnels today were just as infuriatingly blank as the ones he had stumbled through yesterday, giving his thoughts nothing to catch on. So, he tried to focus on the only thing that had helped him sleep last night—Rosemond Street.

He had been gone for a day now. An entire night had passed not in his shop, not next to Eli, but in a cell far below. Were they at all like him? Scared, unsettled, uncomfortable in the strange air? What was Eli doing now—or more specifically, what was he trying to do?

And, perhaps most importantly, was Dawn there to stop him?

He touched his shoulder, confirming that Grim's tracking pin was still camouflaged against his robe there. Aphos hadn't found it, which meant Grim could still track his location. They'd sort out that he was underground eventually, and cooler heads on Rosemond Street would keep Eli from doing anything too reckless. They'd make some sort of plan, to be sure. A careful way into wherever he was.

But he couldn't simply wait for them, not entirely. He'd have to follow the Guild protocol to the letter here—delay the project as much as possible, lead these underground fools on until Rosemond Street could make their move.

Ambrose regarded Cassius once more; his coat had been tailored to widen his shoulders, turning him into an intimidating presence in the empty hall. There was no mistaking him for an officer of Aphos now...but how much did he actually know about potioneering?

Ambrose cleared his throat. "While I'm working, who will I request ingredients from?"

Cassius didn't bother looking behind him. "Me."

Ambrose bit his lip. He had hoped it would be a lackey of Cassius', someone more easily tricked.

"What about more particular ingredients?" he pressed. "I'm not taking any risks with faulty components. If your couriers deliver me anything subpar—"

Cassius' gaze finally flickered back to him in annoyance. "I will inspect them myself."

"And are you Guild certified?" Ambrose latched onto the annoyance, trying to make himself sound as haughty as possible. "How can

I trust your discernment? I've no idea of your background nor your specialty in certain brews, your ability to determine if the ingredient's magical saturation level is satisfactory—"

Cassius stopped and turned on his heel, his coat forming a brief whirlwind around him.

"If something truly isn't *satisfactory* enough," he hissed, "we will have a discussion about your involvement in their procurement. Until then"—he shoved open a door to his left—"you will work here and I will *bring* you what you need."

Ambrose glared at him, then cautiously stepped forward and peered into his new cell.

He had to work hard not to let Cassius see his surprise.

On his walk there, he had formed an expectation of a low and cramped laboratory, full of shadows, rusting equipment, and broken safety regulations. But *this*—this was practically a Potion Con showroom.

Cauldrons of all sizes and metals lined one wall, each with its own set of fume pulls and heat wands on charging racks. All around them, polished tables and cabinets stood sentry, partitioned for cleaning, charging, storing, mixing, and good, old-fashioned thinking. And the dust that plagued the halls was nowhere to be found here—the dark woods and metals gleamed as if they had just been bought and assembled.

The only evidence to the contrary was a stack of journals tucked to one side of the largest desk. Those had certainly been used before, judging by the wrinkles, tabs, and ink stains.

"Go through those notebooks if you like," Cassius said. "Not sure what good they'll be. They're from our last potioneer."

Ambrose perked up. Last potioneer? So, there had been someone before him. Someone who had clearly failed Madam Mila in their impossible task. A dozen questions burned on his tongue. Who were they? How long had they been here? Where had they gone?

But Cassius had neither the time nor the patience for such questions—he continued on in a bored tone. "Oh, and there's this, I suppose."

He tapped a slim wooden box by the doorframe, and the walls disappeared.

The striped stone that dominated the hallway suddenly stopped at the door, giving way to warm wood, flickering sconces...and bright windows, with nothing but fields and flowers outside.

Ambrose approached one of the windows in awe. It all felt so real —thick glass warmed by the midday sun, grass and blue sky stretching far beyond, the smell of lavender and soil beckoning him to step outside...when in reality, all the sunlight and greenery were leagues above him.

He drew his hand away from the wall. It was a prime example of Aphos' specialty, and Ambrose's future task: immaculate illusions. But if he was to truly imitate what Aphos loved—and sold—he needed more than a simple wall panel as an example.

"In addition to ingredients, I'll need a sample of Aphos' current work." He turned on his heel. "An illusion device you find sufficient as an example of what I need to replicate."

Secretly, he hoped for a device he could use to escape. To create a decoy of him brewing, while the real him scuttled away to the surface—

Cassius merely stiffened. "This wall should suffice."

Ambrose pressed his lips into a line. "But how am I to—?"

"I have faith you'll figure it out," he said impatiently. "Meals will be brought to you three times a day, and I will inspect your work twice a week. Give me your list of ingredients tomorrow. Unlike our last potioneer"—his eyes flicked to the old journals—"we will expect progress from you."

"Very well," Ambrose responded stiffly, and Cassius was gone before he could finish, closing the door and turning the lock. Its heavy, final click drew him fully from the sunlit illusion and back into reality—no matter how nice the room, he was still trapped here.

He waited for Cassius' footsteps to fade, then quickly hid Grim's tracking pin in a drawer and headed for the wall panel.

"*You'll figure it out.*" He mimicked Cassius' tone, then tried to pry the panel off the wall. If there was an ingredient he could extract from this and add to a potion, he could fool Aphos with their own work...

But the idea fizzled before it could spark. The panel wouldn't budge.

Now as impatient as Cassius, he set his jaw and made for the journals on the table. There was no point in planning how to delay the project if he didn't know where his predecessor had left off. One could only hope they had been organized, with handwriting he could decipher...

He opened the first journal, and the work within reassured him. Written by a potioneer named Octavia, the notes weren't exactly Guild standard, but they were decent and readable. He ventured through pages of ingredient lists, recipes, little boxes partitioning ideas and thoughts...

And hundreds of small ink doodles.

They started as simple embellishments in the corner, at first—but the farther he flipped, the more he saw them. Vines and flowers running up the edge of the page, tiny little dragons drawn into the margins. They weren't unlike Eli's old doodles on his potion notes, though applied with a little more finesse. A side effect of boredom and isolation, he thought, and flipped to the earliest entry to see when Octavia had begun her work.

She had started almost two years ago.

He grimaced. So, this Madam Mila once had patience—but given his own six-month deadline, it had worn thin under his predecessor's failures.

As he reached for the next journal, something thumped lightly against the door, followed by a muffled curse. He whipped around; a gray face stared at him through the small window in the door, eyes wide. Another curse and the face was gone, light footsteps scampering down the hall.

Ambrose frowned. If they were an Aphosian spy sent to keep watch, they weren't a very good one. He knew little of the spying profession, but he could only assume they shouldn't curse so loudly.

He waited to see if the footsteps returned, but the hallway

remained quiet. Unsettled by both the appearance and the silence, he wandered over to the small box Cassius had touched and set his palm against it. The windows were nice, but he needed something more familiar.

The illusion only took seconds to change, warping seamlessly from bright sky to stone, cabinets, lucky shelves positioned just so by the door... In a blink, he was back in his workroom at The Griffin's Claw. Crystal lanterns flickered in friendly rhythms, while the smoky scent of firewood hung faintly from the rafters. He took a deep breath, then went to the lucky shelf and tried to touch the bronze cat, his favorite lucky charm.

His fingers slipped directly through it and brushed the rough-hewn wall behind the illusion.

A pang shot through him, but he shook it off. He wouldn't be here long, if he and Rosemond Street had anything to say about it. He hung up his potion robes, sorted Octavia's journals into chronological order, and began his work.

He spent his first few days setting up distractions for Aphos: an absurdly long list of ingredients for Cassius and an array of bubbling vials for his workspace. These so-called brews were nothing—hardly more than colorful water, spritzed with harmless ingredients that sparkled in convincingly magical ways. As an apprentice, he had sometimes crafted such distractions when bored.

Now, he made them like his life depended on them.

While the fake vials bubbled and fizzed, he jotted down the guards' rotation outside his door. With only a small window to see through, he had to listen carefully for their approach and exit, but to his dismay, their rotation was consistent. No soft snores, very little card-playing, and only seconds between the exit of one guard and the arrival of another.

There would be no simple escape through the door, then. He had suspected as much.

He stoked the fires under the fake potions and cracked open Octavia's notebooks next. At the very least, he hoped for some idea of where she had stopped, how close she had gotten—but her writing gave no clear answer. As far as he could tell, she hadn't delivered anything close to a successful potion. And the further he read, the more elaborate her doodles became, and the more her notes devolved into strange, nonsensical lists and phrases. Perhaps she had grown more desperate with each failure...or more tired of being confined in this space.

He tried to picture it—picture her working here, standing at this table. But he knew next to nothing about her, apart from her handwriting and how she liked drawing daisies and dragons. Where had she come from? Had she been kidnapped, too? And what exactly did Aphos do with her after they had run out of patience?

The clattering of silverware against metal roused him from his questions.

"Don't bother him," Cassius hissed outside the door.

"I won't!" an unfamiliar voice hissed back.

"I will not have you hanging about like last time. If you say so much as one blasted word to him, I'll—"

"I swear, I *won't*!"

The door opened, revealing Cassius stalking away and a gnome sticking her tongue out at his back.

Well, not quite a gnome. She was gnome-like in stature—short, with folded ears that ended in a point—but orcish in skin tone, gray with patches of iridescence. One tiny tusk poked out from her lower lip, accentuating her pout. She pushed through the door with her hip, then set a tray on the table with another careless clatter.

"Here," she muttered, letting the apple on the tray roll around the bowl of soup. If Cassius was dressed to take up space, she was dressed to take up as little as possible. Her ill-fitting black tunic let her melt into the shadows, while her thin shoes made barely a whisper of sound over the floor. Paired with the strands of charcoal hair hiding her face, Ambrose may not have noticed her come and go at all, had she not chosen to enter loudly.

But even with her features half-hidden, he still recognized her. That gray face had been spying on him for days now, peeking through the window in between guard shifts. How strange—none of the other Aphosians seemed to care much about Ambrose or his work, only about guarding his door and delivering his food.

Perhaps this servant had known Octavia. Perhaps she knew something about the potioneer's origins or fate.

When she turned to go, he held up a hand. "Wait!"

The girl paused, her shoulders stiff. He rushed his words through the precious moments he had left.

"I know you've been looking in," he said. "I was wondering if you knew anything about my predecessor?"

"Who?" she asked, slightly tilting one ear toward him. Ambrose noticed the scarring across the other side of her face, running from the tip of a torn ear to her cheekbone.

"Did you know Octavia?" he tried once more. She nodded. Hope rising, he kept himself still, as if any sudden movement would send her fleeing. "Do you know where she went?"

The girl appraised him, eyes flitting from his worktable to his gold-embroidered robes on the wall—then shrugged. "I'll tell you for a fee."

He sighed. He should have expected bribery; he was locked in a criminal hideout, after all. "I'm afraid I don't have any money—"

She pointed to the piece of bread next to his soup. He blinked at it. "Oh. Um—certainly, if that's what you want."

To his shock, she tackled the bread, ripping it apart and digging desperately into the little dish of butter beside it. When her cautious gaze settled on the door, Ambrose took the cue to ask his questions quickly. "What's your name, and what happened to Octavia?" he asked.

The girl licked butter off her finger. "That's two questions."

Ambrose gestured to the hunk of cheese next to the bread. She nodded—an acceptable deal.

"I'm Nat," she said. "Tavi—or Octavia, or whatever you said—was sent away when Cassius caught her trying to escape."

Ambrose swallowed but kept his expression neutral. "Sent where?"

Nat pointed to the apple on the tray. At his nod, she devoured it instantly, juice dribbling down her chin. Ambrose stared, comparing his vanishing meal to her sunken cheekbones. Gods, had she eaten at all today? Or this week?

"They sent her off with traveling smugglers," Nat finally said, wiping her mouth with her sleeve. "Guys on their way to the Sinking Reach who wanted healing potions on the go."

Ambrose's appetite for his half-eaten lunch promptly disappeared. The Sinking Reach? That expanse of icy wasteland beyond Titan's Nails was as close to a death wish as anyone could get. There was no mercy in that sort of release.

More questions simmered in his head—How was Tavi trying to escape? How had Cassius found out?—but a distant voice bounced up the hallway, and Nat scrambled to her feet, hurriedly tossing the apple core back onto the table. As Ambrose watched the core settle, a risky idea formed in his head. A simple exchange...if he had gauged this servant's interests correctly.

He grabbed the remaining orange on the plate and handed it to her. "What if I could promise you more food? Consistently?"

She reached out on instinct—then stopped, her fingers hovering over the orange. "In exchange for what?"

"Information," he said. "About Octavia and Aphos."

Her gaze narrowed. "Trying to escape won't work, you know."

His heartbeat quickened. "Whoever said I was trying to do that?"

She threw him a flat look. The footsteps outside grew louder, and she turned back to him. "Consistent food?" she repeated.

He nodded. "All you have to do is go along with what I say to Cassius."

She took the orange and pocketed it. "Fine."

Cassius reappeared at the door, eyes flaring when he saw Nat still in the room. "Why are you—?"

Ambrose smoothly stepped in front of Nat and set his hands behind his back. "Ah, you're just in time. I have a request."

Cassius' burning gaze flicked to him but didn't cool down. Ambrose soldiered on.

"I'm in need of a test subject for my potions. Could you spare this servant for my use?"

He heard a noise of indignation behind him and splayed a hand out in a *wait* gesture. Cassius folded his arms. "A test subject?"

"You can't expect me to endanger myself by testing my own work, do you?"

Cassius gave an acquiescing grunt. "How often?"

"Five days a week, two hours a day." Ambrose spun the commands out of thin air. "And I'll need more food delivered as well. Testing often takes energy out of a subject, and my experiments will be frequent."

"As they should be." Cassius straightened, eyes glittering. "With a test subject, I expect you to be able to work faster. I believe a month should be sufficient for your first test."

Ambrose stiffened. He had been ready to enter into one deal today, not two. "I beg your pardon? A *month*?"

But Cassius pressed on. "I'll tell the kitchen you'll need more provisions. Inform me if you need anything more than that." He gave Nat a sharp look. "Come along."

He turned on his heel and swept out without waiting for her. Nat scuttled into the hall, gave Ambrose an inscrutable look, then closed the door.

Ambrose turned to the scrappy leftovers of his lunch with a mix of nausea and pride. A month for a new potion was foolish by any standards, but he certainly wasn't going to end up like Tavi, hiking to her death in the Sinking Reach. He had lied to his captor. Formed an alliance. Gathered *intel*. Eli would be proud of him.

Now he just needed to tolerate a teenager in his lab.

RULE 11:

COMMUNICATION IS KEY

Eli

ELI HATED NAVIGATING The Griffin's Claw without Ambrose.

He hated the empty space behind the front counter. He hated the eerie silence of the workroom without a fire crackling or cauldron bubbling. And he *particularly* hated how the second-floor flat echoed when he and Banneker climbed the stairs, instinctually expecting a presence that wasn't going to be there.

They stood in the flat in silent evaluation. The crystal wall lamps flared to life at their presence but failed to chase away all the shadows, as if the darkness had grown slow and tired without Ambrose there.

"Well, not much to clean up for the Guild helper." Banneker scratched his head at the immaculate counter and bare table. "Should've expected that."

Uncomfortable with looking at the empty chairs for too long, Eli checked his pocket watch. The potioneer the Guild had sent to handle the shop while Ambrose was...away...was going to arrive in a half hour. Whoever it was would be living here, too.

Eli hated that idea most of all.

"Should probably do a grocery run for them," he grumbled, opening the pantry and finding it almost as bare as the table. "But I won't get too much. Don't want them getting too comfortable."

Banneker patted his shoulder. "We'll get him back as fast as we can. Now, if I could get some samples real quick..."

He pulled out a glass test tube and ducked into Ambrose's room. Eli frowned and followed him in. "What are you doing?"

"Just getting some hair," Banneker said, examining the bed. "If I can get enough samples, I think I can set up a way to talk to Ames."

"How?"

Banneker plucked a blue hair from the pillow. "You'll see."

Before Eli could pester him for details, a knock sounded on the front door downstairs. He jogged down the steps and forced himself to remain hopeful. This potioneer wouldn't be in the flat for long, he told himself. He'd just fetch some groceries and swap the linens for them. Get them settled, but not *too* settled...

He opened the door, and his optimism died instantly.

"Xavion?"

Xavion Demachel, holding two suitcases and looking as pleased as if they had stepped in donkey dung, gave a deep sigh.

"Yes, hello, Mr. Valenz." They pushed past Eli, dropped their luggage on the floor, then set their hands on their hips, gold-dusted eyes sweeping over the shop in derision. "Hm. As stiff and boring as ever, I see."

"They didn't send you." Eli gaped. "They didn't."

"They did." Xavion turned and folded their arms. "And before you ask—no, I'm not going to run his shop into the ground. I'm here to sell and replace existing inventory to the best of my ability. Nothing more, nothing less, according to the strictest Guild protocol."

Across the street, the bakery's front door opened, and Tom wheeled across the street at an enthusiastic pace. A tall person, standing by the front counter once more! It had to be—!

She caught sight of Xavion, stared at them with her tilted broom head, then immediately wheeled back into the street.

"You and me both, Tom," Eli muttered. Then, more loudly for

Xavion: "If I see you mess up anything in here—if anything breaks, if anything goes so much as—as *un-alphabetized*—"

"Yes, yes, you'll curse my line and such." Xavion waved him off. "Though I may decorate a little."

"Don't you dare—"

"Merely sprucing up the place, Mr. Valenz."

Eli opened his mouth to detail what exactly would happen to them if they spruced up the place, but Banneker came jogging down the steps, pocketing his test tube.

"Okay, sheets changed, checked the firewood by the hearth, ran the cleaning wand over the washroom." He gave a sunny smile to Xavion. "Has Eli already threatened you?"

Xavion narrowed their gaze. "Yes."

"Good. Then I don't have to make Grim do it." Banneker swept past Eli. "Come on, let the temp get to it. We've got some stuff to make."

Xavion glowered at the word *temp*. Eli gave them a humorless smile and followed Banneker into his shop across the street.

"So, how long will it take until we can talk to Ames?" he asked, wading through the artificer's atelier to the workroom in the back. With all of Rosemond Street now scuttling in and out of the place, Banneker had managed to clear some sort of winding path through the clutter and crates—but there was always still a cannon or two to carefully step over.

"Gimme a few hours." Banneker opened the door to the workroom, where Grim, Sherry, and Dawn were already busy putting materials together. "If we've got everything prepped, that is."

"I think we do." Sherry held up a large jar of grayish goop. "Is this enough?"

"Probably. Dawn, you got the heat wand?"

Dawn stepped away from one of the worktables, revealing a neat array of wands. "Grabbed a bunch from my shop, just to be safe."

"Good." Banneker tugged on his gloves. "Then just a few hours and I can—"

"Hello?" someone called from the front. "Anyone here? I think I have a, uh...something of yours."

Eli stepped back out. Rory the journalist stood at the front door, holding up Tom in a hesitant grip.

"It was tapping on the door trying to get in," she said. "This little buddy is yours, right?"

He expected Tom to squirm out of Rory's grip upon seeing him— but she remained quite content in the woman's arms, swinging her wheeled legs without a care in the world.

If only Dawn could be so comfortable. She was at Eli's side immediately, her shoulders stiff.

"We don't have any updates yet," she said quickly. "So, you'll have to come back later—"

Banneker was already assembling pieces at his worktable. "Nah, this won't take long. If she wants to come in and watch, she can."

"I'd love to." Rory carefully set down Tom and walked in, passing by Dawn with an awkward smile while the wandmaker tried not to make eye contact. Eli looked between them and frowned. The pair had seemed to be having fun at the convention before Ambrose had, well...vanished into thin air. He resolved to press Dawn on the matter the next chance he had.

But Banneker moved too quickly for him to find the time. While Rory asked Eli a few basic background questions—How long had he been dating Ambrose? How did they meet? When had he sold his potion shop to Viola?—Banneker morphed into a whirlwind, laying out the gray slurry, applying heat wands... Within the hour, he proudly laid an expansive sheet of paper before them.

"This is the...communication device?" Rory asked, gingerly lifting up a corner. Banneker gently tore off a small strip and held it up to show the specks of blue within the paper.

"Thought I'd go old-school for this," he said. "It's paper attuned to the dude of brew's location. Small and low magic signature, in case anyone's watching him. There's enough magic in these strips to get a message there and back once. Anything more powerful than that and the magic might get detected by Aphos."

Eli crowded Banneker's shoulder as he wrote the first message:

Hurt? In Aphos? Anyone else in the room? Write here. - BKR

Once the ink was dry, he took another wand and ran it over the paper. The blue hairs embedded in the page lit up, and in a blink, the strip disappeared. Eli held his breath and stared at the table.

Then the paper reappeared in front of Banneker, with different handwriting and different words. The writing was hasty and to the point, but readable:

No Yes No

Eli grabbed the paper and inspected every inch of it, looking for any sign of counterfeit or distress: blood, dirt, wobbliness in the ink... But it was perfectly, precisely Ambrose, down to the calm, straight lines of the *Y*.

He could've kissed the paper if he weren't in front of five other people.

"It's him." He beamed and held up the note. "He's okay."

A collective sigh of relief rippled through the room. Dawn wiped away a tear with her palm, and Sherry leaned bonelessly against Grim. "Thank the gods."

But three words weren't enough for Eli—he handed the paper back to Banneker, heart pounding. "How do we send it again?"

"We can't send that one." The artificer carefully set aside the note. "Like I said, not a lot of magic is stored in this paper. We'll need to rip off another piece to send another message."

Eli's excitement stalled. Banneker's enchanted paper was large but finite. They only had so many messages they could send before their method ran out. They'd have to be careful with what they wrote.

His gaze settled on Rory, who was furiously scribbling in her notebook.

"Fascinating," she mumbled. "Attuned to the victim. Goes right to them..." She looked up to find Eli and the others staring silently at her. "What?"

"You said you know about Aphos," Eli said. "What should we ask him next?"

She closed her notebook and cleared her throat. "Ask if he's in a cell or in a larger room. Rooms are higher up, cells are deeper in the tunnels."

Banneker wrote the question on the smallest scrap of paper possible. The answer came almost immediately.

Room

"Good." Rory brightened. "Makes things easier. And his response time is a good sign that no one else is in the room with him. With any luck, they just want him to make a few high-strength health vials or something, then they'll let him go. Ask him what the commission is for."

Banneker obeyed. The paper vanished, then reappeared again.

Illusion potion. Will delay per Guild protocol

Then, in smaller, cramped letters underneath:

Please get me out

Eli went cold at the second line—but Rory's gaze was fixed on the first.

"No, that...that doesn't make any sense," she murmured, her positivity gone. "Aphos knows illusions. Aphos *does* illusions. They wouldn't need to ask him for..." She handed the note back to Banneker. "Can you ask what kind of illusion potion?"

The answer came back just as quickly.

True illusion

The air in Banneker's workshop dropped to frigid degrees.

"He can't." Eli resisted the urge to crumple the paper. "No one can. It's impossible."

"It was the debate, wasn't it?" Dawn said, hugging her elbows. "They watched him and figured he could turn the theory into practice."

"Well, he's getting out before they can wring anything from him." Sherry had straightened, but held Grim's hand in a white-knuckled grip. "Can he make some sort of guiding potion to navigate himself out?"

Rory snorted. "He'd need a guiding potion, an invisibility brew, *and* a few good weapons to get past the guards and alarms at the surface." When she saw Sherry's stricken look, her voice softened. "I'm sure your man is talented, but unless he's Eban the Bold times five, he's not getting out on his own."

Fear shifted into a desperate energy in Eli's veins.

"Then we'll go down there and get him," he jumped in. Ambrose couldn't swing a weapon, but *he* sure could. He'd plot a route straight to Ambrose, then nab a few of his higher-level brews from the shop. Maybe some of Sherry's armor, too, and Grim's jewelry...

"Sure, if you want to get captured, too." Rory pointed at Ambrose's last note with her pencil. "I don't know what exactly they're up to, but whatever it is, a true illusion will be far more valuable to them than any other kind of potion. Even if no one's in the room watching him, they'll have guards at his door at all times. Regular check-ins, faster demonstration cycles. He's going to be almost impossible to get to when he's in his room, even by Aphosian standards."

"What about when he's out of the room?" Dawn asked, directing her question to the room at large rather than Rory. "Shopping for ingredients or something?"

Rory grimaced. "The markets are messy and overcrowded. There's no slipping in and out of those." She paused, tapping the end of her pencil against her lip. "A demonstration is your best bet. Aphos likes pomp and circumstance. If they want him to show off his work— which they will—they're not going to do it in a potioneer's workroom.

They'll take him somewhere bigger, somewhere fancier. Particularly for something like this."

"Then we'll target that," Grim said. "Banneker, ask him if they've mentioned a demonstration yet."

But Banneker hesitated with his quill over the paper.

"I'd rather not risk too many questions today," he said. "In terms of magical signature, this stuff is about as low-flying as I can make it, but if I push it too far, they might pick up on it. I think we should cool it for a second. Conserve paper a bit."

Eli's heart fell to his feet. He had evidence Ames was alive, was okay—but there were so few words to go on. "I—can I write something?"

Banneker reluctantly ripped off a tiny scrap of paper and handed it to him. Eli took the quill and wrote in minuscule letters, surrounded by even smaller hearts:

Love you. Will get you out. Promise.

RULE 12:

KEEP CALM AND BUBBLE ON

Ambrose

NAT SPUN around on the squeaky stool for the tenth time, sending an ear-jarring shriek of metal through the workroom. Ambrose ran his hand through his hair. "Gods, would you *please* stop that?"

"No." Nat shortened her movements, squeaking back and forth in small, obnoxious bursts—and judging by the grin on her face, that was precisely what she wanted. "You wanted me to be a test subject."

"That was never my actual intention."

"You wanted me to be a *fake* test subject."

Ambrose passed a hand over his face. *He who brews alone* and all that nonsense from his old master was starting to look better by the minute.

"Well, fake test subject"—he turned in his chair—"now that you've devoured both your lunch and roughly half of mine, I believe it's time to uphold your end of the bargain."

This had been their rhythm for the past several days, and Ambrose couldn't claim its beat was leading him anywhere useful. He would ask a question, she would answer in the fewest possible words, and he would gain precious few drops of information about Tavi.

She had been an Aphosian potioneer, he'd learned. Before getting roped into Madam Mila's nonsense, she'd dabbled in medicine. She had been here for two years, aligning with the dates in her notebooks.

And then she had left, and now he was here. Brilliant.

Judging by the half-eaten meal in front of him, he likely had two questions, maybe three, before Nat demanded more food for more prattle. He had to plan carefully. "Was Tavi truly working on the illusion potion while she was here?"

Nat finally stopped spinning around on the stool, settling herself so that her good ear tilted toward Ambrose.

"No idea." She toyed with her ponytail. "She'd give me snacks now and then, let me hang out. Never really explained what she was doing. She was working on something, though." She wrinkled her nose. "Smelled gross sometimes."

"Potions often do," he murmured, tapping his pencil on the desk. Perhaps she had been brewing something without using the fume pull, something that had addled her toward the end. The doodles in the last journal were heavier, more repetitive, covering more of the paper.

Then again, she could have just been lonely and bored. Or dealing with a teenager and a squeaky stool.

"And how was she caught?" he asked.

Nat's face darkened, and she crossed her arms, not looking directly at Ambrose. "Probably doing something dumb," she snapped. "Like anyone who tries to escape."

There was ice behind the words, but Ambrose didn't have time to wait for it to thaw. He took the raisin cake on the tray, cut it in half, and offered her a piece. Nat took it and gnawed on the corner.

"It was weird," she finally admitted. "She was...trying to go down."

"Down," Ambrose repeated. "Not up to the surface?"

Nat shook her head.

"And there's"—he lowered his voice—"no way out going down?"

Nat just snorted and polished off her raisin cake. Ambrose

slouched back in his chair. Tavi must have taken a wrong turn, or was just too desperate for a different way out.

Either way, her failure had landed him here.

"Any more questions?" Nat asked, eyeing the other half of the raisin cake. Ambrose's stomach growled in response.

"That is all, thank you."

She hopped off the stool, ensuring it squeaked one last time, before curling up in the opposite corner and pulling a tiny book from her boot. This was always the end to their daily rhythm—Ambrose sulking and Nat reading. After angling herself away from the door, she flipped through pages and occasionally made a movement with her hand, repeating the motion a few times before turning the page.

A few of the motions he vaguely recognized—but when he tried to ask about it, he was met with a sharp, spiky "Nothing."

He huffed and swiveled back to his workstation. That was fine. He had plenty of sulking to do, anyway.

As Cassius had assumed, the journals were a dead end. Ambrose could hardly see the value in following their doodled gibberish any further, knowing Tavi's fate. His time was better spent brewing a potion that feigned progress for Cassius' check-ins, or making another list of random ingredients to strain his captors' wallets.

He shoved the journals aside and opened his own notebook instead, flipping to a page carefully hidden in the back: his record of notes from Rosemond Street's disappearing paper.

When the first one had appeared by his hand, the blue-speckled paper settling onto the table like a feather, he could hardly believe it. He had responded so quickly he nearly spilled his ink, then spent an eon of seconds holding his breath for the next one, and the next...

He let slip a small grin at Eli's last note, a promise surrounded by lopsided hearts. This proof of life from above was the only thing keeping him grounded. Knowing they were trying, knowing they had found him.

Knowing that they were going to come get him.

But he couldn't sit and brew fake potions all day. If Rosemond Street was going to come rescue him, he needed more information about where he was. Where his room was, where his future demon-strations might take place. Various exits, entrances, where to go, where not to go. But he couldn't see anything of the sort from his room—just a sliver of a dark hall. No, he needed an opportunity, a way to get out of these four walls...

"Hey." Nat popped up at his shoulder. He yelped and nearly fell off his chair.

"*Gods.*" He slapped the notebook closed, one hand on his heaving chest. "Are you a ghost or something?"

Nat stared at him, unblinking. "Servant."

"Understood." Ambrose gulped in a breath and regained his composure. "What is it?"

Nat pointed to the cauldron simmering next to him. "Can I help stir that?"

Ambrose sighed. "No."

"Why not?"

"It's dangerous."

Nat pouted. "Tavi let me touch stuff."

"*Tavi* didn't have Guild rules to follow." Ambrose rubbed his fore-head and stood up. Why did he ever think this partnership was a good idea? "Now, if you'll please stand and take five large steps away from the cauldron, I need to adjust the heat."

She took one step away, still leaning forward.

"Five. Large. Steps."

Nat gave a dramatic groan and obeyed.

"You're so *boring.*" She feebly kicked the leg of her abandoned stool. "If they didn't give you the good food, I wouldn't have taken your dumb deal."

Ambrose's hand stopped midway to the heat wand. "What do you mean, the good food?"

She held up the apple that he had set aside as a snack. "Um, there's no mold, duh."

Ambrose's stomach sank. "I beg your pardon?"

"Oh, right." She took a large, snappish bite from the apple. "Forgot there's no mold up in your city, is there?"

He straightened, wrath toward Aphos already simmering in his gut—but he forced it down. He didn't have all the information yet.

"Nat," he ventured, "do the kitchens...feed you properly here?"

She froze, fear flashing in her eyes, and he realized his tone had been sharper than he intended. "I'm not angry," he corrected, then quickly added, "And I won't tell Cassius."

She folded her arms against herself. "They feed us all right," she mumbled, not meeting his gaze. "Leftovers, mostly. But Cassius said I get the last of 'em since I already get fed the good stuff for being a test subject."

Ambrose suppressed a visceral urge to summon all of Eli's training and punch his kidnapper in the nose.

Of course Cassius had said that. Of course he—*gods*, this girl couldn't be more than fifteen? Sixteen? And she said *us*. How many other servants were being treated like this, while Madam Mila lounged around on her gold throne and threw a literal fortune at a made-up list of ingredients—?

Keys jangled in the workroom door, cutting his silent wrath off at the knees.

"Come along, girl," Cassius said gruffly, holding the door open with one foot. "Time's up. And don't think you've gotten out of your chores, because you've got yours *and* Noah's to do, thanks to that prank you pulled on him."

Ambrose forcibly released his fingers from the fists they had formed. He couldn't punch Cassius—that wouldn't end well for anyone in the room—but there was something else he could do. A way he could help both Nat and himself.

"The markets," he cut in, allowing a bit of edge back into his voice. "My test subject and I will need to visit them this week. The ice vine you bought for me hardly suffices for brews at this strength. If the ingredient is to be useable, I'll need to analyze the color and size myself."

Cassius rolled his eyes. "Just write down what you want, and I'll send the servant out to the market again—"

"And," Ambrose added swiftly, "I will require more food stored here in the workroom for my test subject. What you're currently providing as part of the daily meal is not nearly enough, particularly if you're demanding a demonstration in a month."

Nat stared at him, eyes wide. He forced out a cold smile, focusing on Cassius.

"That is what Madam Mila wants, isn't it?" he continued. "Progress in a month? If I go to her and inform her that I couldn't test frequently enough because of the apparent stinginess of her associates—"

"Fine," Cassius snapped, giving Ambrose a fine-pointed glare. "One hour in the markets tomorrow. And I'm coming with you."

RULE 13:

CONCOCT A PLAN

Dawn

THE MIDNIGHT SNACK no longer had a closing time.

Rosemond Street was there at all hours of the day, whether it was Sherry in line for a morning treat, Dawn swinging by for a midday pick-me-up, or Banneker begging for a half-price slice of pie at dusk. And after hours, the place turned into the merchants' little detective outpost. They tacked Ambrose's notes on the walls, checked his tracker, swapped thoughts and ideas about Aphos...

And, naturally, soothed their stress with cookies.

"Come get 'em, ya loons!" Viola shouted from the comfort of the sofa. "Banneker, you know the drill. Lemon to Sherry, rose to Grim, coconut to Dawn, cinnamon to Eli. Sorry, Rory, I haven't sorted out your flavor yet." She shrugged. "Don't worry, I'll figure it out."

Banneker passed around the treats while Tom wound around his ankles. Dawn took a cookie and, in a bid to ignore the journalist taking notes in the corner, drew up a stool next to Viola's couch. The baker had outdone herself today: the crunchy coconut cookie hid under a velvety coating of white chocolate, dyed pink with hibiscus flowers. Though this particular dessert contained no magic, Dawn imagined herself back on a beach again, enjoying a cool, refreshing breeze.

But the baker herself didn't look particularly refreshed or breezy this evening.

"Pain's still bothering you today?" Dawn asked. Viola had her residual limb propped up while she was laid out on the cushions, ensconced in midnight pillows, double chocolate cookies, and a half-empty healing vial. She shrugged and rubbed her leg.

"Less so, thanks to this," she said, swishing the last of the mint-green liquid in the vial. "But it's all I've got left of Ames' recipe." Her eyes narrowed. "You think that temp is going to make it just as good?"

Dawn wished Xavion had been around to hear the doubt in her voice.

"I'll make sure they do," she reassured her. As she reached out to pat the blanket draped over Viola, a shadow fell over the sofa.

"The temp?" Rory repeated. "Xavion Demachel, you mean?"

Dawn stiffened. The cookie had briefly made her forget that the journalist was in the room, waiting for the street meeting to begin. Even now, she found it difficult to look Rory in the eye without her heart-strings tying themselves in knots. Don't look at her, she told herself. Not the sharp jawline, not the long fingers twirling her pen, and, gods, *definitely* not the flower tattoo peeking out of her jacket collar.

While Dawn fought for her life, Viola wrinkled her nose and snuggled further into her pillow.

"That's Xavion, all right. Dema-shell out for an expensive healing potion," she grumbled. "They almost didn't give me Ames' discount. Can you believe that? Rude." She grabbed another cookie from the tin on her lap.

As Rory nodded along, her collar slipped, revealing more of her tattoo. The delicate flower slowly furled and unfurled along the slope of her neck, while a leaf caressed her collarbone. Dawn's mouth went dry. "Yeah," she said weakly. "Rude."

She had hoped that would be the end of it—that Rory would take her little notebook and her twinkling eyes and go ask someone else some questions—but instead, the journalist looked directly at her and ventured a small, tilted smile.

"Dawn can take Xavion down if needed," she said. Dawn swallowed.

"I can?"

"Yeah. Just a good old glass of water to the face and they're down for the count." Her smile widened. "Or do you not remember your heroics?"

Guilt snarled the warmth in Dawn's chest. Oh, she remembered her heroics, all right. If she hadn't thrown that stupid glass of water, Ambrose might still be here.

"Heroics?" Viola repeated in confusion, but Dawn had already hopped to her feet. Fresh air, she needed fresh air.

"Right. I'm a hero," she rambled. "In fact, I'm gonna go be one right now and bother Xavion about that potion they owe you."

Viola craned her neck to look out the window. "I think they're still closing shop—"

"Then I better go before they forget to bring the bottle over." Dawn stumbled over an ottoman on her way out. "Be right back!"

She reached for the door handle, almost free—but another hand pulled it open for her.

"I'll come with," Eli said, his typical smile not meeting his eyes. "We'll go bother Xavion together."

Under normal circumstances, Dawn wouldn't have doubted his desire to annoy the potioneer, but there was an unspoken question in the way he took her arm and walked with her across the street. She glanced at the half-eaten cinnamon cookie in his hand. Strange—that wasn't Eli's favorite flavor. Eli loved orange dipped in chocolate. Cinnamon was...

Oh. It was Ambrose's.

As guilt tightened in her chest, he finally spoke.

"Dawn," he said, eyebrows raised. She quickly avoided his gaze.

"What?"

"You know what."

They neatly sidestepped a mail dragon together, its buzzing wings giving her time to delay. "I don't know what—"

"Rory," he cut in. "How did you meet her, exactly?"

Dawn set her jaw and shrugged.

"Oh, I don't remember. Just got to talking at the bar at Potion Con."

"Talking."

"Yup."

"Just talking?"

"Mm-hm."

Eli stared at her. Dawn tried to stare back—then broke down with a groan.

"Fine!" she said. "She was in a bar fight, and maybe I helped her a little—"

"Wait, you *what*?"

Her words came out in a flood. "And then we talked and it was great and I stayed with her rather than following Ambrose into the tunnel, and now we're *here* and Ambrose is down *there*!" She gestured to the ground, then covered her face with another groan. Eli pulled her to the side of the street, where the flow of the city couldn't sweep them away.

"Hold on, is that why you keep avoiding her? Because she distracted you for a second?" He laughed, jolting her senses. "Dawn, talking to a hot reporter is nothing to feel guilty about."

She peeked out from behind her hands, her tone miserable. "She's *so* hot."

He wrapped her in a hug, his lingering laughter fading into her curls. "You have nothing to feel bad about," he said. "It's not your fault or Rory's that Ambrose went missing."

"I know," she mumbled into his shirt. Of course she knew that. But it didn't stop the feelings from gnawing at her.

"You know..." The words took on the shape of Eli's grin—a sly and conniving grin—and she quickly untangled herself from his grip.

"No. *Uh*-uh."

"What?" His eyes glittered. Dawn scowled.

"You know what."

She reached for the door to The Griffin's Claw, but Eli caught it first.

"I'm just saying, if she's investigating with us, it's a great way for you to get to know her better—"

"I don't need to get to know her better—"

"Oh, I think you do." Eli opened the door and waved her in. "After you, *hero*."

Dawn glared and stepped inside the shop.

Stepped was a generous word for it—she ventured in, then immediately had to snake around a pile of customers swarming Xavion at the front counter. They had very few potions in hand—but many questions.

"Do you know when he's coming back?" asked a gnome with a medic's armband, both hands gripping the counter. The fur-clad orc behind her nudged her with a sharp elbow.

"They just said he's been kidnapped," he said. "How should they know?"

"But people are looking for him, right?" The human next to the gnome wrapped his arm around her shoulders. "They'll find him, won't they?"

Xavion's response walked across a tightrope of exhaustion and professional politeness. "They are most certainly doing their best," they said, tugging on their glittery sleeve with an air of finality. "And I must go assist. See, my associates"—they gestured to Dawn and Eli with a tight, insincere smile—"are here and I must see to them. So, if you will just make your final purchases, *please...*"

The crowd slowly filtered away in disappointment, leaving Xavion —the temp, the stranger—slouched over the front counter. Dawn bristled on instinct but kept the sharpness away from her tongue for once.

"Street meeting's starting soon," she said, her tone as strained as Xavion's. "You got Viola's potion ready?"

"Of course, of course." Xavion shoved Ambrose's ledgers under the counter and held up a potion, swishing the green liquid. "And before anyone asks, I followed Amby's recipe to the letter. It only took most of the week to find the actual recipe through all his silly notations..."

A week. The phrase settled heavily on Dawn's shoulders. Had it already been a week since Ambrose's disappearance? And at the same time, had it *only* been a week? She had missed lunch with him yesterday. And their weekly tea three days prior. And dinner with Eli before that—

"Great." She took Eli's arm and turned on her heel, unwilling to wind the clock back any further. "Lock up the shop and let's go."

Together, they dragged an unwilling Xavion across the street and into the bakery. Upon seeing Eli come in, Tom rolled up hesitantly to Xavion, the odd not-Ambrose wearing long robes and standing next to Eli.

"Ah," Xavion said, lip curled. "Hello."

They stared down at her. She stared up at them.

Then she turned tail and wheeled all the way over to Rory, where she stopped directly in front of the woman's ankles—or more specifically, her ankle tattoo, an enchanted cuff of clouds that drifted in a circle around her leg.

"Hey, you." Rory bent down and ruffled the bristly top of Tom's head. "How's it going?"

Tom clapped her fork hands together in delight. Dawn stoically took her seat next to Viola, looked at Tom, and patted the top of her thighs.

"Tom!" she called. "Tom, come sit with me!"

The automaton looked at her, then purposefully plopped down in front of Rory's feet.

Traitor.

"Looks like we have everyone." Grim strode over to the corkboard, while the others settled around him. Sherry next to Eli, Eli next to Dawn. The bakery's cleared floor wasn't the same as the cozy hearth in Grim's living room, but it would do for a street meeting in a pinch. "We all ready?"

Xavion dragged a chair noisily away from the group before sitting. Grim let out a small sigh and folded their arms.

"Beake will be out of his cell for his demonstration in a month," they began. "Probably our best shot at getting him out. Banneker, you said you had a thought."

"I liked Dawn's idea from the other day," Banneker said, balancing his chair on two legs. "We go in, we slip him a teleporter, he uses it when no one's looking at him. I just need to figure out how to get the device to bypass their teleport barrier."

"If we're already going down there, why not just grab him and run?" Eli asked, knee bouncing impatiently.

"Teleporting will be both faster and safer," Rory immediately cut in. "If they've got him bound in any way, trying to bring him along will only make it harder for you all to get out of there safely. It's also easier to scope out a good entryway into Aphos if we know it doesn't need to be used as an exit point for three people."

Eli gave a small pout but had no argument. Dawn, for her part, still saw a gaping hole in the plan.

"But who's going in?" she asked. "None of us know the layout down there."

"I can teach you," Rory quickly offered, then tucked her hair behind her ear. "I—I mean, them. You know, whoever's going."

Someone else cleared their throat and raised their hand—Xavion, from their awkward position outside the circle. "Beg pardon," they said without any hint of begging pardon. "I want Ambrose back in his darling shop as much as anyone here, but how exactly are you going to bypass Aphos' teleport barrier?"

"Any Aphosian artificer would know how to do it," Rory said. "I could try a few contacts I know, see if I can get them to spill."

Sherry frowned. "Not that I don't trust your expertise, my dear, but—isn't that dangerous?"

Eli's gaze slid to Dawn, and his sly grin returned.

"Rosemond Street never likes seeing anyone go anywhere alone, you know. Dawn should go with you."

She glared at him with what she hoped was the power of a hundred blast wands—but Rory jumped on the idea, eyes alight.

"Sure!" she started, then sat back. "Only if you've got time, of course. I know you're busy with the shop and all."

"Oh, I can cover the shop if she needs," Eli piled on. "Dawn can charm the pants off your artificer friends, don't you think? And she can bring protective wands. Did you know she came first in this year's city wand competition? And the year before that? And if you read her *30 Under 130* article—"

Dawn's face warmed in embarrassment. Street meetings were not the time for wing-manning. "*Eli,*" she hissed, hoping it properly conveyed her desire to strangle him.

He merely grinned at her.

"And while she goes and helps you"—he tied his plan in a neat bow—"the rest of us can scope out Aphos' entrance points."

"Are you sure you don't need me to help with that instead?" Dawn tried, but to her dismay, the others were already nodding along with Eli's plan.

"Dawn and Rory will work on the barrier bypass, and the rest of us will look for the right entrance," Grim said, then turned to Dawn, eyebrows raised. "If you're comfortable with that?"

Dawn withheld a huff. Fine. *Fine.* If it was going to help Ambrose, she could ignore this woman's wiles for one more evening.

"I'll go." She looked at Rory. "When do you want to leave?"

RULE 14:

GET SOME FRESH AIR

Ambrose

KRAKEN PLAZA, the market square of Aphos, home to shady thieves and smugglers and sneering criminals of all sorts, was...a perfectly normal place.

If Ambrose ignored the stalactites looming above him in the massive cavern, he could almost pretend this was an extension of the Scarrish markets he visited every week. Food stalls lined up in a vented alcove, hawking skewers of dripping meats and bowls of fried mushrooms. The savory aromas warred with the bakers on the other side, crouched behind stacks of pillowy pastries and bread loaves. Cassius led Ambrose and Nat through the middle of the mouth-watering fray, into a haphazard maze of wares. Though no one sold Aphos' treasured illusion devices here—those were far too valuable for a common market like this—there were plenty of potion ingredients to catch Ambrose's eye. Herbs, flowers, crystals...

But his gaze caught more frequently on all of the other goods in the market, the ones less familiar to a topsider like him. Darkvision goggles in all sizes and styles. Jesses and gloves for hunting owls. The farther he walked, the farther the stalls stretched: mushroom and bat compost here, paint for stone murals there, people haggling and chatting and joking every which way...

He briefly craned his neck up at the stalactites and found, far above him, a narrow strip of light, glimmering weakly like a distant river.

Somewhere above, his own markets bustled, and the mere idea of it made him homesick.

He pushed down the bitter feeling and tried to focus on his task: note the routes in and out, memorize any notable buildings or performance spaces, anything that looked like a potential demonstration area.

But his unwilling chaperones had deigned to make that difficult.

"How many more ingredients do you need?" Cassius huffed and snapped his fingers at Nat. "Make yourself useful and carry that basket for him. He's buying things for you, after all." He straightened his coat and continued in a mutter. "Can't imagine why. Kitchens are wasting their food on you already."

In a market like this, the formal lines of Cassius' coat stuck out like a glowing crystal in a dark cave, as did the dragon scale illusions rippling across his shoulders—but he didn't seem to mind. On the contrary, other Aphosian officers began to flit around him, anxious moths to his authoritarian light, and he snapped at all of them in turn.

"Cassius, sir." One such officer rushed up—a short orc in a navy jacket, its cut a simpler, un-illusioned echo of Cassius'. "Inspection of the Redstone entrance is complete."

"And?"

"Illusions are holding well. Fifteen visitors so far, and—"

"Good." Cassius sent him off and swiveled his impatient gaze to the next officer. "You?"

This elf kept up with his pace on equally long legs. "Spoke to that archivist you wanted, sir. They've got potioneering experience. Once they get the right wands, they should be able to copy down his notes within the week."

Cassius gave a short nod—the highest indication of approval

Ambrose had seen all week. "Good. While you're down there with the artificers, could you...?"

Ambrose tried to listen in, to learn when exactly that archivist was going to make a visit—but Cassius stepped farther away, and the chatter of the markets drowned out his words. Ambrose glanced at Nat, who slouched under the weight of his basket. He might as well make use of the brief distance from Cassius.

"Nat," he said, "did Tavi ever go to the markets for her work?"

In a silent show of both spite and bribery, he placed an extraordinary amount of cheese and herbed crackers in the basket, then took the basket off her hands. Her eyes widened, and after a hesitant glance in Cassius' direction, she scuttled over to Ambrose's other side, her good ear tilted toward him.

"What was that?"

"Tavi. Did she ever visit the markets?"

"Oh." She wilted again. "No, I don't think she ever tried. Was too busy brewing or doodling stuff. Sometimes she'd ask me what she should doodle, but she didn't really show me a lot of her drawings." A rare half smile flashed briefly across her face. "I told her to draw me pointing a big fire staff—you know, one of the fireball ones—at Cassius, but she didn't. Drew a bunch of boring leaves instead. Didn't even color all of them in."

As she pawed through the basket and admired the cheeses, Ambrose tried to imagine Nat wielding a fire staff and quickly determined the world was better off without such a scenario.

"But—surely Tavi left the workroom at some point?" he continued, trying to keep his tone indifferent. "For her demonstrations?"

Nat's gaze instinctively flicked toward a path south out of the market: a wide, crystal-lit tunnel. "Sure, but..." Her words trailed off as she reached the ingredient bottles in the basket, and her eyes narrowed in suspicion. "Why are you buying this stuff?"

He blinked. "What do you mean?"

"This." She pulled up a narrow vial filled with dried sunflower petals and shook it. "It's all warm stuff. You know, orangey and yellow.

And all the bottles you've been using are..." She gestured to his robes. "That color. With some purple."

Ambrose gaped at her—she was correct, but how on earth had she noticed?—then he clicked his jaw shut and gathered himself together.

"Potion ingredients come in all colors," he said. "Petals of this kind"—he took the sunflower petals from her hand—"require particular care in their selection. To glean the most magic from them, I had to inspect them first before purchasing."

But his lecture failed. She merely rolled her eyes and took the basket back from him.

"You're not getting out of here," she muttered. "No one does."

Ambrose's hands went cold. If Cassius overheard her—

He lowered his voice to match hers. "I'm *not* trying to leave."

"Sure, sure."

Sharp footsteps approached from behind.

"Are you almost done?" Cassius asked sharply. Ambrose didn't dare look at either of them. It would be so easy for Nat to swing around, point a damning finger at him, and—

She did nothing. Merely tightened her grip on the basket and kept moving, her scowl deepening under Cassius' shadow.

"Almost done," Ambrose said to fill the silence, trying not to let his relief bleed into his voice. "Once I check those food stalls up there, I'll be finished."

He scurried through the rest of the market, piling food into his arms in unspoken gratitude. Anything that Nat's eyes rested on for more than a moment went into the basket: sausages, apples, preserves, confits...

As he was considering little bags of taffy, another officer rushed up to Cassius, their voice wavering.

"Sir," they said, "I have a report from the Madam. She's changed her mind about the luncheon tomorrow."

"Again?" Cassius spun around with a tired sigh. "I've already rearranged security for the event three times. If she changes it one more time—"

He quickly lost himself in berating the poor officer for Madam Mila's choices. Next to Ambrose, Nat inspected the taffy. Nervous energy coursed through him. He had just a moment, but he could use it if he worked quickly enough.

"Pick out which ones you'd like," he instructed Nat, then quietly edged toward the tunnel she had looked at before. If that was where the demonstrations were held, he could take note of the signs, the pathways, any kind of landmark for Rosemond Street...

He ducked a few stalls away, the tunnel becoming clearer with each step. His view gave tantalizing hints of buildings carved into the cave walls and moss climbing up pillars. Something about it felt familiar. Had he been led near there before? If he had, that meant there were other tunnels leading in and out, other opportunities for his rescuers to enter. If he could just find a sign or something—

"*You.*"

A rough hand yanked him backward.

"What do you think you're doing?" Cassius hissed, his face still a splotchy red from his previous tirade.

"I—" Ambrose begged a lie to form on his tongue. Nothing came. "I, um—"

Cassius dragged him away from the tunnel, his grip harsh and bruising. "Your time is up. I won't stand for this sort of time-wasting in the future. You will *remain* in your workroom until she calls for you."

"But what if I—?" Ambrose tried weakly, looking at the sliver of light above for inspiration, help, anything. Cassius swatted his words away.

"Should you need any additional ingredients, my artificers will purchase them for you. Are we clear?"

He shoved Ambrose out of the market and into the dark tunnels. The last hint of sunlight above winked out, leaving him with nothing but dim lanterns and cold shadows. Ambrose swallowed.

"Perfectly clear."

He stumbled back into the workroom, sickened at the sight of the fake walls of The Griffin's Claw all around him. If he truly couldn't leave again for a month, he wasn't sure how he was going to do it. To stay in these four walls, with nothing but scraps of information coming to him from above.

Behind him, Nat silently arranged her new trove of food in the corner. Ambrose tried to gather himself and mimic her, placing his new ingredients in the cabinets. Then he relit the fires under his fake potions, tidied the journals that hid his correspondence with Rose-mond Street...

What was he going to say to them next? Whenever they chose to write again, he'd have nothing to provide, not from Tavi's journals and certainly not from his market trip. No hint or clue as to where he might be taken in a month nor where they could retrieve him.

He tucked the notebooks into a drawer and turned.

"Well, I believe that was more than your required hours for the day," he murmured to Nat, his throat tight. "Thank you. You are dismissed."

But Nat didn't leave. She stared silently at the food, arms folded, her back to Ambrose.

"The throne room," she finally said.

"I'm sorry?"

"Madam Mila's stupid, fancy throne room," she repeated. "You've been there before. That's where Tavi always went for her demonstra-tions. It's closest to the Grapevine entrance and the Forge entrance, if someone wanted to get topside quickly." She finally turned, her gaze boring into him. "You got all that?"

Ambrose's breath caught in his lungs. "I—yes, thank you—"

"You're still not gonna escape, though," she cut in, her words just as stony as her look. "There's no point."

He held his secrets under his tongue and mirrored her gaze. "I wouldn't dream of it."

RULE 15:

COLLABORATE

Dawn

RORY WAS SET to arrive in fifteen minutes, and Dawn had locked herself in a duel with her wardrobe.

Casualties littered the pock-marked battlefield. Colorful dresses and skirts piled up on one end of her bed, deemed too peppy for a waltz into a den of thieves. On the other end, more monotonous articles of clothing dug deeper into their trench of logic.

It wasn't a date. It was a *mission*, and no matter how much she disliked the color gray, she did not need to impress the stupidly hot journalist going with her.

For the third time that evening, she whirled toward the door, instinct drawing her to the rose statue downstairs. Her fingers itched to write to Ambrose, to beg him to come over and help her make a decision.

(His help, while useless in the fashion department, was always objective and comforting and...well, likely on the side of the boring gray skirt draped over her pillow.)

And for the third time, her hand stopped on the doorknob.

Ambrose wasn't going to answer. He wasn't in his potion shop, on the other end of that magic scroll.

That was the whole point of the mission.

Heart empty, she waved her white flag and donned her most nondescript items: dark, loose pants and a gray tunic patterned with subtle dots. Not her prettiest outfit by far, but easy to run away in, at least, should she find herself at the business end of an Aphosian's defensive wand.

Downstairs, the bell above the door chimed, and hesitant foot-steps shuffled into the shop. "Dawn?" Rory called. "You here?"

Excited nerves jolted through her; she tamped them down and cleared her throat.

"Be right there!" she called back, then allowed herself one more check in the mirror.

Still cute, mission or no.

She hurried down the stairs, ensuring her coin purse was tied tightly to her belt. "So, how far away is this tavern? Because if you tell me one of Aphos' hideouts is right around the corner, I'm not gonna sleep for...days..."

Her words died on her lips. Aesthetically, Rory had not gotten the memo about it not being a date.

She had still changed for the occasion. Her hair was dyed brown, her undercut waves grown out, her jewelry and tattoos hidden (a small devastation, but a necessary one). But Dawn had never seen a jacket quite like hers before. Its sawtooth pattern danced in the light, showing off visible silver lines in one angle, pure black in another. And every line tapered perfectly around her body in smooth, sharp lines.

Next to Rory's sleek, understated perfection, Dawn felt like a short little rain cloud—but before she could make an excuse to go change, the journalist bounded farther into the store, taking in the glass cases with unbridled fascination.

"This is a gorgeous shop," she said. "You really make all of these?"

Dawn forced herself to stop tugging at the hem of her tunic. Maybe she looked bland, but her wands most certainly did not.

"Made all of 'em," she said. "I'm looking for an apprentice, though, so one day they might have a few of their own on the shelves."

Rory straightened. "Can't keep all that genius to yourself, I guess." She nodded up at the awards above the shelves and gave a long whistle. "Are all those yours, too?"

Dawn's face warmed. Gods, if Rory was starting the quest like this, how was she possibly going to focus?

"Should we, uh, get going?" She gestured nervously to the street.

"Right, right!" Rory bounded back to the door and held it open for her with a grin. "After you, my lady."

Dawn scurried into the night, letting the cool air warm her burning cheeks. Not a date, not a date, not a date.

Together, they headed south, in the opposite direction of Dawn's favorite hangout spots. More mundane shops crowded the thin streets here, all vying for the small bit of sky the narrower chasm had to offer. In the dim, sporadic crystal light, the unfamiliar space spawned hundreds of equally unfamiliar shadows. Dawn made sure to walk a little closer to Rory as she spoke.

"So, you said you had contacts at this tavern," she said. "They don't know you're a reporter, right?"

"Hells no." Rory pointed to the bronze pin on her lapel, a wand crossed over a wrench. "Over here, I'm Liddy, an apprentice to an artificer in Watchby. I come in now and then when my mentor's here to pick up supplies. You know, stopping in long enough to get a drink and hear the local news. And, in this case, see if anyone knows how to make a teleport device that can bypass Aphos' barrier."

Dawn gave a hum. It was a decent alibi—Watchby was a fairly well-to-do town a few days' ride from the Scar. Rory would blend in among many of the Watchby travelers who came in to shop at The Whirling Wand Emporium.

"This tavern is one of the best spots to look for what we need," Rory continued. "It's been catering to Aphosians for years now. It's not an Aphos-exclusive joint, mind you. The barkeeps just know how to look the other way when needed."

She jerked her chin toward a tavern that Dawn would have otherwise overlooked—a squat, jagged place carved into the chasm wall. It was smaller than The Jumping Ogre, more hunched in stature, with low stone walls and guttering lanterns.

But within, the cheery sounds of a festival bubbled.

Dawn didn't know whether to be frightened or pleased by what she saw through the windows. There were no shadowy figures or whispered schemes here. On the contrary, no one here was even attempting to remain quiet or discreet. A jumbled mass of people danced before a stage on one end, while huddles of friends toasted with large, frothy drinks on the other.

The location was no Jumping Ogre, that was for sure—but the energy within rivaled the Ogre's half-price ale nights.

"What, you thought criminals didn't like to have fun?" Rory extended an arm to her. "Come on. Drinks are on me."

Many thoughts reeled through Dawn's head—*Not a date*, for one, and *Oh gods she's touching me* for another—but she managed to latch on to one of the more practical thoughts bobbing in her mind.

"Wait, wait." She backpedaled. "What's my story, then?"

"Story?"

"If you're Liddy, the apprentice from Watchby, then who am I?"

Rory faltered. "I had a thought on that," she said, then bit her lip. "Now, hear me out. What if we—?"

"Liddy!" A woman with a dull apron and bright smile waved eagerly from the doorway. "Haven't seen you in a donkey's age!"

"Callia!" Rory approached, her grin frozen. "Just, uh, got into town—"

"A lucky one, you are." Callia tilted her head toward the bar. "Jimmy's not out of the whiskey sours yet. Who's your friend?"

The question sounded innocent enough, but Dawn caught the edge in her voice, the suspicion built into the words. Her hand immediately tightened on Rory's elbow. Why had she agreed to walk into an Aphosian bar, of all places? Did she have to make up a name for herself right now? A backstory, an alibi? Would she have to answer riddles in thieves' cant to get one of those whiskey sours—?

Rory gestured to Dawn.

"This is Kerry," she said. "My, um, date."

Somewhere in the back of her head, Dawn's past self cackled wildly as the word *date* bounced around in a panicked echo.

"What extra luck you're in tonight!" Callia relaxed and gestured inside. "Go on, go on. I'll be there to get your drinks in a moment."

Once they were inside the warm, ale-laden air, Rory beelined for a booth in the corner. "Sorry," she muttered, "I meant to ask before I—"

"It's fine," Dawn said, filtering both her elation and her nerves out of her response. "Kerry, though?"

"You know, like Kerighin!"

"Do I look like a Kerry to you?"

They slid into the booth side by side, taking advantage of the relative privacy in the shadows. Rory gave her a sheepish smile.

"You're not a Kerry," she said. "More like an...Allani."

"Allani?"

"Means *beautiful* in Deepriver."

Dawn gave a weak laugh while heat rushed from her neck to the tips of her ears. She couldn't do this. A date-not-date in the middle of a thieves' den, while her friend's rescue hung in the balance.

She fidgeted with her rings and turned her attention to the people around her, all drinking, dancing, and playing cards. She had to focus on them, but how could she? Rory aside, any of these people might have been Ambrose's kidnapper. Maybe they had even seen him that day, toiling away in a dingy underground lab. Her thoughts spun faster, merging fears with memories. Maybe they had peered into a cell at an Ambrose who was pale and scared and begging them not to leave him, begging for *her* not to leave him while she stepped back and—

"Dawn?" Rory's voice broke into her thoughts. "I'm serious. We don't have to do this if you don't want to. If you don't want to sit next to me as a fake date—"

She tried to shake away the thoughts, but they stuck firm. "It's not that," she said. "Really, it's—I'm fine being a date. A fake date. It's just —I'm worried about Ames and..."

The story teetered on the tip of her tongue. There was no point in explaining it. Eli had already told her it wasn't her fault; she should let it go already and move on with her life—

"Wanna tell me about it?" Rory asked quietly, her navy eyes soft in the lamplight. Dawn shook her head.

"I'm just being stupid—"

"You're not," Rory cut in. "Hey, I saw those trophies. I know you're a genius, you can't hide it from me." Dawn gave a feeble smile, and she grinned in response. "Whatever it is, it isn't stupid, and you can tell me about it if you want."

At some point in Dawn's worrying, a whiskey sour and a glass of wine had appeared in front of them. She took the wine and tapped her fingers on the cool glass. "Off the record?"

Rory sat back. "With you? Always."

Dawn both hated and adored how that sounded.

She spoke in between sips. Describing how she had once left Ambrose in a sinkhole in a flash of anger and terrible judgment. Then, in another lapse of judgment, had chosen not to follow him into the hallway during the debates—and how he had landed underground once more as a result, alone and scared, while she remained safe and terribly guilty on Rosemond Street.

"Eli's right," Rory said firmly. "It's not your—"

"Fault, I know. I just can't get it out of my head, and if we're going to get that—that bypass mechanism for the teleporter tonight—"

"Hey, don't worry about that." Rory pushed her untouched cocktail in Dawn's direction. "Here, let's play a game."

Dawn continued spinning her own glass. "What about the contact you were looking for—?"

"He's not here yet. We've got time." She set one arm behind them on the booth. Dawn tried not to think about the warmth coming from her hand.

"All right," Rory continued. "Take five deep breaths and tell me one thing you can see."

Dawn found herself drawn to the one earring Rory had left on—a simple, faceted black stud. A stoic contrast to her tilted smile.

"The lantern behind you," she answered instead. "There's a spider crawling on it."

"Okay, gross. Thanks for telling me." Rory grimaced and shifted away from the lantern, closer to Dawn. "One sip, five more breaths, then tell me one thing you can feel."

Given her proximity, Dawn could now feel the shift of Rory's jacket sleeve against her bare shoulder. The pattern still mesmerized even here in the dim light, its fabric cool and smooth, practically begging for her to run her fingers across it...

"The booth," she said quickly, shoving her thoughts in a different direction. "It's, uh, kinda lumpy." She wiggled to make her point.

"I mean, I prefer the term *cozy*, but..." Rory shifted around and winced. "Point taken."

A quick sip of her wine, then five more breaths. These were easier this time—slower, more regular. And somewhere between the wiggling and the breathing, she had edged even closer to Rory, until their shoulders almost brushed.

But neither woman made an attempt to pull away.

"Last one," Rory said. "One thing you can taste."

Dawn's traitorous gaze went straight to Rory's lips. What would they taste like? Whiskey sour and the warmth of the tavern, or the coolness of the breeze outside, with that hint of mint she kept catching on the air—?

She quickly turned away and gulped down her drink, hoping the liquid would cool her burning chest; then, in a show of pretend disdain, she puckered her lips and set the glass back down with a heavy clink. "At least it's not poisoned."

Rory laughed. "Heard you loud and clear. Next time, I'll take you somewhere nicer."

Dawn opened her mouth to ask exactly what that meant, but Rory's attention suddenly snapped to the crowd, her expression dropping into careful neutrality.

"He's here," she murmured.

Dawn caught a brief glimpse of a gnome maneuvering his way toward the other wall, goggles still strapped to his forehead and soot streaking the edge of his folded ear.

"Jasper. Senior artificer in Aphos," Rory explained. "I've had a few chats with him. Enough for him to remember my face."

"Wanna go catch him?" Dawn asked.

Rory shook her head. "Best if we talk to him after he downs a drink. He's a bit friendlier then. Now, if I could just *see* him finishing his ale, I could time it right..."

Dawn briefly stretched to peer over the crowd, then quickly hunched back in with a practiced air of indifference. Even in such a relaxed space, she was sure prying eyes weren't a good look for a visitor. She drained the dregs of her glass and looked over the crowd before her. Surely there was some way to get closer to him, between the pairs crowded at the bar, the card players filling the corners, the dancers before the tiny little stage...

She stood, a half-giddy idea forming in her head. Two had to play the fake dating game, after all.

"Dance with me." She held out her hand out to Rory, who raised an eyebrow.

"You sure?" she said. "I can't say I have experience dancing on the job—"

"You sure have experience bar-fighting on the job. This'll be easier. All you gotta do"—Dawn grinned—"is relax."

Rory returned the gesture and took her hand.

"If my date wants to dance," she said in a low voice, "who am I to say no?"

They pushed their way to the other side of the bar, where the patrons had given up all pretense of dancing in an orderly line or circle and instead moved however they pleased, several of them raising sloshing wineglasses in a toast to the bards onstage. There would be no smooth moves on the floor here—if Dawn and Rory were going to blend in, they were going to have to do this as terribly as the others. Dawn quickly grabbed two wineglasses off a passing tray and handed one to Rory.

"My lady"—Rory lifted her glass, narrowly dodging a woman's flailing arms—"what do we toast to?"

Dawn raised her wine. "To dancing badly like my best friend's life depends on it."

Rory clinked her glass. "Say no more."

In a delightful excess of Dawn's wildest expectations, Rory Basha of the *Scarrish Post* was an extraordinarily terrible dancer.

"You"—Dawn was barely dancing now, hardly able to move for doubling over in laughter—"how are you even moving your arms like that?"

"Oh, like this?" Rory continued with a perfectly serious expression, achieving a motion somewhere between a flapping dragon and a panicked chicken. "You said someone's life depended on it. I am doing my due diligence. And frankly, I don't see you keeping up your end of the deal here—"

"Excuse you, I've spilled wine on no fewer than three people through practice and sheer force of will!"

"But can your cabernet do *this*?" Rory made a flailing kick that almost struck a passing orc. "I didn't think so, Kerry."

Dawn gave another shrieking laugh and nearly toppled over—Rory grabbed her shoulders to steady both of them.

"All right, all right," she said, grinning from ear to ear. "I'll cool it. Don't wanna show up my date, after all."

Dawn stared at her, relaxed giggles bubbling into nervous ones in her throat. Rory was inches from her face now. If she just straightened and tilted her face up, she could—

Rory's gaze flicked elsewhere.

"Jasper's finally finished his drink," she murmured, barely audible over the dancing crowd. "You ready, my graceful actress?"

Oh. Right. The mission.

Dawn steadied herself and nodded. Rory took her arm once more and led her over to a small table, where the artificer had begun to nurse his second ale. He had taken his goggles off, but their imprint remained deeply set across his wrinkled forehead. And below his dirty collar, his own wand-and-wrench pin glinted in the light, its edges worn and tarnished.

Abandoning all traces of her terrible, jerking moves on the dance floor, Rory slid smoothly into the seat across from him.

"Jasper," she said, keeping her tone short and casual—almost gruff, like she had worked a long day. "How you holding up?"

"Liddy." He briefly raised his mug to her. "Good to see you. Boss send you with the grocery list again?"

Rory leaned back. "Yep. And I'll need at least ten griffins to haul it all back."

"And he won't even use half of it."

"Of course. Needs all that stuff—"

"Just in case," Jasper finished with a snort. It was a path they had clearly trodden before, a conversation as well-worn as his artificer's pin.

But Dawn had never been on that path before, and he swiveled to her.

"Who's this?" he grunted. She pulled up a chair as casually as possible.

"Liddy's date for the evening." She plopped down next to Rory, who gestured between her and Jasper.

"Jasper, meet Kerry. Kerry, Jasper."

Even as she lounged in the chair, Dawn's chest tightened. She was seated directly in front of him now—there was no hiding from any questions he might ask her.

But the artificer seemed to have little interest in dates and instead turned back to Rory.

"Working on any of your own pieces yet?" he asked.

Rory shrugged. "Sometimes." She tapped the table in pretend thought. "Been trying my hand at teleporters lately."

Jasper raised his bushy eyebrows. "Not an easy tinker, all told."

"Right?" Rory slouched in a mix of frustration and relief, so convincing that Dawn half thought she actually made devices in her spare time. "It's so difficult! I don't know how you do it. And *you've* gotta make the device work inside Aphos on top of everything else."

"Time and patience, kid." Jasper took a long sip of his ale. "Time and patience."

Dawn kept herself from fidgeting in her seat. She had neither time nor patience at the moment—not when it came to Ambrose's rescue. In an echo of her feelings, Rory groaned.

"But my boss wants me to get a working one going in three weeks," she pressed. "I'll take any kind of tip you got. Hells, I'll buy you another drink."

That sparked a glint in Jasper's eyes, and Rory hailed Callia before it could wink out. "Beer for Jasper and me," she said, "and another wine for the lady."

Once the drinks arrived, they all hunched closer together around the table.

"For a basic device, it's all in the materials," Jasper said. "If you're not refining the metal first, you're never going to get it to work. But if you're looking to add a special parameter like I have to, you'll need extra help, like this." He pulled a key ring from his pocket. The wand on it was one of the smallest pieces Dawn had ever seen—hardly longer than the artificer's pinky, dangling from the ring alongside a smattering of keys and other trinkets. The construction of the wand —the branched setting, the plain base... Was it a signature device, or a—?

"Using this is another step to manage, but it gets the job done well enough without magical interference," Jasper said, then began to tuck it back into his pocket, reaching for his beer with his other hand. Dawn's heart pounded in her ears. If she could just get a closer look at the wand, hold it even for a second—

"Looks like you've got a break in the fire ruby there," she blurted out.

Jasper paused, his eyes narrowing at her. Rory stiffened in fear.

Dawn took a breath. The only way out now was through.

"I supply gems to her boss." She nodded to Rory. "I know a broken stones when I see one. If you don't adjust the setting, you might have a backfire on your hands." Then, with a shaky breath: "May I?"

She held out her hand. When Jasper didn't move, Rory draped an arm over the back of Dawn's chair.

"Smart as a wyvern, this one." She squeezed Dawn's arm. "If she thinks you've got a break in the stone, I'd let her take a look." For emphasis, she took the back of Dawn's hand and kissed it in adoration.

With a grumble, Jasper took the wand off the key ring and handed it over. "If you think it's gonna blow," he muttered.

Dawn weighed the wand in her palm. It was a signature wand, that much was clear—she could see Aphos' unique sigil carved into the ruby on all facets. The unadorned beech handle would transfer the sigil from the ruby to Jasper's devices, marking them for safe passage through whatever barriers Aphos had set up.

And now that she could see the sigil, every curve and spike and line, she could craft that same power for Banneker.

"Here." She held the wand back out before she could stare at it for too long. "You've got a hairline crack right here. Take it back and get your wandmakers to swap out the ruby, then tighten the setting. Irregular magic transfer from the crack could cause a surge you don't want."

She dropped the wand back into his palm, then discreetly squeezed Rory's hand, hoping her fingers weren't shaking too much.

"This calls for another round, yeah?" Rory hailed Callia once more, relief drenching her voice. "Another beer for Jasper, please!"

After another beer, Jasper forgot all about the cracked gem and wand, instead opting to rant about the price of iron and the slovenly work habits of his fellow artificers. All Dawn had to do was nod along, laugh at Rory's jokes, then slip out of the tavern upon their goodbyes.

Neither of them dared talk until they reached Rosemond Street.

"So, did you get it?" Rory whirled around, face shining. "Did you figure out what Banneker needs?"

"I've got it." Dawn fought back giggles. "I'll write it down right away. Banneker and I can recreate their whole process, I know we can—"

Rory scooped her up into a spinning hug.

"Gods, you're incredible! And you weren't even nervous talking to him. I knew you could relax, I knew you could do it!" She set her down and beamed. "Kerry the gem seller is godsdamned amazing."

Dawn let the praise wash over her from head to toe. "Liddy the apprentice isn't so bad, either," she offered back. "Even if she can't dance."

"Can't dance?' Rory struck a ridiculous pose, then bowed and took Dawn's hand. "I danced exactly as I was told to, my lady."

She regarded the hand as if to kiss it again. Dawn held her breath. There was no audience here, no one to play-act for. If she really did it this time—

Rory gracefully stepped back and let go of her hand.

"Let me know what Banneker says about that wand, all right?" she said. Dawn nodded. Not a date, she reminded herself. Never had been.

"I'll tell you as soon as we've made progress."

"Good. Great. Excellent." Rory hesitated, then stepped away. "Have a good night, Kerry."

Dawn bit back a smile. "Good night, Liddy."

RULE 16:

NOTE YOUR OBSERVATIONS

Eli

THE MORNING after her quest with Rory, Dawn was bubbling over.

"And then we ran back to my shop," she rambled as she strolled next to Eli, her gesturing hands a constant threat to the others on the walkway. "And Rory said I was incredible, and then I stayed up and figured out how I can make the wand"—she tugged a folded piece of paper out of her pocket and flapped it around—"I think we can do it, we can make a teleport device that will get Ames outta there—"

The paper thwacked a passing gnome on the shoulder. "Watch it, lady!"

"Sorry!" Dawn gasped and pulled her hands in. "So sorry, excuse me!"

Eli laughed and gently guided her to the side of the walkway, under the spacious safety of an awning. Dawn's bubbliness was infectious—he hadn't felt this light in weeks.

"I knew you could do it." He pulled out the little bag of cookies they had just bought. "Your reward for your mighty deed, Madam Heroine."

The cookies were still warm and fresh from The Gingersnap Café.

Their intention had been to sit there and lounge in the luxury of desserts and tea, like Dawn often did with Ambrose—but after five minutes at the table without Ames, they left, both silently unsettled.

"I missed these," Dawn mumbled, chomping her way through a cinnamon cookie. Eli hesitated. This was no time to mope. Dawn had just had a major victory.

In more ways than one, it seemed.

He watched her, carefully waiting until she was mid-bite. "So... Rory called you incredible, huh?"

It almost worked—she coughed out a puff of cinnamon, then quickly masked her expression and gave a noncommittal hum. But having four siblings had honed Eli's perception of such things to a fine point. There was more teasing to be done here, he was sure of it.

"And she danced with you," he continued, leaning against the wall. "She sat close to you, bought you wine, you gazed dreamily into her eyes—"

"I did not—"

"You sure it wasn't a real date, Kerighin?"

Dawn chewed faster. "It was a cover. We needed to see the wand to help Ames."

"Sure, sure. And the kiss on the hand, that was absolutely, completely necessary to the cause."

"It *was*!"

"Of course." Eli nonchalantly waved his uneaten cookie. "I mean, that's totally part of *my* adventurer training. Dancing, flirting, seduction, all in the name of getting the quest done—"

"Oh, eat your stupid cookie." Dawn tried to push his hand toward his mouth. He laughed and shooed her away.

"Come on, let's get back and show Banneker your work." He pushed himself off the wall and pocketed his cookie. "I'm meeting Sherry and your girlfriend—"

"She's not my girlfriend!"

"—for the stakeout."

They descended to the chasm floor, slowly picking at the remaining cookies and cinnamon crumbs in the bag. Eli had hoped that both the sugar and the teasing would carry his mood through the stakeout—but the closer he got to Rosemond Street, the more his nerves took over. Dawn had fulfilled her mission and then some. She had gotten them closer to rescuing Ames without breaking a sweat. But the teleporter would be useless if they couldn't find a way in...

And finding a way in was *his* mission.

They made a direct line for Banneker's shop, preparing to part at the door, but Viola caught them first.

"Morning!" she called from the bakery, dusting off the little ramp she had installed for the doorway. "Hey, um—question for you both."

Eli reluctantly slowed down. "Yeah?"

She pointed across the street. "Does Ambrose's shop...always look that sparkly?"

"What?" Eli frowned and twisted around. True to Viola's word, something new flashed high up in the bay window of The Griffin's Claw. That didn't look right—Ambrose always had potions on display, but he never had anything stored so high up near the window.

He turned on his heel and headed for the shop, Dawn close behind. If Xavion had installed extra shelves, they would completely throw off Ambrose's organizing system. The man would have a conniption before he could ever escape Aphos—

He opened the door to find something far worse than extra shelves haunting the shop.

"What in the hells is this?" he demanded.

Xavion blinked at him from the front counter. "Joy and whimsy," they said. "Something Ambrose Beake utterly lacks."

What Eli was staring at was not joyous or whimsical. It was an overwhelming display of trinkets and light-catching baubles hung all across the store. Seashells on string, hanging crystals, twisted strips of colored glass that cast bright caustics across the cabinets and made obnoxious tinkling sounds. Such garish intrusions destroyed—no, *obliterated*—the professional sanctity of The Griffin's Claw.

At least, that's what Ambrose would say. For Eli's part, he didn't actually mind the extra sparkles, but then again, it wasn't his shop.

It was his boyfriend's.

And Xavion Demachel had redecorated it.

Behind Eli, Dawn stepped in and gave a single, large laugh, then clapped a hand over her mouth. "Oh my gods. It's like a spa in here."

Eli whipped around and glared at Xavion. "Take these down. Now."

Xavion didn't look up from the magazine they were flipping through. "When you rescue your prince and bring him home," they drawled, "I assure you I will have every improvement gone from the shop before he sets foot in the door." They closed the magazine and met his gaze. "But not a moment before. I am forced to work here, after all. I might as well make my surroundings livable."

"*You*." Eli held up a finger, then recalled that Banneker and the stakeout were waiting for him. He turned for the door, maintaining his glare. "We are *not* done talking about this—"

He walked face-first into a hanging mobile of seashells.

"Son of a—!" He shoved them out of his face, the shells clinking together in mock laughter. Xavion smiled and waved.

"Have a good evening, Mr. Valenz. Do watch your step."

Eli gave the shells another whack and stormed out with Dawn, his determination cresting in angry bursts. He was going to find a way in, he was going to get Ambrose back, and he was *going* to get that snotty potioneer out of Ambrose's store.

"I could poison them, you know," Viola called from her doorway, leaning against her broom and gesturing to her knee. Now that she had settled on her next cupcake recipe—all-pink, just as Dawn had suggested—her leg was now lined with orange and yellow macarons. "Poison would be easy to hide in a macaron. Or some tea, if I can nail down their favorite flavor."

Eli sighed. The offer was tempting.

"Not today," he finally said. "But I'll keep it in mind."

Eli's stakeout companions had already gathered in Banneker's workroom: Grim, Sherry, and Rory, all clustered around a plate of odd-looking eclairs. Sherry and Rory were both bent over Ambrose's notes from the past few days. Though neither party had anything useful to report recently, Eli had wanted to keep the notes himself, just as a reminder that Ames was out there, alive and breathing.

But Grim, ever the logical one, insisted they keep them in a secure place.

"And you know what entrances he's talking about?" Sherry asked Rory, pointing to one of the notes. Rory marked two spots on a map Grim was holding.

"Grapevine is over here and Forge is over there," she said. "Wherever he got his intel, it's reliable. If his demonstration really is in Aphos' throne room, those are the closest entrances."

"You have a good feeling about either one of them?" Eli asked, itching to take all the notes and stuff them in his pockets.

Rory waggled her head in thought. "Aphos changes their guard rotation often. Makes it harder for folks like us to do exactly what we're trying to do." She chewed on her lip. "We'll need to split up and check both of them today. I'm thinking Grim and Sherry to Forge, you and me to Grapevine."

Grim handed out earrings while Rory spoke. They were little more than dangling teardrop crystals, but the communication spell built into them fizzed against Eli's fingertips as he slid them on.

"Can I write to Ames before we go?" he asked. Sherry tentatively held up the remaining paper. Given their constant communication, they only had a quarter of it left.

A few more days, and they'd lose their connection to Ambrose entirely.

"I suppose you could," she tried, "but—"

"No, no." Eli waved away the question, his heart sinking. "I'll wait. Let's get this done."

They all reached for the eclairs on the plate. They hardly resembled Viola's typical fare—plain shapes, no icing on top—but the soft, golden pastry still made Eli's mouth water.

"What's the spell?" he asked.

"Invisibility," Grim explained. "Viola's ingredients manage a lower magical signature. Harder to detect and won't get in the way of the earrings."

Rory knocked her eclair against Eli's. "Bottoms up."

He ate the pastry in two bites. As he expected, the dessert had been kept plain and simple to keep the magic unfettered, and he hardly got more than a slight hint of vanilla as he ate.

But the rapid tingling from the spell more than made up for it— by the time he finished chewing, his hands were already vanishing. Within seconds, his friends had all disappeared, too: empty air around an empty plate.

"My honorable sir." Rory took Eli's elbow. "May I lead us to the Grapevine?"

Eli grinned. If this was the charm Rory had used on Dawn, Dawn had no chance of resisting.

"Lead on."

Eli quickly learned that the Grapevine entrance was rather aptly named. It took the shape of a perpetually closed wine shop down in the southeastern quarter of the Scar, one he had never noticed before. Together with its discarded barrels, dusty windows, and broken-down furniture within, people hardly gave it a second glance as they walked past. But Rory knew better—she pulled Eli into a stubby little alleyway across the street and waited there.

Given the shallow cover of the alley, he didn't risk speaking out loud to her, lest a passerby overhear the disembodied conversation. Instead, he tugged on Grim's provided earring and directed his thoughts her way.

I don't see any guards, he said. Such a communication tool was more common with adventurers, and Eli was used to the brain-fuzziness that came with it—but next to him, Rory yelped and gave a small jump, disturbing the dust at her feet.

The entrance is closed right now, she said, then reached again for Eli's arm. *Don't get any ideas—they've got strong shields all over the entrances when they're not open. Try to jump through one and you'll be a roast dish by the time you land on the other side.*

Eli grumbled silently; such an idea had been forming despite his better judgment. *Understood.*

Seconds later, a new voice crackled into their heads—Grim's gruff accent, both spiky and distant, as if they were speaking two rooms away. *Got guards at ours.*

Lots of them, Sherry cut in. Rory shifted.

How many?

Silence as Sherry counted. *Five*, she finally answered. Rory hissed out loud.

That's a no-go, she said. *Usually means they're expecting heavy traffic, maybe a big shipment. Too many eyes there. I don't like it.*

Sherry cursed, which under happier circumstances, Eli would have found to be a delight.

Want us to come to you? Grim asked. Rory pulled away from Eli's arm.

Not enough space, she said. A bit of debris fell off the opposite wall, evidence of her leaning against it. *Eli and I will wait here and let you know how this one looks.*

Eli bit back a groan and leaned against the wall behind him. Waiting. His favorite.

He tried his best to watch silently—to scope out anyone who might be giving the wine shop a second look, or pick up any movement from within the store itself.

But after five minutes of that, he wanted to crawl out of his skin, so he opted for kicking a rock in the alley and asking questions instead.

After all, *someone* had to fill in the blanks on what exactly had happened between Dawn and Rory last night, and it certainly wasn't going to be Dawn.

Dawn told me about the outing last night, he said, trying to sound neutrally curious. *Seems like it went well.*

With no body language to pick up on, he honed in on her voice for cues.

Yeah, it went great, Rory answered. *You should've seen her. She completely nailed it.*

The admiration in her voice was genuine. Eli paused, considering his next question—then couldn't help himself.

A fake date, huh?

A nervous laugh sounded through the alleyway before Rory caught herself. *She told you about that?*

She didn't tell me enough about that. He kicked a rock her way. *Just a fake date?*

Silence between them—then she kicked the rock back.

I can't ask out a source for my story.

Eli desperately wanted to call dragon dung on that; he kicked the rock back to her instead. *I asked Ambrose out when we were still working on the commission together.*

Another kick back. *I'm busy—*

Not too busy to dance with her, I hear.

The rock stopped, then did its own little dance on the dust, as if she were rolling it around pensively with her foot.

Look, I like her, she finally said. *I do. I just...have a lot of research going on.*

This phrase was quieter, harder for Eli to parse. He decided to pivot rather than press. There was a lot he didn't know about Rory, anyway.

For Aphos? he ventured. *How'd you get into all that, anyway?*

Into what?

He shrugged. *The magical crimes beat. All your Aphos knowledge.*

Oh, that. Picked it up as a junior journalist working under the writers. You can learn a lot just from reading their notes and articles, following 'em around for a bit.

Her voice had returned to its casual and steady pace, but at her feet, the pebble still rolled around in circles. Eli tried to form his next question—but movement across the street caught his gaze. An elf and a gnome were loitering in front of the empty wine barrels. With a brief, cursory nod to each other, they opened the door and stepped into the shadows of the shop.

Both Eli and Rory straightened instantly, their shoulders bumping together in the narrow alleyway.

Where'd they go? Eli asked, squinting to see the figures through the gray windows—but once they had closed the door, their silhouettes disappeared entirely.

The shop's an illusion, Rory said. *It's all tunnel beyond the windows. They're probably just going in to switch off the shields.*

Sure enough, the pair reappeared moments later, dragging stools and a barrel together to form an improvised card table. Around their feet wound a new companion: a lithe little dog, its thin tail whipping back and forth as if expecting treats to fall from the table any minute.

Eli watched them for a few seconds—but before long, his vision began to swim, and it became harder and harder to focus on the guards. He finally turned away with a wince.

I thought you said they took down the shield.

The roasting shield, sure, Rory said. *The headache's an intentional part of the illusion magic you're seeing. You think we're the first people to try to stake out Aphos' entrances like this?*

They took turns watching the guards' card game, focusing on the entrance until the illusion magic doubled their vision and they had to look away. Their targets were halfway through their game when a pair of orcs finally appeared with a cart, their leathers and furs indicative of a long journey from Hart's Fenn. The illusion magic flickered in its attempt to cloak so many people, and Eli's vision sharpened in relief.

We've got visitors at this one, Eli told Sherry and Grim. *Just two guards and a dog receiving them.*

A magic-sniffing dog, Rory corrected. *Aphos always has a few of them.*

How much of a threat? Grim asked immediately. Rory didn't hiss or hesitate this time.

It's not bad, she said. *The dog can be distracted, and two guards are easier than five. I think we can use this one.* She took a step forward, kicking up a puff of dust. *I just wish I could see if they had a second checkpoint.*

Eli frowned. *A second one?*

Sometimes they have one farther in the tunnel—usually one more guard checking for weapons. If there's no second checkpoint, this entrance would be perfect.

I can check, he quickly offered. Rory set a hand on his arm again.

Don't, she warned. *Between these earrings and the invisibility, the dog could catch you.*

Not if it's distracted.

Eli... That was Sherry this time, a sterner warning underlining her voice—but he was already out in the street, weaving between passersby.

"Tough roads from the Fenn?" one of the guards asked the orcish visitors. His question sounded casual, but his hand never strayed far from the hilt of his sword.

"Easy enough," the taller orc answered in what was more of a grunt than a voice. "A few wild griffins closer to Watchby, but nothing we couldn't handle."

As they spoke, the dog eagerly sniffed the cart, its tail still wagging. Eli dug into his pocket for his half-eaten cinnamon cookie, then sprinkled it on the ground, trailing away from the shop door. The dog went after it, snarfing up the bits before its owner could drag him away.

"Bartleby!" The elven guard gave a heavy sigh. "What have I told you about eating random things on the ground—"

As the guard tried to pull the dog away from the crumbs, Eli swept past him and into the open shop door.

On his first step, the illusion magic pelted him with everything he expected from the shop: dust, strewn papers, the smell of mildew and stale wine. Yet before his other foot could fall, it all melted away. Wooden walls faded into stone, chipped lanterns transformed into bright crystals—and the peeling walls of the shop stretched into a long, shadowy tunnel.

He hurried farther down the path and peeked around the corner.

Even if there was someone there, he could likely knock them out if needed during the rescue—

But no one was there. Just stretches of stone and the faint sounds of water dripping.

No second checkpoint! he crowed back to Rory. *It's clear!*

Rory's voice shook in response. *Good, now get the hells out of there!*

He rushed back to the entrance, its artificial shadows swirling before him. Take that, Oren, he could do stealth after all—

He emerged back into the sunlight, where the guards and orcs still clustered around the cart. All he had to do was hop back across the street, into the alley, then back to Rosemond Street to plan the final—

The dog looked up from the last cookie crumb and barked.

For a split second, Eli hoped the dog had found something magical in the travelers' cart or had spotted a scuttling rat—but the dog was barking directly at him. At suspiciously thin air.

The elven guard looked straight at him, eyes unfocused. "What's there?"

He reached forward, hands going straight for Eli's collar. Eli hurriedly backtracked, but a stack of wooden crates behind him bit into his shoulder blades. Curses streamed through his thoughts. He had nowhere to go, unless he wanted to turn back, brave the Aphosian tunnels, get caught deeper within and thrown into the cells—

As his palms scraped against splintered wood, a clatter of metal tumbled out of the orcs' cart. Something had tugged on the tarp covering the crate, letting loose a stash of weapons previously hidden under a box of apples.

"What the—?" The gnomish guard drew his sword. "I thought I told you no weapons today!"

The elven guard whirled away from Eli. "Hey, what you are trying to pull?"

As he drew his own sword, tiny dust puffs quickly trailed away from the cart and down the street.

Eli, let's go! Rory shouted in his head. He scrambled to follow, leaving the growing chaos around the cart behind.

Are you both all right? Sherry asked. Eli couldn't tell where Rory was in the plaza, so he took to the less crowded ramps, slipping more easily around the people there.

We're fine—

Fine? We almost got caught! Rory snapped, her voice wavering in fear. *I can't be seen by them, I can't afford that—*

What, you think I *can?* Eli gritted his teeth. *I got the intel we needed. There was no secondary checkpoint.*

But now there will be a dozen guards to prevent another breach. That place is going to be swarming the day of the demonstration.

What, so—Eli fumbled down a ramp, his hands shaking—*so we can't use that entrance?*

Not anymore!

Grim was next to curse. *But the five guards at the Forge—*

Will be better than whatever they're going to add to the Grapevine entrance, Rory said firmly. *You either get past those five guards or you don't get to Ambrose.*

Eli skidded to a halt in an empty walkway, anger and regret constricting his chest until he could hardly catch his breath. If he had just listened to Rory the first time, stayed in that stupid alleyway...

I'm sorry, he said, weary and defeated. *Five guards it is.*

RULE 17:

TEST THE SUPPORTS

Ambrose

As soon as Ambrose passed along Nat's information, he threw himself into his potions with renewed energy. Every day, he worked steadily on his fake brew, and every night, he checked his tally marks for the two weeks remaining. There was a light at the bottom of the chasm now—a finite end to his imprisonment.

In two weeks, he would trick his way through Madam Mila's stupid demonstration, Rosemond Street would swoop in to rescue him, and he could forget all about this Aphosian nonsense.

But in the meantime, the Aphosian nonsense came to him.

"Good morning," he called when the workroom door opened. "Or is it afternoon?" He checked the table for his pocket watch. "Never can tell down here..."

"It's lunch," Nat said, slapping down a tray of food on the table. "By evidence of me bringing you lunch."

The raincloud above her head seemed darker than usual today, and he quickly tamped down his own cheeriness. After all, he was supposed to be a prisoner with no hope of escaping. Anything akin to a smile, and someone might catch on.

"Is everything all right?" he asked, keeping his tone carefully indifferent.

Nat slouched down on the stool, picking at a loose thread on her tunic. "Fine."

Ambrose continued his work in silence; he had come to learn that a real answer generally succeeded *fine*, it just needed a few moments to brew.

"There was a fight topside yesterday," she finally said. "A few orcs tried to get into Aphos with a bunch of weapons or something. One guard even said they were trying to get an invisible guy through." She turned on the stool but wasn't at all enlivened by the squeak. "Cassius is pissed."

Outside the door, the guard shuffled and yawned. Nat jumped on instinct, then settled back down with a deeper scowl as if angry at herself for reacting.

Ambrose knew that fear—the anxious edge that came with someone else's sour mood. But before he could try to find a word of comfort she wouldn't scoff at, she swung her legs and nodded at his notes. "You got any questions for me?"

"Not yet," Ambrose said, then quickly added, "but I may think of one soon. Best stay here until I do."

"Okay." Nat didn't have to be told twice—she hopped off the stool and rushed over to her food stash. In seconds, she was settled in with a bag of crackers and her little book, in the relative safety of a room without Cassius in it. Ambrose went back to his notes and ignored the crunch of the crackers. In truth, he had no questions for her— and hadn't for days.

But company was company, even if was just teenage shrugs and eye-rolls.

They both picked at the lunch tray for the next few minutes, each eating and toiling away in their respective corners. Ambrose had his next potion for Cassius ready—a simple trick of a brew, one that inspired a confident aura in the holder—but when it came to the actual demonstration potion, his notes betrayed gaps the size of a sinkhole. How far would he need to carry the deception until Rosemond Street found him? Would they whisk him away the moment he arrived, or would he need to fumble along like Madam Mila's puppet until his heroes appeared?

He gave a stretch and, out of habit more than anything else, walked over to the lucky shelf illusion and pretended to pet the bronze cat. The empty air was disappointing every time, but it was all he had.

"What are you doing?"

Over in her corner, Nat frowned at him in confusion and judgment while munching on a sandwich.

"I..." Ambrose noted the book in her hands and drew himself up. "You know, I do believe I've thought of a question."

"I asked first."

"And that's my sandwich."

They stared each other down; Nat took a large, spiteful bite of sandwich and spoke her next words with a full mouth. "What's your question?"

"That." He pointed to the book. "Is it about sign language?"

She remained silent, her tusk sticking up in pouty defiance.

Ambrose sighed. "I won't tell Cassius."

Her shoulders relaxed a hair. "Yeah, it's sign." She toyed with the corners of the pages. "Just basic stuff. You know, in case..."

She scratched at one of the small scars on her cheek but said nothing more. Ambrose, for his part, had a dozen more questions. Her ear was injured, that much was apparent, but she had never expressed an issue hearing him before. Had she been hiding it from him? Did it hurt her at all?

She'd hate all of those questions, he knew. So, he dared an offer instead.

"I learned a little sign when I was an apprentice," he said, preparing for an eye roll. "I could...practice alongside you, if you'd like?"

Nat fixed him with a hard, analytical gaze—then pointed again at the lucky shelf. "So, what is that?"

Well. Better than an eye roll, he supposed.

"This is an approximation of my lucky shelf back home in my workroom," he said, stepping away from it so she could see it better.

"What's so lucky about it?"

"It's..." He paused, looking over the clutter of plants and trinkets. Most were from past potioneers, but he had added several over time —including the little plant Eli had gifted him last year.

He wondered with a pang if anyone was watering it.

"It's a collection of lucky objects from past shop owners and myself," he continued. "My personal favorite is this one." He pointed to the cat, tucked neatly beside Eli's plant. "The rule is to pet it for luck before you start brewing."

Nat snorted. "And you believe that?"

Ambrose huffed, the pang in his chest growing sharper. "Look, you were the one who asked about it—"

"Okay, sorry!"

"I'll have you know I haven't destabilized a single potion in my entire career—"

Nat laughed. "What, and that's because of the cat?"

Heavy footsteps and squabbling voices bounced around the hall outside, as chipper as thunder and inviting as hail. Nat's laugh died in her throat, and she bolted up in her seat.

"Pet the cat," she ordered, shoving the book down her boot and pointing to the lucky shelf. "Pet all the lucky stuff."

Ambrose froze. "What do you mean?"

But she was already on her feet, checking herself for cracker crumbs. "You don't want him coming into this room, not in the mood he's in."

He didn't need to ask who she meant.

"I assure you, I evaluated the security breach myself," Cassius' voice echoed down the hall, its typical hard edge cloaked in a thin veneer of submission.

"I will *not* have it affect my plans," Mila snapped, her response sharper than all of Cassius' words combined. "You assured me security would be tight, that your charge would deliver."

"And he will deliver—"

"Then show me," Mila ordered. "And tighten our security further." Her knifelike footsteps continued down the hall at a brisk pace. Ambrose held his breath, hoping the other pair of steps would go along with her, far, far away—

Cassius barged into the room.

"Show me what you have," he said, his voice back to its honed hiss. He looked like he hadn't slept the night prior, his hair in tangles and purple bruises dragging down his eyes—but the anger and fear in his stare was as bright as ever.

Ambrose didn't want to think about how he had taken out those emotions on servants like Nat.

"Of course." He hurried over to the worktable and lined up the potion bottles, while Nat took a stiff, neutral pose by the door. "I've been expanding on Octavia's work. Her principles were sound, but her use of ingredients was leading her off track. You see, she was trying to utilize a solution involving hyssop oil to create a precipitate that she would then cleanse and crush into a—"

"Just tell me what you have so far," Cassius snapped; Ambrose was already dancing on the edge of his temper. He swallowed and held up the last bottle, still warm from the cauldron.

"I've combined two illusion components so far, with the third on the way." He uncorked the bottle. The energy packed into the glass melted into the air in invisible waves, filling him with an unearned sense of confidence and optimism. It wasn't his usual sort of brew—adventurers rarely bought something with so subtle an effect—but it still seemed to work on Cassius. His shoulders rounded instantly, and the stress lines on his face smoothed out.

"Two of three?" he asked, bending down to peer at the bubbles in the brew. Ambrose capitalized on the man's mood with a practiced lie.

"Octavia only managed to perfect one and a half senses," Ambrose said. "I will manage three for Madam Mila by the first demonstration."

Cassius' eyes narrowed; Ambrose didn't dare move.

"I'll have my archivist copy your notes tomorrow." Cassius finally straightened, then added, "And you'll present your work next week."

Ambrose's heart stuttered, and he scrambled to recork the bottle. Clearly, he had over-indexed on the confidence element. "I beg your pardon?"

"Mila wants results faster."

"I cannot perform miracles simply because she wants results faster," Ambrose said, his own voice turning snappish out of fear. "You assured me I had four weeks before the demonstration, and now you've cut off an entire week. I cannot do it—"

Without the air of the confidence potion, Cassius' stress settled back into his body like an angry weight. "Then perhaps I'll pay a visit to Eli," he said smoothly. "Or Grim or Sherry."

Ambrose broke, anger spewing from his tongue. "You get their names *out* of your mouth—"

Cassius' hand was on his collar, gripping the fabric until it crumpled. Ambrose flinched, but no blow came. The threat had already been made, and judging by Cassius' infuriating smirk, he knew it.

"Next week," he repeated, then strode out of the room, closing the door with a final slam.

Ambrose glared at the door, the bottle shaking in his hand. He was going to punch Cassius himself. No, he wasn't—he was going to have Eli punch him first. *Then* punch the man himself—

"What are you going to do?"

He jumped. In his anger, he had forgotten Nat was in the corner, hiding in the shadows, her wide eyes on him.

"I..." he started; the words died on his tongue. He didn't know. The Guild's protocol to delay the work had failed miserably, and all he had to show for it were a few fake potions. He couldn't cram a month—realistically, six months—of experimental work into a week to deliver something that could fool Madam Mila.

Not alone, at least.

He set his lips into a thoughtful line. An ally was in order, certainly, and said ally only had one prerequisite: they needed to hate Cassius enough to break a few little rules.

If he judged wrong, his next words could sink him.

"Nat." He drew himself up. "How would you like to help me pull one over on Cassius?"

She broke into a grin—the first one he had ever seen on her face.

"What do you need me to do?"

RULE 18:

TAKE CONTROL

Dawn

DAWN HAD NEVER SEEN Eli so anxious before.

"What do you mean they pulled up the demonstration?" he said, gripping the final corner of Banneker's enchanted paper until it crumpled. "It wasn't supposed to be for another two weeks!"

"Did he say anything else?" Sherry peered over his shoulder.

"Nothing." He handed her the note, then ran both hands through his hair. "Is there anything else we can say to him? Any other note we can send?"

Banneker fidgeted with a leather bracelet around his wrist. "That was the last of our paper. I could try to come up with another way—"

"It's too late at this point," Grim cut in, setting a heavy hand on Eli's shoulder to anchor him in place. "Beake got us the important information—we've got one week to prepare and we know where he'll be. Now it's our turn to put the plan into motion."

An uncomfortable silence settled over the workroom, leaving only their thoughts, the distant bustle of Rosemond Street, and the scratch of Rory's pen on paper. The same taut concern crossed all their faces, Dawn's most of all. There was no plan. Just like Banneker's paper, they only had scraps to work with. A few disguise ideas here, an entrance strategy there…

And a signature wand that hadn't even been started yet.

But while Dawn's nerves paralyzed her, Sherry's drove her into harried action.

"Well, I've got the clothing for Grim and Eli." She dragged Viola and a reluctant Xavion to a table piled with fabric. "This jerkin and cloak should match the travelers we saw at the Forge entrance. I'll add some armor underneath the cloak, naturally—"

"And I'll get a disguise spell going." Viola nodded to energize herself. "Yeah, we can do this. Xavion, do you have the extracts we talked about?"

The potioneer rolled their eyes and handed over a bag of clinking crystal. Viola dug into it and pulled out a tiny vial.

"Hm." She held the clear liquid up to the light. "Good. Keep this up, and I might make you your favorite dessert one day."

Xavion snorted. "As if you know my—"

"Earl grey cake with fernberry jam, lavender buttercream, and candied rose atop a vanilla cinnamon glaze."

Xavion swallowed, their voice shaking. "N-no, that's—that's not it."

Viola smirked. "Thought so."

In the other corner, Eli and Grim had gathered for quite the opposite discussion.

"I still think we can sneak in a weapon if we're careful," Eli murmured.

"That guards will be looking."

"We'll make them invisible, or—or shrink them." His eyes glinted at the idea. "Sherry might have something, actually… Hey, Sherry!"

The whirlwind left only Dawn and Banneker in the middle of the sawdust-covered floor. She turned to the artificer, but he was already lost in his own planning, muttering to himself as he gathered a pile of scraps and baubles before him.

"If I can reactivate this with…" He hefted a copper scrap in his hand, then tossed it aside. "No, if I combine these parts with the old wand parts I salvaged...?"

His mutterings ran in useless circles. When Dawn forced herself out of her own nerves and joined him at the table, he gave her a weak nod.

"Hey," he said, rummaging through a small heap of old cannon parts. "Just seeing if there's another way to contact Ames."

"You don't have to do that."

"But the paper wasn't enough." He weighed a copper screw in his palm. "If I had made it differently or found some way to stretch the materials—"

Dawn carefully took the screw and set it on the table. "Don't worry about it," she said. "I'll get you that Aphosian signature wand today, and you can start work on the teleporter."

His eyebrows rose. "Wait, today?" he repeated. "But I thought you hadn't started."

A true observation that Dawn staunchly chose to ignore.

"I'll get it done," she reassured him. "I'll be back by tonight, I promise."

She strode out of the shop, exuding cool confidence for his sake—then broke into a frantic run as soon as she reached the street.

She could do this, right? She had done more with less in the past. It would be just like her days studying for apprenticeship finals, only this time she was making a completely unfamiliar wand using notes from a post-fake-date fever dream. It was completely and totally under control.

"Dawn!" Rory called after her. "Wait up!"

An excited tingle shot up her spine, but she didn't dare stop or turn around. No, *no*, under *control*—

"Can't stay!" she called back, fiddling with the key to her shop. "I have to make this wand for Banneker."

"I know." Rory jogged up next to her. "Let me help you."

Dawn made the mistake of looking at her—at her friendly, eager smile, her soft undercut. The way she leaned against the shop wall, waiting for Dawn to open the door with fumbling hands.

There was no part of her that wanted to rebuff Rory's company, but...a wandmaker's workshop wasn't entirely journalist-friendly.

"You got a wandmaking certificate?" she asked, tearing herself away to regain control over the door key.

Rory shrugged. "No, but I can help with something, right?" She folded her arms. "If you're going to finish the wand in one night, you can't do it alone."

Dawn grimaced. Doing it alone was better than setting Rory near sparks and sharp objects all night. Then again... She slowly opened the door in thought. She'd have an apprentice soon: someone just as clueless and just as eager. Having Rory around would simply be good practice.

At least, that's what she told herself as she ushered Rory inside.

"Come on in," she said. "First step is snacks."

As Dawn suspected, Rory was a natural at the snacking part of the project.

"All right." Rory rubbed her hands together over a table in the loft. Ember the salamander perched on her shoulder, napping through her gestures. "I grabbed what I could from your kitchen and the food cart on High Vine. Oh, and"—she picked up a chocolate cupcake—"nabbed some half-price desserts from Viola."

Dawn's mouth watered. "Anything enchanted?"

"Mundane. It was all she had left."

A mild disappointment—she had been hoping for another calming petit four, or maybe one of those extra-jolty espresso cookies Viola sold every morning.

"You've prepared a feast." Dawn nodded solemnly. "Ember, do you approve?"

The salamander licked his eyeball in response. Rory winked. "High praise."

As they dug in, Dawn continued filling pages of her notebook with thoughts on the signature wand. The wand itself wasn't complex, but Banneker's teleporters were already filled to the brim with magic components. To make a signature stick, the wand needed to be elegant, efficient...

"The sigil itself doesn't contain any magic," she rambled aloud, pacing around the table while Rory carefully constructed a plate of cheese and crackers. "It's just a marker, a signal that Aphos' barrier magic picks up on. If the device doesn't have the right sigil, the barrier won't let the magic through, and Ames won't be able to get out."

"Well, you saw the sigil yourself." Rory's tongue poked out as she balanced a slice of salami atop a cracker tower. "You can just recreate it, right?"

"It's more than that." Dawn's shorthand scribbles grew more incoherent. "The vessel—that's the wand part that everyone thinks of—has to communicate it clearly. Perfectly, or else the marker won't take. And all my wand components have magical properties of their own. Throw them together wrong, and the wand could backfire."

She glanced at Rory—the journalist was watching her pace, her chin on her hand and a soft smile on her face. Dawn blinked. "What?"

"Uh, nothing! Here you go." Rory grabbed the cracker plate and handed it to her. "So, what does all that mean?"

"It means..." She stopped to admire the little snack tower. Rory was an excellent snack assistant—delivering edible architecture, already perfectly formed and ready to go.

Wait. Perfectly formed. Her wand shaper, of *course*—

She tossed aside her notebook. "It means," she repeated with a grin, "that I get to pull out one of my favorite tools."

She eagerly led Rory into her workroom. The little square was hardly bigger than Ambrose's workroom, and paltry compared to Banneker's, but she prided herself on how she made it work. Many of her tools and tables were fastened to the wall or on wheels, ready to shift at a moment's notice. On her busiest days, she could set up three workshops in one with her myriad of configurations.

But today, all she needed was one folding table on the center wall. She unfolded it and locked the legs with a flourish.

"Behold!" She gestured to the table with both hands. Rory had her notebook poised, eyes bright.

"Yeah, I'm beholding." She nodded along. "What, um...is it?"

"It's an automatic, gem-powered wand shaper," Dawn said proudly. "Bought it a few years after I inherited the shop from my old mentor, to celebrate another year of not running this place into the ground. This"—she patted the smooth wood—"will shape my wand for me."

She could understand Rory's lack of applause. By itself, the table didn't appear to be much—just a wooden surface with a series of leather straps and a small divot in the center. But with an added gem and a decent wand base...

She set a raw fire citrine in the divot, then perused her cabinet of wand bases. She had many pre-turned wands, but those were all finely carved and polished, a process that often whittled down the raw power of the wood in favor of balancing the magical effect. But this wand required clarity over balance, so she instead opened her drawer of raw dried branches. This drawer smelled like a forest she had visited once, along with the charcoal-like smell of wand magic. She inhaled deeply, then selected a branch: beech, with smooth bark and a smattering of knots in the wood.

"This"—she pointed to the table with the branch—"will help the wood grow around the gem, rather than me having to install the gem into the wand." She secured the branch with the leather straps. "These sorts of wands are way more powerful than my usual stock, but they're also harder to control. The only folks who request this sort of work are my veteran customers."

Rory grinned. "And people looking to break into Aphos?"

"And heroes looking to rescue their friend," Dawn corrected, then dragged over a chair. "Can't turn this bad boy on yet, though. Sigil's gotta go on the gem first."

"Sigil. Right. Need me to step out for that?"

Dawn paused from sifting through her carving tools. Unlike

much of her work, carving was a quiet activity. If she did it alone for too long, the silence began to itch at her ears.

Typically, this was where Ambrose would help. Every now and then, he'd write to her on the rose statue, giving her an excuse to step away and take a break. But in his absence...

Perhaps Rory could help a little further.

"This might be a weird ask—"

"Not weird!" Rory pulled up a stool and plopped down on it. "Ask away."

"It helps to talk while I'm doing this sort of work." She laid out her tools. "Normally I talk to Ames or Eli, but..." She caught sight of the tattoo on Rory's neck, the petals slowly unfurling. Magical tattoos like that were never a casual decision—there had to be a good story behind them. "Could you tell me about your tattoos while I work?"

"Oh. Yeah, of course."

Rory stood up, and Dawn quickly realized that if she wanted to focus on her task, she had asked for precisely the wrong thing: because Rory was taking off her jacket.

Part of her hoped she was wearing a long-sleeve shirt under the jacket, perhaps another few layers—but what remained left just enough to her sprinting imagination. The clingy, sleeveless top showed off a menagerie of tattoos running up and down her arm, some shifting and swaying, others static.

And menagerie wasn't an exaggeration. Nearly all the tattoos were of animals, though a few other flowers and clouds formed a dreamy setting around them. Dawn couldn't help but stare at the large tattoo spread across her left shoulder blade: a sea turtle, drifting slowly on an invisible tide, a wavy line undulating below it.

Carve, Dawn reminded herself. More carving, less staring.

As she selected her first tool and steadied the gem on the table, Rory began to speak.

"The sea turtle was my first one," she said. "My dad's family symbol."

She knew she was supposed to be carving—but Dawn couldn't help but take another peek at the tattoo. The unique shape of the wavy line under the turtle was too familiar. She looked up at Rory's head, where a similar line had been carved back into her undercut. "It matches your hair," she said, delighted by the discovery. "It's a Deepriver symbol, right?"

Rory looked just as delighted at Dawn's connection. "Yeah. Grew up near Blue Marsh Island. Can't say that island's my favorite, though. I once stole my dad's boat and nearly sank it in a night race there..."

As she spun a tale of daring drunkards on dinghies, Dawn focused on the gem—for real, this time—and carefully traced the Aphosian sigil into every facet, all while learning about Rory's adventurous childhood. Compared to her current career, her upbringing had been decidedly non-academic. There was schooling somewhere in there, of course, but most of her stories centered on working and playing along the shores of the Deepriver, and a carefree life with her father. He figured greatly in her past: his dorky humor, his unkempt beard, his leisurely pace.

Dawn kept waiting for a mention of her mother in the tales—but none came.

"Was your mom with you in Deepriver?" she ventured when Rory had stopped to take a sip of water. Rory hesitated but didn't lose her energy.

"Oh, she left a while back." She leaned in to inspect Dawn's work. "That looks gorgeous. You ever think about going into Grim's line of work?"

Dawn didn't dare think about how close Rory was, how the warmth of the woman's arm seeped under her skin. She held the gem up to the light instead, carefully dusting off each sigil. She did love working with gemstones, that much was true—but there was a satisfying heft to wands, a particular satisfaction in aiming and using them, that she could never get from a necklace or a ring.

"Nah," she said. "Grim's bracelets can't shoot fireballs." She stood, and the absence of Rory's warmth was both a relief and a disappointment. "Ready for me to start up this wand shaper?"

"Absolutely. Where should I stand?"

Dawn pointed to the large metal sheet propped up in the corner. Rory deflated.

"But I'm gonna miss all the fun," she said. "It's not like you're welding anything, are you?"

"It's more dangerous than that." Dawn tapped the gems embedded in the sides of the table. "These pull energy in order to make the branch grow, and they don't care what energy they pull. You'll be safer behind the shield."

Rory still didn't retreat. "Wait, what about you?"

Dawn had to suppress a smile at the concern. "Oh, I've got gloves and a charged druzy it'll pull energy from. I'll be safe, don't worry."

Rory narrowed her gaze. "Okay..."

She finally slipped behind the shield and ducked down until only the top of her purple hair was visible. Dawn tugged on her thick leather gloves and placed her charged amethyst at the head of the table. The gems flashed once, already hungry for its energy.

"All right," she called, pulling her activation wand off the wall. "It'll just be a few minutes."

She waved the wand over the table, then set both hands on the branch to keep it steady. All around her, the gems bathed her in their light, pinks and purples and oranges creating a raucous spotlight. Under the leather straps, the branch grew as if she were watching a full spring season pass in seconds. It stretched toward the carved citrine, tiny branches cautiously dipping around and over it in a twisting, natural cage. Dawn kept her hands firm and her eyes on the growth. About halfway through, now. Once the branches thickened enough to properly pass along the magic—

The light within the amethyst guttered.

"Oh, no," she breathed. Not daring to take her hands off the branch, she twisted around, looking for a druzy to swap in. She thought she had fully charged it, but if the energy didn't hold out before the magic was complete—

The purple light flickered once, twice, then went out.

She had no time to move or even breathe—the gems around the table latched onto her energy, their greed far too strong for her gloves to block. Her vision tilted; her knees buckled. But she could no longer release the branch if she tried, far too tied into the magic now. The spell would hold her until it finished—

Or it finished her.

"*Dawn!*" The shield behind her clanged. Two arms grabbed her, and suddenly, a second energy pulsed under her skin, sating the magic's hunger. Through her daze, she expected a rush of warmth, but lost herself in cool water instead. In rushing rivers and deep shadows, the scent of petrichor and soaked stone—

The spell released her, and both of them tumbled back, a tangle of arms and heat. Dawn flinched, expecting to strike the stone floor— but Rory's arms caught and held her inches above the ground. For a suspended moment, they both stared at each other, breathing in exhausted, shaky gulps.

They were fine. They were both fine.

"You all right?" Rory finally managed.

Dawn wasn't sure there was a response that properly communicated *My crush both fed me crackers and saved my life, how do you think I'm doing?* But in the absence of the right wording, she squeaked out a thoroughly unconvincing "I'm fine. You?"

Rory's breath steadied. "Good. Yeah, good." She blinked at her own arms, still securely holding Dawn. "Gods, sorry. I just—wanted to make sure your head didn't hit the floor—"

"Appreciate it."

They awkwardly untangled from one another, their legs both wobbling. Dawn leaned against the table and finally gathered the wherewithal to check the entire purpose of this work, and the thing that nearly killed her: the signature wand.

Though its source of energy had been...unorthodox...the wand shaper had done its job perfectly. The sigil-carved gem was now encased in a cage of strong wood, and the narrow end of the wand glimmered with tiny flowers and green buds. She unstrapped the wand and held it up.

"There it is," she said, pride fighting through her exhaustion. "All ready for Banneker."

She handed the wand to Rory, who gave a delighted, disbelieving laugh.

"I get it now," she said. "All the trophies and the certificates..." She gestured weakly with a limp arm. "When this story comes out, I'm gonna need a whole side article just about you."

Heat rushed to the tips of Dawn's ears. "You helped," she tried to deflect. "What about an autobiography on page three? A full-page spread all about the woman behind the words?"

Rory laughed again. "Please, no one wants her."

"I do."

The words passed her lips before she could think—and once her thoughts caught up, every one of them screamed for her to deflect again, to sweep them away somehow.

She stubbornly let them hang in the air instead.

As they remained, a charge built up around them. Rory's gaze darted to her lips and stayed there, and Dawn could have sworn she took a step closer—

A knock sounded on the shop door below.

"Dawn?" Banneker called out. "You in there, my swan of wands?" A pause. "I'm gonna keep brainstorming that one."

The charge in the air broke; Rory cleared her throat and handed back the wand.

"Here," she said. "Better get this down to him. He'll be so pleased with it."

Dawn took it and stepped back. "Sure," she said weakly.

But in that moment, that wasn't who she wanted to please.

RULE 19:

PEER REVIEW

Ambrose

AMBROSE CORKED the final potion bottle with all the grace and dexterity of a drunken griffin missing a wing.

He had minutes until Cassius arrived to test his work, which was roughly equal to the amount of sleep he had gotten last night. When the door swung open, he jumped and gave a yelp.

Nat froze in the doorway. "Are you...good, Mr. Ambrose?"

He slouched over the worktable. "Is that coffee on the tray?"

"I think so?"

"Then yes, I'll be fine." He shoved the last vial into place and grabbed the cup from Nat's tray before it could hit the table. It wasn't good coffee by any standards—like everything else in Aphos, it bore a savory hint of mushroom—but it was hot and sharp and did the trick.

"Thank you for bringing this," he breathed, wanting to melt into the chair and attempt a power nap before Cassius arrived. But there was no time—Nat hadn't yet been briefed on her role. He could collapse later after this was all done.

"I have everything ready for you." He ushered her over to the worktable, where a fizzy blue bottle sat politely next to a neat stack of notes. "You'll drink this for the test. I took the liberty of flavoring it with fernberry—I hope that's acceptable."

Nat picked up the bottle and tilted her head. "What's a fernberry?"

His sleepless brain fractured.

"I—it—" He rubbed his face. "It'll taste fine, I promise. Now, what you drink will have absolutely no effect on you. While Cassius is looking at you, I will be taking these." He pulled up his sleeve to reveal three tiny vials in a makeshift wristband, each one wrapped in leather to avoid clinking. Nat's eyes widened.

"What, all of them?"

"All of them at once," he said. "Then I'll control the illusion in front of you."

"Oh." Nat grinned and tapped the vials with her free hand. "Cool."

Cool wasn't how Ambrose would describe the absolute abomination of an idea that should revoke his Guild license—but if this was what he had to do to make it to the demonstration tomorrow, to keep going as normal until the rescue...

He'd live with the guilt.

Voices approached the door. Nat quickly took her place on the chair by the wall, and Ambrose tugged down his sleeve. "What sort of mood is he in today?"

Nat shrugged. "He didn't threaten to fire anyone today. That's about as good as you're gonna get." She frowned at the chair. "What exactly do you want me to do during this whole illusion thing? Just sit here?"

Ambrose cursed—an excellent thought he should've had days ago. He was never one for theatrics.

"A bit of a performance would help." He bit his lip. "Why don't we—"

The door swung open.

Cassius strode in, talking to a squat gnome hurrying at his heels. "This will be short. Follow along, copy his notes, then deliver them down to the archives. Gods willing, they'll be more useful than Octavia's gibberish."

"Of course, sir. I'm sure they will be, sir." The archivist gave a small bow and scurried over to the table, looking eager to be lost in the relative shadows opposite his boss. As for Cassius, he glanced at the array of chairs in disdain and remained standing; the illusory spikes along his sleeves mimicked his mood.

"Walk me through it," he ordered. "What will we see in the demonstration tomorrow?"

Ambrose shoved down his exhaustion and nerves.

"If you stand here..." He directed Cassius to the spot right in front of Nat, who donned her best scowl. "This is the best vantage point to see the illusion. I'm still working to improve on its dimensions and clarity, but this should be enough of a proof of concept of my progress—"

"Fine, fine." Cassius folded his arms. The archivist gathered up Ambrose's notes, his nose buried in the paper. With all eyes elsewhere, Ambrose himself carefully stepped behind Cassius and drank the three vials on his arm. They all burned on the way down, each one worse than the last, and settled in his chest in heavy, tangled threads of magic.

Gods, this was going to hurt later.

"First," he said, keeping his voice steady, "the test subject will drink the potion."

Nat feigned a glare as she uncorked the bottle; the role of unwilling experiment came naturally to her.

"Drink it all at once," he ordered, trying to play his part. "Not a drop left."

She scowled once more, then did as he said. Briefly, her eyes lit up at the bright, fizzy flavor—then she recalled her role and gave a dramatic shudder.

"Ugh, what's it doing to me?" She tugged at her collar. Ambrose pulled on the magic threads inside him and focused on the air in front of her.

"Now," he continued, "the test subject will think of a dragon."

Nat furrowed her brow, and Ambrose stretched his thoughts to align with the motion. In a blink, a tiny dragon appeared before Cassius, floating in the air on constantly flapping wings. He wasn't quite able to make it mimic the dragons Tavi had often doodled in her notes—this one was rounder, more like the mail dragons he used to see every week—but he hoped it was enough of a nod to her, wherever she was.

Nat gasped at the sight of the dragon, then resumed her frown, focusing hard on it. Cassius bent to inspect the illusion from all angles, as if the test subject wasn't even there.

"Looks good enough." He sniffed. "No holes in the illusion, no distortion from different angles. But I'm not seeing anything particularly special about it." He snapped his fingers at the archivist. "Have you been reviewing the notes? Do they align with what we're seeing?"

The archivist hesitated; Ambrose hid a smile. His notes, while technically showing the correct process for each component of the illusion, were buried under every citation, corollary, and bit of technical jargon he could think of. If the archivist came away from this without at least a mild headache, he would be impressed.

"I—I believe so?" the archivist squeaked. Cassius rolled his eyes and strode over to review the notes.

"At least there aren't any of those infuriating doodles," he muttered and flipped a page. "Is this it?"

As they sifted through the notes, Nat leaned forward. "*Psst!*" she hissed at Ambrose. "What do I do now?"

He tried to keep his voice low. "Next is the—"

"What was that?" Cassius called. Ambrose straightened.

"Nothing."

The archivist flipped the pages over. "So, I believe what we're seeing here is shown in these steps..."

Ambrose bounced on his heels, pressing his lips into a line. Nat's theatrics would sell the next steps, of course—he only needed her to know what they were.

The magic from the second vial, the sound component, swirled in his ears like whispering smoke. The more it swirled, the heavier it hung in his skull until his head throbbed. He winced, then caught Nat's gaze and tugged on his ear.

"*What*?" she mouthed.

"*Sound*!" he tried to mouth back. This only earned him a confused look. He huffed and searched around the room for something that would help him—

He caught the edge of her signing book hidden in her boot.

"*Wait*," he mouthed, then clumsily spelled out the word *sound* with his fingers. The attempt was horrendous—he had to stop and start several times, and he was fairly certain his *N* was actually an *M* —but after the third attempt, her face lit up.

"Oh!" she said, then clapped a hand over her mouth. Ambrose coughed to hide the sound.

"If you'll review the next step of the illusion?" he called to Cassius, who stepped back into place. The archivist slumped in relief.

"On with it," Cassius demanded. Nat held up both hands to the floating dragon illusion.

"I'm feeling...my ears tingling..."

Ambrose redoubled his focus on the dragon, tugging on the magic until the smoky feeling in his head threatened to escape his ears—then all at once, it surged into the illusion. The dragon gave a tiny roar, its tail lashing with a sharp, audible *thwip*. Cassius once more analyzed all angles of the illusion, but the sound was perfect. No tin-like undertones, no stuttering in the roar.

"That's two elements, then," he declared. "Where's the third?"

"I believe—ah, here's where he notates the third component," the archivist said proudly, then faltered. "Or perhaps it's here. No..." He flipped the paper. "On *this* page."

Cassius sighed and joined the archivist once more. As the magic dug more heavily into Ambrose's system, his vision doubled, and he leaned heavily against the table for support. But he couldn't stop now —smell was the next and final component.

He quickly caught Nat's gaze and pointed to his nose. To his surprise, she nodded and fumbled back a word of her own: *Smoke*?

He leaned more heavily on the table and nodded. *Fast*, he tried to sign back. He couldn't hold onto this magic for much longer. There were three Nats swimming before him now, magic clogging his ears and nose and threatening his throat—

"It's almost like," Nat said loudly, her eyes darting to Cassius, "almost like I can smell the smoke, you know?"

Ambrose could hardly take in a breath now, but that didn't matter —he pulled on the magic with all his remaining strength, and as the tiny dragon released a billowing plume of flame, the pungent smell of charcoal and woodsmoke filled the air.

"Behold!" Nat said, unabashedly proud of herself. Ambrose wiped the sweat from his brow with a shaking hand.

"This sort of illusion can last for at least twenty minutes," he explained, his professional tone strained. "My attempt to add the element of touch requires more finesse, but for a complex moving object fully controlled by one user within sight of it, you can clearly see how it is an improvement upon my predecessor's work."

"I see it." Cassius walked around the dragon again, expression shadowed. Ambrose held his breath. Gods, if the man deliberated any further, he was going to collapse right in front of him—

"Madam Mila will be pleased about this progress," Cassius finally said. "It's sufficient for the amount of time you've had. We'll move forward with tomorrow's demonstration for the Madam and her advisors."

Ambrose released the illusion. Chills immediately rippled over his body, weakening his limbs and churning his stomach. "Understood," was all he could manage.

"I'll come retrieve you and the test subject tomorrow at noon. Make sure you have another brew ready by then." Cassius reached the door and snapped at the archivist, who gathered up his copied notes with a little jump and scurried out behind him.

As soon as the door closed, Nat leapt from her seat. "It worked! It really worked! How did you—?"

Ambrose rushed to the nearest cauldron and hurled into it.

"Mr. Ambrose?" Nat knocked on the door. "You good now?"

Ambrose was splayed out on the floor of the washroom, scrunching his eyes closed. He wasn't sure how long he'd been in here. Minutes? Hours?

"More water," he called weakly.

Nat came in with more than water—she had thrown together a tray with a washcloth, too, and a small pile of fresh mint leaves from his own stock.

"Sorry the potions got you bad." She carefully set the tray down by his arm, then glanced back at the workroom door and grinned. "But how *cool* was that? He totally bought it!"

He groaned and threw the damp washcloth over his forehead. He was getting nauseous again just thinking about the brews he had drunk.

"The Guild can never know," he mumbled. "That was a crime against potioneering. They'll never let me on the debate stage ever again..."

Nat tentatively patted his arm. "I don't know what you're talking about, but I think of all the people in this place right now, you're the least criminal."

"Does that include you?"

"Well, I've been stealing half your lunch for the past two weeks, so..."

Gods, two weeks. Was that all? The words settled in his stomach like a stone. Rosemond Street felt so far away. Months away, at least. It didn't help that they had never responded to his last note, the one crammed into a corner of the paper. Had they received it? Would they show up tomorrow?

He chewed on a mint leaf, its sharp zip jolting his thoughts out of the downward spiral. He couldn't think like that. He'd just have to tweak his recipe for tomorrow, ensure it wouldn't make him hurl all over Madam Mila's throne...and Rosemond Street would be there, somehow.

He slowly pulled himself to his feet and staggered into the work-room. He expected Nat to be gone, or reading in her corner, but she was at his worktable, humming to herself and putting away empty vials and ingredients in the correct order. Mint by the marjoram, silverweed by the saffron...

She had been helpful. More helpful than she realized, even if she didn't think he could ever escape. And if he did escape tomorrow, if he found freedom...she would be staying behind, still under Cassius' rule. It didn't sound fair, but—certainly she had a life here beyond her work, didn't she? He couldn't just tear her away from it.

Gods knew he was aware of how well that generally worked out.

"Nat," he ventured once she put away the last of the bottles, "does your...family also work in Aphos, under Cassius?"

A blanket of silence fell over the room. Nat's humming stopped, and her shoulders tightened.

"No," she said. Ambrose inwardly flinched. He knew that type of *no*. That was a *no* he was far too familiar with.

"Apologies." He held up both hands. "I shouldn't have asked—"

"It's fine," Nat retorted. "Look, if you're feeling better, I should go."

"I am, but—"

She turned to go—but he couldn't leave it like this, not so close to his escape.

"Wait!" He hurried over to the door and set a palm on it. "I...I understand not having a family you want to talk about. Really, I do. I won't ask again. And..." He released the door. "And thank you for your help today. For everything. I appreciate it."

Nat stared at him, her gaze both young and far older than her years had earned.

"My help won't be enough," she said. "No one can get to you down here."

He swallowed. "I know—"

"No, you don't." She yanked the door open with a stony expression. "I'll see you tomorrow."

RULE 20:

EXTRACT

Eli

ON THE DAY of the demonstration, all of Rosemond Street was closed.

"Magical deep cleaning!" Sherry shooed away a disappointed customer. "Shops'll be back open tomorrow, don't you worry."

Eli waited for her at the bakery door, bouncing on his heels to shake off his excited nerves. Sure, the other shops might open tomorrow, but The Griffin's Claw was going to stay closed for a week, during which Ambrose wasn't going to leave his sight, or if he was being honest, the bedroom—

"All ready?" Sherry shuffled up to the bakery. Eli gathered himself back together. Best not to think about the coming week too much. Not until Ambrose was back in his arms.

"Almost." He gave her an encouraging smile and opened the door for them both.

Today, the bakery smelled of cinnamon and anxiety. Viola struggled to wave at them over the people already clustered around the front counter.

"Just finished a batch of Ames' cookies!" she called. "Your pies are on the table!"

Grim, Eli's rescue companion for the day, had already found the pies—but rather than eating the slice, they were waving it around in their hand, a rhythm to go along with the directions they were reciting.

"North past the markets, then east. Don't go up the stairs, go down the left fork—"

"And the throne room will be in the plaza," Rory finished for them. "You can't miss it once you're there."

Grim lifted the pie to their mouth, then paused. "And you're sure the paths haven't changed? You said you couldn't go into Aphos—"

"Just trust me on it." Rory held up both hands. "And you remember what to say to the guards?"

Grim's gaze narrowed. "Trust me on it."

"All right, all right. Eat the pie." Rory hopped away, gravitating back to Dawn and Xavion at the front counter. "Xavion, you ready to go back to your day job?"

Xavion glared at her. "I'm already packed."

"Can I quote you on that?"

"No."

Part of Eli was tempted to join Dawn and the others at the front counter to talk through his nerves. The much greater part of him begged to down the entire pie in one bite and sprint down to Aphos.

He compromised and ate the pie in two bites.

Regret struck him instantly. This wasn't one of Viola's normal pastries—the disguise magic baked into the fruit filling had turned the cherries bitter, leaving a horrible, chalky aftertaste as the pie slid into his stomach. He closed his eyes and shuddered, and across the table, Grim gave a rumbling laugh.

"Should've warned you beforehand," they said. Eli opened their eyes and found that it wasn't Grim standing with him at all.

The jeweler's silhouette still remained, of course—large and intimidating, their head nearly brushing the ceiling. But their face had completely morphed—nose pointed, cheekbones narrowed, a silver ring studding thin, arched brows. There wasn't a single speck Eli could find and claim some sort of familiarity.

He touched his own face to see if anything felt different, but Banneker made the revelation for him.

"Hey, dude of not-brew, lord of swords, you—*ah!*" He gave a shout and almost fell off his stool. "Blasted dust, Viola's good." His hand clutched his heart. "If I didn't already know your aura, I'd have no idea it was you."

"Will have to tweak the recipe to account for auras next." Viola winked. "You both look great."

As they donned Sherry's protective costumes and Grim's communication earrings, Banneker presented both of them with two leather bags.

"Your teleporters and invisibility potions," he said, dropping the bags into their palms. Eli's eyes widened—each one was hardly bigger than his thumb.

"Enchantments," Banneker explained. "Don't worry, everything inside will pop back to normal size as soon as you fish 'em out of the bag." He leaned in. "So far, I've been able to fit a whole couch in there. Hard to take it out, though. I'm working on it."

Eli carefully secured the bag to his belt, checked his clothing one more time, then turned to the door. In just a few hours, Ambrose would be—

Someone tackled him in a wide, fierce hug.

"Oof!" He steadied himself. "Dawn—?"

"You get him back, okay?" She buried her face in the fur covering his shoulder, her voice shaky. "You be safe and you get him back."

Eli wrapped her in the tightest hug he could manage. "You know I will."

———

Much like the Grapevine entrance, the Forge entrance to Aphos was named after its illusory location.

The fake forge didn't look much better than the fake winery. Rusty tools and worktables had been pushed to the side, the old, soot-steamed furnace cordoned off with rope. And just like at the

Grapevine, Eli's eyes struggled to focus on the place. His gaze desperately wanted to slide right off the forge to look at the more aesthetically pleasing flower shops and millineries on either side of it.

Grim's low voice pulled him away from his growing headache.

"I'll say the words," they said. "Then we'll take the potions once we're inside."

Eli couldn't say he was disappointed not being the voice of the party—as Sherry and Grim had observed before, there were five guards in plain clothing milling about the forge, every one of them checking visitors and carts thoroughly. If it were up to him, he'd just knock them all out and sprint into the tunnel—but he didn't much feel like fighting the entirety of Aphos today, so he kept himself steady and got in line next to Grim.

"Some kind of event today," one of the guards said in apology to a visitor ahead of them. "Cassius' orders and all."

Half the visitors in line grumbled knowingly in response. Eli and Grim echoed them and nodded along.

"Well?" The fourth guard waved them closer. "What have you got?"

Grim kept their expression stoic as they pushed their cart forward for inspection.

"The usual," they grunted, their tone both professional and brusque. "Pears, canvas, candles, and soap."

Naturally, there were none of those things in the cart—Grim's words were merely cant for devices of all sorts, most of them broken relics taken from Banneker's shop. Metal scraps, bags, rope, and tools, all stacked amidst a few more mundane sundries to keep the cart looking normal to Scarrish passersby.

"Good, good." The guard wandered around the cart, then gestured to two other guards. "Check them for weapons."

For a moment, Eli hoped these men would give them a lazy glance and wave them in—but the visitor ahead of him quickly dashed his hopes.

"Do I really have to empty all my bags?" she whined; clearly an artificer of some sort, she had at least a dozen pouches on her person.

"Cassius' rules," the man beside her drawled, just as enthusiastic about the order as she was. Eli's hands went cold.

He only had the one bag, the one, tiny bag—but if he emptied it here, the quest would be over before it had begun.

While his guard wasn't looking, he quickly unfastened the bag from his belt and tucked it up his sleeve.

"Think we can find a good tavern once we're in there?" he casually asked Grim, yawning and stretching one arm across his chest. Grim caught sight of the leather cord peeking out from his fingers, and their eyes widened.

"I'm sure we'll be able to find one," they muttered, clapping Eli on the back a little too hard. Eli quickly dropped his arms, swapped the bag to his other hand, and brushed against Grim. As he had hoped, their hand was right there beside him, already reaching for the bag.

"Anything on your belt?" Eli's guard droned. Eli adjusted his cloak, showing his empty belt. A flash of movement off to his left— Grim was now leaning against the cart, hands empty.

"Belt?" their guard asked. Grim rolled their eyes and showed off a similarly empty belt.

Eli let out a long, quiet sigh of relief.

"They're good to go," Eli's guard called and stepped away from both of them. Grim took hold of the cart once more, preparing to push it into the illusory wall at the back of the forge—

"Wait!" The first guard held up a sharp hand, peering into the cart. Their hand dove into the pile of goods and rummaged around. Eli instinctively reached for a dagger that wasn't there. He knew he should have convinced Sherry to shrink a weapon—

"Aha." The guard pulled up a growler of beer, fresh from The Jumping Ogre, and gave a wicked grin. "Event tax. I'm sure you understand."

The other guards laughed. Grim scowled and gestured Eli forward.

"Come along," they said. "We've got business inside."

Eli gave a stoic nod and strode into the tunnel.

They walked straight into the darkness, not daring to utter a word until they had passed at least five crystal lanterns and the bustle of the street had softened into a hum.

"Here." Grim pointed to a cluster of stalagmites, their points barely visible in the shadows. "Stash the cart and take the potions."

They shoved the little cart into the shadows—Eli giving a small, silent goodbye to the perfectly good beer and cheese inside—then plucked the tiny vials from their sneaky little bags. Before drinking, he checked Xavion's looping handwriting on the label:

Don't fail.

"Thanks, Xavion," Eli muttered, and downed the potion in one gulp.

For a brief moment, his face tingled—the effect of Xavion's invisibility striking Viola's disguise magic—but after a moment, he was grounded once more, waving his invisible fingers in front of his face.

"Got a short walk ahead of us," Grim's disembodied voice warned. "Activate the teleporters as we go."

Grim led the way around the tunnels, following Rory's directions down ramps and around noisy markets. As Eli followed closely, his fingers worked to activate the teleporters—little armillary spheres of bronze and copper, each ring both cool and sizzling with Banneker's teleport spell. He pulled on each one, then handed one back to Grim and tucked away two in his pocket.

One for himself, and one he would slip into Ambrose's hand.

The plan was ostensibly simple. Sidle up to Ambrose as he left the demonstration, slip him the teleporter, then wait for him to use it once in his cell. He'd then be whisked off straight to Sherry's living room, into the arms of his friends and, most importantly, Eli—and this nightmare would be over.

They reached the plaza, its carved columns and bright crystalline statue a mockery of the government square topside. Eli forced down his nerves and focused on what he had learned in training: keeping his steps quiet, balancing his weight, keeping hold of Grim just in front of him...

But when they reached the door of the throne room—the largest and most gilded facade—all thought of training flew out of his head.

"Here for the demonstration," a man with a sharp voice and jagged haircut said to the guards, unruffled by the thick columns and toothy carvings peering down at him. A short, willowy girl stood stiffly on his left, and on his right—

Ambrose.

At first glance, he looked just as he had the night of the debates. Potion robes, professional posture. But his face spoke not of lively debates but draining commissions and late nights. Shadows weighed down his eyes, and the crystal light threw a wan pallor across his cheeks.

Eli hurt from everything he was holding in. His chest burned for the shout he couldn't make; his arms ached for the embrace he couldn't give. He couldn't even take a full breath as the guards opened the massive stone doors and Ambrose stepped away from him, fully ignorant of his presence.

A buzz at his ear precluded Grim's voice in his head.

Focus. I've got the door.

Grim jumped ahead of him. As soon as Ambrose and his companions entered the room, the orc leaned all their weight against the door, an invisible and confusing doorstop to the two guards flanking the entrance. As the guards struggled with the door, Eli slipped inside.

In. You?

A moment later, he heard the shuffle of fabric behind him.

In.

The stone door closed behind them.

Though the plaza outside had taken its cues from the bright Scarrish squares above, the throne room lounged in a style that was pure Aphos. The moving carvings leering down at the floor, the way every footstep clinked on the mosaic tile below... There was nowhere to hide in a place like this. Every guest, whether they liked it or not, was laid bare before the golden thrones on the dais.

And today, everyone on the thrones stared at Ambrose. At *his* Ambrose.

"Thank you all for gathering," a woman in the center drawled to the advisors around her, her honeyed words as sharp as the corners of her throne. "Cassius, if you would?"

The man who had accompanied Ambrose pressed a hand against one of the columns, and a breeze whiffed around the dais. Satisfied by whatever the effect had been, he gestured for Ambrose and the girl to take the space before the thrones.

What was that breeze? Eli asked.

Not sure, Grim said. *I don't like it. We should try to get Beake in the hallway, not here.*

But that air was near the thrones, not him—

Not taking any chances. They tugged on Eli's arm and guided him to the wall, where the scant shadows gave them a faint illusion of safety. They watched as the girl—a gnome? An orc? Eli wasn't sure—drank a potion. A moment later, a small dragon illusion formed in front of her.

Eli impatiently tapped his fingers against his leg, glancing between the thrones and the door. Grim's idea made sense, but it was still a risk to get back through the doors undetected. And the other, smaller doors on the sides—what if Ambrose took one of those paths instead? What if they couldn't fit through, or one of the guards felt them pass?

Bile rose in Eli's throat. Those doors looked like a greater risk than simply grabbing the man twenty paces away from him.

"It looks so real," one of the throned advisors said, leaning forward in his chair. Circular patterns rippled through his long coat, as ephemeral as the carvings on the walls. "And this was all one potion?"

The dragon belched fire, and the smell of charcoal filled the air. Not one, not two, but three perfect illusion components, all in one potion. The advisors all burst into chatter amongst themselves.

"We can work with this—"

"Mila, I never thought I'd see the day."

As they all squawked, Ambrose paled further. Eli tensed. The girl had stepped away, and that man Cassius hadn't yet approached him.

He was alone before the dais, and everyone else was distracted.

Grim, we have to get the device to him now, Eli hissed.

No—

No one's near him. I have a clear path.

The woman in the center, Mila, finally stood, her expression smug. "Take him back," she ordered Cassius with a wave of her hand. "My advisors and I have much to discuss. We'll need another demonstration soon. A larger one."

"What timeline should I give him?"

"A month should suffice."

Cassius bowed and moved toward Ambrose, closing the gap. Eli's heart pounded in his ears. If Cassius had him by the arm on his way out, they'd lose their chance, they wouldn't be able to slip him the device. He had to do it, now, now, *now—*

He sprinted forward, one step, two, three—

And struck a wall.

It was invisible until it was too late; a sheer, shimmering barrier curving around the demonstration area. At first, it did nothing, other than knock Eli back onto the floor. He froze, regained his breath, scrambled to his feet—

Then the shield reverberated in alarming spirals of red, a blaring sound accompanying their constant rhythm. Magic detection.

All the guards in the hall looked his way.

Eli! Grim shouted, but he was already off. Sprinting around the shield, desperate to find a way in, to still get to Ambrose—but Cassius was now planted in front of him.

"Cassius?" Mila hissed at him. "What was that—?"

He pointed to the guards, his face growing purple. "Fan out and find whoever it was!"

Eli couldn't breathe. He couldn't do it, he was stuck, he had failed. *Grim!*

Get out! Grim shouted in his head.

But Ames—

I'm not risking them capturing you too. Get out now! That's an order!

Eli cursed, grabbed the teleporter in his pocket, and pulled.

RULE 21:

RECALIBRATE

Dawn

BEFORE THE RESCUE, Rosemond Street had debated for an hour on where to calibrate Ambrose's teleporter.

The Griffin's Claw was presented first and pulled first, given the...decoration improvements...Xavion had made to it. The bakery was another option—Ambrose would be hungry, Sherry insisted—and Grim's living room yet another.

In the end, Sherry's flat won out as the destination. The place was quiet, set back away from the street, and, well, if Ambrose *was* hungry, Sherry's kitchen was right there, already filled with his favorite snacks.

But by the time the rescuers returned, the merchants had already devoured half the food in a stress spiral.

"I should've gone," Sherry muttered, throwing down a playing card. "Should've just taken a vial for my bad hip and gone down there with my hammer."

Dawn, Banneker, and Rory were huddled with her at the dining table, pretending to play a game of Unicorn's Gambit as a distraction while Tom sat in Dawn's lap. In reality, no one was actually paying attention to the score, the next player, or even which card they were playing. At one point, Banneker had tossed in a muffin wrapper instead of a card, and no one batted an eye.

"Ambrose would be furious with you if you got hurt down there," he reminded Sherry, playing two cards—decidedly against the rules, but no one called him on it. "*I* should've gone down. I've got enough hand cannons to blast apart a few rock walls—"

"Can't save Ames if he's trapped under a rockslide," Dawn muttered, gripping her cards tightly over Tom's bristly head. She didn't even remember what the symbols in her hand meant. Was a five of chalices covered in cupcake crumbs good or bad?

Not that it mattered as long as Grim and Eli were still in Aphos. When she checked her pocket watch for the tenth time, Rory set a gentle hand on her wrist. "They'll have gotten to the throne room by now," she reassured. "They know what they're doing. Ames'll be back here in minutes."

"I know, I know." Dawn took a deep breath and pulled the chalice card from her hand. "I can't help it, I'm just—"

Before the card could fall, a flash of light burst from the far side of the living room and out tumbled two figures.

Only two.

Everyone at the table jumped to their feet, but Dawn's legs were shaking, barely able to hold her up. "What *happened*?"

Eli was already rambling tearfully—not to them, but to an incensed Grim.

"I'm sorry, I thought I could—"

"I told you to hold off!"

"If I had known there was a shield there, I wouldn't have gone!"

Banneker leapt to help Eli to his feet. Sherry reached for Grim, but they launched to their feet on their own, their face contorted in fury.

"Just a minute of waiting, that was all you needed to do—"

"How do you think I feel about this?" Eli shouted, his voice choked. "He was right there, I could *see* him, and we—" He covered his hands with his face. "He was right there…"

"Are either of you hurt?" Sherry wavered, hovering close to them. Grim grunted a short negative. Eli didn't respond, not even when Tom rolled up to his feet and tapped his leg.

Dawn leaned heavily on the table, her insides a shattered gem: sharp and painful, no matter how she moved or where her mind went.

She should say something. Comfort Eli, help Grim, *anything*. Surely it had been an honest mistake. Surely, they could try again.

But anger and devastation made for a wretched mixture of unwise words, and before any of them could leap out of her mouth, she found herself outside, walking back home on a road that didn't feel right under her feet.

"Dawn?" Rory called after her. "Dawn, it'll be okay. He's not lost forever—"

"How do you know that?" she snapped. She didn't slow down, nor did she need to; Rory's legs were longer than hers and caught up easily. "What if they saw Grim and Eli? What if they realized Ames was trying to get out, and they're—they're punishing him, or moving him somewhere else, or..."

She yanked uselessly on the door to her shop, torn between hiding in the loft and walking all the way to the end of the city and back. But neither was going to help with the pain because Ambrose wasn't in the loft nor in the Scar, and gods, Eli had even *seen* him and had come up empty-handed—

Rory pulled her into a hug, making no mention of Dawn's heaving shoulders or the tears streaming down her face. She simply stood there, a silent pillar of support, until all of Dawn's awful, stabbing emotions had melted into Rory's shirt and onto the street.

"Here, let's go inside." Rory finally pulled back and pushed a curl off Dawn's forehead. "Can I make you some tea? Coffee?"

Dawn wiped her face and shuffled into the shop. The wands all glittered at her like ever-present friends, but that wasn't what would comfort her right now. With a tired hand, she pointed to the back cabinet behind the counter.

"You know"—she sniffed, giving Rory a wan smile—"I keep a good vintage back there for bad customer days."

Rory squeezed her shoulder. "Bad customer day it is."

A half hour later, they both slumped on the floor behind the counter, passing a wine bottle between them. Rory had her feet propped up on a stack of old wand boxes, her tear-stained jacket now dried off.

"I really do mean it." She took a swig of the wine. "About getting another shot at saving Ames, I mean. If he did well during the demonstration, they'll make him do another one soon." She handed the bottle back to Dawn. "I'm not walking away from this story before it ends happy."

Part of Dawn wanted to sink into her moping, to wallow longer in the loss—but she could feel Rory's attempt to tug her out of that mire, and she reluctantly went along with it.

"We'll need to find another way to talk to him." She grimaced after her next gulp of wine—too dry for her liking. "We don't have any paper left. If we could make more..."

"I wouldn't recommend it." Rory toyed with a scrap of fraying ribbon on the floor. "Ambrose has proven his worth to Aphos now. They might be watching him more closely. If someone catches him scribbling on disappearing pieces of paper, they'll make his life a nightmare."

Dawn let out a slow breath and sank back against the counter. All the tears had left her exhausted, and the wine certainly wasn't giving her a boost. Her mind begged for sleep, but given the shadows still pacing in her thoughts, she knew she'd have nightmares of her own that night. Of Ambrose, definitely. Probably him stuck in sinkholes again. Or hidden in the shadows, just out of her reach, while she called for him, tried to talk to him—

An idea slammed into her like a charge from a blast wand.

"Wait." She straightened, nearly dropping the bottle in her hand. "Dreams."

Rory frowned. "Dreams," she repeated slowly. "What about them?"

"We can communicate to him through *dreams*." Dawn grabbed the ledge of the counter and hauled herself to her feet. "Then it wouldn't matter if they're watching him during the day—he can talk to us at night."

"Oh." Rory's eyes widened. "*Oh.*" She scrambled to her feet, kicking aside the wand boxes. "Can you actually do that? Do you have a wand for it?"

"Not exactly, no." Dawn grabbed an old receipt to write on. "But we can link waking minds with Grim's earrings. So, why not dreaming minds?"

"And there's already magic that affects dreams, right?" Rory added. "Prevents nightmares or something? What if you combined the two?"

"Yes, *exactly*." She scribbled across the back of the receipt, her stubby pencil flying. If she combined heartstone with sleeping embers, then combined it with some of Banneker's tools or Xavion's potions...

"We can do this." She beamed at Rory, her ribs suddenly too small for her heart. "We can make this work, we can talk to Ames again—"

Rory yanked her into a hug that lifted her off her feet, an impulsive and energetic reflection of everything Dawn was feeling. "You're brilliant, you know that?" She laughed, letting her down with a breathless grin. "Just amazing and incredible and—"

The hug wasn't enough, not this time, not with all the emotions swirling in Dawn's chest. She let the feeling pull her forward, back into Rory's arms, her hands reaching for her face—

With tears still salting her lips and hope dancing on her tongue, she kissed Rory.

It wasn't her finest kiss. In her eagerness, she may have leaned in too hard, pushed too soon—but Rory didn't seem to care. She gave a small, delighted squeak and pushed right back, her hands circling around Dawn's waist.

And when they pulled away, Rory laughed, bright and delighted and almost disbelieving. "Could I—?" She fought down another giggle. "Could I get another go at that?"

She dipped down and cupped Dawn's face for another kiss. This one was slow and soft, but the more it deepened, the more Dawn could taste Rory's impatience on her tongue, the burning desire to sink even further. It tasted of wine and bad dancing and fleeting glances, and the brief, cool rush of a river.

When they finally parted, Dawn could barely breathe.

"Listen," Rory said huskily, her mouth still inches from Dawn's. "I know you've got friends to save and all that. But...you think we could do this again sometime? On a date, maybe?"

Dawn bit back a laugh at it all—the terribly alluring tone, the awfully dorky words. "Real date or fake?"

"As much as I loved bringing you to a terrible tavern with lumpy seats and bad wine..." Rory pulled away and scrunched her nose in fake thought. "I dunno, I'm thinking real this time."

Dawn thought her chest might explode, but she couldn't tell what burned hotter: her desire to whisk Rory off on a date, or the written ideas now crumpled in her hand.

"Soon," she promised. "A real date. No fake names."

Rory gave her another kiss, eager and happy and threatening to melt Dawn into a puddle. "You sure about that, Kerry?"

Dawn made a face, securing one more laugh from Rory, then reluctantly pulled away to reach the rose statue. In an impatiently slanted scrawl, she scribbled all of the merchants' names at the top of the paper, then her message underneath:

I've got an idea.

RULE 22:

DREAM BIG

Ambrose

As soon as the door closed, Ambrose collapsed on the workroom floor, ignorant of the dust and the frigid stone against his palms.

He wasn't supposed to be back here, in the windowless room with a cruel mockery of his home covering the walls. The plan had failed. The people, the objects, whatever magic had set the shield alight had been them, he knew. It had to be them. It was too well-timed, so close, so godsdamned close.

But whatever their plan was, it hadn't been enough. And he was still here, with a pounding headache, a new demonstration date, and no end in sight.

He ignored Nat's footsteps as they rushed past him into the wash-room, each step jarring the pain between his ears. She had been right —he couldn't escape, after all. He didn't bother getting up, instead waiting for the snide *I told you so* to commence. It didn't matter— words couldn't hurt any more than what already stabbed at both his thoughts and his chest. He should have done more, tried to bring something that would help them. Perhaps if he had tried to run through the shield himself or fight off the guards—

"Water?" Nat bent down and placed a mug near his head. He slowly pushed himself to his knees and drank, the cool water doing little to soothe any of his aches.

"Thank you," he mumbled weakly, not meeting her gaze. The smug jeers and crowing would come soon. It was only what he deserved.

Instead, she settled cross-legged across from him and bit her lip.

"Those invisible attackers," she said. "Cassius said they must have come to steal the potion, but..." She fidgeted with the top of her boot, where her book was hidden. "They were coming for you, weren't they?"

He didn't have the energy to lie.

"Yes," he mumbled. "They were trying to save me."

He braced himself for the response—a derisive snort, a laugh— but she blinked at him instead, eyes wide.

"*Trying*?" she repeated. "They almost *did* save you!" An odd smile spread across her face, and she hopped to her feet, arms flung out in wide gestures. "Do you know how many intruders have made it to the throne room in my whole life? One. *Maybe* two, if you count Igor, but he was a parrot—" She swept her hands to wipe the words from the air. "Whatever. Point is, your friends got closer than almost any of Madam Mila's enemies. Your friends almost saved you."

Ambrose looked around in confusion. Had he been thrown into the right room? Had he fallen into some mirror dimension where Nat was being...positive?

"Yes," he said slowly, "I suppose they did."

"Will they try again?" she pressed. Still adjusting to his new reality, Ambrose drank the rest of the water, then set his palms on the cold floor.

"Yes," he said. Of that much, he was confident. "They won't leave me down here."

Nat drew herself up and extended a hand down to him. "Okay," she said. "Then I want a new deal."

Ambrose rubbed his forehead. "Nat, I'm not sure I can secure more food for you—"

"Not food. *Out.* I want out. I'll help you prepare for the next rescue as long as you take me with you."

He stared at her. He must have fainted back in the throne room, and this was all a strange vision. "Are you...quite sure?"

"Yes."

"You want to help me escape?"

"Yes."

"And this isn't..." He glanced at the door. "This isn't a trick to get me in trouble with Cassius?"

Her face darkened. "That man can stick himself right up a dragon's fiery ass."

Ambrose laughed and pushed himself to his feet. He didn't know exactly how she would help, or when the rescue would be, or much of anything, apart from his splitting headache.

But if he turned this new partnership down, he deserved to stick himself right up...where Nat had said.

"I accept the terms of your bargain." He shook her hand. "Let me show you how to preheat a cauldron."

The new deal between them absorbed much of the next few days. Whenever Cassius wasn't sending an archivist to copy his latest notes, Ambrose taught Nat the basics of potioneering.

Unfortunately for her, the first lesson was about safety, which she detested.

"What, you gotta turn that thing on every single time?" She wrinkled her nose at the fume pull. "Ugh, that's so annoying."

Ambrose glared at her. "Would you rather brew a potion or hallucinate dancing mushrooms over its fumes?"

"I mean"—she pursed her lips—"okay, I *should* say brew a potion, but..."

The second lesson was about heat wands, which, as he feared, she absolutely adored.

"Which one's the hottest one?" She eagerly hopped up to the wand rack. "Does it shoot fire? Can we tweak it to shoot fireballs?"

Ambrose sighed. "May you and Dawn never meet."

Nat twirled the high heat wand between her fingers. "Who's Dawn?"

With such an enthusiastic subject, the lessons moved quickly—but as the days passed, Ambrose couldn't say where exactly his plan was headed. Without any communication from Rosemond Street, he had no way of knowing what sort of potion would help them the most. He had no clue what to start brainstorming, what to test, what to plan for...

And beside him, his new partner was getting impatient.

"Well?" she said as she flicked a wand, sucking the flames out from under a test cauldron. "When can we start getting to the good stuff?"

"The good stuff?"

"Yeah. The real potions and brews and"—she looked at the door and lowered her voice—"whatever else is going to get us out of here."

Ambrose cleared his throat to hide the emptiness in his thoughts. "Allow me to think on it tonight," he said. "We can start making a plan tomorrow. Is that acceptable?"

Nat snorted. "Sure, sure. Tomorrow's good."

As soon as she left for the evening, he climbed into bed, hoping that his half-asleep thoughts muddled against the pillow would surface something useable. He couldn't wait on Rosemond Street—he had to start something himself.

But thoughts of recipes and notes slowly morphed into memories of Eli, both sweet and painful, which in turn took the shape of daydreams. Of Eli breaking down the door, sweeping him away, back into the bright daytime...

He fell asleep in the imagined warmth of a patch of sunlight and Eli's arms.

When he woke next, he was standing in Grim's living room.

The setting of his dream wasn't particularly unusual. These days, his dreams often threw him into various rooms around Rosemond Street. His shop most often, Dawn's shop next. Then the bakery, his friends' houses, their various workshops...

But none of his dreams had ever been this vivid before. The faded rug sank softly under his feet. The fire crackling in the hearth warmed his legs. Even the very air bore the familiar scent of Grim's place: pine, fresh linen, and a lingering echo of Sherry's sugar cookies.

"Ames?"

Ambrose whipped around. Dawn sat on Grim's wide, squashy couch in one of her lovely sundresses. She stared at him with a teary smile, her hand covering her mouth.

His breath hitched. How rude of his inner thoughts—to paint his best friend as both beautiful and sad.

"Gods, do I miss you," he said. It didn't matter what he said, did it? It was just a dream. "Please don't cry. I'm sorry the dream made you this way. If I could think up some cookies or something, maybe that would—"

Dawn leapt from the couch and hugged him tight.

He stopped breathing.

This wasn't a hug from a dream. This one felt too real—the tickle of Dawn's hair against his chin, the way her arms nearly broke his ribs. And there was a new smell, a faint whiff of soot and amber, which had no place in either Grim's room or Dawn's perfume. He frowned, forcing his sleep-heavy mind to reach back into his conscious thoughts. Soot and amber... He had smelled those before in combination...

Back when he was brewing a communication spell.

"Dawn?" Her name cracked on his tongue. "Dawn, is that you?"

She released a sob into his shirt. "It's me. I'm talking to you through a wand we made —"

He broke down into her shoulder. They had done it. Those ridiculous, wonderful, loving, brilliant fools had found another way to reach him.

He wanted to drag them all into this room and stay there forever.

But when he finally pulled away, thrilled and tear-stained and utterly exhausted, the room had thinned. If he squinted, he could see through the walls into gray nothingness. "How long do we have in here?"

"I'm not sure." Dawn wiped her cheek. "No more than an hour, I think. The wand build was just a test." She gave a weak laugh. "Tomorrow won't feel great for either of us."

"Headaches?"

"Think more along the lines of our old pre-certification all-nighters."

Ambrose grimaced. There was a reason those days of incessant study and exhaustion were far behind him. "No matter. I'll brew an energy potion tomorrow. But, quickly—did someone try to save me the other day?"

They settled on the couch, the worn cushions threatening to devour them whole.

"Eli and Grim," Dawn said. "They were trying to get you a tele-porter while invisible."

"Eli?" Ambrose's voice threatened to break all over again. So, Eli had really been right there. Paces away from him.

Dawn quickly took both of his hands in hers. "He says he's sorry and he feels terrible about it. He thought he saw an opportunity to get to you and he took it."

Ambrose sniffed. "Gods, that sounds like him," he warbled. "I miss him."

"He misses you too," Dawn said. "We all do. Now, while we've got some time left, will you tell me everything?"

And Ambrose did.

Dawn held up a hand. "So, wait, how'd you end up babysitting a teenager while also being kidnapped?"

"It was my idea," Ambrose said. "She knew Octavia, the potioneer before me. I thought she could give me information about her."

"Was Octavia close to actually making what Aphos wants?"

"Not at all. I can barely comprehend her last few journals. Aphos' archivist couldn't understand them, either."

"Have they told you why they want a brew like that?" Dawn asked. "Don't they have enough illusion magic to sell off?"

Ambrose scoffed, a vision of Cassius' many coats coming to mind. "Enough to wear like jewelry, apparently," he muttered. "I don't know. They haven't told me why, only that they wanted it, and that they never got it from Octavia." He leaned back against the couch and folded his arms. "At least her doodles are mildly entertaining. She liked to draw dragons in the corners of her notes."

Dawn gave a hum. "Rory doodles in her notes sometimes."

"Rory? That's the reporter who's been helping you?"

"Mm-hm." Dawn's eyes glittered, but she offered no further information on that point. "She just draws spirals and stuff, though. Nothing like dragons."

Ambrose narrowed his gaze at her, quietly filing away a note to press her on Rory next time. "Tavi eventually got quite good at the dragons," he continued. "Nat wanted her to draw her with a fireball wand, but I never found that particular artistic commission in the margins."

"No?"

"No." He shrugged. "She just kept drawing leaves and flowers. She didn't color them all in, either. She only filled them in at random...intervals..."

He sat up, his own words clanging in his head. Now that he said it out loud, that didn't sound quite right. The leaves and flowers she always drew...they were never randomly placed on the page, were they? He always found them framing a small recipe or a stack of notes, perfectly aligned with every line of text. And that archivist—

the one who had constantly reviewed her work, who didn't understand a word of it. What if his confusion had been intentional?

What if Tavi's silly, idle doodles had never been silly nor idle?

"Ames?" Dawn said. "You okay?"

"I have to check on something," he said. "Gods, I hope I remember it when I wake up. But"—he stood up—"you will try to rescue me again, won't you?"

"Eh, I dunno." Dawn feigned a skeptical look, then slapped his leg. "Of course we will. We just had to find another way to talk to you first."

His joy bubbled over. "So, you'll talk to me like this again? Every night?"

"I'll need to improve the wand before it can be used every night." Dawn reached for his hand in reassurance. "But I promise. One of us will show up as often as we can."

Eli, Ambrose thought, his heart stumbling. He could talk to Eli.

The room around them flickered, then held. Dawn's voice grew more urgent. "What will they have you do next?"

"Another demonstration," he responded quickly. "A bigger one. Cassius mentioned something about an oasis after we walked out— could you ask Rory what that means?"

"Of course." Dawn stood with him. "We'll come up with another plan. A better one. Can you still pretend to make their potion while you wait?"

He nodded, his mind buzzing even as the corners of the room flickered again. "I'll try. You'll be safe up there?"

"Says the guy living in a crime syndicate." She wrapped him in one more hug, tight and warm. "I love you."

Ambrose squeezed her as hard as he could, feeling her warmth slowly fade and willing it to stay just a second longer. He wanted to remember his idea in the morning, yes—but he wanted to remember this hug most of all. "I love you, too."

A Beake CPM
Tri-Illusion Potion
In Three Parts

Part 1: Sight

high viscosity
is normal →

Part 2: Sound

nebula-like
formations will appear
around step 27 →

Part 3: Smell

frost will disappear
30 min after brewing →

nat was
here!
:)

Procedure

1. Preheat cauldron to level 250.

2. Prepare rinceweed by slicing stems vertically.

Observations

→ THIS IS NOT GUILD-
APPROVED. DO NOT
MAKE THIS POTION.

Pg 1

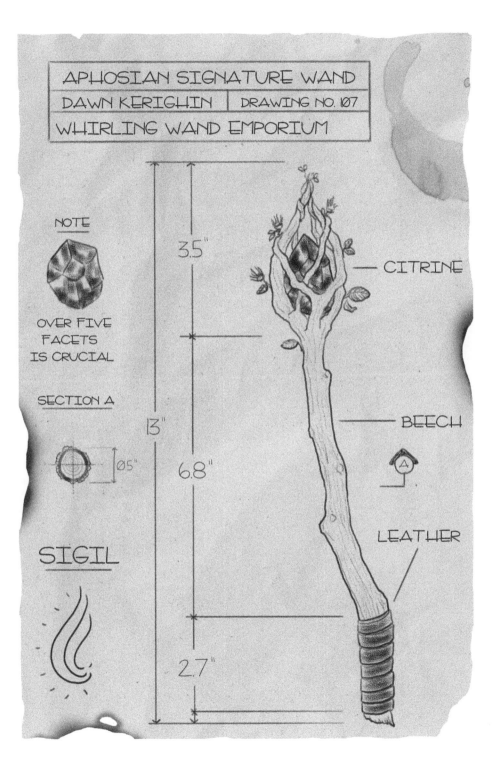

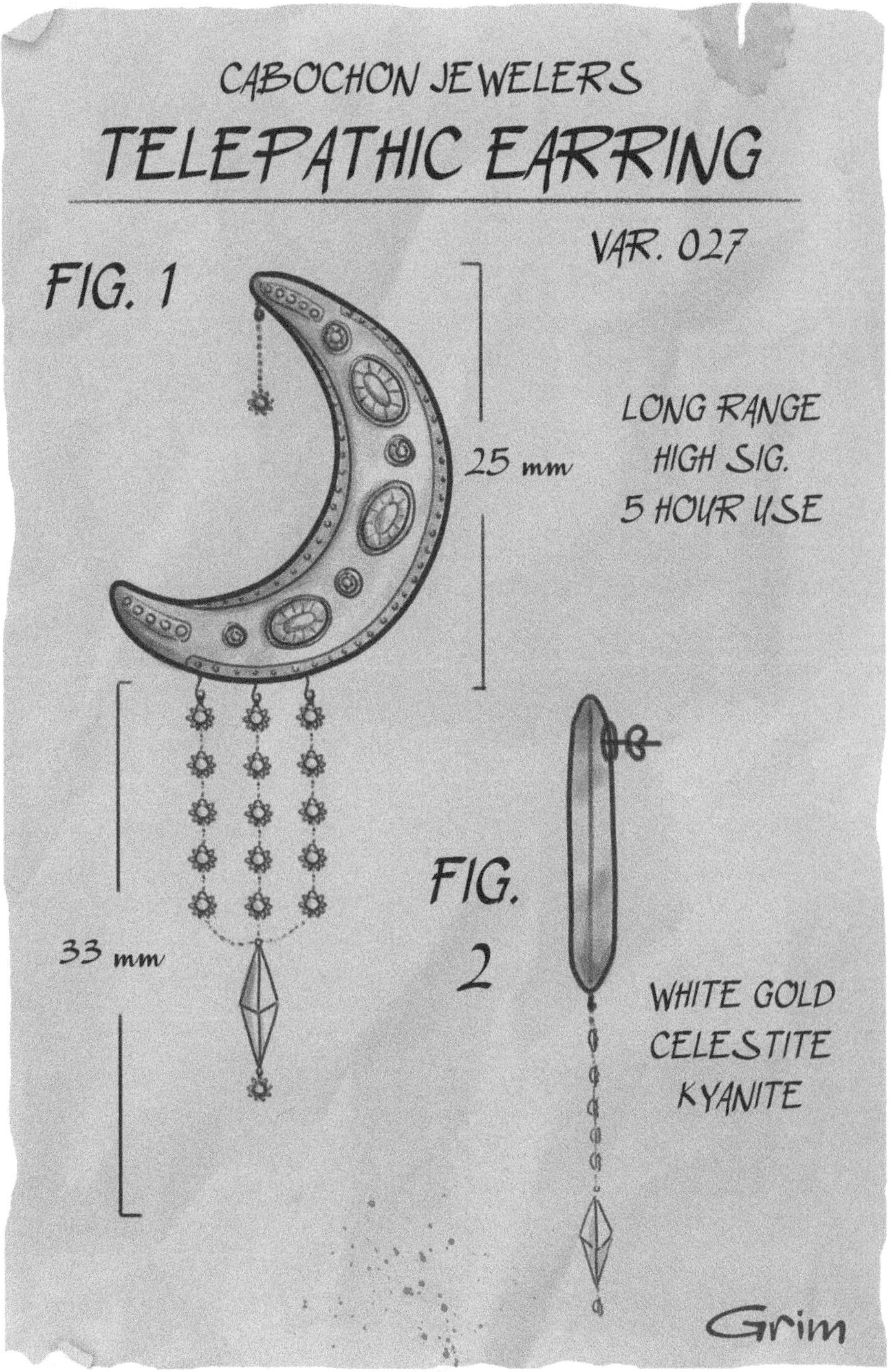

CABOCHON JEWELERS
TELEPATHIC EARRING

VAR. 027

FIG. 1

25 mm

LONG RANGE
HIGH SIG.
5 HOUR USE

33 mm

FIG.
2

WHITE GOLD
CELESTITE
KYANITE

Grim

PLATE I

TITLE: SHORT-DIST. TELEPORTER

UP TO TEN CHARGES
LVL. B DISTANCE

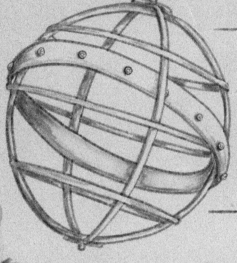

——————— ATTUNED COPPER

——— TWICE-CLEANSED
IRON

——— GEMS FOR
ACCURACY

——— INTERIOR SILVER INLAY
PROVIDES STABILITY

POSSIBLE MODS:

METAL COMPONENTS
CANNOT BE
INTERCHANGED

CONSULT CABOCHON
JEWELERS FOR
GEM MODS

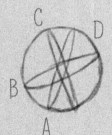

LONGER DISTANC[
STRONGER CHAR[
ANTI-NAUSEA
FOCUS ON RE-USE D[

Banneker

Beachy Dreams Cupcake

sugared flowers!!

what kind?

~~violet~~
~~rose~~
~~pansies~~
~~begonias~~

need more icing dye

reminder: buy more baking cups

FLAVORS

passionfruit
coconut
vanilla

MAGIC

dual sensation
illusion

VIOLA

recipe on back

True Illusion Potion

OCTAVIA GRAY

[ ] - to buy!!

INGREDIENTS

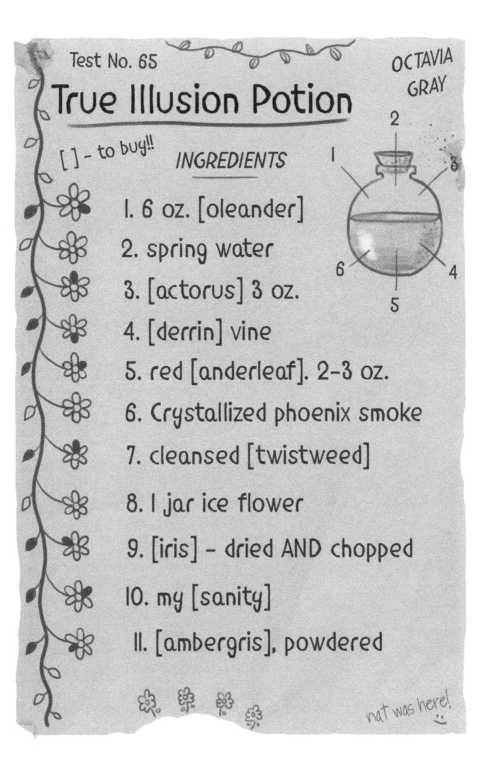

1. 6 oz. [oleander]

2. spring water

3. [actorus] 3 oz.

4. [derrin] vine

5. red [anderleaf]. 2-3 oz.

6. Crystallized phoenix smoke

7. cleansed [twistweed]

8. 1 jar ice flower

9. [iris] - dried AND chopped

10. my [sanity]

11. [ambergris], powdered

nat was here! :)

RULE 23:

TAKE A FIELD TRIP

Eli

ELI WASN'T sure what he was more ashamed of: the failed rescue or the fact that he had absolutely no hand in cobbling together Dawn's new dreaming system.

"It shouldn't be me talking to him next," he muttered to Dawn as he walked next to her in the lavender fields. "I screwed up the rescue, and all of you scrambled to fix it. It should be Grim next, or Banneker, not me—"

Dawn slapped his arm. "Ames doesn't want to see Grim or Banneker. I mean, I'm sure he does, but—you should've seen his face when I mentioned you. If we don't let him see you next, he's gonna climb out of the dream and hunt you down himself."

He bit back a smile and let Dawn walk ahead of him on the narrow deer path, all of Rosemond Street now wandering single file through the fields. Dawn's conversation with Ambrose had only been a few days ago, and the morning after, Eli had brought her a pot of coffee and begged her for every detail: how Ambrose looked, how he sounded, what they talked about.

But it wasn't enough.

"When do you think you'll have the next prototype?" he asked. "If you need me to break into The Griffin's Claw to brew anything—"

"I heard that," Xavion called from behind them. Eli ignored them.

"It's all right, we've got it handled," Dawn said. "Well, Grim does. They're making something way better than my wand."

"Rather you not set the bar that high," Grim muttered ahead of them. "Eli, I'll get it to you in a few days."

Grim and Rory were leading the charge for the day's little escapade—a quick jaunt to what Rory called the Oasis.

"We're not far now," the reporter shouted back to the merchants trailing her like ducklings. "You'll know it when you see it."

"Why am I here, again?" Xavion grumbled, tugging their gauzy robes off yet another bramble.

"This is a street effort," Sherry huffed from the back of the line. "And you are part of the street."

Just ahead of Xavion, Viola floated effortlessly above the uneven path on an enchanted, cushioned chair—one of Banneker's own prototypes for ease of travel.

"How's it working?" Banneker walked alongside it, squinting at every angle and poking the little handles on the sides. "I can always recalibrate it when we get back."

"Works great," Viola said. "Just needs a nice little ghost pattern on the cushion." She delicately unwrapped a mini cupcake she had brought with her. "Xavion wants one next."

Xavion yanked their robe off a lavender bush with an audible rip. "I'm doing perfectly well on my own, thank you."

Viola gave a bemused *hm* and floated on. Just in front of her, Dawn called up to Rory, "What do you mean you'll know it when we see it?"

Rory turned and winked back at her. "Like I'm gonna ruin the surprise."

Dawn stifled a giggle and kept walking. Eli glanced between the two of them, a new, delightfully distracting thought simmering. Dawn had been...*particularly* happy upon sharing that dream idea she had brainstormed with Rory. Giggly, even. Giddy, one might say.

He had been so focused on Ambrose, he hadn't done his due diligence in interrogating the friend right in front of him. It was time to fix that.

"So"—he lowered his voice—"how's everything going with you and Rory?"

"Hm?" Dawn took a second to drag her eyes off Rory. "Oh. Fine. It's fine."

Eli grinned. "Just fine? How...exactly did you and Rory brainstorm that dream idea? I missed some of the details."

Dawn shot him a look; he folded his hands in front of him and donned his most innocent face.

"It's nothing—" she tried.

"Oh, no, it's not nothing."

"It's—I don't want to sound like—like I'm bragging in front of you while Ambrose is—"

Eli stopped walking. "Oh my gods, you kissed."

"*Shh!*" Dawn scrambled to cover his mouth with her hand, though the ecstatic sparkle in her eyes gave her away. "Not so loud!"

Eli laughed through her hand. "You're telling me everything when we get back, are we clear—?"

"Okay, *okay!*" Dawn pulled her hand away and glanced around at the others. "But when we get back. If Sherry finds out, who knows what she'll—"

"Did someone call my name?" Sherry asked.

"No!" Both Eli and Dawn called back, and walked along arm in arm, both of them stifling grins. This was what he needed, Eli thought. A lovely, wholesome tidbit of gossip to take his mind off its constant replay of the failed mission. If it meant he could go more than an hour without thinking about it, he'd demand every possible detail from—

The crackle of magic in the air stopped him in his tracks.

"Damn," he mumbled, waving his hand through the air. The magic was invisible, but tingled around his fingertips like static. "Rory, you weren't kidding."

Just as she had promised, the wide sinkhole ahead of them had announced its magical presence before they could even see into it. Rory stopped a careful distance from the edge, her hands on her hips.

"Here it is," she said flatly. "The Oasis."

Eli edged closer to the sinkhole, careful not to go much farther than Rory. He caught a glimpse of ragged walls, bursting foliage, and delicate streams of water falling down into the depths—and beyond that, a shadowy stone dais.

"Aphosian royalty's little gem of a sunroom," Rory said, derision dripping from her words. "And where they'll show off their new potioneering toy in a month. Now, there's no shield down below, but up here..."

She picked up and tossed a pebble into the sinkhole; a shield flared where it struck, briefly glowing red before fading once more.

"It's exactly like the shield you saw in the receiving room," she said. "Keeps anyone from sneaking in through the sinkholes connected to Aphos. The fact that they added one to the throne room, though, was a surprise to me. They must've tightened security there."

Banneker appeared at Eli's shoulder. "Can we deactivate the big guy?"

Rory grimaced. "Probably, but they're well-monitored. Deactivating it might send up a bigger flag than you want it to." She folded her arms. "If you really want to get in undetected, your best bet is to go in as a guest at the demonstration."

Dawn sidled up next to Rory—not too close, but not too far, either. "So, we steal an invitation, then," she said. "You want to go out together, do our bad dance routine, steal an invite or two?"

"Yeah, go out together," Eli muttered just loud enough for Dawn to hear. She nudged him hard in the ribs.

"Well..." Rory hesitated. Eli had expected her to agree immediately, particularly given who was asking—but to his surprise, she shifted from foot to foot instead. "I don't think I can. Aphos only invites its richest clients to these sorts of things, and they don't exactly hang out in ground-floor taverns. They're all people who do business with Mila—I mean, Madam Mila—personally."

"But you know where we could find them, right?" he pressed. "If you have names—"

Unexpected anger flashed across Rory's eyes.

"Of course I have names," she snapped. "But they didn't come easy, and they're far too close to my—" She cut herself off and scowled. "Her inner circle. If any one of them finds out I'm sniffing around, I'm done. All my contacts, all my—"

"It's all right." Dawn set a hand on her arm. "You've already risked yourself by getting us this far. We'll figure something else out."

Sherry jumped in to help, her tone smoothing the air. "What if we didn't steal an invitation at all?" she offered. "What if we forged one and used that to fool the guards?"

They all murmured in agreement at that. Even Rory's unease dissipated.

"That could work," she said, "if we get the details right."

"And we'll need disguises again." Viola nodded eagerly, the floating cushion bobbing with her movement. "New ones. I'll need some new extracts..."

Somewhere in the fields, Xavion groaned. Dawn held up a hand.

"We should talk to Ames about this first," she said. "See if he can find anything else out about the demonstration before we get too far." She tugged on Eli's sleeve. "You wanna tell him all about it when you see him? Or will you get too *distracted*"—she wiggled her fingers here —"and forget?"

Eli snorted. "Come on, I'm a professional. I won't forget."

Eli had to remind himself upwards of twenty times that week that he had actual messages for Ambrose apart from love and sweet nothings.

"Okay," he said, pacing back and forth in front of Grim's couch— this was not a time for remaining still. "I gotta tell him we know what and where the Oasis is. We're gonna forge an invitation to get in and grab him. He just needs to tell us if he hears anything else about the demonstration." He stopped and looked over at Grim, who was hunched over the kitchen table. "What am I missing?"

The orc didn't look up from their work. Their bulky arms blocked whatever they were tinkering with, but Eli could still see their furrowed brow and the tiny silver caustics dancing across their fingers.

"The street updates," they said, not missing a beat.

"Right." Eli rattled them off on his fingers. "Sherry bought him some new tea for when he's back. Banneker says his horoscope is looking good for the week. And Xavion hasn't burnt down the shop yet. Anything else?"

Grim finally stood up and wiped off their hands.

"Tell him I said hang in there." They grunted and handed over their work. "Now, put this on and go to sleep already."

Eli stared down at the shining crown in his hands: a bright circlet of silver, interwoven with deep blue crystals and gold flowers. A piece fit for royalty, not for sleeping. "Grim, are you sure?"

"What, sure it'll work?" They shrugged. "The dream might be shorter than what Dawn could manage, but you won't need three pots of coffee to survive the next day. And since my living room is, well…" They waved to the sparsely decorated walls. "Just think about a better setting when you go to sleep and you'll probably see it in the dream."

"No, I know it'll work," Eli said, afraid to move his hands for fear of breaking the piece. "But—it's incredible. You didn't have to do this much just for a communication device."

Grim scratched their beard and gave a noncommittal grunt, but the pride in their eyes was clear. "Couldn't have anyone thinking my detail work is slipping in my old age. Now, go on." They nodded to the couch, where a blanket and pillow were waiting. "Get to sleep. I'll have pancakes ready in the morning."

When Eli next opened his eyes, he was staring up at the night sky, the stars his new blanket.

He had thought very hard about what he wanted the dream to be like before he drifted off to sleep. He had considered imagining The Gingersnap Café, or The Griffin's Claw, or, cheekily, Ambrose's bedroom—but then he recalled that Ambrose had been locked underground for weeks now and might appreciate a bit of fresh air and clear sky.

He pushed himself to sit, the weave of the picnic blanket underneath him tickling his palms. No sign of his boyfriend yet—just the nighttime lavender fields swaying in the breeze. He hoped Ambrose wasn't staying up late brewing something. Grim had said the spell wouldn't last as long, and if he forgot any of Rosemond Street's messages while waiting—

Footsteps crunched in the brush behind him. Eli scrambled to his feet, heart already hammering. There was Ambrose: standing in the fields beyond the blanket, rubbing his eyes and squinting at all the flowers sparkling in the moonlight.

(It was a dream, after all. Eli figured he might as well make it romantic.)

"Where...?" Ambrose turned to Eli and froze. "Is it—are you—?"

"Real," Eli breathed. "It's me, I'm here—"

Ambrose fell to his knees, and Eli couldn't run to him fast enough.

"It's okay!" He skidded to his knees and wrapped Ambrose in a hug, grabbing fistfuls of his rumpled tunic. "It's okay, I've got you."

Ambrose clung to him in turn, his tearful, rambling words buried in Eli's shoulder. "I love you, I missed you, I've thought about you every day—"

Eli started planting kisses everywhere in response. His hair, his forehead, his cheek—

When he reached his lips, a shock bolted through him, as if he had forgotten what Ambrose's kiss tasted like.

He didn't recall how they reached the picnic blanket after that. He only vaguely remembered murmuring broken phrases in return—

love, apologies, reassurances. All he could focus on was Ambrose's body: his lips, his hands, the warmth that melted him wherever they touched...and the desperate look in his eyes when he pulled away.

"I—" Eli tried to catch his breath. "The others, they didn't want me to forget—"

Ambrose cupped his face with both hands, eyes crinkling, his smile both pleading and loving.

"With all due respect to them," he said firmly, "*later.*"

He crushed his lips against Eli's one more time, and for a moment, Eli gladly forgot all about the others.

Much later, when the night sky betrayed hints of gray nothingness beyond it, they huddled under a blanket, watching shooting stars cross the sky in glittering shards.

(Another personal touch of Eli's; he was particularly proud of that idea.)

"I suppose a sinkhole doesn't sound too bad," Ambrose mused, once Eli told him about the Oasis. "If it's as fancy as it sounds. Do you really think you'll be able to go in as guests?"

Eli peppered his shoulder with kisses. "That's the plan."

Ambrose briefly closed his eyes, then reached up and adjusted the circlet on Eli's head. "You should wear this when you go in. It makes you look like a prince."

"The Prince and the Potioneer. Classic tale."

"It could be if you get that reporter to write it," Ambrose said. "Rory, right? Dawn mentioned her a few times."

Eli grinned. "Mentioned her a few times, did she?"

Ambrose frowned. "Wait, what does that mean?"

Eli's grin sharpened to a wicked point. Ambrose gasped.

"No."

"Yes."

"Did they—?"

"*Yes.*"

Ambrose sat up. "And I'm *missing* it? Get me out. Get me out of Aphos right now. I had a moral imperative to help Dawn land a girlfriend—"

"I'm trying to cover that for you!"

Ambrose ignored him, running both hands through his hair. "Do you know how much I was looking forward to this duty? How much counter-teasing I owe her from last year? If I miss this opportunity now—"

"Don't worry about it." Eli reached for him, already missing his warmth. "We'll break you out at the Oasis and you'll get to tease her about it every day."

With a grumble, Ambrose reluctantly curled up next to Eli again, watching the stars in renewed silence. But Eli knew the man was holding a question on his tongue. He'd recognize that little frown anywhere.

"You know," he ventured, "Dawn said that you had some sort of idea when she spoke to you. Wanna tell me more about it?"

He was on the right track—Ambrose's frown line deepened before he responded.

"I..." He watched one more star go by. "I'm looking further into Tavi's journals, and..." He took a breath. "Are you at all familiar with any dragon species in Aphos?"

The question threw Eli off entirely.

"Well, there's the snub-nosed dragon, I guess," he said. "And those rock pygmies that got reintroduced last year. Why do you ask?"

"It's nothing," Ambrose said. "At least—it's possibly nothing. I'll tell you once I know more." He paused. "You will visit again, won't you?"

Eli kissed his cheek. "Grim'll have to pry this crown outta my cold, dead hands," he said. "Unless Sherry asks nicely for it."

Ambrose traced another shooting star with his gaze, then intertwined his fingers with Eli's. "How is the rest of the street doing? Will you tell me about them?"

"They're doing great. Viola's torturing Xavion as best she can."

"I knew I liked her for more than her baked goods." Ambrose ran his fingers over Eli's knuckles. "I just want to hear about something other than the rescue or potions. I spend most of my waking hours thinking about all of it."

"And in the waking hours when you're not?"

Ambrose bit back a smile. "I'm thinking of you."

"Never knew you to be the corny sort."

"Alas, the deep, dark dungeons have changed me."

Eli ran a thumb under his jawline and kissed him, silently begging the dream to allow him a few more minutes of corniness. "The dungeons haven't made you less handsome."

"What a relief," Ambrose said, his dry tone hitching at each of Eli's traveling kisses. "You see, I've been trying to seduce the guards to break free, and it simply hasn't been working."

"It would work on me." Eli circled his arms around Ambrose's waist. "Wanna practice?"

Their lips met again, deep and earnest and pleading—then Ambrose smiled through the kiss, his breath brushing against Eli's.

"I'd love nothing more."

RULE 24:

DEEPEN YOUR RESEARCH

Ambrose

AMBROSE SPENT his waking time brewing and his dreaming time being far more social than he had ever been in his previous life.

"We do miss you," Sherry said, adding sugar to her tea. They sat in her kitchen in this particular dream. Buttery light streamed through the window, and a fresh pie sat on the sill. As far as illusions went, Ambrose thought, dreams allowed for particularly good ones. He could hear the murmur of morning passersby out on the street, and the chair cushion under him crinkled just as he remembered it.

It was a shame Aphos wanted their illusions in real life; a dreaming illusion potion would've shaved weeks off his work.

"We all miss you." Sherry reached over the table to squeeze his hand. "I've been inviting the children—Dawn and Eli," she corrected herself, "but it's not quite the same without you."

"I'm a terrible tea guest," Ambrose said. "You always say I never talk enough."

Sherry's eyes twinkled. "But you always mean what you say."

The walls of the kitchen briefly warped. The dream was slowly fading, and their teatime together was coming to an end.

Sherry stood and cleared their plates—a habit she clearly couldn't shake, even when sleeping. "I wish I had more updates for you, but Banneker's still working on the forged invitation. You'll tell us when you have any news on your end?"

Ambrose hesitated. Eli had asked him a similar question, and in truth, he still didn't know how to respond.

"I'll tell you when I have something," he finally said. "Something conclusive."

But thus far, Tavi's journals were anything but.

Once he began to look at the patterns of her doodles—to analyze what leaves were inked, which flower petals were filled in—much of her code became easy to unlock. She had indeed placed specific doodles on specific lines, to mark what letter to pluck from her otherwise nonsensical recipes. Once he had the letters properly assembled, they formed notes, certainly—but ones entirely unrelated to potions.

Right, down steps, 2 lefts, down tunnel was extracted from a fake note about alchemical bonds.

Dragon plasma was hidden deep in a nonsense recipe for mint flavoring.

And, most strangely, *get him out* came from an anti-headache recipe, followed by a list of nearby villages and half-formed thoughts on how to erode chains.

Ambrose had checked that last note over and over, ensuring he had decoded it correctly. It wasn't *get out*, but *get him out* specifically. And that list of villages that went along with it—they were all far from Aphos, yes, but dangerously remote, nestled in heavy woods filled with beasts.

Tavi's other clues weren't much clearer. Her list of directions never stated where they went, and the mention of dragon plasma befuddled him, particularly after Eli's response about the lack of dragons in the area. Plasma in useful, magically relevant quantities only came from large dragons—frightfully large dragons—and he had never seen anything of the sort anywhere near the Scar.

A fact he was usually quite thankful for.

Every day, he flipped further through the notes, scouring for more codes to crack—but at some point, Tavi must have shifted to a different code, cutting his knowledge short.

"Nat," he called, "did Tavi ever repeat anything strange?"

"What?" She turned, her hand halfway to the bronze cat on the lucky shelf. "Oh—no, not really. Didn't talk a whole lot. Just wrote and drew a bunch."

"Helpful," Ambrose muttered. He'd just have to keep working away with the code he had. "Do you mind swapping out the potions on display?"

"After I pet the cat."

"Naturally."

Nat pretended to tap the illusory statue on the head, then swapped out the faded fake potions for ones she had brewed herself: fizzy bottles that gave off a pleasant scent and were vibrant enough for an untrained eye to assume they did something magical. Once the bottles were swapped and cleaned, she hopped onto the stool next to Ambrose and pulled out her book.

"Okay," she said authoritatively. "You get a sign, and I get a question."

This was a growing habit of hers—constantly making new deals in order to pester Ambrose with questions about his life outside of Aphos. He didn't have the heart to tell her he'd answer the questions without such a deal. She seemed to be having too much fun with them.

"Ah, I get a sign," he mused. "What shall you be showing me today?"

She placed a flat hand near her lips, then swept it down and out. "Thank you."

He repeated the sign back. She waved. "No, a *flat* hand. Yeah, there you go. Wait..." She checked the book. "Yeah. That's it."

"A masterful lesson indeed."

"Mm-hm." She slapped the book shut. "My turn. I get a question."

"I am quaking in my robes."

She wiggled on her stool. "Do other people help you brew stuff back on Rosalind Street?"

"Rosemond Street," Ambrose corrected. "And no. Eli will sometimes keep me company, however."

"Eli?"

"My boyfriend."

Nat gasped. "You have a *boyfriend*?"

Ambrose stifled a laugh; a year ago, past Ambrose would have been just as shocked. "I do."

The questions came rapid-fire after that.

"What's he look like?" she asked. "What does he do? Does he make magic items, too?"

Ambrose held up a hand. "I thought I brought you on to answer questions, not ask them."

Nat groaned and spun around in her stool—recently greased, so it made not a sound. "You're so boring."

"It's quite easy to be boring when you're not allowed to leave the room."

Nat made a face. "No, I'm pretty sure you're just boring."

As she continued spinning, a spark from their conversation buried into his thoughts. He paused, staring into the distance to mentally walk back through his words, to sort out what was in them.

Ah, wait—leaving the room.

He flipped back to Tavi's decoded notes. She had directions listed here, along with ingredients not available in the workroom and references to a mysterious man and chains. If she never left the workroom to even go to the markets, how had she come across her information?

"If a boring man may deign to ask one question?" he asked Nat loftily. She stopped spinning, which he took as a yes. "Did Octavia leave the room for anything other than demonstrations?"

"No, how could she?" Nat said. "She always had guards."

He suspected as much. But for a talented potioneer, there were other ways...

A Captured Cauldron 221

"And what did her potions look like, toward the end?" he asked. "You mentioned they smelled terrible."

"I mean, most of them did. But the last ones she made weren't too bad. They were green with gold swirls."

"And do you recall what they smelled like?"

"Kinda..." She scrunched her nose. "What's that thing you put on lamb? Madam Mila eats it all the time."

"Mint," Ambrose answered without thinking. Green and gold, with the smell of mint. He knew precisely what that potion was—an astral projection brew, most certainly strong enough for Tavi to project herself out of the workroom and wherever she wanted.

Tavi was a madwoman.

"What's that face?" Nat asked.

Ambrose roused himself from his thoughts. "What?"

"Your face. It's your thinking face, but worse."

Ambrose shot her a look. "I do not have a thinking face."

"Then what are you not-thinking about?"

He hesitated, just as he had with Eli's questions. Astral projection was risky—and it wasn't just his life in the balance now; it was hers, too. Best not to broach the subject before it was necessary, nor expose her to damning information just yet. After all, he hadn't even told her about the magic dreams.

"I'm thinking about your next potion lesson," he lied.

Nat gestured at him. "See? Boring!"

He rolled his eyes and signed a flat *Thank you.*

As Nat laughed at him and made one more rotation on the stool, someone knocked pitifully on the door.

"Mr. Beake," the archivist started, "I'm here to—"

Cassius pushed the door open for the archivist. "Gods, man, I don't have all day. Copy the notes and let's be off."

Ambrose quickly flipped his notes to his fake brewing pages and stepped aside for the gnome to shuffle in. "Pages fifty-seven to sixty are new and complete."

"Thank you, thank you." The gnome slid on his gloves and carefully turned each page, waving a wand to copy the text onto fresh sheets of paper. While he worked, Cassius folded his arms and wandered about the workroom, glaring at everything he saw.

Nat sat very still, not daring to look at him. His gaze swept right over her—and landed on Tavi's journals.

"What are you doing with these?" he asked. "You've far surpassed her progress."

He plucked one from the table, handling it like a dirty rag. Ambrose stiffened and sorted carefully through his words. He wasn't done with them yet—best to reaffirm Cassius' opinion that they had little value.

"Merely checking them for anything I might have missed," he responded. "Octavia was prolific in trying new recipes, even if none succeeded. Potioneers often come across half the right answer, only to stumble across the second half much later." He turned to the bottles, rearranging them to look busy. "Unfortunately, I cannot yet confirm Tavi had any half-right answers."

Cassius grunted and tossed the notebook back on the table—but his gaze lingered on them.

"You have three weeks left," he said, then turned to the archivist and pointed to the notebooks. "Take that woman's journals with you as well. Copy them and review them again."

Ambrose's hands went cold as the archivist gathered the books into his gray satchel. "No—" he started out of instinct.

Cassius' eyes narrowed at him.

"No doubt you'll find little of value," he finished. "Like I did."

Cassius gave him a sharp smile. "If there are any half-right answers in there, we'll help you find them."

Ambrose could do nothing but glare at the door as they left. He highly doubted that archivist was going to crack Tavi's code—but he'd be damned if Aphos uncovered the meaning of the secret notes before he did. Whatever she had discovered had not only been worth writing for later reference but had also been coded. It had been price-less, at least to her.

It had to be a way out—or at least, a way to help them escape. Help them *both* escape.

He flipped to a new page in his journal. Yes, Tavi was a madwoman for astral projecting her way through a mazelike criminal hideout.

And he was going to follow in her footsteps.

RULE 25:

SIFT WELL

Dawn

"A NYTHING IN THAT CABINET?"

"No, nothing here. You?"

"Nah." Rory pushed a drawer closed, the wood creaking under the weight of a dozen thick file folders. "Damn *Post*. You'd think they'd actually be good at archiving after how many years in the business..."

Dawn peered into the cabinet in front of her—nothing but old inkwells and a coat—and shut the door. The sound echoed in the office of the *Scarrish Post*, the cluttered maze of desks devoid of writers for the evening. To her relief, no one was staying late tonight, chugging coffee and writing furiously toward a harsh deadline. The empty silence allowed them to sneak about Rory's workplace at their leisure, doing the only thing they could to help the mission: search for records of an old Aphosian invitation.

It had been Rory's idea. If any of her predecessors on the magical crime beat had managed to secure evidence of Madam Mila's past events, they may have done their due diligence and archived an invitation—something Banneker could mimic for his own work.

Across the room, Rory checked another drawer, grimaced, and shoved it closed with her hip. "If we weren't doing this on the sly, I'd have a word with our archivist about this. I could have sworn they'd documented one before."

She wandered over to Dawn, her gaze scanning the room—when she caught sight of a desk in the corner, she lit up. "You know, I might've grabbed it ages ago for my research. Mind checking my desk for me? It'd be in the drawer on the left."

Dawn nearly agreed—then saw an opportunity and wrinkled her nose in disdain. "Another search? Hm, gonna have to pay a toll for that."

Rory raised her eyebrows. "A toll?"

Dawn leaned forward and tapped her cheek. Rory laughed, cupped Dawn's face, and planted a kiss on her lips.

"Toll paid?" she murmured.

Not in the slightest, Dawn wanted to say, but the office wasn't going to stay empty forever.

"For now," she said. "Toll might go up later. You never know."

Rory winked. "I'll take my chances."

They parted once more, Rory to a cabinet, Dawn to the desk—but to her dismay, she could barely see the drawer Rory had mentioned. Piles of papers and journals spilled over the edge of the table, with an assortment of trinkets struggling to hold them in place. Half-dead plants, empty coffee mugs, and bronze desk puzzles had formed ranks to keep the avalanche of debris from falling. Atop the highest stack, a glass sphere filled with an ever-crashing wave presided over the inky, sparkling mess.

Dawn winced at the desk disaster but couldn't bring herself to judge it—the area behind her own front counter didn't look much better most days.

She carefully swapped the glass sphere for a little round planter, then held up the glass. It had a delightful heft to it, and the magical wave within shifted with the angle of her palm. "Where'd you get this from?"

Rory glanced over her shoulder. "Oh, that? That's from my dad.

Gave it to me before I moved back to the Scar. Can't say the Deepriver is ever that clear or pretty, but it's a nice reminder of home."

Dawn frowned. "When did you live in the Scar?"

Rory buried herself halfway into a cabinet. "Just a few years when I was little," she called back, her voice bouncing around the wood panels. "Hardly remember any of it, to be honest."

Dawn set the sphere down and excavated the drawer, finding a hefty stack of papers organized by date. She flipped through what she could, searching for a magically copied invitation or—gods willing—an original.

But she found nothing—just lists of arrests, peacekeeper reports, and the odd grocery list here and there. When she called out as much, Rory cursed. "If my desk doesn't have it..."

"I can keep looking," Dawn offered. Dusty folders spilled out of the cabinet Rory was buried in.

"Son of a wood-eating dragon—" she started, then briefly pulled her head out. "Sounds good!"

Dawn checked the other drawers in as methodical of a fashion as she could manage, given the mess. The stacks all contained faded copies of past articles, many related to the Deadleaves and Harfoots, but mostly about Aphos: inner wars in the syndicate, new devices coming out of their underground markets...

After scanning a dozen or so articles, they all began to melt together. She rubbed her eyes and flipped through them more quickly, and it was only through her speed that she noticed a new pattern: not just Aphos' name, but the appearance of Madam Mila, head of the syndicate. The sketches of her had been dashed out quickly to satisfy a deadline but remained elegant in what they had achieved. Dark hair swept behind her shoulders, sharp, unwavering eyes, aging gracefully as the years went on... She looked familiar, but Dawn couldn't place it.

Eventually, her search caught up to the more recent past: handwritten notes from this year's Potion Con. She stopped and read through them. Rory's notes on the fluff piece about bodyguards had quickly devolved into scribbles about Ambrose's kidnapping:

the vanishing, the ensuing chaos, the ring and the cloth in the tunnel...

She tried to read further, but a ripped scrap of paper had been taped over the original notes, blocking her view. Though torn from something else, she could still see the *Scarrish Post* letterhead and the name F.C. Grayson, Editor in Chief across the top, just above the scrawled message:

> *Story not worth it. Stop and move on to the Jameson arrest, then come back once the peacekeeper's dug up the potioneer—or once Aphos has dumped him back into his shop.*

Dawn stared at the note, a cold unease growing in the pit of her stomach. That wasn't right—Rory was doing all this for the story. She had been working on it this whole time, hadn't she?

She checked under the paper and around the other piles, searching for another note from the editor. Something telling her to pick the story back up, to follow the trail again—

Rory pushed up against the cabinet with her whole body to force the door closed. "I'm not getting anything here. Any luck on your end?"

Dawn fought against her unease. The editor's note was weeks old —and even if Rory had been told to drop the story, did it matter? She had volunteered to help. Put herself at risk multiple times at the tavern, the stakeout...

Of course Rory wasn't going to drop it just because her editor told her to. That wasn't who she was.

"Nothing." She slid the papers back into place. "I'll tell Banneker we couldn't find anything useful. He'll make something work."

"Sorry, Banneker." Rory meandered over and leaned against the desk. "You...okay?"

"Yeah." Dawn shook herself out of her thoughts. "Yeah, fine. You?"

Rory's smile tilted upward. "Fine. So, did that toll go up?"

"Hm." Dawn mimicked her posture. "I think it did."

"Oh, whatever shall I do?"

She pulled Dawn against her and ducked down for another kiss, far deeper than the last one. Several breaths and two traveling hands later, Rory had her pinned against the side of the desk, her fingers skirting just under the hem of Dawn's tunic.

Dawn reluctantly recalled where she was and managed to pull away.

"We're at work," she blurted out. "Literally, we're at your work."

That fact did nothing to dim the glint in Rory's eye. She gave a hum and pushed a strand of hair out of her face. "There's a decent wine bar around the corner that should still be open," she murmured. "Wanna go check it out?"

The back of Dawn's mind was still latched onto the editor's note that lay not two feet behind her—but a good bottle of wine would settle her thoughts.

And a few more kisses of the desk-pinning variety wouldn't hurt, either.

"Only if it's better than that Aphosian stuff," she said. Rory took her hand and intertwined their fingers.

"Oh, it wasn't so bad." She tilted her head. "I recall that wine making us both excellent dancers."

Dawn allowed herself a grin and pushed all other thoughts out of her head. "Then let's see where this wine will lead us tonight."

RULE 26:

MAKE A BACK-UP PLAN

Eli

"Okay, Tom, you go over here." Eli pointed. "No, not that way, *that* way. Toward the cannon."

Tom zoomed deeper into the maze that was Banneker's shop, then paused.

"Good," he said. "Now, I'm gonna sneak up on you, and if you hear any sound, you have to turn around and wave your arms."

Tom waved her fork arms in excitement.

"Yes, exactly like that." Eli gave her a double thumbs-up, then shooed her along. "Now go, and I'll come find you after I count to ten. Ten, nine, eight..."

Tom wheeled off into the artificer's abyss. Technically, Banneker's shop was open to customers, but given the lack of adventurers in town to purchase cannons and nets and other violent sundries, the slow day gave Eli and Tom the run of the place. Every now and then, Banneker would pop his head out of the workroom, remarking on a horoscope he had read or asking about ink preferences for the forged invitation—but at the moment, he hummed and clattered away in the back room.

Leaving Eli to do a little work of his own.

He waited a few extra seconds, then tiptoed in Tom's general direction, mentally running through all the advice his adventuring party had given him. Stick close to walls and heavy objects. Breathe through your mouth. Remain steady and *frustratingly* silent and *painfully* slow—

"I've got it!" Sherry burst in through the front door. Eli stumbled and banged his knee against a defunct whirligig.

Just above the crate ahead of him, Tom's hands popped up and waved.

"Sherry!" Eli tried to admonish her, but it didn't stick—she had already made a beeline for Banneker's workroom, brandishing a silky waistcoat.

"I didn't get rid of this old thing after all," she said proudly. Eli followed her into the room, where she laid out the waistcoat alongside a pile of clothing. "This should be about your size, Eli. Granted, it's an older pattern, but it should do the trick."

The clothing she had gathered here for the next venture couldn't have been more different from the bristly furs and tough leathers of their first rescue attempt. Everything here either shone, sparkled, or begged to be touched. Eli carefully picked through gold-embroidered waistcoats, silky tunics, a dainty half-cape...

All in service of them blending in with Aphos' inner circle.

"I'll stitch in what armor I can," Sherry reassured him. "I've got a few pieces thin enough to fit under the cape, at least. You won't go in defenseless, I'll tell you that."

"Gotta make sure they can get into Aphos first," Banneker called from across the workroom and held up two sheets of paper. Ink stained his fingers and arms, but he didn't seem to care. "Ready to test these out?"

One by one, Rosemond Street trickled into the room—Grim first, then Dawn, Viola, and Xavion. While Banneker laid out his test invitations, Eli huddled with Dawn nearby. His nerves about the rescue were bubbling up again, but if he began pacing one more time, Sherry was going to chain him to a chair—so instead of walking, he distracted himself with his favorite topic of the month:

Dawn's love life.

"You"—he poked her arm—"were going to tell me about how that wine date went days ago."

Dawn leaned back against the table. "I told you we didn't find anything at the newspaper office—"

"I know that. What I don't know is anything about the wine bar you hit up after."

He expected her to gush, for the floodgates of gossip to open and distract him—but instead, she hesitated.

"It was great," she said. "The atmosphere was lovely, and Rory knows her wines."

"Oh, is that what they're calling it these days?"

Dawn snorted and slapped his arm. "Oh my *gods*."

He laughed along with her, but the details she had provided were far too lean for his liking. That was all right—perhaps the details were too saucy to bring up in merchant company.

"We'll go to the café this week and chat about it," he said. "Ames'll want an update, too."

Dawn shot him a look. "Wait, you told him about Rory?"

"Of course I told him." He grinned. "*You* were depriving him of this news. And you'll be thrilled to know he's absolutely devastated to be missing out on all the teasing."

Dawn groaned and covered her face. "I was trying not to make him feel worse than he already does."

He tugged her hands back down. "Worse? He demanded every detail. Held me at knifepoint about it. Summoned a knife from the dreamscape and everything. I don't know how he did it—"

Xavion cleared their throat from the corner, cutting into Dawn's laughter.

"If anyone still cares, I have the testing solution ready," they drawled. "Please utilize it now so I can go back to the interminable myriad of high-level potions our dear Amby insists on stocking."

They all gathered together as Banneker took the solution and set it beside his creations: a set of forged invitations, some written in gibberish, others blank, and yet more written in an approximation of an invitation.

"I tried to make invitations that would magically imitate what the guards expect to see," he explained. "As long as it's not the first invitation they've seen that day, they should pass muster and get you inside."

"As long as the invite passes their illusion test." Viola took the spray bottle from Xavion. "May I?"

Xavion nodded. "To be clear, I don't know Aphos' exact formula, but this is a rather basic solution to indicate whether an illusion is present. One spray should do it."

Viola carefully sprayed each invitation with a light mist. They all waited, watching for any change in the text, any curl in the paper...

One by one, each invitation turned black at the edges, even the blank one. Banneker cursed under his breath.

"Back to the drawing board," he muttered, then looked at Grim. "How much time we got left?"

"Two weeks."

Banneker let out a louder curse; Dawn tucked her arms against herself with a queasy expression. Forcing himself to stay in place, Eli toyed with his earring, his nerves a reflection of the curled and broken invitations.

But he refused to lose hope so close to the rescue.

"We'll come up with a back-up plan," he said, trying to cut into the silence with confidence. "If the invites don't work, we'll just pivot."

"You're right." Grim ran a finger along the edge of the closest invitation; it shattered into black dust. "If we can't get in this way, we're going to need to sneak in again."

Eli rubbed his knee, which still ached from his failed stealth practice earlier. Pivoting no longer sounded like a good idea—but Grim wasn't wrong, either. Without a working invitation, disguises would be useless, brute force even more so.

But stealth was how he had failed Ambrose the first time.

Tom tugged on his pant leg; he picked her up and hugged her close, hoping the gesture would help glue his insides back together.

"We'll figure it out," he said, though he wasn't sure whether he was reassuring the room or himself. "We promised him."

RULE 27:

UNCORK

Ambrose

THOUGH TIME HAD no real meaning in his windowless workshop, Ambrose prided himself on his precise bedtime.

It was one of the only ways to ground himself to some sort of routine while in captivity—he lived by his mealtimes and the ticks of his pocket watch. Unless he had to spend extra time brewing something for Cassius' check-ins, he made sure he was in bed at the same time every evening, with a watery cup of tea and a desperate wish for a nice book to read...

Until his loved ones started visiting in his dreams.

Now, all thought of leisurely reading in bed had vanished, and he had to fight not to burrow under the covers right after dinner. The sooner he went to sleep, the sooner he could see Rosemond Street—and tonight, he thought of nothing but them. He barely held out an hour after dinner, then eagerly climbed into bed, wondering who he'd see and what sort of setting they'd think up. His dream surroundings had become increasingly fantastical every night—though there was a limit to what the circlet's magic could achieve. Banneker had tried to set his dreamscape in the clouds once, which only held for half an hour. Viola had dared to summon an enormous cake to sit on, with fondant chairs and teacups filled with buttercream.

(Delicious, until it all melted away a minute later.)

But his dream tonight was, at a glance, more realistic. He stood on the walkway in front of Widdershins' Books. Whoever created the dream had captured the details of his favorite bookshop perfectly: the stained-glass flowers adorning the window, the strong whiff of coffee and paper flowing in from the chipped doorway.

As Ambrose took a deep inhale of the intoxicating scent, Eli stepped out of the shop, a bouquet of flowers in his hand.

"Hoped you would like it." He grinned and leaned against the doorframe. "Happy anniversary."

The bookshop air in Ambrose's lungs went stale. "Anniversary?"

While his bedtime had once been precise, his recollection of the actual days was hazy at best, limited to the series of rough tally marks he maintained at the top of his notebook. Had their one-year anniversary already arrived? His heart twisted. Gods, he'd had ideas for the event and everything. He was going to close the shop for the day, wake Eli with pastries and coffee from Viola's—then they were going to picnic in the fields, attend a show, make out somewhere they weren't supposed to...

And now he had nothing to offer. He couldn't even summon a gift into his hands, like Eli had done.

"I'm sorry," he croaked. "I didn't mean to forget. I can't—I wish I could..."

While he choked on his words, Eli approached with his bouquet —a bright, stunning array filled with lavender and sunflowers.

"It's all right," he said, the circlet across his forehead as beautiful as the flowers he held out. "I'm just glad I get to see you today. We'll plan something better for when you're back—"

Ambrose cut off his words with the only thing he could give: a kiss, pressed like a rose petal against Eli's lips, while his fingers delicately traced his cheekbones. He tried to keep the gesture light, happy, something anniversary-worthy—but as soon as Eli pulled on his waist, his despair pushed him forward until he had one hand tangled in Eli's hair and the other grabbing fistfuls of his shirt.

"I love you," he managed between kisses. "You deserve so much more than this."

Eli's laugh vibrated against his neck. "Ames, I don't even deserve *you*."

Eventually, Ambrose recalled that Eli hadn't summoned an entire illusory bookstore only to be pinned against its outer wall, and with rumpled flowers in hand, they meandered into the shop together. Out of instinct, their path took the shape of a normal bookstore date —starting at the new releases first, then moving to the romance novels on the maroon shelves deeper in. While the front of the shop appeared normal, Eli had taken a few fantastical liberties with the dreamscape in the back. The flowers draped over the romance shelves looked real, quietly furling and unfurling in a velvety, perfumed rhythm as they walked past. Next to the shelves, the shop had been expanded to accommodate a cluster of comfortable furni-ture: deep couches and cushioned armchairs, each paired with steaming cups of tea.

An excellent idea for real life, Ambrose thought, if Widdershins ever scrounged up the coin to renovate.

When they eventually settled on the couch together, he hoped they could continue their pretend date for a while—but then the walls flickered, and the flowers stuttered in their movement.

He couldn't wait any longer. He had to ask about the rescue.

"How are the preparations going?" he asked, trying to keep his tone even. As he was falling asleep that night, notes on astral projec-tion spinning in his head, he had desperately hoped the Rosemond Street team was making strides of their own. The very idea of projecting his way through the tunnels of Aphos was so risky, he still hadn't dared utter a word of it to Nat. But if Eli, Dawn, and the others had made progress, perhaps he wouldn't need to try it at all. He could just sit back, brew more fake potions, find a few more ways to annoy Cassius before his inevitable departure...

But when Eli spoke next, his voice was tight.

"Good," he said. "Banneker is...still trying to figure out how to get Grim and me into the demonstration. But he's close."

Ambrose frowned. That was Eli's lying tone—the overconfidence, the slightly higher pitch. "How close?" he pressed.

Eli shifted against the cushions. "He's still trying to come up with a foolproof invitation to get us in. No luck so far."

"And if he can't?"

Eli cleared his throat. "We'll sneak in like last time."

Ambrose's chest tightened. Sneaking into this demonstration, through Cassius' beloved security, past all of Madam Mila's guests... He didn't dare try to calculate the chances of success. It would only make him want to hurl into a cauldron again.

Eli must have read the thoughts on his face, for he took Ambrose's hand in both of his. "I know it sounds dangerous, but however we get in, it'll work this time. We're not letting you go, I promise you."

"I know," Ambrose said quickly. "I know you'll do everything you can. I just..."

He swallowed. There was no getting around it now—if Eli was going to take on the risk of the rescue, he would have to take on a risk of his own.

"I'm going to find something that can help," he said. "You won't be alone in this."

Eli frowned. "Is it the dragon plasma Tavi wrote about?"

"I can't be sure." Ambrose took a breath. "But whatever it is, I'll find it for us."

The bookshelves began to melt, then stabilized once more. Eli leaned in and kissed him, the gesture tainted with desperation.

"No more rescue talk," he murmured. "Not much time left. Can't have your last thoughts be about the rescue—you won't sleep well."

He ran one hand through Ambrose's hair, the other dipping down to his waist. Ambrose closed his eyes, drinking in the movements.

"What should I think about, then?" he mumbled back, a smile skating across his mouth. Eli captured it with his, then slowly pushed him down into the couch cushions. Already, he had succeeded in his mission—between the weight of his body and the soft kisses trailing down his neck, Ambrose couldn't form a single coherent thought about the rescue, other than what he could do to this man after it was done.

But that didn't stop Eli from pressing a thoughtful hum to the base of his throat, one that sent vibrations down his veins and through his whole body.

"Nothing," Eli finally said, slipping his hand under Ambrose's shirt. "You think too much. I want you to relax and think of nothing at all."

Ambrose cupped his cheek, his thumb stroking his jawline. "As if I could focus on anything but you right now."

Eli gently tugged on his hand and pressed a kiss to his palm, lingering on the heart line—the first place he had ever kissed Ambrose. "Focus on me, then."

Ambrose gladly sank into the cushions and obliged.

Despite Eli's attempts to quiet his mind, Ambrose tossed and turned the latter half of the night, his rest shattered by growing nerves. Nerves about using the astral projection potion, certainly. About following Tavi's instructions, venturing into guarded territory, to find a man or an ingredient or who knew what.

But nerves of a different kind intertwined with those thoughts. To make the complex potion, he required the help of his assistant—and he had a cold, sinking feeling that his assistant wasn't going to like his reckless plan.

So, when Nat came in with her tray of food, his anxiety barely let him last a second.

"Sorry I'm late," Nat said, closing the door with her hip. "Fran wasn't cleaning the stupid bowls fast enough and managed to blame it on me, so I had to—"

The words flooded out of Ambrose all at once.

"I'm afraid I have to go." He held up his projection notes. "I have to go find whatever Tavi found."

Nat paused in confusion, then set down the tray. "Mr. Ambrose, did you sleep last night?"

"Yes. I mean, no. I mean—sort of." He pinched the bridge of his nose, took a breath, then grabbed the coffee from the tray and took a grounding sip. "The potion you described to me the other day, with the green and gold swirls."

"And the mint."

"And the mint," he said. "I recognize it. Tavi was making an astral projection brew. I've decided to make one myself and investigate Tavi's directions. To...find whatever it was she found."

Her gaze immediately sharpened into a fine point. "You can't. That's stupid."

Ah, the blunt feedback he had come to enjoy from her. He quickly summoned all the counterpoints he had drummed up in the early hours—there had to be a way to get her on board with this. She had agreed to other stupid plans, hadn't she?

"I realize it's risky," he said, "but if I find something useful, it could help with the rescue—"

"You'll get caught!"

"*And*," he soldiered on, "just think about how foolish Cassius will look. He'll think I'm stuck here, when in reality I'll be out exploring his domain, discovering whatever it is he's trying to hide." He was particularly proud of that argument. It had worked in the past, after all. "Think of it like a prank, just a rather large one—"

To his shock, Nat's face crumpled.

"No!" Her voice rattled the tray on the table. "It's not a prank! It's a stupid idea, and you'll get killed and you'll leave me here just like she did!"

She stood before him, fists clenched, tears rolling silently down her face. Any remaining words in Ambrose's argument died in his throat.

"What—what do you mean?" he asked quietly. He took a step forward; she flinched.

"Don't."

He silently gestured to the table. She wiped her face with her threadbare sleeve and slumped into one of the chairs, her breath still hitching with emotion. Ambrose carefully took the seat across from her, every movement weighed down by his heart sinking to his feet.

He had misjudged this. He had terribly misjudged this.

"Nat..." He took the cream roll on the tray, cut it in half, and set the larger portion in front of her. "Will you tell me what happened?"

She stared at the roll and folded her arms, determined not to meet his gaze. "What happened when?"

When Tavi had gotten captured, he wanted to say. But there was far more to her tears than that. "Whatever you want to tell me," he said, then waited patiently. Words like these didn't come easily.

He would know. He had kept them bottled up his whole life.

After what felt like an hour, she finally took the cream roll and began picking it apart, sniffing back tears. "You asked about my family," she mumbled. "I don't have any."

Another shaky breath, another few crumbs on the table. Ambrose waited.

"Dad left years ago. Business outside the Scar. Didn't come back. Happens sometimes," she said, trying to shrug off the pain apparent on her face. "Happened to most of the other servants."

Ambrose nodded. Nat wiped her face again.

"Mom went foraging in one of the sinkholes a year later. Went missing. It's how I lost my..." She gestured with a shaky hand to the scars over her ear. "Tried to find her and fell down in the caves. Hit some rocks real hard. Woke up dizzy and couldn't hear anything from that side."

She shook her head. The roll was mostly gone now, nothing but torn pastry and vanilla cream. "Then I met Tavi, and she said she was gonna escape. That she could bring me with her."

Ambrose's heart was in pieces on the floor.

"And she was caught," he said quietly. Caught going down—wherever Tavi's decoded notes were directing him.

"Yeah," she mumbled, her voice thick and empty. "She got caught. And if you try to do whatever she did, you'll get caught, too, and I'll

—" She gestured to the door, her gaze still fixed on the table. "I'll be stuck here without...without anyone."

The words bounced inside Ambrose's chest, striking old wounds. Some buried, some scarred, some as fresh as when they were first cut.

He steeled himself and cut the sandwich on the tray. "I know what that feeling is like."

She snorted. "No, you don't. You have people trying to rescue you right now."

"I have them, certainly. But before that..." He placed half the sandwich before her, along with a glass of water. "I don't know where my parents are. Haven't since I was eight."

She finally lifted her gaze to his face, eyes wide. "Really?"

"Really."

"But..." She reached for the sandwich—but instead of disassembling it, she nibbled on the corner. "I thought...I don't know, I thought you worked in the family business or something. Or had rich parents that hired teachers for all that potion stuff."

Ambrose gave her a ghost of a smile. "Indeed?"

"Yeah. The kinds of parents with your certificates on the walls. Bragging about you at parties and stuff."

The words simmered bittersweet in his ears. When he thought of proud, doting people, he didn't think of his parents. He thought of Rosemond Street.

"That is a nice thought," he said. "But I'm afraid that isn't the case. I was"—he should just say it, say the spiky, sludgy word—"I was abandoned when I was young. I was looked after by others, whom for all intents and purposes, I'll call my family. But my true parents are decidedly not bragging about me at parties." He gave her his half of the sandwich. "However...I couldn't have been abandoned on a better street. You're going to love everyone on it. I promise you that."

"Yeah?" Nat said quietly.

"Yes," he said. "I don't make empty promises. I must do everything I can to help with the rescue, including following what Tavi did. But no matter what I find or what happens, I *will* be getting you out of here, all right?"

She had no argument this time—just fresh tears and a wobbly smile, both of which she tried to wipe away. "And your friends will let me?" she said in a small voice, as if asking would sour the answer. "Join the street, I mean?"

"Let you? Once they meet you, they'll be begging to dote on you." He returned her smile. "You'll get to meet Eli and Dawn, and have tea with Sherry and read horoscopes with Banneker—"

Nat gave a weak half laugh through her tears.

"I mean it," he said. "Would you like to meet them?"

She nodded.

"Good." He stood up and gestured to the sandwich. "Now go on and eat up. Astral projection potions are no easy feat, and I will require the valiant help of my assistant so that it doesn't singe all my hair off."

A lightness settled over his shoulders as she took a large bite, mischief glimmering once more in her eyes. "What if I want it to singe all your hair off?"

"Hm." He tapped his chin and pointed to her stash of food in the corner. "I do get rather hungry when brewing. Perhaps I'll take a look at the candy left in your stores—"

"You wouldn't."

He hummed and wandered closer to the stash. "Oh—is that taffy I see? Dawn loves taffy. I should try a piece on her behalf—"

"Nuh-uh!" Nat chewed faster through her sandwich. "I'll help, I'll help!"

Ambrose laughed. "Eat up first," he said. "After all, you only have two weeks left to enjoy the magic that is Aphosian cuisine."

RULE 28:
TEST THE HYPOTHESIS

Dawn

DAYS LATER, once Dawn could afford to close her shop for a long lunch, she found herself attending the Scar's most serious picnic.

"I really don't think we need to sneak through the entrances this time." Eli knelt down on the scratchy picnic blanket beside her and Rory. The Oasis lay paces beyond them, its magic shield humming a silent tune. "Let's find a way to turn off the sinkhole's shield, sneak in once it's down, then grab Ames and Nat before Aphos can react."

"Nat," Dawn repeated, her eyes on the sinkhole. "How in the hells did he pick up another person for us to rescue?" She stabbed her fruit salad with her fork. Sherry had packed them all the accoutrements for a nice picnic—fruit, cheese, homemade cookies—but they had barely touched any of it.

Well, except for the cookies. Half of those were already gone.

"He wouldn't give me the details." Eli topped off Rory's glass of sparkling fernberry juice. "Only that she needed to escape with him."

Dawn let out a small *hmph* and nibbled on a cantaloupe square. Ambrose had been adamant when he had broached the subject with her, too. He hadn't exactly explained Nat's full story, but had made it clear in his most serious, most Ambrose-y tone: they were rescuing her, too, or else he'd go back in for her.

"Man's not afraid of a challenge." Rory clinked her glass against Dawn's. "You're up for testing the shield, right? You brought your box and everything."

She leaned against Dawn's shoulder, her proximity far more reassuring than her words. Dawn was sorely tempted to stay at her side a little longer—but Eli's eyes widened at the mention of the box.

"What'd you bring?" he asked. Dawn reluctantly moved away to drag a leather case into the center of the picnic blanket. She threw off the clasp, and the soft, treated leather gave way to a neat row of wands, sparkling in a rainbow of colors.

"I've been thinking about the shield, too," she said. "I could run a test to see how sensitive it is, if we want. Did you bring the potions I asked for?"

Eli eagerly unclasped several vials of swirling turquoise from his belt. "Ready for invisibility round two," he said, then quickly looked at Rory. "I promise I won't try to sneak anywhere. I just wanna get close while we try out the wands. See how Aphos security reacts."

Rory evaluated the sinkhole, bit her lip, then popped the cork off one of the vials and poured it into the dregs of her juice. "We'll be fine as long as I don't have to drag you out of that hole myself."

Dawn drank the potion alongside her, not daring to move closer to the sinkhole until she couldn't see her own hands or toes. The magic gave a delightful tingle on the way down; she briefly wondered if that was part of Ambrose's original recipe, or if that was an element Xavion had added to the brew.

"Come on." She gathered up her wands once the tingle had evaporated from her hands—she needed her grip steady for this, after all. "I'm not gonna risk running the clock on these potions."

They took position close to the edge of the sinkhole; Rory toward one bush on the north side, Dawn and Eli toward shrubbery on the south side. Dawn tried to listen for Eli's footsteps and keep a careful distance behind him—

"Ow! That was my foot!"

"Sorry!" She reached out to steady his invisible form and poked him in the ribs instead.

"Oh my gods, just—just take my hand—"

"I can't see your hand!"

They eventually managed to duck behind the bushes in one piece, Dawn desperately hoping Rory didn't overhear any of that. While she rolled out the wands again and plucked the first and smallest one from its setting, Eli gave her a nudge—a thoughtful, intentional one this time.

"Hey," he said, keeping his voice soft. "You sure Rory's okay with being this close to the sinkhole?"

Dawn's movements slowed. She'd had the same thought when organizing the picnic, but when she'd brought it up with Rory, the journalist had insisted she attend.

"Yeah, she's cool with it," she said. "Why?"

"Nothing," Eli said quickly. "It's just—last time, she was afraid of getting caught by Aphos."

"She just wants to preserve her intel." Dawn weighed the wand in her hand. "And her safety. I mean, everything we're doing here is crazy, and she volunteered to—"

"No, I get it." Eli paused. "How do you think she came to know all that stuff, anyway? I mean, she knows everything from down there but says she can't go in herself."

Defensive spikes formed on her tongue in support of Rory; she forced them down.

"Research," she answered. "She's said it before, she's a journalist and she shadowed the other—"

"I know, I know." Eli took the second wand—Dawn watched it float from its setting and settle in midair. "Can't wait to read her story about the rescue once it comes out."

Her defensive air dissolved. The story—the one Rory's editor had told her not to write. The one she must have been writing anyway in defiance of her boss.

At least, that's what Dawn told herself.

She pushed aside her thoughts. "The story will be great."

Even so close to the sinkhole, it was still difficult to see the details in its depths. Unlike the rugged sinkhole she and Ambrose had ventured down last year, this one had been carved and trimmed, with delicate, cascading plants and colorful shrubs carefully planted in the crevices. Down at the center of the sinkhole, a round stone dais peered back up at them, and around it circled two indistinguishable figures. Guards, she assumed. Her grip tightened on the wand.

"Watch out for how they react," she whispered, then flicked the wand.

A tiny string of sparks shot toward the bubble-like shield. They skittered ineffectively along its surface, causing not so much as a flicker. The figures down below did nothing.

She nodded and tucked away the first wand. The lack of reaction made sense to her—that particular caliber of wand was meant to be the equivalent of a tiny bird landing on the shield. If it reacted to something as small as that, the guards' time would be thoroughly wasted checking nonexistent threats.

Eli flicked the second wand, Dawn the third. Each time, the sparks grew brighter, stronger, more magically intrusive—

On the fourth wand, the magic finally tangled. The shield wobbled and rippled against the sparks, red spirals fanning across its surface...then it vanished entirely.

"Great," Eli whispered. "Let's keep count, see how long it takes for the guards to react—"

"All right now, let's see what's goin' on."

A gnomish guard appeared directly in front of Eli and Dawn.

Dawn cursed, then clapped a hand over her mouth. Eli froze, his fingers tight around her arm. Neither dared move—the guard stood only paces away from them, chomping on a sandwich and looking around the fields.

"Anything?" someone shouted from deeper in the sinkhole. The guard gave one more look, eyes carefully sweeping the horizon, landing directly on the bushes...

He shrugged.

"Nothing!" he called back. "Turn the thing back on."

He disappeared in a blink. Eli released Dawn's arm, and the bushes rustled against his movement. Dawn scrambled to stick close to wherever he was headed. "Eli—"

"I just wanna get a closer look!"

She caught up to his invisible warmth and peered over the edge with him. The gnome reappeared at the bottom of the sinkhole, teleport device shining in his hand. Next to him, the other guard shifted a curtain of vines and pressed on a wall panel.

Eli pulled Dawn away just as the shield turned back on—iridescent, idle, and utterly immutable.

They slipped away from the sinkhole and clumsily regrouped with Rory at the picnic blanket, where Dawn fidgeted with her stack of rings. The gnome had only taken a second to appear; his surveillance five more seconds; the guards' reaction three seconds more.

Far too little time for them to sneak in and out that way, unless Eli wanted to risk rushing and falling to his death.

"We could make it work," he tried nonetheless. "If we set up a rope, then rappel down right when they turn off the shield—"

Dawn shivered. "What if the shield severs the rope?"

"And it's not just a matter of getting down." Rory draped an arm around Dawn's shoulders, the tips of her fingers rapidly becoming visible again. "You'll have to turn the shield back off in order to escape—and by that time, the whole place will be crawling with guards. You'll have too much on your hands as it is."

Dawn curled in against Rory. The idea that she could watch Ambrose's entire demonstration from above and not reach him burrowed deep into her gut. Beside her, Eli sighed and flopped heavily onto the blanket. Rory poked him with the toe of her boot.

"Look," she said, "you can still get to Ambrose through the normal entrances. I can map you a direct path and keep it as short as possible. If you go in while invisible again—"

"I *can't*," Eli blurted out, then passed a hand over his face. "You know how that worked out last time. I'll just—I'll just mess it up again."

Dawn's throat tightened. With that sort of mindset, no one was going to see Ambrose ever again. She reached forward and tugged his hand off his face.

"Listen," she said firmly. "When you snuck in the first time, you almost made it to him. You got all the way to the throne room. You *saw* him. You didn't know about the shield, and you almost had him—"

He glared at her. "Yeah, I *know*."

"I'm not saying that, I'm saying"—she huffed—"that this time, you just have to take a few more steps and you'll really have him." She squeezed his hand. "You can do this."

"Yeah," Eli mumbled. "That's what Oren always says about my stealth practice."

"And he'd be right," Rory added. She took his other hand and placed a small stack of cheese and crackers into his palm. "Those adventurers wouldn't be taking their time to teach you if they didn't think you were capable of learning."

"Exactly." Dawn took the top half of the crackers and ate them herself; the bitter grimace on Eli's face finally broke, and she smiled at him. "You can do everything else an adventurer can do. You can do this, too. For Ames and Nat."

"And Nat." Eli took the remaining crackers and stuffed them in his mouth. "I swear it, if he adds anyone else to my rescue list, I'm leaving him down there and he can do all the heroics himself."

RULE 29:

FIND THE SECRET INGREDIENT

Ambrose

AMBROSE STOOD over the cooling cauldron, carefully ladling swirls of green and gold into a bottle.

"Does this look familiar?" He turned to Nat behind him. Normally, she stood right next to him when he brewed, tracking his every move and asking questions. Today, she hunched paces behind him, arms folded.

"Yeah," she mumbled. "Looks exactly like hers."

Ambrose quietly reassured himself that it couldn't look *exactly* like Tavi's—his was textbook perfection, if he did say so himself—but he bottled it up without further comment. "I understand you're nervous," he pivoted, "so I took the liberty of brewing something for you as well."

He strode over to the cabinet, pushed aside the alphabetical array of vials, and pulled out a tiny bottle tucked in the shadows. Nat stiffened.

"You want me to astral project with you?"

"Not at all. This is an invisibility potion, enhanced with silence and anti-tracking components. I can't promise it tastes any good, but it's the strongest I could possibly brew it. If I don't come back—"

Her jaw tightened. "Don't say that."

He kept his voice firm. "If I don't come back, or if they catch me and send me away, use this and make your way directly to Rosemond Street. Ask for Sherry first at Plackart and Faulds Armory and tell her I sent you. Do you understand?"

Nat bit her lip.

"I need you to repeat it for me, please."

She sighed. "Sherry at Plackart and Faulds Armory on Rosemond Street."

"And if I do make it back?"

"I'll keep both eyes on you at the demonstration."

"Precisely." He smiled and handed over the bottle. "I'll see you soon."

He climbed into bed while Nat gathered up his dinner tray and left the room. As soon as she stepped into the hallway, she stumbled, letting the tray and plates clatter across the floor. The guard's silhouette in the window gave a startled jump.

"*Dammit*, girl," the guard hissed. "Pick that up!"

"Would go a lot faster if you *helped* me pick it up."

The guard grumbled and bent over. Ambrose took the green and gold bottle, still warm from the cauldron, and drank it in one gulp.

The brew immediately affirmed his decision to take it lying down. Nausea and vertigo struck immediately, his limbs too heavy and too light all at once. He screwed his eyes shut and kept them closed until the effects wore off—and when he opened his eyes, he was standing by the bed, staring down at his body. To anyone looking in, he appeared to be sleeping soundly.

It was a good start, at least.

He held up his hands and inspected his handiwork. Most projections were translucent to begin with, but he had tweaked the recipe to make himself barely there—so much so that anyone looking at his projected self might first assume he was a trick of the light.

"While I've got you," Nat chattered loudly outside, "I wanted to ask if we could stock anything different for lunches."

"Why me?" the guard grunted. "I don't talk to the kitchen folk."

"Don't talk to the—?" Nat sputtered. "Gary, you're dating the chef!"

"No, I'm not!"

"Dragon dung. Can't you just tell her to make something other than sandwiches?"

"But she *likes* sandwiches—"

Before either of them could launch into a diatribe on lunch meat, Ambrose took a deep breath and launched himself through the wall.

Quite literally through it. His projection passed through the stone with hardly more than a shiver and a brief moment of darkness—unpleasant, but fast. He froze in the middle of the hall, whipping around to check his surroundings. The guard had his back to him, with Nat standing nearby. Her attention barely flickered to Ambrose; he nodded to her and sprinted down the hall.

Sticking close to the walls, he repeated Tavi's directions in his head as he went. Right, then down the steps, take two lefts, down the tunnel...

The tunnels here stretched farther than he expected, forcing his thoughts to hold fast to the directions like a lantern in the shadows. When Nat had said Tavi was going down, she truly had been descending—the long pathways boasted a steep decline, forcing him to skitter carefully. He tried to keep an eye out for any indication of what he might be walking into. Barred cells, perhaps, for the chained man, or a storeroom filled with plasma.

But the directions ended at a tiny, dark crevice in the wall.

He looked around, searching for a sign or a door...nothing. Just a shadowy nook leading into nothing. If he had been wandering undirected, he would have passed right by it.

But Tavi had led him here, so he steeled himself for discomfort and wormed his way into the shadows.

This particular path was just as unpleasant as the wall jump and several times as long. The poky rock wall kept jabbing through his astral form, the force somewhere between a tickle and a hard push, while the darkness forced his eyes to strain for something that wasn't there. He gritted his teeth, held his breath, and pushed onward. If he ever managed to meet Tavi, he would have several words for her, none of them polite at this moment—

He stumbled out into the back of the largest cave chamber he had ever seen.

At first glance, it reminded him of where he had found Dawn's star shine moss—but while this chamber was twice as large, it was half as grand. The moss that clung to the walls here didn't gleam or sparkle. It was dull and overgrown, covering the jagged rock with dim, pillowy softness all the way to the top of the chamber. A glint of silver winked at him from the very top—a narrow slit in the cave, allowing one shaft of pearly moonlight to pool in the center of the room.

And bathing in that moonlight, silent and still, was a dragon half the length of Rosemond Street.

Ambrose pressed himself against the wall on instinct, every muscle in his body preparing to turn and run—but the beast wasn't simply napping there. It had been chained to the floor with heavy iron manacles, surrounded by worktables and bottles and tubes hooked under its scales. In a slow, steady rhythm with the dragon's breathing, liquid pumped from the dragon to the glass, roiling in iridescent waves. The liquid itself was difficult to look at, as were the dragon's scales: bright one moment, then dark and deep in another, blending in with the moss around it.

Ambrose slowly ventured away from the wall, fixated on the iridescence in the tubes. That liquid had to be the dragon plasma Tavi had so dearly wanted—but what she actually wanted it for, he had no idea. He didn't recognize it as an ingredient, nor were any of the bottles labeled—

"How much did we extract today?" a voice floated into the chamber. Ambrose leapt behind a stalagmite and ducked down. Seconds later, a pair of artificers shuffled into the room, one holding a clipboard. These artificers clearly didn't work on tunnels or wands, like the tired, soot-streaked workers he had spotted in the Aphosian markets. Their bronze artificer pins shimmered in the moonlight, their cheeks were free of grease, and dust only gently clung to the bottom of their shoes.

The first artificer flicked a bottle of plasma as they walked by, while the second grimaced at her clipboard.

"Not enough to fuel all of the Madam's orders," she said. "The numbers are still following Finley's estimates from last year. With the constant harvesting, its hibernation is beginning to stall. At this rate, we won't get any plasma by next year."

"And we've already upped the nutrients in the moss?" the first one asked. The second pushed her hand into the soft green moss covering the wall.

"As much as we could. Either the dragon's not absorbing them, or it's not enough nutrients to keep the plasma replenished."

They both let the information hang uncomfortably in the air until the first one sighed. "So, what do we do?"

"We hope that potioneer knows what he's doing." The second one tossed her clipboard onto the worktable. "Or we'll be out of illusions to sell by the end of the year."

Ambrose stared at the liquid slowly filling the glass bottles. The plasma was Aphos' secret ingredient. It was what made their illusions so potent...and endangered.

Anger bubbled up inside him. That was what he was meant to replace. Instead of a dragon chained to the floor, it would be him bound to his worktable, creating illusion potions until he deteriorated just like this poor beast—

He forced himself to focus. Knowing what the plasma was didn't help him understand why Tavi had wanted it. It was valuable to Aphos, certainly, but even if she could use its power herself, illusions alone wouldn't have helped her or Nat escape. And what about that man Tavi had written about? He squinted at the shadows around the room. He saw no prisoners here, other than...

His eyes fell on the manacles around the dragon's limbs. Tavi had wanted to erode chains so she could escape with this person to the outer villages. Remote outer villages filled with dangerous beasts like...other dragons.

She hadn't been looking to harness the plasma for herself, nor free a man. She had been looking to free the dragon itself—Aphos' entire source of power and wealth—and take down the entire system with her.

He slid down to the floor, cold stone pressing in all around him.

This wasn't a way out. He could feel Tavi's reasoning here as surely as if she stood next to him—the desperate need to escape, the potential to free more than just herself, the potent desire to leave this place in ashes behind her... But that desire had burned her in the end. She couldn't free this dragon, and neither could he. He didn't even know where to start, and he had less than two weeks until the demonstration.

Nat had been right. His attempt to follow Tavi had come to nothing.

He slowly stood up and made for the crevice, his breath ragged, his growing panic making him woozy. He just had to—had to get back to his room, that was all. Had to get back to his room and think up another way out of this mess—

Then the artificers circled around the dragon and headed straight for him. In a frantic move, he scurried and leapt not behind the stalagmites but behind the dragon instead. He backed up against its massive frame, its cold scales freezing the tips of his fingers.

"Can we delay our next report?" The first artificer led the way back out of the room. His partner shrugged.

"I can try, but the boss is scheduled to report to Mila after that potioneer's show or something..."

Ambrose tried to retreat deeper into the shadows, away from the corners of their eyes—but upon running his hand back along the scales, his finger caught on one of the sharp tips.

"*Ow!*" he hissed on instinct and whipped his hand back. His astral form couldn't bleed, of course—but a tiny bit of his flickering self clung to the tip of the scale, like a wisp of smoke escaping from a candle wick.

It sank into the scale, and the dragon moved.

It wasn't a large movement—it didn't rear its head, nor even open its eyes. Its chest merely expanded once to release a long, heavy sigh. Still, Ambrose didn't dare move. If the dragon woke, if the artificers turned at the movement and spotted him...

But they didn't bother looking back. After a few seconds, their silhouettes disappeared down the tunnel, and after a minute, the dragon's breathing resumed its glacial cadence.

Ambrose stood there one minute longer, a prisoner stealing the shadow of another prisoner, before offering a silent apology to the dragon and slipping out through the crevice.

He sprinted through the tunnels, ignorant of whatever walls or lanterns happened to slip through his form on the way back. He'd have to tell Nat what he had seen, of course, but she would be devastated to learn he had found nothing that could help them. Or would she take the opportunity to gloat about it? He never could tell with her—

A new voice in the tunnel made him skid to a halt.

"Why haven't you reported back to the kitchens?" Cassius demanded.

"I, um"—Nat's voice wavered at a higher pitch with each syllable —"I had to test a potion and it took longer than I thought it would."

The guard scoffed. "Please. She was talkin' up a storm not a minute ago."

Ambrose peered around the corner. Nat had managed to keep Cassius and the guard angled away from the door, but her conversation wouldn't last much longer. He ran straight for the wall, panic driving every step. He could do this, he could make it in without so much as a whisper—

He passed through the door just as Cassius whipped around.

"What was that?"

Ambrose threw himself into his own body. A moment of darkness, a sharp intake of breath—then he was sitting up in bed, looking at Cassius charging into the room.

"What were you doing?" Cassius demanded.

Ambrose squinted blearily at him. "Sleeping?"

"No, you weren't. You were..." Cassius looked around, his sharp gaze piercing the shadows of the workroom. Ambrose choked on his own heartbeat. The cauldron—he hadn't yet cleaned the dregs of the potion from it.

Both of their gazes landed on the cauldron at the same time, the warm iron still marked with splotches of green and gold.

"This..." Cassius ran a thumb along the metal, red rising from his cheeks to his ears. "What is this? I've seen it before."

Ambrose staggered to his feet, trying to summon nonsense words with a tongue thick with fear. "The active ingredient in that brew had to be boiled at night in order for its potency to—"

But Cassius wasn't having it this time.

"You." He snapped his fingers at Nat. "*You* were a part of—of whatever this was. Get to the kitchens and stay there. Someone else will be taking your place in the rounds."

Nat backed away. Ambrose's heart seized. He couldn't lose her, not now. Not when they both knew so little about their own rescue.

"You can't," Ambrose demanded. "She's—she's been essential to my testing—"

"Then I'd be happy to double the guard so you can test on any one of them as needed," Cassius hissed. "And during the demonstration, I will test your potion myself. If I get a hint of fraud, *anything* less than what the Madam is looking for, I am sending you straight to the Sinking Reach. Are we clear?"

Ambrose started forward, but Cassius had already stalked back into the hall, his grip tight on Nat's arm. "Let go of me!" she shouted. Cassius half threw her down the hall in response, then glared back at Ambrose.

"I will send for you in a week. Be sure you are ready."

"Am—!" Nat tried; Cassius slammed the door before she could finish, leaving him standing in the dark silence of the workroom.

He didn't move when their footsteps disappeared, nor when the guards rotated. He remained stuck in his thoughts, mired in anger aimed sharply at himself. There was no magic ingredient waiting for him beyond the walls, no trapped sage pointing him to the way out. He was back where he started...and he had lost Nat.

He finally managed to break himself from the spot behind the door—first walking, then pacing, then climbing back into bed, his thoughts ragged and heavy. There had to be someone in his dreams, someone who could fetch what he needed—or, rather, who he needed.

So, when Dawn appeared in his dreams that night, the bright light of The Gingersnap Café all around her, he didn't hesitate to take the chair opposite her and make his request.

"Dawn," he said. "I need to talk to Xavion."

RULE 30:

ISOLATE THE COMPONENTS

Dawn

TYPICALLY, Dawn woke up after her dreams with Ambrose bearing a brief feeling of normalcy. A fleeting assurance that everything was fine, that Ambrose was really just down the street, brewing his morning potions and ready to meet her for coffee and gossip about his latest customers.

But seeing him the night prior, shaken and scared and spouting strange requests, she woke up wishing she could huddle under the covers and go right back to bed.

"Have a nice day!" she called to her last customer before lunch, her voice strained and eyes bleary. It didn't help that all of Rosemond Street was frantically discussing Dawn's observations through the rose statue, its light distracting her from her shop duties. She flipped the store sign to *Closed*, then opened up the statue's scroll to check the latest in the conversation.

I don't like it, Viola had written, followed by an unfamiliar script, one unnecessarily flowery for something as simple as the rose statue.

You *don't like it?* Xavion had written back. *He asked to speak to me! What could he possibly want from me? I know nothing about Aphos! I will not have the pressure of this damned rescue fall on me—I'm already quite saddled with his infuriating number of level seven brews, thank you very much.*

The next message was from Banneker's shop, but the writing was in Eli's blocky hand.

When I last talked to him, he kept mentioning dragon plasma or something. I kept trying to tell him just to lie low, not do anything, we'll get him out ourselves.

Not do anything? That was Grim's handwriting, the letters large and perfectly aligned. *You really thought Beake was going to just sit there and wait for us?*

Sherry's response came as Grim's words were still appearing on the paper. *Dawn, did it sound like he was in danger?*

Dawn could feel the scared tremor in the question, and she tried not to echo it herself in her response.

He didn't say much, but I don't think so. Then, after a thought: *How about I bring some wine over tonight? I've got a bottle from my birthday I've been waiting to open. Think we all need it.*

The responses rolled in immediately.

yes please
Oh, thank the gods.
Just one bottle?

The bell over the door tinkled, drawing her away from the statue.

"We're closed—!" she started, then smiled, relief settling on her shoulders. "Oh. Hey, Rory."

"Hey." Rory grinned. "Just thought I'd stop by." She pulled a bouquet out from behind her back—wildflowers from the Elwig Market, spilling out of twine-wrapped paper in a joyous burst of pink and purple. Dawn's nerves evaporated just looking at them.

"You have no idea how much I needed these." She gave Rory a kiss and took the flowers. Rory nodded to the statue, which still flashed a frenetic white.

"Does it have anything to do with that?"

Dawn sighed as she dug up a vase, then placed the flowers next to Ember's water dish. The phoenix salamander slowly blinked and reached for the thickest stalk, testing his weight on them.

"I talked to Ames last night," she said. "I don't know what's going on, but he's not doing great, so..." She reached up on her tiptoes and pulled the wine bottle off the shelf. "Sounds like I gotta dust this off for tonight. You wanna join?"

She silently begged Rory to say yes. The last time she had pulled some wine off the upper shelf, it had earned her their first kiss.

But Rory hesitated, setting both elbows on the counter. "I would, but I've got to work late tonight. My editor wants an update on the Ambrose story as soon as possible."

All at once, the nerves that had unspooled at the sight of the flowers coiled back up in her stomach. That wasn't true. She had seen the note. She *knew* that wasn't true.

Her chest tightened. She had to call it out, but the words lodged in her throat, unwilling to lead herself down that path. While she floundered, Rory reached for the wine bottle.

"But if I can manage to get out of work at a decent time"—she glanced out the window—"maybe I could—"

"I saw the note," Dawn blurted out.

Rory's shoulders tensed...then slumped, and she turned back around. The silent gesture only made Dawn's heart pound harder.

"I saw it on your desk," she continued. "I know your editor rejected the story on Ambrose weeks ago. Why are you still working on it?"

Rory straightened, her gaze on Dawn's face wavering. "I wanted to help. I couldn't just leave, not after knowing he was kidnapped—"

"You didn't know him then," Dawn said, "and you didn't really know me, either."

"But I knew how to help—"

"And how do you know how to help?" Her questions were picking up speed of their own volition, plucking at her doubts and Eli's questions. "You've only been in the Scar for a few years, and yet you know everything about Aphos. You can't go down there, but you gave us perfect directions. Look, I can't say I'm not grateful, but..." She took an uneven breath. "Please be honest with me. What are you really doing here?"

Rory set the wine bottle on the counter with a quiet *thunk*.

"I haven't...only been in the Scar for a few years," she murmured, her gaze fixed on the wine label. "I did grow up in Deepriver, but before that, I was born here." She took a breath. "In Aphos."

Dawn thought back to the articles piled on Rory's desk, the repeated images of Mila, the head of Aphos. The shape of her eyes, the angle of her nose... She searched Rory's face. "You're related to that woman, aren't you? The leader?"

"That woman," Rory said, tapping her nails on the counter, "is my mother."

Her ensuing words came out in a desperate tumble.

"I don't—I'm not *with* Aphos, all right?" she said. "I hated that place. I knew what my mom was doing, and I—I left when I was a kid to go live with my dad. I never lied about any of that. But I couldn't..." She toyed with her jacket sleeve. "I couldn't just let it go, knowing what she was doing down there. I got into reporting and came back to the Scar to work on the magical crime beat, hoping I'd..."

The sourness of the hidden truth laced Dawn's words. "You'd what?" she said. "Take down Aphos yourself?"

"I don't know," Rory retorted, then immediately softened as she ran her hand through her hair. "Take down *her*, at least. She doesn't know I'm here. If she finds me out, finds out what I'm doing, I don't...I don't know what she'll do to me. If she'll kick me out, or try to—twist me into coming back..." She waved her hand, batting her own fear out of the air. "So, I did what I could without stepping foot inside Aphos. I gained contacts, tracked her work through their gossip. Meddled where I could."

Dawn let her words sink in. Rory was no spy or enemy, she told herself. She was on their side, helping Ambrose while simply trying not to get caught herself.

But one of the words had its claws in her, refusing to let her relax and allow the revelation to pass.

"Meddle," she repeated. "Is that why you're helping us? To meddle in her affairs?"

Rory swallowed. "Look, if Ambrose is rescued, it'll be a huge blow to her stupid little empire—"

The claws deepened.

"Empire?" Dawn recoiled. "He's not a—a *pawn* for you to move around. He's my best friend."

"I know that—"

"Have you just been using all of our work to get back at your mom?"

Rory stared at her—then her expression went cold.

"Oh, like you haven't been using my knowledge to get him back."

"You offered!" Dawn gestured to the bakery outside. "*Weeks* ago! When did your editor reject the story? Before you even stopped at our door?"

Rory remained silent, her lips in a line. Dawn's thoughts uncoiled while her nerves tightened painfully.

"Was the rest of it real?" she asked, her voice warbling. "The dancing, the stories, the kiss—or was I just a pawn, too?"

"A pawn," Rory repeated with an icy, barking laugh. "As if someone like you could ever be a pawn—"

"I certainly feel like one," Dawn spat. Anger grew behind her eyes, thorns building up in her teeth...

She released her tight grip on the edge of the counter. No, this wasn't the sinkhole. She wasn't going to do anything she would regret.

"Please leave," she managed, every word shaking. "I just—please go."

Rory opened her mouth...then snapped it shut, backed away, and left the store, the bell above the door clanging lifelessly above her.

Dawn stared at the *Closed* sign swinging on the door handle. Through tears, she opened the wine bottle and scrawled a messy note on the statue scroll.

Change of plans. Someone come drink with me now.

RULE 31:

DEBATE

Ambrose

AMBROSE WENT to sleep and found himself, bewilderingly, on the debate stage at Potion Con.

"Oh, come on." He rolled his eyes and looked down at the other end of the stage. "Really?"

Xavion shrugged. "I didn't know what else to project."

"You could've projected anything." Ambrose folded his arms. "A field, a street, a tavern—and you chose this? What, did you want to try for a rematch now that I have nowhere to run?"

"I wouldn't"—Xavion smiled sharply—"*dream* of it."

Ambrose desperately wanted to punch them.

"Now," they said, wandering toward him with their hands folded behind their back. "What has the great Ambrose Beake running to me in his time of need?"

"Well, I've been kidnapped, if you haven't noticed."

"I am running your shop. I believe I have noticed."

"Then you'll be delighted to know that I'm trying to aid in my own rescue," Ambrose said. "And...I need your advice."

Xavion's eyebrows rose.

"Consider it a debate topic, of sorts," he added quickly. "I'll give you my ideas on what I should brew and you tell me why they won't work, until we find one that will."

Xavion straightened and took their normal position on the stage. "Very well. What's the purpose of this potion of yours?"

"Something that can get Nat and me out in case Rosemond Street can't help me."

Xavion stared at him but didn't question the premise. "And what did you have in mind?"

Ambrose mentally ran through the notes he had jotted down and hidden under his mattress, as if that would help him remember them better. "Flight, initially."

Xavion shook their head. "There's a shield over the sinkhole. You won't be able to fly out."

Ambrose had guessed as much, based on what Eli had last told him of his plans—but he had to rule it out to be safe. "A teleportation brew, then."

"I've seen Aphos' unique teleport signature myself," Xavion said. "You won't be able to apply it to a potion."

"Invisibility?"

"There is nowhere to go in that sinkhole. Turn invisible before them, and they will simply catch you."

Ambrose started to pace; Xavion remained still on the other side of the stage. How infuriating—to be standing in a sinkhole the day of the demonstration, so close to the sky and to freedom, only to not be able to reach it.

He rattled through his other notes, other potions that he had less confidence in but had to rule out to keep his mind from going in circles—and, of course, nothing worked. Xavion, in their usual way, found flaws in every single one of them, shooting them down without effort. Ambrose had hoped this sort of conversation, if one could call it that, would gradually coax out a grand idea, a unique, masterful brew that would buoy him to victory—

But nothing came, and by the end, they stood there in silence on a stage without an audience. Xavion hadn't moved, but their expression had fallen, their stance less haughty.

"It isn't going to work," they said quietly. A desperate fire flared in Ambrose's chest.

"I have to do something—"

"Are you sure you cannot make what they want you to?" Xavion asked. "Actually make a passable true illusion potion for them?"

Ambrose snorted. "What I made for them at the last demonstration was a Guild-defying disaster, a mere stopgap to fool them. I can't actually make a true illusion potion, not by myself in a—a stupid, windowless room—"

"You wouldn't be doing it alone." Xavion stepped forward. "You have your knowledge, what you wrote down of your predecessor's old notes, and unfortunately for myself"—they took a breath—"you have me in this illustrious dreamscape."

Ambrose looked around him—at the convincing illusion the circlet on Xavion's head had built. The solid floorboards under his feet; the sound of his voice bouncing off the makeshift walls; the faint smell of the food court wafting in from the tunnels...

"Wait," he said. "Is there a way I can do this? Create this sort of illusion in reality?"

"Certainly not," Xavion said, their retort instinctive. "The circlet's magic is too specific. Its components are entirely dependent on the delicate interactions between..." They looked around them and trailed off, their mind taking the same path as Ambrose.

"Delicate interactions that could be smoothed..." Ambrose grinned. "By esther?"

Xavion couldn't help themself. "Shut up."

"So, I was right?"

"No."

"Tell me I'm right."

Xavion huffed and took one more hard look at the room; their silence was a victory in and of itself.

"How long do you have to make this potion?" they finally asked.

"One week."

Xavion sighed, then cracked their knuckles. "Then thank all the gods you're Ambrose Beake, because no other potioneer I know could pull this off."

RULE 32:

RUN MORE TESTS

Dawn

ROSEMOND STREET HAD five days until the rescue, and every shop radiated a forced cheeriness.

Customers milled thoughtfully between stores, taking little heed of the strangely quiet artificer, jeweler, and potioneer. The usual lunchtime crowd gathered around the open-air forge, watching Sherry work with a taut smile on her face.

And in The Midnight Snack, Viola compulsively cleaned, the metal foot of her leg clinking all around the shop.

"Still can't believe it about Rory," she muttered when she got close to Dawn's table. "Here. On the house." She set a cup of tea in front of Dawn, the plate adorned with a hibiscus flower and a vanilla cookie. Dawn gave her a wan smile.

"Appreciate it," she mumbled. In the spare time she had before opening her own shop, she had decided to post up here in a little corner of desserts, sadness, and denial. She wasn't alone, either—Eli had arrived minutes later and promptly placed Tom in her lap.

After all, it was difficult for a corner to be sad if Tom was there.

"You tell me if you need anything else, all right?" Viola patted her shoulder, smiled at Eli, then headed straight for the broom propped against the wall.

Yesterday, all of the merchants had devoured both the bottle of wine and the news about Rory in minutes. Banneker had sworn up and down that he should've seen the signs in his tea leaves. Sherry had courageously talked Grim out of confronting Rory directly, only to then swear she was going to do it herself. Eli had…

Well, in the moment, he had rushed off to the bakery and ordered a dozen emergency cupcakes, but this morning, the news seemed to have caught up with him. He slouched over the table, his coffee going untouched. When Tom reached for the flower on the teacup, he took it and wedged it between her broom bristles—but it barely brought a smile to either of their faces.

"She didn't just lie to you," he finally said. "She lied to all of us." His gaze darkened. "What if she *had* been working for Aphos? She knew our every move for weeks."

"She isn't working for Aphos." Dawn rubbed her face in exhaustion. Her warring thoughts had kept her up all night, turning her last conversation with Rory like she would the handle of a wand until her mistakes came out shiny and unmissable. "She was trying to help."

Eli gave her a look.

"She was!" Dawn retorted. "She just…"

"Was using us?"

"And we were using her right back." She sighed and sipped from the tea—there was no spell in the drink, but the floral notes in the tea helped wake her a little. She used the brief moment of wakefulness to force her thoughts in a different direction. There was no staying in the corner of sadness forever—there was a rescue plan to finish.

And that plan was barely limping along.

"Any word from Banneker on the invite?" she asked hopefully. Eli shook his head.

"No progress," he said flatly. "No working invite, no way in."

Dawn hugged Tom closer. If Rory wasn't here—and despite looking out the window every few minutes, she wasn't—then someone would have to take the rest of the mission into their own hands.

And she certainly couldn't mope while Ambrose's life hung in the balance.

"Come out to the tavern with me tonight," she said without thinking. "The Aphosian one down south."

Any of the merchants would have balked at the idea—it was too risky, so close to the rescue—but Eli perked up immediately.

"What do you have in mind?" he asked. Dawn crunched on the vanilla cookie in thought.

"Rory never said who Madam Mila's inner circle was," she said, "but someone else in that tavern has to know, right? We'll just get a drink there and ask around."

Just. As if it was a night of dancing and not a dangerous venture into a criminal hideout.

But as she hoped, Eli drank his coffee in two gulps and grinned. "See?" he said. "Who needs Rory? We've got you as our spymaster."

Dawn wouldn't go that far, but at least she wouldn't have to visit the tavern alone.

She set Tom down on the floor and straightened the flower in her bristles. "Leave around nine?"

"Nine it is." Eli scooped up Tom, then extended a hug to Dawn when she stood up. "Hey. I know I probably won't be as good of a date, but I can dance and throw a punch with the best of them."

Dawn smiled and punched his arm. "Knew there was a reason Ames kept you around."

———

Hours later, they descended to the tavern, already in over their heads.

"Wait, so I need a fake name?" Eli asked. Dawn rolled her eyes.

"Yes, you need a fake name. You can't just go in there and say, 'Hey, I'm Eli Valenz, Scarrish adventurer-in-training—'"

"What's your fake name, then?"

Dawn bit her lip. "Kerry."

"Kerry?" Eli's laughter bounced down the street. "Like Kerighin?"

Dawn tried to laugh along with him, refusing to admit the fake name had grown on her.

"Yeah, it was dumb." She brushed off his words. "But you have to think of one, too."

"Fine. Um..." Eli looked around. "Jerry?"

Dawn stopped in the middle of the street. "We are not going in as Kerry and Jerry."

Eli threw up his hands. "You're the spymaster here. *You* think of something!"

Dawn resumed her pace, hoping something would come to her as they walked—but the warm light of the tavern was fast approaching, and she had nothing in her head.

"I don't know," she rambled. "Corey?"

Eli gave her a sideways look—but at the door, Callia was already waving from her post.

"Kerry, wasn't it?" she called. "Come on in, come on in. Got some good bards tonight."

Dawn took Eli's arm and pasted a smile on her face in return, not wanting to think too much about why Callia had memorized her name so quickly, nor what she could possibly do with that information.

They clambered into the booth in the corner, the same one Rory had led her to weeks ago. The place hadn't changed; the cushions remained lumpy, the spider still toiled away by the lantern, and the wine...

Dawn took a sip and pursed her lips. Yep, still sour.

But next to her, her new partner-in-crime wasn't making a move to soothe her nerves. He was just as anxious as she was—gaze darting around, leg bouncing, his cold beer slowly warming in the tavern atmosphere.

"All right, so who are we talking to?" he asked, watching everyone who came in. Dawn pushed his drink toward him.

"We aren't talking to anyone until you try to act normal," she said.

"Take a sip or something. If you're making me nervous, you're going to make them nervous."

He reluctantly acquiesced and took a sip. While he drank and tried to lounge back against the lumpy seats, Dawn observed the bar at a more leisurely pace. There were indeed new bards onstage, a pair of fiddlers and a drummer, catering to several drunken dancers reeling in wide circles. But the other patrons looked about the same. The orcs playing cards, the gnomes huddled in the opposite corner...

Ah. And Jasper the artificer, nursing his beer.

She leaned toward Eli. "That's the guy we talked to. Goggles and artificer pin, on the other side of that column."

Eli quickly pushed aside his drink. "Okay, let's go—"

"Hold on." She grabbed his arm. "We have to wait until he's done with his first drink. That's what Rory did."

"We can't." Eli lowered his voice. "Look at him again. He's gonna bolt any second."

She let her gaze casually flit elsewhere first, then observed Jasper once more. He hunched forward over the table, spinning his beer mug, eyes flicking over every inch of movement in the tavern.

She'd be surprised if he even finished his beer before leaving.

"Fine," she said. "Let's go."

She led the way over to Jasper, keeping her pace slow, her expression light. The artificer's eyes flashed in recognition, but he didn't bother accompanying it with a smile.

"Evenin'," he muttered, adjusting the goggles on his forehead. "No Liddy today?"

Dawn gripped her wineglass tighter. Damn these Aphosians and their good memories.

"Not tonight, no," she said. She didn't dare sit down at his table yet—but while they were on the subject, she could dare a question. "Has she, um...been here recently?"

Jasper shrugged. "Not in the past week or so."

Dawn nodded; Jasper sipped his beer. Eli nudged her, gaze urgent.

"So"—she aimed for a more direct tactic—"you hear about that demonstration in the Oasis next week?"

Another blunder. Jasper's eyes narrowed immediately.

"Maybe," he said slowly. "What about it?"

Behind him, an elf glanced back at her, and the orcs at a nearby table all stiffened. Dawn swallowed, cognizant of the hole she had just stepped in. They were all just as on edge as Jasper was, ready to leap up from their drinks at a moment's notice. Even Callia was flashing nervous smiles and hurrying between tables faster than before.

Something must have happened—and she could use that to her advantage.

"What do you know about it?" She sat down across from Jasper and leaned in with a look of concern. "Liddy and her boss are just as scared as everyone else. I just got back into town, and I gotta know if a storm's coming. For her sake, you see." She checked Jasper's beer—only half-full. She hailed Callia. "Another beer, please?"

That was the key—Jasper's shoulders unwound as soon as his next beer was in front of him. As he wiped foam from his mouth, Dawn kept up her concerned facade, while Eli quietly took the seat beside her.

"Tell Liddy not to throw her wrench over it," Jasper finally said. "It's the rest of us that's got to worry about it. So long as her boss is keepin' in Cassius' good graces, she'll be fine."

"Cassius?" Eli frowned. "What's he doing?"

Jasper glanced at him for the first time, looking his plain merchant's garb up and down. Dawn set a hand on Eli's arm.

"Corey," she said. "Potioneer's apprentice." Then, for her own satisfaction: "He's very new to all this. Has hardly learned his level one's."

Eli kicked her under the table; she bit back a smile.

"Potions, eh?" Jasper scratched his beard. "That's exactly what the demonstration is for next week. Problem is, someone stole Lady Free-heart's invitation, and she's making a sooty stink over it."

Dawn froze in confusion. "Someone stole her invitation?"

Jasper nodded. "Stole it right from under her nose in Aphos," he said. "Normally, I don't give a damn fire blast who's going to those things, but if it's Cassius' problem, it's suddenly everyone's problem."

Dawn sipped her terrible wine. All well and good for Lady Freeheart to have lost her invite, but she needed the name of someone who still had theirs in hand. "Who else normally goes to those events?"

But Jasper was already rattling on, the beer urging him in the opposite direction. "Cassius sent folks to check all my workers' bags today. Can you believe that?" He snorted. "As if any of us would want a peek at a potion we couldn't afford in ten lifetimes. That damn man just doesn't have anything better to do with his time. He hounded the wandmakers, then the markets, then the—"

Next to Dawn, Eli shifted impatiently. "Yeah, we hate that guy," he said. "So, who else might be—?"

It was no use.

"And then," Jasper barreled on, "he has the gall to tell everyone to be on their best behavior next week!" He threw up a hand. "Me 'n' mine have never caused a lick of trouble for him. When that one giant spider got into the tunnels, who was first to take it down?" He jabbed a finger down onto the table. "Not him, that's who. In fact, it was my older brother Nic who—"

In desperation, Dawn set her glass down hard. "Fascinating. Does *Nic* know anyone else who might be attending the—?"

Up onstage, the bard's tune changed.

What had been a lightly rolling dance suddenly veered into something jangling and off-putting, almost out of tune. Everyone in the tavern straightened—then began to chug their drinks and rush for the exits.

Eli stiffened. "What's that?"

"Damn, you are new," Jasper muttered. "Cassius is coming. Best get out now."

Dawn gripped her chair. She couldn't leave—she had no information yet, nothing to go off of. "But—"

"Good evenin'." Jasper clinked his mug against theirs, drained the dregs, then shuffled off along with everyone else. Eli tugged on Dawn's arm.

"Come on, we have to go, too," he muttered. "As much as I want to wait around here and punch him, we can't afford to have him see us."

"But we didn't get any—!"

"We'll figure it out later." Eli's nerves had vanished now that danger was approaching. He pulled her to her feet, his grip strong. "Let's *go*."

Dawn tossed back the last of the city's worst wine—then slipped into the night with him, sour and empty-handed.

RULE 33:

APPLY BINDING AGENT

Dawn

DAWN COULDN'T STOMACH the thought of delivering her failure straight to Ambrose that night—but it was her turn to wear the crown.

"I'm sorry, Sherry." She stood in the doorway of her shop, her sniffles making an embarrassing echo in the empty nighttime street. Sherry held the wooden box that Banneker had built for the circlet, but she couldn't bring herself to take it. "I can't do this tonight. I can't see him."

What was she supposed to say to him? That they still had no invitation? That they were going to sneak in and hope for the best? He'd hate it, *hate* the idea of Eli risking himself like that again. And an angry Ambrose was a risky Ambrose—an Ambrose who would get caught trying to get himself out instead.

But Sherry didn't take the circlet back. She stubbornly held the box out, eyes shining. "You have to. The only way we lose him is if we stop trying." She pulled Dawn into a hug, her voice unsteady. "Sleep well and tell him we love him."

When she left, Dawn closed the door and clicked open the box.

The circlet gleamed up at her, freshly polished and resting in a bed of blue velvet. She toyed with one of the crystals. What would be worse —the heartache Ambrose would get from her news, or the heartache of her not appearing at all?

As the pain in her chest sharpened, a hesitant knock sounded right behind her.

"Dawn?" a voice called.

The sharp pain twisted and cut. That was Rory, inches away from her.

Dawn gripped the box tight. She couldn't do this, not now. "Not tonight." She took a ragged breath. "I—I want to talk to you, just... It's a bad time."

"I know it's a bad time," Rory continued, the door muffling her words. "But if you open the door for just a second, I can explain myself."

"I can't..." Dawn wiped her cheek. She wasn't sure how much she could—or should—tell Rory anymore. "The plan isn't... It's not working, and I have to tell Ames that—"

"That's why I'm here."

Something slipped under the doorframe and poked Dawn's heels: a piece of paper, neat and pristine, with a golden kraken insignia shining at the top.

She bent down and read the text.

As one of Madam Mila's most valued clients, you are invited to the exclusive—

Dawn snatched up the paper with trembling hands. The invitation. Lady Freeheart's invitation.

It hadn't been taken by some random thief. Rory had descended into Aphos and stolen it from right under her mother's nose.

She yanked open the door. "It was *you*—"

Her words cut themselves short. Gods, Rory had never looked so handsome as she did at that moment. Warm light from the street-lamps caressed her face, and her hair fell over her forehead as if she had run her hands through it a hundred times on the way here. And her eyes, pleading and lovely, couldn't have been further from the calculating coldness of Madam Mila's portraits.

A hundred words prepared to pour from Dawn's chest—but Rory's came rushing out first.

"I know Ambrose isn't a pawn," she said. "I know he gossips with you while you work, and you write to him about every little thing. I know you once got caramel apple in his hair when you were thirteen and he didn't talk to you for three days. I know he's the best at what he does and you're even better, and *you*—" A desperate smile spread across her face. "I have never once thought of you as anything less than magnificent. You're incredible, and beautiful, and the best terrible dancer I've ever seen, and I..." She gestured to the invitation in Dawn's hands. "I want you to get your best friend back, and I want to be standing by your side when you do." She gulped in air, eyes shining. "If you'll have me."

Dawn gave a cracked laugh. She had started crying at some point in the speech, and it was all she could do to keep her tears from falling on the invitation.

"Of course I'll—" she tried, but before she could finish, Rory leaned down and kissed her, letting her words melt into pure relief. Of course she wanted this grinning, reckless, thieving vigilante by her side. She had wanted it from the start.

When she finally pulled away, she kept a firm grip on Rory's waist, not daring to let her slip back into the night.

"It's my turn to talk to Ames tonight," she said. "Will you stay with me?"

Rory dropped one more kiss on her forehead. "I'd love to."

In her excitement, the dreamscape built quickly around her—her own wand shop, morning light blazing across the glass cases in a spray of rainbow caustics. She threw open the door, like she had just done for Rory, and looked for Ambrose out in the street. "Ames?" she called. "Ames, you here—?"

"Over here!" he called in a strained voice. "Over—oh, son of a wood-eating..."

She turned to find him behind her front counter, reaching for the wine bottle she traditionally kept on the top shelf. His hand went through it once, twice, and he cursed again, slouching against the shelves.

"I'm sorry," he mumbled. "I thought I could get it down for you."

"I...appreciate the thought?"

But before she could ask for details, he walked straight through the counter and wrapped her in a hug.

"Sherry told me about what happened with Rory," he said, her hair muffling his words. "I'm so sorry."

She held back a laugh. "There's no need to be sorry, Ames—"

"She lied to you." He pulled back, frowning. "I know she was trying to help, but to think that—"

"Really, there's no need to be sorry." She squeezed his hands and grinned. "She just secured us our invitation. We're breaking into the demonstration and getting you out."

Ambrose blinked. "You're serious?"

She couldn't help it—she bounced his hands up and down and began to chant. "We're getting you out, we're getting you out—"

Ambrose laughed and hugged her again, far tighter than before. But when he stepped back, he was back to his serious self once more.

"If you're truly going to be there..." He ran a hand through his wild, overgrown hair. He clearly hadn't bothered to trim it in weeks, nor was he paying attention to the sky-blue stubble dusting his jaw. "If you really do have access... I'd like to try talking to everyone at once. Soon. Do you think Banneker and Grim can boost the circlet's magic?"

She forced herself out of her celebratory state of mind and back into a semblance of thinking. "I can ask," she said, mentally running through what she knew of the enchantment. "We probably wouldn't have very long to talk, with more people in a dream. Maybe twenty minutes at most—"

"I can make that work." His gaze unfocused, then snapped back into place. "Yes, I can make that work."

Dawn hesitated; she hadn't seen this sort of Ambrose since their apprenticeship finals. "What are you working on down there?"

He gathered himself and shook his head. "I'll tell you when we're all together. I promise." He forced out a smile. "In the meantime, will you take care of yourself?"

Dawn reached up and rubbed the stubble on his jaw. "Like you're one to talk."

He winced. "I've been meaning to shave it."

"Don't, it's cute."

"I'm quite sure it isn't. Please don't tell Eli—"

Dawn laughed. "But he wants you to grow a beard!"

"Precisely." He took her hands once more. "You'll talk to Banneker and Grim tomorrow?"

"We'll throw a whole dream party just for you."

His smile tilted. "For once, I cannot wait."

RULE 34:

ADD FINISHING TOUCHES

Ambrose

AMBROSE HAD NEVER WORKED SO hard on a potion in his life.

He had three cauldrons going at all times, the ink stains on his hands dripping from the heat. He either inhaled his meals in one bite or left them to sit for minutes or hours or days—he had a foggy sense of time without Nat, windows, or a real sleep schedule. Even Cassius glanced at him sideways when he came to survey his handiwork.

This wasn't exactly what Dawn would call taking care of himself, but if it got him and Nat to Rosemond Street, it would be worth it.

The only times he dared retreat to his bed were the times he thought the others might be able to contact him. He napped for a half hour here, a few minutes there, hoping the darkness would turn into friendly faces.

And two days later, the friendly faces appeared—all of them.

The merchants had clustered into The Jumping Ogre, taking over a long table at the back of the tavern. The table groaned under the street's favorites—cheese rolls, fruit pies, stews flanked by stacks of crusty bread...

Ambrose walked into the tavern to find them already digging in.

"Who wants a roll?" Sherry stood and held up a platter. Banneker reached for one; she swatted his hand away. "Not you, you've already taken three. Eli?"

She tossed one to Eli at the end of the table. He took a bite and grimaced. "It hardly tastes like anything."

Ambrose cleared his throat. "If you don't want it, I'll take it."

Eli whipped around. "Ames!"

He scrambled out of his seat as fast as he could, but the others were closer. They all piled onto Ambrose at once, smothering him with hugs, cheek kisses, and loud babbling in his ear.

"Look, I think we've got about a half hour in this dream," Banneker rambled, "and we're all gonna have wicked headaches tomorrow, but it's worth it for you." He grinned. "I'm liking the beard, by the way."

Eli hummed in agreement and kissed his scratchy jawline. "Keep it, *please* keep it—"

"No."

"But it's so handsome," Sherry cooed; he wriggled away.

"Someone help me," he tried weakly—but in truth, he was fighting back tears. They were all here—even Rory, sticking tightly to Dawn—and he wanted nothing more than to simply sit and ask them about their days. To chat with them for hours, then retreat back into the welcoming quiet of his potion shop.

But the minutes were already slipping away, and he couldn't indulge in anything beyond staying close to Eli's side, holding his hand in a tense grip.

"I must thank you all for coming," he said. Everyone stepped back and fell quiet for him. "I have an idea for how both Nat and I can escape during the demonstration while giving Aphos the brew they want..."

His eyes fell on Rory. She did look like Madam Mila, didn't she?

"...and making your mother terribly angry in the process," he finished.

Rory grinned. "We're all ears."

The night before the demonstration, a potion bottle sat in a silk-lined box, polished and perfect and completely ready for Cassius.

"One true illusion potion and the entirety of my research." Ambrose pointed to the journals stacked neatly next to the box. "The brew achieves sight, smell, and sound, as you have already seen, along with touch and taste for relevant illusions. You'll also find that your archivists can easily follow the instructions inside to duplicate my work for their records."

Cassius took the box and journals, his smile lofty and smug. "I see you learned what was best for your self-preservation," he said. "Madam Mila and her guests look forward to seeing your work tomorrow."

Ambrose maintained a straight face and a steady posture. So did he.

As Cassius swept off, a servant approached with a tray of food. To his constant disappointment, it wasn't Nat—it hadn't been ever since his failed astral outing.

"Here," the servant mumbled, then quickly scurried away. When she slipped out, a breeze slipped in, and the door caught a moment before closing.

Ambrose's stomach grumbled—he had accidentally ignored the last meal brought to him—but something forced him to freeze in place. A distinct sense that he was being watched in the empty room.

He waited several seconds, surveying the air around him. Then, when nothing appeared, he ventured a small, "Hello?"

Someone in the room cursed.

"How did you know?" Nat whispered harshly. "I thought I was doing a good job of being sneaky—"

Fear and relief seized him all at once.

"What are you doing?" he hissed, searching the air frantically for any sign of her. "Where are you? How long have you been invisible?"

A hand tugged on his sleeve.

"About fifteen minutes. Why?"

He grabbed her shoulders, glaring at what he approximated to be her eyes. "That potion only lasts for thirty minutes. If you want to escape now, you need to leave immediately—"

"Escape?" she said. "I just wanted to bring you some raisin cakes."

Raisin cakes, fresh and warm from the kitchens, suddenly piled themselves onto Ambrose's dinner tray.

"I saw they hadn't given you any in a week," she continued, "and the trays almost always came back full. Don't tell me you've been eating my stash of candy instead."

"Nat," he said, gripping her shoulders tight. "You're *invisible*. What on earth are you doing? Why aren't you *leaving*?"

He could feel her tilt her head; strands of hair that never stayed in her ponytail fell onto the back of his hand. "I'm not leaving you behind, Mr. Ambrose."

Ambrose blinked back tears. Gods, he didn't deserve her. He didn't deserve any of them.

"Get to the demonstration tomorrow," he said.

"I'll try—"

"You must." He swallowed. "Promise me you'll be there."

"Okay, okay! I will. I'll be there."

"Good."

Footsteps haunted the hall once more—the other servant, come to pick up the tray. He let go of Nat's shoulders and immediately lost all sense of where she was.

"I'll see you tomorrow."

RULE 35:

INFILTRATE

Eli

THE MORNING OF THE RESCUE, Eli found himself leagues outside of the Scar.

Rosemond Street had taken no chances on their cover. They had ridden into a neighboring village the night before, disguises and devices in tow, then joined the city-bound crowd of travelers the following morning.

"Remember not to say much when you get to the entrance," Rory said, coaching Sherry, Grim, Eli, and Dawn from within their gilded carriage. She gestured with Banneker's forged invitation as she spoke —a perfect match to Lady Freeheart's. "You're rich and important. There's no need to be polite, understood?"

"I can do that," Sherry said confidently. Dawn threw her a skeptical look. "What? I can!"

Next to her, Grim rolled their eyes and shifted the bejeweled belt across their hips. Eli could barely recognize the pair; they had already donned their costumes and wolfed down their enchanted disguise desserts. *Undercover butter buns,* Viola had called them. Respectfully,

Eli thought she should workshop the name—but there were bigger things to worry about at the moment.

"Now, after you show your invite at the entrance," Rory continued, "stick to the middle of the group and act like you know where you're going. The guards out front won't bother checking faces or names, but you don't want someone like Cassius looking too closely."

"What about those dogs that caught you at the Grapevine entrance?" Grim asked, nodding to Eli. "Kid's gonna be walking in with half our inventory strapped to 'im. They'll sniff him out in a second."

Rory waved a hand. "They don't have those dogs here—just their wands to check invitations. Half of Madam Mila's guests use her illusion devices just to hide their wrinkles. If Aphos tried checking them over with a guard dog, they'd get migraines from all the barking."

The carriage slowed to a halt; Eli's nerves spiked.

"Stopping at the crossroads, ma'am," the driver called. "Just like you asked."

Rory reached for the door, then paused. "Earring check?"

They all quickly touched their earlobes, ensuring Grim's mind-linking earrings were all in place. Eli checked both of his studs—light gold, almost blending in with his ears. He generally preferred a nice dangling quartz, but they would've stuck out against his servants' attire.

"How about you?" Dawn turned to him, her smile unsteady. "You have everything? Teleporters, invisibility potion, wand—?"

"Checked a dozen times, got it all."

She gave him an overly tight hug. "You can do this."

Eli returned the gesture with just as much force. "See you soon."

Dawn took Rory's arm, and with a twist of the copper teleporter in her hand, they both disappeared back to the Scar. Eli slipped out of the carriage and took his place on the sideboard as Sherry and Grim's servant. As soon as he settled in, Sherry flipped up the window.

"You all right out there?" she whispered.

Eli grinned. "What did Rory say about being polite?"

"Right, right, sorry." She paused. "Wait, I wasn't supposed to apologize, was I—?"

Grim sighed and flipped the window closed for her.

The carriage bore them not to the main elevators of the Scar, but to the southern ones, where the chasm narrowed. In snobbish fashion, they abandoned their carriage and hired a palanquin on the ground floor, throwing about coins like they meant nothing in order to ride to Aphos in style.

"You know how many cheese rolls those talons could've bought us at The Jumping Ogre?" Grim grumbled to Sherry once they disembarked. "Or how many good northern ales—?"

"That's quite enough," Sherry whispered back. "We're here."

Eli gazed up at the entrance. There would be no slipping into an abandoned winery or broken-down forge this time—Madam Mila's guests were far above that. No, *this* entrance bore the grand illusion of a fine Scarrish hotel, replete with stone columns and balconies dripping with flowers. It would have fit right in amongst the government square or the posh Myrtle Plaza up in the northern quarter—if it weren't for the subtle carvings of krakens along the tops of the columns.

"Welcome, welcome." A guard in a fine silk waistcoat held out a gloved hand. "Your luggage, if you please?"

But Rory had coached them well—the man didn't expect anything like luggage to sully his perfect white gloves. Grim drew themselves up to their full height, elbowed Eli out of the way for good measure, and placed the invitation and another talon in the guard's hand.

"I see, I see." The guard flicked a wand over the paper, its writing perfectly aligned with Lady Freeheart's stolen invitation. Eli stiffened. In his own head, he hadn't yet ruled out the use of force when it came to getting inside. If the man gave them so much as a sideways look, he would gladly clobber him, run in, down the invisibility potion early, avoid every single guard in Aphos...

"Very well." The guard handed back the invitation and pushed open the golden doors. "Enjoy your stay."

Eli barely suppressed a sigh of relief. No clobbering necessary.

Sherry and Grim gave the guard stiff nods and proceeded forward, Eli following close behind. Once they moved into the marbled lobby, he expected the illusion to give way to the rough-hewn tunnels he had seen before—but even the real tunnels here had been gussied up for Aphos' richest visitors. They strolled along smooth obsidian paths, past golden braziers shaped like krakens.

"Goodness," Sherry muttered, veering a little too close to one of the braziers. "Are these wax-casted, do you think—?"

Grim quietly pulled her back to the middle of the pathway.

Before long, others joined them in the tunnel—people draped in half-capes and furs, gold thread glittering in the kraken light. Eli didn't dare look the well-dressed visitors in the eye, but did manage a few subtle nods in solidarity to the servants following along. The other guests' presence wasn't unwelcome—the growing crowd allowed Sherry and Grim to blend in more seamlessly—but his time in the crowd was rapidly coming to a close.

You recall what Nat's supposed to look like? Sherry asked, looking straight ahead and keeping her lips pursed. Grim adjusted their cloak.

Gray half-orc, ponytail, one tusk, dark clothing, they responded. Nat was their responsibility today, leaving Ambrose entirely to Eli. Just the idea of it made his chest tighten, so he quickly diverted his thoughts to the next part of the plan. That was all that mattered—the next step, and the step after that, and the step after that...until he reached Ames.

Hopefully.

Rory, we just passed the statue, he said, frowning at the wrought-iron kraken curling its tentacles up and around the ceiling. *I'm ducking out at the staircase ahead, right?*

Yes, Rory's voice floated in, far thinner than Sherry and Grim's due to her distance. *The path narrows there. Duck into the stairs like you're making space for the others, then take the potion before the guards pass.*

Eli glanced back down the tunnel; a pair of guards strolled at the end of the glittering group, no doubt making snide remarks behind their gloved hands. He'd have fifteen seconds at most before they passed.

Got it, he said, then stuck his hand in his pocket and angled himself close to the upcoming staircase, an alcove of black marble winding up into the shadows. True to Rory's word, the tunnel did indeed narrow just before it, clustering the guests closer together while the servants scrambled to make the appropriate space for their employers.

A picture of the perfect servant, Eli ducked into the staircase and bowed to Sherry and Grim as they passed—then retreated up into the shadows and drank the invisibility potion in one gulp.

He pressed himself against the wall, willing himself to sink into the darkness, for the magic to work faster. One second passed, and his feet vanished. Five more seconds, and he could barely see his hands. Ten more seconds—

"That everyone?" one of the guards muttered. Eli froze, his heart thundering. The guard next to him toyed with her gloves and looked up into the staircase. For a moment, she stared directly at the curved wall Eli was hiding behind, her expression unreadable.

"Looks like it," she finally said, and continued on with her partner. "Hey, did you see that stupid little hat that one countess had on, with all the feathers? What'd she do, nap in a chicken coop?"

Eli waited for them to pass, a hand on his pounding chest—then slipped down the staircase and followed them without a sound.

Between the guards' constant gossip and the guests' low murmurings, there was plenty of noise to muffle his footfalls, letting him focus on keeping a safe distance from others in the tunnel. Avoiding servants darting in from alcoves, keeping away from dust and pebbles that might betray his steps...

When he reached the blinding light of the sinkhole, he had to press himself against the wall again until his eyes adjusted.

Now that he was seeing the Oasis from below, rather than above, he could soak up every detail of the place. It wasn't a normal Scarrish sinkhole, with thin stairways and treacherous footholds. This one had been terraformed by illusions into a peaceful beauty. Waterfalls trickled down from the top, gathering in a crystal-clear stream that ringed the edge of the floor. By the guests' platform, the central base had been built up into an intricately carved dais, dappled with light streaming through the land bridges above. And all around them, ivy spread luxuriously along the walls, and blooms spilled over the uneven ledges.

Eli hated that it was one of the most beautiful places he had ever seen.

He ripped his eyes away from the lush greenery, only briefly glancing at the platform where Sherry and Grim gathered with the other guests. He no longer needed to follow them. His goal was on the other side of the sinkhole, behind the columns that lined the outer path: the control panel for the shield, hidden behind a patch of carefully cultivated ivy.

Not that Rosemond Street would be blasting in through the top of the sinkhole, as he had once hoped—that was still too risky, given the teleporting sentries—but a disabled shield, however brief, would stoke the ire of one man in the Oasis.

One particular, ornery man who needed to look away from Ambrose for just a second.

"I don't care if you already made a round. Do another one," a voice snapped. Eli slowly inched toward the voice—there was Cassius, hovering like an angry wasp in an alcove.

"I will *not* have anyone sneaking into this event," he continued, his gaze boring into the poor officer in front of him. "Do another invisibility sweep while I get the potioneer."

"On it."

After Cassius stalked off, the officer placed a finger on her bracelet—a circle of chunky blue stones overpowering her wrist—then unclipped a wand from her belt.

All around the outer path, fellow guards touched their own bracelets and dug out their wands.

What are they doing? Grim asked. They slouched on the platform with the others, looking for all the world like a curmudgeonly merchant waiting for the show to start—but they'd caught the guards' movements immediately.

Invisibility sweep, Eli answered, sweat beading on his brow. He should have expected something like this after his failure in the throne room. He should have asked for some sort of deterrent from Banneker or Dawn—

It isn't too late to back out into the tunnel, Banneker called. Eli looked up at the edge of the sinkhole—it was impossible to tell through the gauzy shield, but he knew the artificer was there with Dawn and Rory, looking down at them. *If you head out now—*

I'm not leaving, Eli snapped. *Dawn, you got eyes on these wands?*

A pause; Eli thought he saw a tiny shift beyond the shield.

I'm looking, she said tightly. *They've got a low radius. Strong, but short, probably twelve paces. Give them a wide enough berth and you can get past them.*

Sweat trickled down the back of his neck in time with his short, nervous breaths. If even one of them caught him...

You can do this, Dawn said. *We trust you.*

He curled his hands into fists, then let them go, releasing a long, slow breath. He could do this—he didn't have a choice.

Moving carefully and quietly, he judged each guard's rhythms before they approached. When their wands swung right, he dodged left; when they checked the ceiling, he rolled right under them. He was over halfway across the sinkhole now, weaving around columns, ducking into alcoves—

Cassius reemerged onto the path with Ambrose in tow.

"This way," he ordered—and walked directly toward Eli.

Eli dove behind a large planter overflowing with flowers and ferns. He carefully separated the fronds to watch them approach—Cassius in his sharp-lined coat, Ambrose in his potion robes, the shadows heavy under his eyes. A guard with a detection wand followed close behind, her rhythmic sweeping angled away from Eli. All he had to do was wait. Just wait, let Ambrose pass, let the path to the panel clear out...

The trio moved closer. Ambrose was only paces away now. If Eli reached out, he could brush the fabric of his robes. His heart screamed, begged him to activate the teleporter in his pocket, to make this all end here and now, right under Cassius' nose—

But that wasn't the plan. Eli crouched lower behind the planter, closed his eyes, and breathed. Let him go—he'd get his chance later.

A waft of cauldron metal and woodsmoke curled around him, tempting and taunting...then it faded. He opened his eyes. Ambrose, Cassius, and the guard had passed, leaving no one between him and the hanging ivy.

The panel was an open target.

He sprinted to the wall and pulled Dawn's wand from his pocket. Even for something like this, she had made the wand beautiful—gems polished, her signature swirls and turns on the handle. She had even added a cheeky little kraken carving at its base.

He smiled, touched the tip of the wand to the panel, and gave a small flick.

A tiny jolt of recoil shocked his hand, and up above, the bubble-like texture of the shield flickered and disappeared. One second later, a guard near Eli muttered a curse and pulled a teleporter out of his pocket.

Shield's off, Eli called. *Get out of sight of the guard headed up top.*

The answers shot back immediately from his allies above.

On it!

Done.

Outta sight, outta mind.

He rushed back toward Cassius and Ambrose, keeping his steps light. His targets now waited by the steps of the dais—Ambrose perfectly still, Cassius constantly shifting.

"The Madam will give her speech first," he muttered to Ambrose. "Then you will give a *brief*"—he glared harder here—"explanation of your work, then I will drink the potion."

Eli took shelter behind a column, bouncing on his heels, waiting for his moment. Finally, an officer strode stiffly toward Cassius, their pace on the verge of a nervous jog.

"Cassius," they said in a low voice. "Report from up top."

Eli set his foot back and prepared to run.

"What is it?" Cassius said. The guard's eyes flicked upward. Cassius cursed.

"How long?"

"Just a few seconds—"

"And why is it not back on?"

The guard swallowed. "Can't seem to get the panel to work, sir."

Eli balled his hands into fists, willing the man to just *move*—

And he did. Cassius cursed once more, then strode off toward the panel. One step, two steps, three—

Eli lunged for Ambrose.

RULE 36:

EVAPORATE

Ambrose

AMBROSE TOOK A STEADYING breath and closed his eyes, anxiety and joy twisting like vines inside him. Eli had made himself known, then disappeared, having completed his part of the plan flawlessly. Ambrose was still in Aphos, yes, but he now knew he wasn't alone: Rosemond Street was here, too, above and all around him.

He opened his eyes, set his jaw, and fixed his gaze on the stone dais ahead. He was nearly there; all that was left was to finish his part of the plan.

Madam Mila's audience on the other side of the dais was far more luxurious and far less skeptical than her advisors in the throne room. They eagerly chatted and milled about their own platform, showing off spotted furs and bold, dripping jewelry. But Ambrose had no interest in them—he searched the servants' huddle instead, a crowd of plainly dressed people checking nervously to see if their employer had summoned them. He examined the huddle for a flash of gray, a scarred ear, a messy ponytail...

Ah—there she was. Nat was little more than a shadow weaving in and out of the flock of servants, glancing hopefully in his direction. He caught her gaze, gave her a subtle nod, then quickly turned away.

"Mila wants us to start," Cassius growled next to him. His eyes also wandered, but they were pulled upward, toward the gauzy shield now present at the top of the sinkhole. He nodded in tightly wound satisfaction, then handed Ambrose the potion box and pushed on his shoulder. "Get up there. *Now.*"

Ambrose took his place at the center of the sun-warmed dais, where moss grew in the cracks of the carvings. The sunlight was a small comfort, its heat drawing out the smoky scent of cauldron metal and charcoal left on his robes. As soon as he stopped, Madam Mila swept out in front of her guests. Not to be outdone by her visitors, she was bathed in sheer, cool layers of blue and white, each translucent trail of cloth fluttering and flowing behind her. Over her hair, drops of blue marble on silver netting provided sparkling, foamy flecks to her waterfall-like silhouette.

When she raised both her hands, her audience fell silent.

"My dearest guests," she said, gladly filling the quiet with her own sharp voice. "Aphos has stood the test of time for centuries now. But it is not in our nature to be complacent with our work, is it?" She paused, looking each of her guests in the eye. "It is time for Aphos to push for advances that the above-world cannot—*will* not—even consider. It is time for us to embrace the future and what we previously thought was impossible.

"We are all familiar with partial illusion potions. They are limited in their capability and difficult to combine with other magics. If one is to create an apparition to your high standards—why, we all can think of a hundred easier ways to do it, and we sell all of them in our shops." Another smattering of laughter. "But a true illusion potion— something not just equal to Aphos' current capabilities, but superior —may not be beyond our grasp. It will take time yet, but we are proud to show you our progress into the impossible."

Ambrose opened the box with shaky hands—no, focus, *focus*— and pulled the potion out of its cushioning. Cassius had provided him with a beautiful bottle of cut crystal, a specimen as impressive as the magic within.

A waste, Ambrose thought, for people like this.

"I present to you a true illusion potion." He held up the bottle. "Measured for and controlled by an adult of average humanoid height. Its onset is classified as rapid, with the potential to be instantaneous after further experimentation. Based on my observations, the effect will last up to fifteen minutes, again with the potential for improvement."

He received mostly blank stares in response. Madam Mila's smile tightened.

"Demonstrate it for us," she commanded.

Sharp nerves cut into his chest. "Very well."

He uncorked the bottle and smashed it on the ground.

Glass shattered in a rainbow at his feet, and a hundred tiny dragons burst out of the wreckage. All glittering, all furious, weaving in and around him in dizzying displays of magic and color. They expanded in a spiral and spewed purple flames into the carvings at Ambrose's feet until he was wreathed in cold amethyst fire. The air rippled above the massive display, morphing and mutating his audience's faces—

But he could still see Madame Mila's horrified expression and the deep red in Cassius' cheeks.

Perfect.

"You thought you could actually keep me here?" he shouted through the sound of roaring fire and beating wings. "You thought you could trap me underground forever, scaring me into doing impossible tricks for you?"

One of the guards tried to move forward; a dragon snapped at him, and he staggered back.

"You took your potioneer from the wrong street," Ambrose hissed. "Now, if you will *excuse* me, I have a shop to run."

"Get him!" Cassius leapt for him first, batting away the glitter, ignoring the false flames. His hand grabbed Ambrose's forearm—

And went straight through it.

"Get me?" Ambrose gave him a wild, unhinged, victorious smile. "My dear Cassius, I'm already gone."

And he vanished into thin air.

RULE 37:

REGROUP

Eli

"Find him!"

"Where'd he—?"

"Spread out!" Cassius yelled above the din. "He must be in the tunnels. He couldn't have gone far!"

Eli watched the chaos from the top of the sinkhole, his heart soaring. Above him, the birds sang. Below him, guards and guests ran into the tunnels in a panic. And beside him, his boyfriend sank into his arms, warm and real and so very, very present.

"It's done." Ambrose sagged against his chest, his limbs shaking in Eli's tight grip. "Gods, I'm going to feel that potion tomorrow."

"Here." Banneker uncorked a medicine bottle and handed it to him. "Grabbed it from your shop. Figured it might be a doozy."

Eli wasn't the only one holding Ambrose up; Dawn helped prop up his other side while he gulped down the bottle. "Did you see Cassius' face when you disappeared?" She shook his arm back and forth. "Oh my gods, I want it as a painting."

"We'll commission one for the shop when we get back." Eli kissed his cheek. Ambrose breathed a happy sigh and melted into him all over again.

Grim and Sherry's hands; they both acquiesced and let go, sending her stumbling into the lavender.

"So sorry, dear." Sherry quickly reached down and helped her up. "I know it must be a terrible shock."

Nat frantically looked around her and settled on the only familiar person in the circle: Ambrose, still glued to Eli's side, his smile wide and exhausted.

"I told you," he breathed, his shoulders sagging in relief. "I promised I'd get you out."

"You're..." She stared. "I'm not..." She stepped back, taking in where she was. The strange, smiling people. The bushes and flowers tickling her legs.

The wide, wide sky all around her, holding nothing but birds and clouds and sunlight.

She broke down into tears.

"It's all right." Ambrose pulled away from Eli and knelt in front of her. "Nat, you're all right."

She tried to nod, to say something—but only tears came out. Ambrose gave a soft laugh, one of the softest things Eli had ever heard.

"I'm afraid we're a little too close to Aphos for my liking," he said gently. "Would you like to see Rosemond Street?"

She gave a large sniff and managed a true nod this time.

"Good." Banneker pulled out his teleport device and twirled it around his finger. "'Cause you're not gonna believe the amount of stuff Viola baked for you."

The Midnight Snack was a tearful whirlwind of activity the moment their feet struck the floorboards.

Viola shrieked the moment she saw Ambrose. Tom tilted full speed at the poor man's legs, only to crash right into Grim, who was currently fighting for hugging space with Sherry, who had, in turn, elbowed Dawn out of the way—

"You already got to hug him!"

"What if I want another one?"

—Leaving Rory to maintain a semblance of thought and gently extricate Nat from the loving fray.

"Okay, so that's Dawn," she said, pointing out the woman currently throwing elbows with Banneker on her way to Ambrose. "His friend, the wandmaker."

"He, um…" Nat tried to wipe away her tears. "He mentioned her a lot."

"And that's Eli—"

She gasped. "*That's* Eli?"

Having no earthly idea what that meant, Eli opted for excavating Ambrose from the huddle of loved ones and gently pushing him toward the counter full of baked goods.

"I didn't know what you'd want first." Viola trailed along, still stubbornly hugging Ambrose's waist. "So, I made everything."

Everything was an understatement. Viola had stacked her entire inventory on the counter. Three-tiered cakes, precarious stacks of cookies, cupcakes in a rainbow of colors and flavors…

Just like Nat, Ambrose hurried to wipe tears off his face. "This is —I can't thank you enough—"

"Oh, like you need to thank us." Sherry waved a hand and began ushering everyone else toward the desserts. Her disguise had faded, revealing her normal, beaming face. "Please, please, eat up, everyone."

The street gladly dug in—save for Nat, who stuck to Rory's side, fidgeting with the hem of her tunic. Eli squeezed Ambrose's hand, picked up a chocolate cupcake, and brought it over to the nervous half-orc.

"We can be a lot sometimes," he said, handing her the cupcake. Nat gave a weak laugh and took it.

"I know," she said. "Mr. Ambrose warned me."

His heart burst. Oh my gods, he was *Mr. Ambrose.*

"If it helps," he said, glancing back at Sherry, "Sherry has a room all ready for you, if you'd like to stay on the street."

Sherry scurried over, maternal smile still glowing. "It was my eldest daughter's," she added, "so I hope you don't mind paintings of mermaids on the walls. If you'd like to take your cupcake with you and see it?"

Nat stopped partway through unwrapping her cupcake. "Wait, it's a whole room to myself?"

"Of course it is."

While Sherry and Rory ushered her off to quieter, less crazed spaces, Eli gravitated back to Ambrose. He had expected the man to be double-fisting cinnamon cookies by now—but he was holding Tom instead, smiling at the room and its muted chaos.

"Not hungry?" Eli asked. Ambrose took a breath.

"I...I'd like to see the shop first," he said. "I don't think I'll feel... I'd just like to see it."

Dawn shot Eli a fearful look over her slice of cake.

"I'll go make sure Xavion's ready for visitors," she said quickly. "It'll just be a second—"

"No, no." Ambrose set Tom on the ground. "There's no need."

Sweat formed on Eli's brow as he followed Ambrose across the street. He had in no uncertain terms instructed Xavion to remove all of their stupid decorations from the shop that morning, but if that potioneer had decided to keep up their trinkets as a joke—

Ambrose opened the door and stopped.

"Hm," he said. "Appears clean enough."

Eli peeked over his shoulder and let out a sigh of relief. Everything was back to normal—not a single shell nor sparkly bit of glass was in sight. Xavion had even given the place an extra dust and polish, until it looked like Ambrose himself had cleaned it.

"Amby." Xavion descended from the stairs, suitcase in hand. "It's good to see you alive."

Ambrose set his jaw, but he kept his tone polite. "Thank you for all the assistance. I do believe I am in your debt."

Xavion's grin sharpened. "Do you mean it?"

"Unfortunately, I do." He held out a hand. Xavion shook it, nodded to Eli, then headed out the door.

"Well, Rosemond Street has been lovely, but I must be off to grander endeavors. Do call on me next time you get kidnapped, yes?"

They gave a short bow, then sauntered off down the street, whistling aimlessly.

Ambrose sighed. "I don't want to think about how that debt will come back to haunt me," he muttered.

Eli snaked his arms around his waist and kissed the back of his neck. "Then don't think about it."

To his surprise and delight, Ambrose was too impatient for slow, loving gestures. He spun in Eli's grip and kissed him hard, his hands already finding their way under his shirt.

"Come upstairs with me." His words brushed across Eli's lips— then they were stumbling upstairs, hands traveling, kisses landing wherever they could manage. Far too eager, Eli pushed him up against the bedroom door, one hand tugging at Ambrose's belt while the other reached for the door handle—

They tumbled into the bedroom and froze.

The entire bedroom ceiling was hidden under hanging decorations. All of Xavion's shells and mobiles and suncatchers—they were all here, dangling low enough to brush the tops of their heads, tinkling in mock laughter.

Eli couldn't help it; he laughed along with them. Xavion had, in the most precise technical sense, followed his instructions.

"Xavion," Ambrose rumbled. "*Xavion!*"

He sprinted out of the room and down the stairs, Eli laughing and stumbling to follow. "Ambrose, no—"

"I'm going to get them!"

"Ames, please—"

"I'm going to wring their neck with my own two hands!"

But when they skidded out into the street together, Xavion was gone, their glittering robes and aimless whistling nowhere to be found.

RULE 38:

HIRE A HELPING HAND

Ambrose

ONCE AMBROSE and Eli finally rolled out of bed in the morning and made a decadent breakfast in the kitchen, Ambrose opened up every window in the flat.

"Oh, come on," Eli called from the sink. "I didn't burn the bacon that badly."

"It isn't that." Ambrose kissed him on the cheek. Normally, he wouldn't dream of opening more than one window in the place, for fear that the ever-present Scarrish dust would permanently settle over everything he owned. But after weeks away from wind and sunlight, he couldn't get enough of both streaming through the windows in abundance—a cool reassurance and a warm blanket all at once.

He basked in it for a long moment, then headed for the stairs, rolling up the sleeves of his tunic. Eli looked up from the sink again, his gaze sharper this time. "You're not opening up the shop, right?"

"I'm not," Ambrose said, his steps buoyant. "Just thought I'd take a look around before we go to the café."

He nearly laughed as he said it—how quickly he could settle back to normal. Breakfast with Eli, the café with Dawn, a tea later with Sherry and Grim and Banneker...

He stopped halfway down the steps. Someone new, someone very much not part of his old normal, was wandering around his shop.

"Sherry said I could come in," Nat said quickly, pulling her hand away from a crystal bottle on display. "But if I should go—"

"No, no." Ambrose joined her on the floor. "Of course, you can come in. Please, have a look around."

Her shoulders rounded, and she slowly began to wander, peering into each cabinet. "So...this is it? The Griffin's Claw?"

"This is indeed it." Ambrose fiddled with his sleeve. It was a far cry from Aphos' dark shadows, certainly—but there was always a chance she wouldn't like it. "How was staying at Sherry's?" he ventured.

"Good," she said, her voice unusually bright. Her gaze kept swiveling from the store to those outside of it—passersby, wagons, mail dragons... She watched it all in fascination.

"Sherry's nice," she finally continued. "She made me pancakes with fernberries in them."

"That is one of her specialties." He took her side at the bay window. Viola had already opened her bakery and was busy ushering customers inside. She waved at Ambrose, like any normal morning; Ambrose waved back.

Nat tapped the window. "Do you always get this much sun?"

"Typically," he said. "Unless it rains, of course."

"Rain," Nat said almost reverently—then practically pressed her nose to the glass to peek at the clouds above. "Will it rain soon, do you think?"

Ambrose laughed. "I can ask Banneker. He enjoys keeping track of those sorts of things." He glanced behind him at the door in the corner. "Would you like to see my workroom?"

He opened the door and gestured for her to go in; the warm crystal lamps flared happily at her presence. Nat immediately gasped in delight.

"The lucky shelf!"

She ran over to it and reached for the bronze cat—but quickly pulled her hand away.

"Is it bad luck?" she asked. "If I pet it when I'm not brewing anything?"

"Not at all."

Her grin returned, and she petted the cat between its ears.

"It's not as big as your room in Aphos," she commented, finally taking in the rest of the space.

"Not as large, no," Ambrose said. "But I'd like to think it's superior. See this?" He tapped the fume pull. "I've adjusted this one to absorb far more smoke than the Aphosian one. And this over here, the wand rack..."

He guided her through all his favorite devices, sparks of joy racing through him. He could stand in his workroom again, arrange things how he liked, show off his lovely ingredient cabinet...

Then he realized he was filling Nat's first hours of freedom with dry technical ramblings, and he quickly drew back.

"Apologies," he said. "I'm sure none of this is all that interesting."

"Hm?" Nat looked up from his ingredient cabinet. "No, it is." She smiled. "I like it."

While Nat continued to wander, Ambrose toyed with an empty vial on the table in thought. It had been nice to have some assistance in Aphos, hadn't it? And ever since Eli had stopped accompanying him while he brewed, he had...well, he missed the company sometimes.

His workroom was small, to be sure, but it could fit two people. Eli had proven that last year.

"Nat," he said, "I realize you might not have considered it yet, but...what would you like to do in the city? If you choose to stay, of course."

"Oh." Nat picked up a wand from the recharging rack and weighed it in her palm. "I, um—I guess I'll need to find a job. Not serving food, though," she added quickly. "I don't wanna do that again."

Ambrose raised his eyebrows. "Was I that terrible to serve?"

"You were the worst one."

Ambrose's smile faded back into nerves—gods, why was he so nervous about this? "You know..." He fidgeted. "Potion shops don't serve food."

Nat raised an eyebrow. "Okay."

"And you could work in a potion shop," he said, his words picking up speed. "This potion shop, I mean. I—" He took a steadying breath. "Would you be at all interested in apprenticing here? For me?"

Nat dropped the wand in shock, then cursed and scrambled to pick it up.

"Hold on, hold on," she said, her gray cheeks blushing a darker gray. "You want me to be your apprentice?"

"Yes. I mean," he rambled, "I do promise I don't regularly brew illegal potions. The Griffin's Claw is completely above board. And I can also promise there will be no one barging in to threaten us, unless it's Banneker coming in to read our horoscopes for the week. And—"

"I'll do it."

"And I can set up a stash of food for you right here, if you..." He stopped. "Wait. You'll do it?"

Nat grinned, her entire face alight. "When do I start?"

RULE 39:

DREAM BIGGER

Ambrose

WEEKS LATER, Ambrose lounged in a bakery booth, devouring a cinnamon cupcake and weighing in on another important decision.

"I prefer this one," he said. "They're clearly the most organized."

"But this guy"—Eli lifted a piece of paper—"already has experience making wands."

Rory snorted. "Apprenticeships are all about getting experience, not coming in with it." She tapped a third paper. "This girl got her application in first *and* sent in a whole presentation on her goals for improving wand safety mechanics."

Dawn nudged her. "You just like the fact that she wrote a lot of words."

"'Course I like a lot of words." Rory shrugged. "And I like being right. You should choose her."

Nat swung by the booth, a garishly orange cupcake in hand. "So" —she lifted the corner of one of the apprentice resumes—"when do I get to interview the candidates?"

Dawn laughed. "You wanna interview them?"

"Um, yeah." Nat took an authoritative bite of her cupcake, frosting smearing her tusk and upper lip. "I'm the senior apprentice on the street. I think I should get a say."

Eli raised an eyebrow. "How many potions have you brewed, again?"

Nat's eyes darted around. "Um, none at the moment, but—"

Dawn pulled her resumes away from Nat's orange-stained fingers. "I think I'll handle the interviews myself, thanks." She nodded to the cupcake. "Has Viola figured out your flavors yet?"

Nat proudly showed off the half-eaten dessert: bright purple jam filled the inside of the eye-watering cake.

"Orange and fernberry," she said. Before she could react, Rory darted out with a pinky finger, grabbed a tiny swipe of the icing, and licked it.

"Gods." She shuddered. "The sugar in that could kill a troll."

Nat downed the rest of the cupcake in one bite and ran off. "Viola, do you have any more?"

Ambrose rolled his eyes and continued enjoying his perfectly reasonable cinnamon cupcake at a perfectly reasonable pace; but next to him, Eli was slowly growing more fidgety, refusing to touch his chocolate cookie or cup of coffee.

Ambrose knew exactly why—and it was time to put him out of his misery. He set down his empty wrapper and turned to Eli.

"Eli," he said pointedly, "do you have something you wish to tell the table?"

Dawn's gaze whipped up from the resumes. "What? What is it?"

Under the table, Eli squeezed Ambrose's hand in thanks. "So, I kinda went to training today and—"

Dawn shrieked and leapt out of her seat, drawing startled looks from the bakery's other patrons. "You got it! You got the quest!"

Eli's face was a lantern. "Tracking some poachers down south," he said proudly. "They're hunting the local rock phoenix population. Oren picked me and Hickory to go."

As always, Ambrose's mind lurched back and forth between pride and anxiety. "He'll only be gone for a week," he said, mostly in reassurance to himself. "Enough time for me to catch up on all the potions Xavion refused to brew while they ran the shop."

"A whole week of tracking poachers?" Rory grinned. "Too bad it's not more local. I'd love to cover it."

Ambrose smiled. "From what I understand, you've got plenty to cover here."

Upon his return, Rory's editor had—quite conveniently—discovered the error in his ways and pushed her article out the following day, not batting an eye over the many little lies she had woven into the story to edit out her own involvement. And the piece had been a hit, drawing eyes to both Rory and Ambrose. The moment he had turned the *Open* sign on his shop, the place had been swamped with customers, questions...and wildly inaccurate rumors.

Some rushed in asking if he had really fought off a dozen guards at once. Others wanted to know how he had set fire to the whole place during his escape, laughing maniacally in its ashes. One particularly curious customer asked if he had been an illusion the whole time, or if he was even an illusion now, and his real self was sunning on a beach by the Trapping Sea to escape Aphos' revenge.

(Ambrose had reassured most of the customers that Aphos had what they asked for—an exceedingly complex, impossible-to-parse recipe for the illusion potion was technically in their hands. But after Eli's encouragement, he hadn't entirely denied the rumors regarding the fire. Eli thought the air of dangerous mystery suited him.)

But today, the potion shop was closed, giving him a rare moment of respite amongst friends and the silent, un-intrusive pastries.

"We have to go out and celebrate," Dawn squealed to Eli. "To The Jumping Ogre. Or dancing—"

"I won't say no to some dancing." Eli turned to Ambrose. "Will you come out with us?"

The very idea made him want to take a nap.

"As much as I love celebrating you," he said, "I believe I will stay in tonight."

"Oh, don't worry." Eli kissed his cheek and lowered his voice. "I can think of other ways to celebrate."

Dawn stared at them. "Really? Right in front of my macaron?"

———

That night, after Eli had come home from dancing and crashed into bed next to him, Ambrose tossed and turned, his thoughts drifting through the following day's plans. He'd visit the market, put in an order for a new wand, continue teaching Nat about heat levels for brewing...

The thoughts finally trickled away and he fell asleep, finding quiet comfort in the fact that his dreams weren't going to whisk him away or cause him headaches anymore. But the dreams themselves were still present, flitting in and out. He caught odd glimpses of a cave. Of scales flashing in a patch of moonlight, of moss and darkness and sharp shadows.

Amidst the scales, a deep golden eye cracked open.

Hello?

Ambrose jolted awake with a gasp, his heart stuttering. It hadn't been so much of a voice as it was a feeling—a reaching out, a question mark formed into a language he understood. He had never heard nor felt anything quite like it.

"Ames?" Eli mumbled sleepily, reaching out to touch his arm. "You okay?"

But the feeling was already gone, vanished into the night. There was no moss around him, no shadows. Just the whisper of wind outside the window, the rustle of sheets, and Eli's warmth curling around him.

All real, all comforting, all decidedly above ground.

Ambrose shook his head and huddled into Eli's chest. "I'm fine," he said. "Just a dream."

WANT MORE?

Did you enjoy *A Captured Cauldron*?

Spread the word and leave a review!

Want more cozy fantasy romance?

Sign up for my newsletter to get free stories, art, and release updates:

https://rkashwick.com/newsletter/

Also written by R.K. Ashwick:

The Lutesong Series

Keep an eye out for the final chapter in the Side Quest Row Series!

PSST! OVER HERE!

Did you catch the code hidden in this book?

Visit rkashwick.com to claim your prize!

ACKNOWLEDGMENTS

At the risk of sounding too much like Banneker, sequels are a *trip*.

Sequels never behave, listen, or go remotely according to plan. But I wasn't alone on this journey, and I have many people to thank for getting this book (and my sanity) across the finish line.

First, to my alpha, beta, sensitivity readers, and puzzle testers: Laura, Joe, Emma, Kalynn, Amber, Jenna, Zoe, Sebastian, and Luna. Thank you for your wisdom and insight. As always, this book wouldn't be what it is today without your guidance.

To my copy editor Kim Halstead and my proofreader Stephanie Slagle: one day, I'll learn punctuation. One day.

To my cover design team at CoverKitchen: thank you for continuing the *Rival* cover style across the series with grace and finesse.

To my husband Joe, who can no longer keep track of what book I'm writing: thank you for being patient and baking me cookies.

And as always, to my writing group, online writing community, family, and friends: I love you.

ABOUT THE AUTHOR

By day, R.K. Ashwick herds cats in the animation industry. By night, she writes, bakes, and herds her literal cat around her living room. She lives with her husband (and said cat) in California.

For more information, visit https://rkashwick.com/.

Milton Keynes UK
Ingram Content Group UK Ltd.
UKHW041431121224
3628UKWH00044B/810